His eyes narrowed. "Exactly where are you going with this, Rosa?"

"I have fulfilled my part of our original bargain. My debt to you is repaid. It is time to strike a new deal."

"Now? Here?" he said in a fierce undertone. "On this roof, with a dozen soldiers patrolling the grounds?"

She smiled. *"Sí."*

"I don't agree. Give me the journal, Rosa."

She lifted the book. Instead of passing it to him, she reached out and dangled the journal over the edge—directly above the heads of the three soldiers sharing a smoke below.

"What are you doing, you little hellion?"

"Opening a new round of negotiations."

"This is not open for discussion," he hissed.

It infuriated her that he refused to acknowledge her role or take her wishes into account. More determined than ever, Rosa shifted her hand. The journal now dangled precariously between her thumb and forefinger.

Derek froze. "Rosa," he whispered, "hand over that book. Now."

"Not until we come to an agreement."

"What the blazes do you want?"

"I want you to take me, and my godfathers, with you when you leave Cuba. Our lives are in danger after aiding you. I want to be part of the search for this Spanish galleon. And when we find her, I want a share of the treasure."

ALSO BY KRISTEN KYLE

Touched by Gold
The Last Warrior

Kristen Kyle

PROMISE
OF GOLD

BANTAM BOOKS

PROMISE OF GOLD

A Bantam Book / April 2002

ISBN 0-553-58415-4

Published simultaneously in the United States and Canada

Bantam Books are published by Bantam Books, a division of
Random House, Inc. Its trademark, consisting of the words
"Bantam Books" and the portrayal of a rooster, is Registered in U.S.
Patent and Trademark Office and in other countries. Marca Regis-
trada. Bantam Books, 1540 Broadway, New York, New York 10036.

PRINTED IN THE UNITED STATES OF AMERICA
OPM 10 9 8 7 6 5 4 3 2 1

To Sally:
For passing on to me your love of books and
reading... the seeds of my imagination.
Without that, I wouldn't be writing today.
Thanks worlds. I love you, Mom.

To my Lord...
I may be the dancer, but You are the Dance.

To the treasure hunters of the late twentieth century. Their real-life adventures triggered more ideas than I could ever dream of fitting into this story.

PROMISE OF GOLD

PROMISES OF GOD

Chapter One

Havana, Cuba
Early June 1898

THE JUGGLER TOSSED the burning torches into the air in an outstanding display of skill, catching the unlit end of each before sending it up again in a circle of yellow flame. Suddenly, he stopped all four and plunged them dramatically into a waiting bucket of water. The dying torches hissed in protest. With a flourish, the juggler bowed.

The eighty dinner guests burst into enthusiastic applause.

Derek Christopher Carlisle, Viscount Graystone, concealed his sigh of impatience. He clapped along with his fellow guests, honoring his upbringing as a gentleman and the lessons of diplomacy that his father had taught him were so essential to achieving one's goals in a foreign country.

Derek sat back against the red brocade of the richly upholstered chair, his fingers gripping the carved armrests. Beneath the floor-length white linen covering the long table his leg jiggled with the anticipation and irritation he dared not show. He would play his host's game, though it qualified as a bloody nuisance.

He recognized the unceasing string of entertainers for what they truly were.

Delay tactics.

Don Geraldo de Vargas was toying with his guest of

honor, building the suspense and trying to seize a position of power in the upcoming negotiations. The Spanish sugar baron hadn't expanded on his inherited wealth, nor maintained his position in Cuban society, by being dull-witted. Surely he had guessed that the heirloom documents in his private collection must be worth a great deal if Derek had sailed all the way from England in search of them.

Whatever the price, Derek was willing to pay it.

He possessed the monetary resources. What he didn't have was the one essential item he'd been tracking down for a year.

He prayed that Don Geraldo didn't understand the true worth of his ancestor's journal.

Derek picked up his cut-crystal glass and swirled its contents. The wine clung to the inside of the glass before sliding smoothly back down. The rich, fruity aroma teased his nostrils. The respite in the entertainment allowed conversation to rise among the guests, droning like a swarm of bees. All these people were strangers to Derek, except for the two highest-ranking members of his crew relegated to the far end of the huge U-shaped table.

Slanting his blue-eyed gaze to the left, Derek covertly studied his host's classic Spanish profile. A thick mustache and neatly trimmed goatee accented a bold nose and rigid jaw. Don Geraldo's walnut-brown coat matched the hair brushed straight back from his broad forehead. Silver hair streaked down the center of his goatee, and similar flecks dusted throughout his collar-length hair. An ivory satin waistcoat stretched across his slender torso. The right questions around Havana had revealed that the don was a cruel taskmaster, demanding maximum work in the sugar-cane fields while paying as little as possible . . . just the type of Old World inequality the Cubans were rebelling against.

Cold distaste slid through Derek. In his world travels he'd crossed paths with more than one self-proclaimed tyrant, making it natural for him to sympathize with the

Cuban revolutionaries . . . or anyone fighting for equal opportunities and the right to govern their own lives. The only way to gain an advantage with a man like de Vargas was to approach negotiations from a position of strength.

"Very impressive, Don Geraldo," Derek commented. "This food is excellent, the wine superb. My compliments."

The don waved a hand with token modesty. "*Gracias*, Lord Graystone. I am pleased that you are pleased."

Expectancy tingled beneath Derek's skin. "I am amazed you chose to honor me with this occasion."

"You are an aristocrat, like myself. You are a guest in my country. It delighted me to invite you to stay in my hacienda. What other reason is needed?"

What other reason, indeed, except to keep a close eye on me and manipulate the situation to your advantage. "You certainly put on quite a celebration on such short notice. My ship sailed into port only yesterday."

"We Spaniards are always looking for an excuse for fiesta, *señor*." De Vargas stroked his goatee. A sapphire large enough to choke a cat sparkled from his right hand. "We do not allow ourselves to become too serious about life."

Derek tried not to let de Vargas see his irritation. The sly fox couldn't resist a poke at him, contrasting the Spaniards' love of fun with the staid attitude of the British. Although de Vargas intended the comment as a slur, Derek couldn't argue with the assessment. A lingering sense of responsibility and duty constantly threatened to crush the lighter side of his spirit, leaving him feeling as if he couldn't breathe . . . until he embraced the wind behind the wheel of his ship, or spent days searching through historical archives, or plunged his hands into fresh dirt as he sought to extricate something precious and ancient from the earth's secret hiding places. Archaeology gave his life purpose and an excuse for adventure . . . in a word, freedom.

Then again, he could aptly remind Don Geraldo how the English traits of bulldog stubbornness and daring had enabled them to defeat the Spanish Armada and drive the

Spaniards out of most of the New World. The antagonism between England and Spain extended back centuries.

If de Vargas knew what Derek was really after, and why, the antagonism would run even deeper.

Derek took a sip of wine. "The entertainers have been excellent. Quite a variety. Where do you manage to find them all?" he asked, thinking of the tedious string of musicians, singers, contortionists, and magicians. He also hoped the question would prompt the don to reveal when they could abandon the preliminaries and simply get down to the business that had brought Derek across the Atlantic.

With a tilt of his head, Don Geraldo indicated the central area between the tables. Eight men entered the room. Each pair carried a large square slab of wooden flooring.

"The best is yet to come, Lord Graystone. You are about to witness one of the greatest art forms to come out of Spain. One of my favorites."

Curious despite his cynicism, Derek watched the men arrange the wooden flooring in a large square before the head table. It resembled nothing more exciting than a dance floor.

An elderly man, clearly Spanish from his olive-toned skin, entered the room. He carried a guitar and a chair. Setting the chair on the far side of the flooring, he sat down and devoted his attention to the instrument. Gray-haired head bent, shoulders hunched, he caressed the guitar as if it was his one true love, softly testing the tuning of the strings. Rich tones like aged whiskey drifted across the room. The compelling sound drew Derek's interest for the first time that evening.

"So, *señor*," interjected Don Geraldo. "Tell me again how you eluded the Yankee *bastardos* guarding our harbor."

Derek reluctantly tore his gaze away from the guitarist. He took note of the bitterness in the don's voice. *Negotiate from a position of strength.*

"Ah, yes, the Yankee blockade. This Spanish-American War must be damned inconvenient for you. Actually, there was no need to elude them. When the crew of the *Eagle* hailed us, I simply showed my papers, proved that we were not carrying weapons or smuggled goods, and they let us pass in peace. But not before Captain Bancroft and I shared dinner and a toast. Capital fellow. The wine, alas, was not as fine as this."

One corner of Don Geraldo's lip lifted in a sneer. "*Perdoname* for my not understanding your casual attitude toward the Americans. After all, they stole a valuable source of income from the English crown in their War of Independence, then proceeded to issue you an inglorious defeat in the last war."

Derek suppressed a sigh. He could thank Elizabeth I and generations of English royalty for souring relations with the Spanish and making his job more difficult. But if Don Geraldo wanted to stand toe to toe and match subtle insults, he could accommodate him and still maintain a veneer of diplomacy.

"Dealing with Napoleon in 1812 was a slightly higher priority. Damn good thing that Wellington and his troops came along to push the French out of the Peninsula, or Spain might be under French rule now . . . and thus Cuba. That would have been disagreeable for you."

A muscle twitched alongside the don's nose and tugged at his mustache. "I can think of a worse rule to be under," the other man hinted.

Derek smiled at the aspersions cast on Queen Victoria and countered, "Indeed. I assume you find these Cuban rebels a persistent lot of ruffians."

The game was only beginning—point and counterpoint, like the thrust and parry in the sport of fencing at which Derek excelled. But their positions of power were fairly evenly matched. Don Geraldo desperately needed money, since the Yankee blockade had cut off his ability to ship sugar and other crops. On the other hand, if Derek failed to convince de Vargas to part with the journal, hundreds of hours of research might have been in vain. The primary focus of his life for the last four years would sputter and die, not unlike the juggler's flaming torches.

Don Geraldo tugged on a gold chain draped across his waistcoat. A brass ring with an ornate key attached slid from a pocket.

"The key to my collection room," he explained. "I hope we shall be able to put it to good use tonight." Unhooking the ring from the chain, he held the key up, dangling it from his manicured fingers enticingly.

Derek's expression remained bland from long practice. "I have no doubt it shall be put to its intended use before the night is over."

Don Geraldo smiled without humor. He set the key on the table beyond his place setting, next to a crystal vase containing half a dozen red roses. Derek's hand tightened around his wine glass. He stubbornly directed his gaze forward. Although he noticed the guitarist watching them, every fiber of his body was keenly aware of that key.

It lay there, taunting him, a scar against the white tablecloth and amid the fine crystal and china. His palms itched. How tempting it would be to sneak back later, spirit away the key while Don Geraldo slept, and avail himself of the journal without needing to deal further with this pompous aristocrat. Something inside Derek instantly recoiled, appalled by the direction of his thoughts. Steal the journal? Carlisles prided themselves on their integrity.

Dammit, he would acquire that journal through honest means, or not at all.

The guitarist's hand strummed across the strings in a dramatic flourish. The rich chords hushed the crowd. The time had arrived for the next entertainer.

More delays. Derek resolved that he would spend the endless dinner plotting strategy, his next move in countering Don Geraldo's evident hostility toward anyone of English origin.

At least, that was Derek's plan before the young woman appeared in the doorway opposite.

She entered the room and paused to speak with the guitarist, commanding attention as much with her regal bearing and the confident tilt of her chin as the outrageously daring dress she wore. Derek had never seen a gown like it. It cut away in the front, just below the knees, revealing shapely calves sheathed in sheer black stockings. Black flounces gathered dramatically along the lower edge of the burgundy gown, sweeping back in a short train and moving sinuously with every graceful step she took. Although Derek felt a twinge of disappointment as he tore his gaze away from the trimmest ankles he'd ever seen, his regard moved irresistibly upward.

The gown's neckline scooped modestly below the delicate line of her throat. There was nothing demure in the way the bodice hugged her trim torso and full breasts. The tight sleeves opened at the elbows in flowing bells lined in black satin, imitating the hemline.

A sheer black lace shawl was draped over her head, yet failed to conceal the ebony hair hanging to her waist. Tendrils of hair at her temples were waxed into a curl against either cheek. Another black strand curled down the center of her forehead like an ornament. Lines of kohl bordered vivid green eyes that needed no accents.

Silence reigned in the room. The audience seemed to hold its collective breath.

The woman advanced to the middle of the wooden floor, then struck a dramatic pose. With her black leather shoes at right angles, she held one arm overhead, her wrist and hand curved in a way that was both rigid and graceful at the same time. Words of encouragement burst from the enthralled onlookers.

She stared at the floor, seemingly oblivious to the spectators. She licked her lips, leaving a sheen in her tongue's wake.

A sensual shudder rippled up Derek's spine, warming him like the brush of a Caribbean summer breeze. Her lids drooped languorously over her eyes, her expression reminiscent of a woman lying among mounds of pillows, replete after a round of fervent lovemaking, boldly watching her lover retrieve his rumpled clothes. The hairs on his nape prickled with awareness.

"Flamenco, Lord Graystone," Don Geraldo whispered in a reverent tone. "The dance of the *Gitanos*. The true expression of passion."

Gypsy dance. The guitarist began again, coaxing the soul from his instrument, entering into a song that seemed to celebrate life yet weep for its struggles at the same time.

The woman began to move, slowly and sinuously at first, her arms and hands accenting the music.

"The dancer is one of the best in Cuba," added the don. "Alas, not as *excellente* as her mother. The mother was a legend in my country. But the daughter makes up the difference with her great beauty, no?"

"On that we can agree, Don Geraldo," Derek murmured.

He couldn't tear his gaze away as the pace of the music increased. Her heels drummed the floor in a staccato beat that perfectly complemented the lush rhythm of the guitar. She moved with a unique combination of power and grace. The dress hugged her torso, failing to disguise even the slightest movement.

She was arresting, a figure of sexual intensity . . . and the last thing Derek needed to monoplize his attention while everything he'd strived for depended on keeping his wits about him. His goal hung in the balance. The merest thought of dalliance held no place in his plans.

She danced to the edge of the floor nearest him. Several members of the audience began to clap in rhythm with the music. Her right arm rose in an arc that raised the shawl before her face like a sheer curtain.

Her gaze met Derek's through the black lace.

His mouth went dry.

As she continued to dance, her gaze did not leave him. Was it his imagination, or was she dancing for him now?

Her heavy-lidded eyes examined his face, then dipped lower, encompassing his shoulders and chest, lingering. She watched him as if she beheld something unique and wondrous.

Derek gripped his wine glass to conceal the slight trembling of his fingers. Is this what a woman felt like when a man undressed her with his eyes—embarrassed, awkward, yet filled with a strange exhilaration?

His body hardened in a rush. Perspiration broke out across his chest, dampening his otherwise crisp white evening shirt. The drum of her heels, the clapping, the strum of the guitar—all combined with the coursing of his blood and the pounding of relentless desire. It was madness, this desire, this deep and shadowed wanting for a woman he'd never touched, whose voice he'd never even heard! But his typically reliable logic failed to quiet the throbbing in his body.

Without warning, she stepped off the dance floor and whipped the lace shawl from her shoulders. She threw one end toward the table. Derek froze in expectation. Was this a wanton invitation? His thoughts leaped forward, entertaining a fantasy of the dancer stretched across his sheets, her lithe body wrapped in nothing more than this sheer black lace.

The free end of the shawl fluttered downward.

It settled across Don Geraldo's shoulder.

Derek's pent-up breath slid silently from his chest. He felt oddly deflated . . . and angry. At himself. He'd allowed himself to be tugged along, all for a meaningless flirtation.

De Vargas chuckled, fully enjoying her attention.

Derek gulped a swallow of wine to disguise his scowl.

The woman stepped up to the table. Although the carpet muffled the beat of her heels, she continued to dance, turning and swaying, leaning against the table once to smile at the host. Her interest remained exclusively on Don Geraldo . . . as if her flirtation with Derek had never existed.

She was nothing more than a coquette. To this black-haired vixen, he was just part of the game, the entertainment. Acquiring the journal was the only goal worth his attention.

She retreated toward the wooden floor, drawing the shawl with her. The lace slid off Don Geraldo's shoulder, then off the table like rippling black water. The audience's eyes remained riveted on the dancer.

For Derek, however, the magic had been shattered. He no longer shared the audience's fascination. Instead, he sensed something amiss. His attention sharpened on the space before Don Geraldo's plate.

The key ring was gone.

His gaze flashed to the woman. The clever little thief!

She started to turn away and resume her dance.

Derek quickly plucked a red rose from the vase. He didn't want to see her arrested, but neither was he going to allow her to make off with that key.

"*Señorita,*" he called out.

Her head jerked around, revealing the raw tension beneath her playful demeanor.

The key landed on the carpet with a soft clink.

The sound was only infinitesimally audible over the energetic strumming of the guitar. Derek glanced around. No one else, most importantly Don Geraldo, seemed to notice.

He held out the rose. "A flower for the beautiful *señorita.*"

A look of sheer annoyance—just as quickly concealed behind a false smile—flickered across her face. The flash of defiance in her eyes implied she knew he held the power to expose her. Yet she lifted her chin and approached, accepting the dare. Derek felt a reluctant flicker of admiration.

She didn't reach out her hand to accept the rose. No, nothing so tame. To his astonishment, she took the stem of the rose between her even white teeth.

Her lower lip touched his thumb, as soft as one of the red petals crowning the flower. The bold move mowed down his cynical defenses like a broadside of cannon. Desire slammed into him, coiling a demanding heat into his lower body. A groan threatened to rise in his throat.

He lingered before liberating the rose, keeping her there, willing himself not to reveal how deeply she affected him. Her eyes widened. She looked confused, as if astonished by the unexpected results of her ploy, or perhaps dazed by the intimate contact between her mouth and his thumb.

Nonsense. She must be damn clever to exact such swift, bittersweet vengeance like a skilled wanton, then manage to act the role of innocent.

He released the rose with a muttered curse.

Applause and laughter broke out from the audience. The dancer spun away, still holding the rose between her teeth.

She returned to the floor and finished the dance. With a final flourish, she tossed the flower.

It landed in the middle of Derek's plate.

Then, with a flick of her skirt, she departed through the doors. She scorched the air in her passionate wake . . . at least that was how Derek felt as he struggled to draw breath into his overheated body. Desire clashed with anger and a patent disbelief in his own raw response. Dammit, he didn't lose control like this. Ever. His liaisons during his sojourns in England were carefully thought out, well-executed seductions, the resultant relationships mercilessly short-lived.

A beringed hand reached in front of him, startling Derek from the sensual thrall.

Don Geraldo lifted the rose and smelled of its fragrance. "Exquisite, is she not?"

Derek struggled to make his voice sound neutral. "Quite unique. What is her name?"

"She goes by the name La Perla."

"The Pearl. How charming." How inappropriate, he concluded inwardly, to compare her to the smooth, uncomplicated purity of a pearl. She should be called the Carnelian, for the rich red of that dress and her bold flirtation, or the Emerald to complement those flashing green eyes.

"That is the end of tonight's entertainment. Come, let us attend to business, Lord Graystone," offered Don Geraldo, saying the very words Derek had anxiously awaited for hours.

The Spaniard reached for his key ring. He frowned sharply when his hand encountered nothing but empty tablecloth. His gaze shot to Derek, laced with suspicion.

Instantly, Derek said, "I believe the key accidentally caught in the lace of La Perla's shawl, *señor*." He peered over the table. "Indeed, there it is. No harm done."

Don Geraldo's expression relaxed only slightly. He sent a servant around the table to fetch the key. He then rose and bid his guests good night, encouraging them to enjoy conversation and the remainder of the meal.

Derek followed, but not before sharing a meaningful glance with his first mate and navigator dining at the far end of one arm of the table. They knew what to do should he not return within a reasonable time.

The don led the way down a long hallway decorated with plaques of crossed swords. Two guards followed several paces behind. Periodically, Derek passed other guards stationed in recessed doorways. Don Geraldo's private army was very much in evidence, suggesting that he was a great deal more worried about the threat of the rebels than his dismissive attitude let on.

"Tell me more about your ship, Lord Graystone. Why is she called *Pharaoh's Gold*?"

"Egypt is the first place my father, the Earl of Aversham, took me on his extensive travels." *And the place I learned archaeology at his knee.* "He had a particular fascination for Egyptian antiquities."

"Your ship appears to be very fine, very fast."

"She is adequate for my needs."

The route took them up two flights of stairs to the only

section of the building with a third floor. As they climbed, Don Geraldo asked, "Yet you could have outrun the Americans if you wished, no?"

Now I see where you are going with this. You're looking for a fast ship to make good your escape from Cuba should the war go badly for the Spanish. Well, you shall not have my pride and joy. "We could have outpaced the American ship, perhaps, but not necessarily her artillery," Derek retorted, his tone discouraging.

"You have no cannon?"

"Small, deck-mounted brass guns only. Limited range. *Pharaoh's Gold* is a ship of exploration, not a naval vessel."

At the end of a short hallway, Don Geraldo stopped before a heavy door. "But you mentioned that you have sailed the world for many years," he insisted, sounding irritated. "How did you protect yourself from pirates?"

"My charm and charisma?"

De Vargas's upper lip curled in a sneer.

"Or perhaps flying the Union Jack has made the difference. Pirates know that to prey on English ships only invites the wrath of Her Majesty's Royal Navy down upon their heads."

"It was reported to me that your ship sailed quickly into Havana harbor, *señor,* even though her sails were nearly slack from the dropping winds at sunset."

"*Pharaoh's Gold* was built to my specifications. She is equipped with the latest in screw-driven propellers . . . not a common thing in smaller vessels, to be sure, but available to gentlemen with deep pockets and the necessary designs. Thus, she is not at the mercy of the winds, nor as unwieldy as the large steamships with their paddle wheels. I have a fascination for science, you see. I seek after the latest inventions."

"How interesting." Don Geraldo's lips curved in a feral smile.

Derek had cautioned his six-man crew against the eventuality of the enemy hungering for *Pharaoh's Gold,* particularly during a blockade that was strangling Cuba's economy. The deck guns were mounted and primed. Additional weapons in special hidden lockers belowdecks had been broken out. His first mate, Timothy Rutherford, and navigator, Geoffrey Stockbridge, knew better than to linger over dinner or consume too much wine. It wouldn't be the first time someone attempted to steal his sleek, prized schooner. He knew he could count on his handpicked, multitalented crew.

Don Geraldo slid the key into the door.

The snick of the turning lock riveted Derek's attention. A shiver of anticipation raced down his spine.

The Spaniard pushed open the door.

"I believe this is what you came for, Lord Graystone."

Chapter Two

¡Stupida! How could I have been so careless as to drop that key?" Rosa Constanza Wright raged as she stormed out into the deserted hallway. The audience's loud applause faded behind her.

"Calm yourself, *niña*," her great-uncle, Esteban Ortega, urged as he followed close behind. He slung the guitar across his back. The leather strap stretched across his broad chest and a rounded belly that demonstrated too much of a fondness for *cerveza*. But age hadn't dulled the lightning genius of his fingers upon the guitar strings. "Spotting Don Geraldo removing it from his belt was a fleeting blessing, an advantage I did not expect. I suspected it must be the key to his valuables, for he is known for keeping it with him at all times." He shrugged. "Now we shall merely go back to my original plan."

"*Sí*," Rosa agreed reluctantly. "But it would have made things so much easier. We could have unlocked the door, then slipped the key back before dinner was over and it was missed."

"Your beauty enthralled Don Geraldo. It would have been effortless, no?"

"If only that cursed rose had not been stripped of its

thorns." She snapped her fingers for emphasis. "I wish it had been full of thorns. Very sharp ones."

Esteban's lips twitched beneath a thick mustache that had once been a glossy black, but was now heavily salted with gray. "That would have been rather hard on your mouth."

Rosa flicked one hand in a gesture of dismissal. "If the rose had pricked the Englishman, he would have tended to his own business, nursing his wounds, instead of interfering in mine."

"So the gringo *was* the reason you dropped the key. I suspected as much."

Rosa wrinkled her nose. "He startled me."

"Better that than reveal you to de Vargas, *niña*."

A welcome calm filtered into Rosa's heated blood. Curse her temper! Thank goodness for Esteban's logic and insight. "This is true," she acknowledged softly.

"So instead you flirted with him, an *hombre* who is a complete stranger to you," Esteban scolded.

Her gratitude evaporated. "I wanted to shake his composure after he spoiled my efforts at retrieving the key," she said defensively. "It worked, too. Did you not see the color that rose in his cheeks?"

"If a flush heated his face, it could only have been from lust. The *hombre* was attracted to you. You must be careful. Wealthy, indulged nobles such as he cannot be trusted to control their baser urges. You know I have tried to protect you from such things. Did you not see how his eyes followed you during the dance?"

Oh, yes, she had noticed. How could she not notice a face so handsome that the man must have left many broken hearts in his wake? Strong cheekbones, firm mouth, glossy blond hair, and those eyes—as blue and unpredictable as the Caribbean Sea over shifting white sands. Something in the Englishman's quiet intensity had captured her, teasing her into testing the power of her femininity by dancing only for him.

That is, before he ruined everything by being the only one to spot her sleight-of-hand trick.

"You are an innocent, Rosa," Esteban added. "You are a lady, and I am certain you would not act brazenly."

Brazenly. What a tempting taste of freedom that would be. "Why do you insist on calling me a lady? *Gitano* women are not considered ladies."

"They are in this family. You have noble Spanish blood flowing in your veins from your mother's side. Never decry your heritage. Remember that your grandmother, though from one of the oldest and richest families in Seville, did not hesitate to run off with my brother for the sake of love."

"Yes, *tío*," Rosa agreed obediently, though secretly she cherished the story of her grandparents' flight to Cuba. Grandmama Constanza's family had been furious that she dared give in to passion and marry a Gypsy flamenco dancer. They had disowned her in a heartbeat. But that did not lessen the wonder of her adventurous, romantic life . . . a life that seemed as distant from Rosa's mundane existence as the stars.

"My niece raised you as a lady. Despite Michael's and Dickie's damaging influence on you, I shall continue to do so."

The impact of boot heels sounded on the tile floor.

Esteban's hand tightened on the guitar strap. "*Silencio.* Someone is coming."

A guard, dressed in a gray and green uniform, turned the corner. "Señorita La Perla. *Señor,*" he greeted them. His gaze never strayed from Rosa. "Are you having difficulty finding your way out? Allow me to escort you from the hacienda."

Rosa tensed, knowing that Don Geraldo's private army was under orders to prevent entertainers and guests from wandering into private sections of the hacienda.

They had no intention of leaving just yet.

"*¿Cómo se llama?*" She smiled, perhaps a bit too brilliant considering the nervous butterflies colliding with one another in her stomach.

He blinked, then squared his shoulders. "Juan, *señorita.*" Stalling for time, she extended her hand. "I was hoping to stay longer . . . perhaps have a tour of Don Geraldo's beautiful home. Surely the don would not mind if you accompany us?"

Juan captured her fingers in his palm. "I would be going beyond my duty, I am afraid." He raised her hand and pressed his lips fervently to her knuckles. In a lowered voice, he added, "I watched the first part of the flamenco before my rounds took me away. The way you dance heats a man's blood."

Esteban cleared his throat . . . loudly.

Juan straightened abruptly. He dropped her hand. "Is Señor Ortega your . . . er, grandfather?"

Esteban scowled. Rosa suppressed a chuckle. If there was one thing the dear man hated, it was being reminded of his age. Any mention that he would turn seventy next month soured Esteban's always volatile mood. "He is my great-uncle, as well as one of my three godfathers."

A crease appeared between Juan's brows. "Three?"

"Sí, tres." A long-suffering sigh rose in her chest. "The other two are cronies of my father, who sailed with him many years before he died."

"Rosa is quite well protected," Esteban pointed out.

Rosa glanced over the guard's shoulder, spotting two figures creeping up behind him. She touched Juan's forearm, holding his attention. Apologetically, in anticipation of what was about to happen, she explained, "The others are former smugglers, though from their stories they would try to convince you they once sailed with pirates. Either way, they are quite irredeemable. I despair of their behavior."

The shorter of the two stealthy old men raised a club and struck a sharp blow to the back of the guard's head.

Juan crumpled to the floor.

Rosa winced in genuine sympathy. "I am so sorry," she whispered to the insensate soldier.

Esteban squatted down and checked the man's pulse. He glared up at Dickie. "You did not have to hit him so hard."

"You call that hard?" Dickie Hunt exclaimed with a

snort. In a rough accent he claimed to have earned in the dockside haunts of every port between New Orleans and Boston, the old salt challenged, "Is the bloke bleedin'?"

"No."

"Then I didn't hit him too hard, you old coot."

"Stop bickering," Rosa ordered in an impatient whisper. "We cannot afford to draw attention. Hurry. Tie and gag him. And for mercy's sake, do not be rough about it."

"We can hide him in a storage room Michael and I found while we were waitin' for you. Just down that side hall there."

"Good. I shall change clothes in there, as well."

Michael O'Shea's six-foot-two frame twitched in surprise. "In the same room?" he exclaimed. He patted her shoulder. "Now, colleen, I'm thinking maybe you haven't thought that one through. I mean . . . what about your modesty?"

Folding her arms, Rosa quipped, "What alternative is there? Shall I change here in the hallway?"

Blushing, Michael dragged a large hand down his face. The action knocked his black hairpiece askew. He hastened to rearrange it over the bald area dominating the top of his head. Michael fixated on the notion that the false hair was essential to his self-esteem, not to mention his colorful reputation with the widows of Havana. Personally, Rosa thought he looked more sophisticated without the hairpiece or any other effort to deny his sixty-seven years.

"We shall cover Juan's eyes," Esteban suggested.

Rosa looked heavenward. "The man is unconscious, tío."

"He might not stay that way. Your reputation is at stake. We take no chances."

How well she knew that, to her profound frustration. Their protectiveness was stifling. But if it became known that she'd been moonlighting as a thief for several years, she would have no reputation left anyway. "Very well, cover his eyes. But let us hurry."

Michael and Dickie each grasped one of Juan's arms and dragged his limp body to the storage room. They tied the poor man with an efficiency that demonstrated perhaps not all their stories of piracy were exaggerated.

Michael handed Rosa a carpetbag. Dickie closed the door.

As she unbuttoned the burgundy dress, Rosa couldn't resist a cautious glance at the still sleeping Juan. Feeling suddenly awkward, she turned her back. Her excessive modesty irritated her. How did she expect to one day live a life of adventure, full of daring flirtations with handsome men, if she couldn't keep from blushing before one who was blindfolded?

She danced flamenco, which was about passion and the deepest emotions life had to offer, yet experienced no passion in her own life. The heritage of generations stirred in her veins, filling her with a strange restlessness. If only her mother, Mercedes, had lived long enough to explain these things. Many stories told how her mother could mesmerize men with her dance. With a snap of Mercedes's fingers, they would fall under her spell, a power she relished—until an American sea captain named Alex Wright came along with his brash self-confidence and laughing green eyes and swept Mercedes Ortega off her feet.

Rosa wanted that kind of excitement.

Only when she performed flamenco did her godfathers let down their collective guard. They were worse than old, conservative *dueñas*. At four-and-twenty, she was long past the age for a nursemaid.

She longed to test the power of her femininity.

She'd been ambitious in her choice of target tonight. Since his arrival yesterday, rumors of Lord Graystone's wealth and dashing good looks had swept through a city hungry for news other than rebellion and blockades.

At first she'd tasted victory. Graystone's gaze had locked on her, heating in a way that made her almost painfully aware of her own body. His male beauty and the flattery of his regard had filled her with a heady sense of exhilaration. Never before had she danced with such intensity. The daring flirtation had almost been successful, until strange feelings interfered. When her lips had accidentally touched his thumb on the rose, a sudden shiver of awareness had snatched away her breath. The tingling sensation that dipped from her belly to her legs had nearly destroyed the rhythm she needed to finish the dance.

How could she expect to mesmerize men when she grew clumsy and shy under the regard of one pair of cool, arrogant blue eyes?

Angry now, Rosa's movements grew jerky as she slipped out of the dress. She pulled her trousers, blouse, and boots from the bag. Quickly, she donned the concealing black clothes and shoved her flamenco outfit and shawl in their place.

She couldn't allow thoughts of Lord Graystone to affect her concentration. It was time to put the acquired knowledge of the hacienda, the guard routines, and the location of the vault room to good use. Dickie, Esteban, and Michael had bemoaned their "sacrifice" of courting drinking comrades among the retired guards, consuming large quantities of *cerveza* and whiskey, and seducing three of the older maids who worked in the hacienda.

Rosa felt relieved that they hadn't felt compelled to reveal any more details of how they came by their information.

She stepped out of the storage room.

"Are you ready?" Esteban whispered.

Rosa nodded with reluctance. She would never grow accustomed to the guilt she felt about stealing. Regrettably, she was not the flamenco legend her mother had been. Dancing did not provide enough money. The affluence and comfort of her childhood had disappeared with her parents' untimely deaths.

Fear slithered through her stomach, as well. Thievery thus far had consisted of picking pockets and, only when necessary, minor robberies of the island's wealthy landowners.

The burglary of Don Geraldo's rumored valuables was the most daring—and most dangerous—one she'd yet to attempt.

Her three godfathers gathered round. They immediately began their customary campaign to convince her that she was doing the right thing.

"You know how the Cubans hate Don Geraldo," Esteban pointed out. "He works them to death on his plantations."

"Then pockets most of that lovely money for himself," Dickie added, stroking his dense white beard. "It's a bleedin' shame, that sort of greed."

"You see, now?" Michael concluded with an encouraging smile. "You'll be like that medieval fellow, what stole from the rich and gave to the poor. The Cuban rebels being the poor in this case, not to mention our humble selves."

"Robin Hood is an English fable, Michael, not Spanish," Rosa explained patiently.

Michael's thick salt-and-pepper brows pinched together. "Now, don't go letting yourself be fooled. That's just English lies for you. Robin Hood was an Irish hero, born and bred. Had to be, to thumb his nose at the English and make such mischief."

They were dears for trying to make her feel better about her role. She couldn't break their hearts by letting them know their arguments made little difference.

Stealing was simply something that had to be done. So they could eat. So she might keep a roof over the heads of three old men who could no longer work. Her godfathers had raised her from the tender age of seventeen when her mother's demise from a mysterious fever had come within days after Michael and Dickie returned with news of her father's death in an accident at sea. Rosa had always felt that grief had taken away her mother's will to live.

They crept down the hallways, avoiding the guards, heading for the large open courtyard in the center of the hacienda.

Esteban's *Gitano* heritage led him to regard thievery as

something merely expedient to survival. Michael's background of poverty in Ireland, and Dickie's history as a waterfront rat, had founded a perception of their right to relieve the rich of ill-gotten gains. Her own father had been a blockade-runner during America's War Between the States, for pity's sake. But she could not share their casual attitude, even though they'd recognized her talents and taught her to steal.

The energetic dancing that kept Rosa trim and strengthened her body also provided her with the athleticism to climb trellises and shimmy down drainpipes. Sensitive fingers equipped her with the means to pick locks and open most safes. If only she could use such skills doing something she was proud of!

These three men were all that remained of her family. She would do whatever necessary to provide for her loved ones.

Until she found a way to put aside enough money to endow their declining years. Only then would she find freedom and a chance at a life of her own. Only then could she assuage her deepest fear that something might happen to her, leaving her godfathers unprotected and uncared for.

"We're here, angel girl," Dickie murmured.

Rosa blinked, focusing on her surroundings. She'd been so engrossed in her thoughts, she hadn't noticed when they emerged outside in the courtyard. The two-story hacienda surrounded them on three sides, framing an open block of night sky awash with stars. A nine-foot stone wall closed in the fourth side, providing limited access to the courtyard through two gates.

Plants and ornamental trees grew in profusion. Flowers filled the air with sweet perfume. Water splashed into a fountain in the center. The marble pillars supporting the upper verandas added a whimsical touch to the classic Spanish architecture. Each smooth pillar was carved from a different stone—black, burgundy, green, rose, cream, gray, and other beautiful swirling patterns.

Esteban handed Rosa a belt holding the tools of her shameful trade—a dagger, hood, rope, a pouch holding a candle and flint, and a cloth bag to carry her spoils. She buckled it around her waist.

Michael stepped close. "Ready, now?"

Rosa nodded grimly.

Michael interlaced his fingers. Rosa slipped her left foot into his cupped hands. With a quick boost, he hoisted her up until she grabbed the cold stone balustrade along the second-floor veranda. With a flex of her arms, she pulled herself over.

As previously agreed, her three godfathers slipped out of the courtyard, retreating through the eastern gate to hide in the stables. Staying here would leave them exposed to the guards who came through every ten minutes on scheduled rounds. The threesome would return to help her at the allotted time.

She ran down the veranda, as lithe and silent as a cat. She stopped at the last pillar in the corner and looked up. According to their information, an isolated room—the only third-floor level in the hacienda—held Don Geraldo's most prized valuables. The only openings into the room were through an inner stairwell deep in the house, or through a window that opened onto the roof. Michael had charmed the upstairs maid and coaxed the information from her with heated kisses.

"And this from the three men who have chased off my every suitor," Rosa muttered to the sympathetic sliver of moon.

Grabbing the thick coil of wisteria vines that grew up two stories of marble pillars, Rosa climbed to the roof's edge.

"THIS IS MY family collection," explained Don Geraldo, "gathered over many generations since my ancestor settled in Cuba in 1622."

Derek drew a long, slow breath, clamping an iron control on his enthusiasm. It wouldn't do at all to succumb to this urge to dash into the room like a boy at Christmas. He knew how to remain cool and in control—just as he did any time he negotiated for the privilege of excavating priceless artifacts.

He always won. He always got what he wanted.

He only wished he was as fearless and controlled in all aspects of his life.

Don Geraldo moved through the brightly lit room. The two guards remained stationed on either side of the door. With evident pride, the Spaniard pointed out his collections of weapons, porcelain figurines, jewelry, and paintings.

Derek followed, diplomatically making appropriate comments. In reality, he glanced over the cases and displays with little interest. Something else entirely had captured his full attention. A bookcase stood at the far end, its shelves crammed with books, some in excellent condition and some brittle and crumbling at the edges.

Don Geraldo stopped before the bookcase.

Despite his outward reserve, Derek's heart rate leaped.

"You say you are particularly interested in purchasing naval documents, Lord Graystone?"

"Yes. Manifests, journals, nautical maps. You did say you possessed such documents from the sixteenth and seventeenth centuries?"

"Indeed." Don Geraldo stepped back to provide access. "You must see for yourself, of course."

Derek pulled down books at random, flipping through pages and confirming their authenticity. Impressed, his interest in the entire collection quickly became more than a façade. But that didn't preclude the fact that his current goal was solely fixed on one particular journal.

As Derek picked through the books, searching, the don commented, "Many of these are not unique, I am afraid. They are copies of ship documents kept here in Havana for safekeeping. The originals sailed on to Spain with the fleets, where they are now stored in the Archivo General de Indias in Seville. Perhaps you are aware of this great library?"

"I have heard of it." Actually, he had spent countless hours in the Archive of the Indies doing research.

His gaze locked on a book with a brown leather binding. The gold letters printed on the spine had nearly faded completely away.

A prickling sensation spread through the pads of Derek's fingers. As casually as possible, he pulled the book from the shelf. Stiff leather and brittle paper crackled as he opened it to the middle. He inhaled deeply, cherishing the familiar smell of aged parchment. Scanning the yellowed pages, he translated a few words from the looping scrawl of archaic Spanish. He turned to the beginning, to the title page. The author's name leaped out at him. Excitement bubbled up in his chest, effervescent, nearly explosive, like a shaken bottle of champagne.

So, the journal did indeed exist.

Regrettably, it would take hours to translate the text and derive any useful information from the author's description of historic events. He hoped to do that at his leisure.

Derek reached up to slip the book back into its place on the shelf. Once he offered for the entire collection, Don Geraldo need never know that the possible existence of this one book had led him here, ever since he'd uncovered mention of Gaspar de Vargas and the journal in the archives.

"Oh, my, what is this doing here?"

Without warning, Don Geraldo grabbed the journal before Derek could put it back.

Derek froze. He felt certain he hadn't betrayed his interest. What had gone wrong?

"My sincere regrets, Lord Graystone. This journal should not be shelved with the others and is not for sale. It was penned by my ancestor Gaspar de Vargas." Don Geraldo paused. His gaze, sly and searching, fixed on Derek's face. "Gaspar survived the wreck of *Nuestra Señora de la Augustina*."

The bottom dropped out of Derek's stomach at the mention of the Spanish galleon's name.

It took all his willpower to keep his expression neutral. He suspected that the Spaniard was probing for a reaction, testing how much Derek knew of the journal's significance. Anger immediately rose, pricking like stinging nettles.

Don Geraldo opened the journal, balancing it on the palm of his hand. "You see? The book is written in a very old form of Spanish. Have you seen such writing before?"

"I have some familiarity with it," Derek replied stiffly. It had taken him more than a year to learn to read similar script in the archives.

Bloody hell. He had played the game perfectly, not showing his hand. Unfortunately, Don Geraldo had held the trump card. While Derek had been hoping that the don hadn't bothered to examine a dusty old book handed down through the generations, the fox had known the potential value of the journal's contents all along.

Derek glanced away, concealing his frustration and silently reviewing his options. A flicker of movement at the room's only window caught his eye, a darker shadow against the night. Derek frowned. What could possibly be out on that steep roof? A nest of ravens, perhaps?

Don Geraldo spoke, reclaiming Derek's attention. "My ancestor describes where the *Augustina* went down, the reefs that claimed the ship during the hurricane. He barely managed to cling to floating wreckage until he was rescued."

The Spaniard was definitely angling for information. Coldly, Derek challenged, "Was your ancestor the *Augustina*'s pilot, *señor*?"

"Nothing so humble." Don Geraldo sniffed, offended. "He was one of the passengers. A nobleman. The horror of being the only survivor among so much death encouraged him to make Cuba his permanent home."

"The Caribbean is a vast sea with reefs beyond counting, all of them treacherous. Without a pilot's knowledge of
navigation, it is unlikely this journal will offer sufficient
clues to pinpoint the wreck's location," Derek countered.
By itself, that is.

He spoke from brutal, time-consuming experience.
He'd spent four summers searching for the sunken galleon,
using other clues gleaned from archive records, without
success. The other accounts, some almost contradicting one
another, left several square miles of ocean near the Florida
Keys as the possible site. He hoped the journal would provide the additional cross-reference he needed to narrow
down his search.

Don Geraldo's smug expression faltered. "But Gaspar
was there. He also saw other ships of the fleet founder and
sink in the hurricane."

The *Consolación,* the *Atocha,* the *Santa Margarita* . . .
how well Derek knew the names of other treasure galleons
lost in that ill-fated *flota* of 1622. "Hurricanes themselves
change landmarks, build beaches, tear them down."

"Nevertheless, the *Augustina* has never been found. It
would be worth it for a man who, say, had the right equipment and knowledge to partner with the man who held the
journal, no? The search could prove quite profitable."

A proposed partnership. Such had been de Vargas's intention all along . . . through the dinner and the inter-
minable string of entertainers. Cold fury sliced through
Derek. Had the beautiful flamenco dancer been a particularly sly addition to seduce him into cooperating?

"You are talking underwater salvage, Don Geraldo.
That is rather more complex than sailing over the wreck
site and saying 'Oh, there she is.' "

The don scowled at Derek's sarcasm. "But it can be
done," he insisted. He leaned in closer, fully warming to his
subject now, greed sparkling in his brown eyes. "Even in
the sixteen hundreds, was not the cargo from lost ships of-
ten recovered using pearl divers and diving bells?"

The man had certainly checked his facts, much to Derek's mounting frustration. "That was on ships that had gone down within a few months or years of the salvage effort . . . before the pounding sea ripped apart the hull and scattered the cargo, before worms devoured the wood and coral overgrew the artifacts, before the heavy weight of any metal sifted down beneath a barrier of soft white sand. You're talking about a galleon that sank over two hundred and seventy years ago."

Don Geraldo growled impatiently, "If these difficulties are true, then why are you here? Why do you seek the journal and the *Augustina*? You describe such salvage as impossible."

Dangerous. Challenging. Not impossible. Derek arched his brows. "I don't recall saying my intent was to recover a sunken ship, *señor*. I merely came here for historical documents, some for my personal collection and the remainder to go to the university at Oxford. If you are so convinced of the journal's authenticity, why have you not hunted the *Augustina*?"

White lines appeared in De Varga's tightly pursed lips. He turned away.

Derek experienced a flicker of redemption. It seemed that the don had sought the wreck, yet failed, either through his own lack of expertise or inadequacies in the journal, or both. De Vargas needed the clues Derek possessed.

Don Geraldo hunkered down on his heels before a large safe. He concealed the dial with his shoulders as he worked the combination. Derek caught a glimpse of papers and velvet jewelry boxes as the don set the book on a shelf. The heavy metal door closed with a thump and a hiss of the dial.

Derek exhaled slowly as he watched the journal locked away, bracing against the acidic burn of regret in his gut.

Nevertheless, he knew he was making the right decision in letting it go. Split the unique and priceless cargo of the *Augustina* with someone who was only interested in the monetary value? Dammit, he'd sooner cut off his arm. What about the artistry behind the artifacts? What about the history, the stories told by items sheltered by sand and sea for 270 years?

Perhaps his other references would prove sufficient this time around . . . with a great deal of unexpected luck. At least he could eliminate the failed sites of prior years. Although that still left an intimidating expanse of underwater terrain, he would soon take delivery of some new, experimental equipment that would help in the search. There was still a chance of success on his own.

Don Geraldo rose. "We shall continue this discussion in the morning, Lord Graystone. Perhaps I may convince you to reconsider my proposal."

Derek didn't hold out much hope for a change, but as long as there was a slim chance of purchasing the journal without selling out his integrity or his right to the entire cargo, he was willing to give it one more try. His arguments had planted the seeds of doubt. He'd witnessed the uncertainty deep in Don Geraldo's eyes. If he could convince the greedy tyrant that money in the hand was worth more than a lengthy, risky search . . .

At the very least, he would insist on a closer examination of the journal. Perhaps it held the answer he sought . . . and perhaps not.

He nodded. "In the morning, then."

Chapter Three

THE CURVED TILES of the roof, nested together like scales on a fish, pressed painfully into Rosa's knees and hands.

A shiver of nervousness rippled down her spine as she crawled upward. Glazed tile roofs were notoriously slippery. One careless move and she could tumble all the way down until she hit the cobblestone patio far below. The ceramic tile was also fragile. Too much weight on a weak spot could break one with an audible snap, alerting the guards.

A light glowed in the single window of the third-floor room. That didn't bode well at all. Rosa gnawed on her lower lip. The longer she had to wait for the room's occupant to leave, the greater her risk of discovery.

Reaching the window, she eased her head around the edge.

A start of surprise lanced through her body.

Don Geraldo stood in the center of the room, a book cradled in his hands. Two armed guards maintained a watchful position by the door. But it was the sight of the room's fourth occupant that inexplicably caused Rosa's heart to race.

Lord Graystone's broad shoulders seemed to fill the room. He stood with legs set slightly apart, as if braced against the pitching and rolling of an angry sea.

He glanced toward the window.

Rosa ducked her head with a gasp. The incident with the key had demonstrated that she shouldn't underestimate the Englishman. After several seconds, when he failed to raise the alarm, she edged back up to peer into the room.

He faced Don Geraldo again. This would be her last chance to admire the clean, strong lines of his face and his sun-kissed blond hair. The man was arrogant and troublesome, but she couldn't deny that he was a feast for the eyes.

Although Lord Graystone's expression remained calm, muscles flexed in the sculptured hollow behind his jaw. His hands clenched into white-knuckled fists behind his back. Something had inspired a silent fury in the man. But what? His narrow-eyed gaze fixed on the book in the don's hands.

A book? Rosa leaned forward, her curiosity aroused.

Don Geraldo squatted in front of a large steel safe.

She watched eagerly as the don positioned himself with his body between Lord Graystone and the dial . . . which provided Rosa an unrestricted view of his hand. The dial was too far away to accurately make out the combination, but she could see enough to approximate the turns and the numbers.

Don Geraldo placed the book inside. Rosa's interest mounted. The mysterious book must be valuable if de Vargas considered it worthy of locking in his safe. He closed the door and stood.

Lord Graystone left the room, his expression unreadable. The guards extinguished the light, then followed. The door closed behind the last man.

The don and Lord Graystone might be fellow aristocrats, but there was certainly no love lost between the two men. Graystone apparently wanted that book.

Rosa smiled. Not if she beat him to it.

Pulling the slender dagger from her belt, she eased the blade between the window and its frame. The latch slipped and clicked. She held her breath. When no one rushed into the room to challenge her, she opened the window and crept inside.

She pulled the candle and flint from the pouch at her waist. Once lit, the stubby candle provided just enough illumination to guide her but not enough light to create a telltale glow beneath the door.

Slowly, she prowled the room, searching for relatively small items she could carry and later convert to coin. Most of the items in Don Geraldo's collection were large. It angered her that he hoarded such wealth when Cuban peasants suffered. She might be Spanish by blood, but she had been born here in Havana. Her heart was with the Cubans.

She pulled the black cloth sack from her belt. A silver plate was the first to go in, then a set of candlesticks, a pair of gold earrings, and a small ring set with an emerald. In a low drawer, she discovered a set of flatware dulled by tarnish and a film of dust. She selected neglected or common pieces she felt would not be readily missed. Over time, Esteban and his contacts could sell the items without raising suspicion.

Kneeling before the safe, she turned the dial clockwise. When it neared the range of numbers where Don Geraldo had made the first stop, she slowed and pressed her ear to the metal door. When it hit sixteen she felt, more than heard, the deep click that heralded a turn in the tumblers.

She turned the dial counterclockwise, searching likewise for the second number. When the tumblers adjusted again, she released a long sigh. Reversing the spin, she eased up to the last range of numbers. The tumblers settled into their final position with a satisfying sound.

"*Gracias,* my beauty," Rosa whispered.

She turned the handle. The door opened. She shifted the candle, casting angular light and shadow through the cluttered contents of papers and velvet jewelry boxes.

Her hand went straight to the book that had held Lord Graystone's interest. Perhaps he would pay well to acquire it. After their clash at dinner, she would enjoy demanding the maximum amount of money he was willing to part with. Or perhaps she would deny him the book, and sell it on the black market.

She lifted the book out, fascinated to discover that it was quite old. Although the brown leather cover showed the stains of frequent oiling, hairline cracks ran throughout.

Rosa opened the cover.

Her brows snapped together in a frown.

The book was written in Spanish, but unlike any she'd ever seen. There was no punctuation. Sentences seemed to start but never end. She studied the script at the top of the page. This was the memoir of one Gaspar de Vargas. It was dated in the year of our Lord, 1622.

Her gaze scanned down the page. A few relatively familiar words took shape. She caught a reference to a ship, a storm, and the deaths of many people.

Surprise shuddered across her shoulders and down her back. A sunken ship. The year 1622 fell within those halcyon days of Spanish power, when silver and gold poured from a ransacked continent and the flotas set sail from Cuba.

Madre de Dios.

Did directions to a Spanish treasure abide within these pages? Her heart raced. Her hands trembled.

All thought of selling the book fled.

Although it seemed like a wild hope, this book might lead to more money than she'd ever dreamed. Enough to secure her godfathers' futures. Enough to travel beyond the limits of her island home. She loved Cuba, but since her parents' deaths she'd longed to visit Spain and the rest of Europe that Esteban described so eloquently, and to see her father's beloved homeland of America.

Why not pursue the dream, however far-fetched?

However long it took, she would decipher the writing and uncover the clues hidden within. Until then, the book would remain her secret. Just a hint of its significance would send Esteban, Dickie, and Michael into a frenzy. She winced at the disloyal thought. She didn't want to imply her godfathers were greedy. They were just . . . focused on acquisition.

She closed the book and carefully slipped it into the bag.

All that remained were the jewelry cases. Stacks of black velvet boxes filled half the safe. She picked through them, discovering necklaces laden with diamonds, sapphires, and emeralds. Her disgust grew with each box. This was true greed. Don Geraldo had been holding back on his workers' wages, citing the Yankee blockade as the cause, while hoarding such riches. At least she and her godfathers supported the rebels and shared what they could with their less fortunate neighbors.

She ignored the more elaborate necklaces and earrings, knowing they were too distinctive to sell without raising comment. Among the cache, however, she discovered a simple pearl choker with three strands, a dozen gold bracelets and rings, and two pocket watches. These joined her other spoils. Finally, she restacked the boxes in the order she found them.

Snuffing out the candle, she retreated to the window. She crawled out onto the roof and used her knife to return the latch to its original position. She poured the melted wax into a crack between two roof tiles, concealing any evidence of her presence. Then she tucked the candle back in her pouch.

Stretching out on her belly, Rosa began to work her way down the roof headfirst with the bulky bag.

DEREK STEERED AWAY from the hallway leading to his bedchamber. He was far too restless to sleep.

Attempting to acquire the journal had been a gamble, he knew that. But, dammit, he wasn't accustomed to losing. Typically, his charm, his diplomacy, or his money turned the odds in his favor.

He should have anticipated that Don Geraldo would understand the journal's true worth and attempt to manipulate the situation to his advantage.

He had to get outside, into the open. Little demons of frustration hammered against the inside of his skull, demanding an outlet. He needed to shake his fist at the moon, or perhaps bang his stupid head against a wall. Just when he needed them most, his fencing foils were back on his ship.

Any place beyond the walls of the hacienda was off limits unless he wanted to run afoul of the guards. Derek headed for the courtyard. The moment he stepped outside, he drew a deep breath of the comforting scents of water, moist earth, and old stone.

The lack of lights allowed a dense wash of stars to show against the night sky. Water cascaded into a fountain in the center, spilling from a stone vase held by a scantily clad Venus. Leaning his back against a gray marble pillar, Derek tilted his head against the cold stone.

"Bloody hell," he said softly.

He'd narrowed his search to a section of the Florida Keys. He was so close. He could feel it in his bones—the excitement, the tingle of anticipation that instinctively hit him before each significant discovery. All he needed was that damn journal to nail down the location of the wreck, shaving weeks, perhaps years, off his search.

But he wouldn't sacrifice his principles. The last thing he wanted was a snake like de Vargas coiling his way around a legitimate expedition. Derek despised treasure hunters whose only goal was wealth . . . not the preservation of art or history, but merely the value the artifacts would bring at auction.

Nuestra Señora de la Augustina had carried a unique and priceless cargo. It was just the type of colossal, career-making find he'd always dreamed of.

A gate latch clicked. Derek came instantly alert. A uniformed guard started across the courtyard.

Folding the lapels of his black coat across his white shirt, Derek stepped silently into the dense darkness behind the pillar. It seemed wise not to challenge the thinly veiled hospitality of this place. Don Geraldo evidently lived in fear of the Cuban rebels.

The guard passed by, humming to himself. The starlight rippled faintly along the barrel of the rifle slung over one shoulder. Derek's gaze followed his every step. The man exited the gate on the opposite side.

The closing of the gate triggered an entirely new set of sounds. A faint scratching disturbed the silence. Suddenly, an opaque silhouette descended against the sky, its uneven shape blocking out a section of stars. It was a black bag, its sides distorted by lumpy contents. A rope secured its neck.

Derek's brows snapped together. His gaze shot directly overhead, tracing the rope to its origin. A pale face peered over the edge of the second-story roof. A waxed lock of dark hair formed a curl against the wraith's forehead.

The flamenco dancer.

Intrigued, Derek hung back, blending with the shadows.

The bag began to swing gently. At the far end of one outer swing, the girl abruptly let out slack in the rope. The bag landed in the nearest garden plot. Its contents settled into the soft dirt with a muffled clink of metal. With a flick of her wrist, the dancer tossed the rope after the bag. It slithered downward to disappear into the bushes.

Derek's mouth twisted cynically. It would seem the Gypsy practiced other skills besides dancing. Her attempt to pilfer the key had only been a portent of bigger things to come.

He glanced up again. The pale oval of her face had vanished. Not to worry. She must be on her way down. She would hardly leave without her bag of booty.

Derek folded his arms. A smile of anticipation banished his earlier scowl. Leaning one shoulder against the pillar, he crossed his boots at the ankles and settled in to wait.

ROSA PUSHED BACK from the edge of the roof. The lingering warmth of the afternoon sun, absorbed by the clay tiles, soaked into her chest and belly.

Although the guard would be back, the pattern of his rounds granted her ten minutes to climb down, retrieve the bag, and make good her escape. Plenty of time.

Now for the tricky part. She had to climb back to her access point, then reach feet first over the overhang and find her footing among the tangle of wisteria vines. Turning around, so that her head once more pointed toward the crest of the roof, she began working her way sideways toward the corner.

Without warning, the tile beneath her left boot slipped.

The sudden loss of that critical hold threw Rosa off balance. She started to slide down the roof.

Rosa clawed at the tiles. The glazed ceramic offered no solid purchase. Before she could even think to scream, her legs shot out into open space. Her body bent at the hips. Her legs dangled. The roof's edge jabbed painfully into her hipbones. The angle helped slow her plunge for one critical second. But it wasn't enough to stop her fall. Her torso followed the weight of her legs, heading for oblivion.

With one last desperate surge of strength, she grabbed for the lip of the roof.

And held on.

Closing her eyes, she thanked God. But she wasn't out of danger yet. The two-story plunge to the cobblestones below wouldn't kill her, but she could easily wrench a hip or break an ankle. Thus crippled, how could she elude the guards?

A rhythmic clicking sound caught her attention. Her eyes flew open. The loosened tile slid down the roof. If it crashed against stone, the noise would lead the guards right to her. How many more things could go disastrously wrong tonight?

Rosa sucked in her breath as the tile shot past her. Its momentum carried it in an outward arc, straight into the nearest garden. Thankfully, the thick plants muffled its landing.

Her hands ached with the effort to hang on. She caught her lower lip between her teeth.

The swirled pattern of brown marble met her gaze. One of the second-floor pillars stood just in front of her, offering a slim chance . . . though the marble column was set back a good three feet beneath the overhang. If she could wrap her legs around it, she could slide down to the balustrade.

Gritting her teeth, she raised both legs and caught the pillar between the toes of her boots. Concentrating fiercely, she worked her feet forward, searching for a sufficient grip on the smooth marble surface.

"You might as well let go. I shall catch you."

The cultured masculine voice startled Rosa.

She glanced down . . . which proved a mistake. The shock of seeing Lord Graystone standing directly below broke the tenuous grip of her hands. Her boots slipped from the pillar. Her mouth opened on a silent cry as she plummeted downward. The awkward angle terrified her. She was going to hit on her back.

Rosa landed against something hard, all right, but it wasn't quite as unyielding as stone.

Although the Englishman staggered back a step, he managed to brace himself against the sudden impact of her body landing in his arms. Rosa's lungs filled with a shocked gasp. Her skin tightened, drawing into goose bumps at the sensation of lean muscle and sinew supporting her knees and shoulders.

Her bemused reaction vanished the instant she recognized a hint of mockery in his remarkable blue eyes. His sandy brows rose in two infuriating arches.

"Ah, the flamenco dancer," he drawled. "Out for a bit of exercise, señorita?"

His sarcasm struck her senses like a mouthful of pepper seeds. She started to squirm.

"Put me down," Rosa demanded in hushed tones.

"You've had a bit of a shock. Maybe you shouldn't be in such a hurry to stand."

He whispered as well, as if he understood the necessity of not alerting the guards. That only added to Rosa's acute embarrassment. Had he concluded that she was up to something dishonest? Well, why shouldn't he guess, when she was creeping about dressed in black and falling off the blasted roof?

"Do not be ridiculous. I am fine. Now, let me go."

He released her legs, but he held on to her waist and slowly, slowly, let her body slide down his until they faced one another. Her belly pressed intimately against his. Her breasts flattened against a chest that was far too solid and muscular to be caged in elegant evening clothes.

It seemed like forever before her toes touched the ground. Heat radiated into her body from every point at which it made contact with his, curling into a strange knot of tension low in her belly. No man had ever dared hold her this close before, certainly not with her godfathers in the vicinity.

She felt torn between congratulating him and uttering an outraged protest at his boldness. Before she could find her voice, he released her and took a step back.

"Better?"

"Yes, I . . . thank you for catching me." Suddenly, her entire body started to tremble. The belated reaction to her terrifying fall settled in with a vengeance.

Her knees buckled.

Lord Graystone caught her. For the second time in a matter of seconds, Rosa found herself pressed against his chest.

"I warned you not to take things too fast."

But timing was critical. The guard. If he discovered her here . . . "You must let me go."

"When I am sure you can stand on your own. Not before. You're still shaking."

Wildly, Rosa suspected that the trembling no longer had anything to do with her fall. The light shudders passed through her body every time his deep voice vibrated against her skin.

"You danced for me tonight."

Wariness shot through Rosa. She mustn't forget that this man held the power to expose her to Don Geraldo. "What makes you think that?" she hedged.

"A room full of dinner guests, and you barely took your eyes from mine. Why?"

She would never admit how devastatingly attractive she found him. Nothing would complete her humiliation more effectively. Lifting her chin, she retorted, "Does your arrogance always lead you to draw such faulty conclusions?"

"Derek. My name is Derek Carlisle. You should know the name of the man you tried to seduce with your dance."

Rosa stiffened. It angered her when people drew the wrong conclusions about her heritage. "Flamenco is art, not a form of seduction. It is an expression of deep emotion, of joy, sorrow, and—"

"Passion?"

"Yes, passion most of all."

His left arm tightened around her. Rosa realized her mistake when his other hand slid into her hair and eased her head back. His thumb brushed her cheek, causing an unsettled feeling to bubble up inside her chest.

"No . . . I . . . that is not what I meant. Not that type of passion."

"Why me?" he asked roughly. "Because I sat next to Don Geraldo and formed a convenient excuse for you to draw near and attempt to steal his key?"

She licked her lips nervously. His gaze traced the movement of her tongue. "Sí. You looked so easy to beguile."

"Easy? As in dull-witted and simple to manipulate?"

"As in desperate for a woman," she countered recklessly.

Something dark and dangerous flashed in his eyes. "Really," he said in a low, silky tone. His gaze ranged boldly over her face. "Then isn't it a bloody lucky coincidence that I happen to find one in my arms right now?"

His head descended. His mouth boldly covered hers. Although firm, his sculptured lips were the texture of velvet. They moved over her mouth, tasting, teasing, mapping every contour. Every brief, stolen kiss she'd ever received from a past suitor seemed chaste in comparison. She kissed him back, too stunned to do otherwise. The mastery of his lips demanded a response. When her lips moved, boldly matching his own, he pulled her closer into the circle of his arms.

Without warning, he broke the kiss. Rosa's hands gripped the sleeves of his coat. But he didn't pull back. He kissed his way down her jaw, then moved to her neck. Delicious shivers rippled across her shoulders. She tilted her head, giving him better access. He obliged, trailing kisses down the taut line of her neck. Then his teeth closed gently on the juncture between her neck and shoulder.

Rosa's eyes nearly rolled back in her head. If Derek Carlisle was desperate for a woman, it certainly wasn't from a lack of experience or the inability to ignite passion.

She wanted his kisses to go on and on.

She could do this all night.

Rosa's eyes flew open. All night? Was she insane! The guard was due back soon.

Derek's cheek rubbed lightly against hers. Rosa stilled, enthralled by the sensation of closeness, of intimacy. His nose nuzzled her ear. Something melted deep inside. Perhaps . . . maybe just a little longer. She could spare another minute. What other chance would she have to explore these sensations? She'd never realized desire could be so—

He bit down lightly on her earlobe. The tips of her breasts tightened and something tugged in the most womanly part of her body. Her breathing sped up, coming in shallow pants.

His breath fanned across her cheek. "What is your name?"

"Rosa," she whispered. What harm could come from revealing her given name? She shivered, delighting in the wild tingles that danced down the backs of her legs. Of its own volition, her body arched into his. Her arms curled around his neck.

His hands slid down her back to cup her buttocks, squeezing firmly. A whimper escaped her throat. At the sound, his hands flexed, massaging her buttocks in a way that caused Rosa's thoughts to scatter. Tilting her hips, he pulled her even closer. The hot ridge of his arousal pressed against her belly.

Light exploded through Rosa's mind like fireworks.

Then Derek's low, seductive voice spoke close to her ear.

"So tell me, what valuables did you find in Don Geraldo's collection room? What do you have in the bag?"

Chapter Four

ROSA PLANTED HER palms against Graystone's shoulders and shoved with all her strength. His grip loosened somewhat, but he did not release her.

"How did you guess?" she hissed.

"There is only one room on the third floor of the hacienda." He looked up at the spot where she'd fallen. "I would have thought an accomplished thief such as yourself could enact a more graceful exit."

His criticism stung. His ready assumption of her guilt wounded her already sensitive pride. She snapped, "What business is it of yours?"

"I am a guest in Don Geraldo's home. I should report this theft."

"Why would you do that? You are no *amigo* of the don. I saw the expression on your face up there, the hands fisted behind your back. He angered you."

Graystone's hands shifted to her upper arms in a tight grip. "So, you crept in after we left. What did you steal?"

His fierce intensity intrigued her. He evidently wanted the book. It was her leverage. "A few things from the safe."

"You managed to break into that safe? Bloody hell." He

gave her a little shake. "Did you find a book? An old journal with a brown leather binding?"

The frustration in his voice pleased her. It was infinitely
more satisfying than the mask of indifference he'd adopted
after breaking off their kiss. It infuriated her that he seemed
untouched by an embrace that had rocked the ground beneath her feet.

"Is it valuable? Perhaps I could sell it." He drew in a
sharp breath. Rosa added deliberately, "Why would I bother
to weigh down my bag with a heavy, dusty old book when
there was money and jewelry readily available?"

"That is not an answer to my question, you stubborn
little hellion." He transferred his grip to her arm. "There is
one way to find out. Shall we take a look in the bag?"

Rosa's eyes widened in horror. She didn't want him
taking any of her hard-won spoils, particularly not the book
with its intriguing mysteries. Nor was there time for this.
She was crazy for taunting Graystone when she should be
making good her escape. What was it about his sophisticated
hauteur that made her want to shatter his perfect control?

Kneeling, he loosened the neck of the bag with his free
hand. Rosa leaned in the opposite direction, pulling against
his hold on her arm and preventing him from reaching too
far inside. He managed to reach the pearl choker. He drew
it out and held it on his palm.

"What do you anticipate this is worth?"

Quite a lot. Without thinking, Rosa snatched up the
necklace and dropped it down the front of her blouse.

Derek froze, startled by her quick reflexes and her
provocative solution to the problem. He pictured the
choker inside her blouse, slipping down through the
scented valley between her breasts. His mouth went dry.

"Are you challenging me to retrieve it?" he asked
hoarsely.

"You would not dare!"

On the contrary, his fingers tingled at the idea of sliding his hands over silken flesh. Some inner demon urged

him to take up her challenge and see how she would react. Would she slap his face, or melt in his arms again?

Instead, he reached for the bag. "Actually, I'm more interested in—"

The even cadence of a man's stride sounded against the cobblestones.

A sense of danger shot down Derek's spine. How could he have let himself become so distracted? He'd even missed the advance warning of the gate latch. He'd abandoned his wits to a pair of luscious lips and a beautiful face, letting time slip away rather than staying alert for the guard's return.

Rosa's eyes rounded. Her mouth opened in a soundless expression of dismay.

Derek responded instinctively to the threat of discovery. Rocking back on his heels, he pivoted, uncoiling to his full height as he turned. Rosa hunkered down behind him, next to the bag, obscured by the shadows and her dark clothing.

He spared a quick glance over his shoulder. She was pulling a black hood over her head, concealing her identity while leaving him exposed to the guard. Swift anger shot through him. She certainly came prepared for subterfuge. No logical reason explained this strange urge to shield her, except of course the need to protect that bag and the possibilities it represented. Did she have the journal, or not?

She gathered the bag to her chest. Her shoulder brushed a sensitive area on the back of his thigh. A sensual tremor shot to the soles of Derek's feet. His whole body still vibrated like a tuning fork after that scorching kiss.

"Señor Carlisle?" the guard called out. The young man approached, his rifle cradled against his chest.

"Yes?" Derek attempted to sound bored.

Rosa started to inch away. *Not so fast, you little hellion.* Derek thrust his left hand behind him. His fist closed around the first thing his fingers came in contact with.

Soft material filled his hand, with something inside that

bunched and shifted within his grip. It was the hood, along with her hair, Derek concluded with satisfaction.

That should keep her still.

She tugged. He held fast. She dug her fingernails into the back of his fist. It required all of Derek's willpower to maintain the pleasant, neutral smile on his face.

"Dinner is over, *señor*. The other guests are calling for their carriages and leaving the hacienda. I am much afraid that Don Geraldo would be displeased to find you here unescorted." The guard glanced nervously over one shoulder. "*Por favor*, if you would only return to your room."

"My apologies. I just stepped outside to enjoy a cheroot. Beautiful night, don't you agree?"

With his right hand, Derek reached into his inner coat pocket. He used the movement to conceal a wince as his captive continued her silent assault on his hand. He pulled out one of the slender cigars he'd hoped to share with Don Geraldo when they finalized the sale. His inquiries around Havana had reported that this particular brand was the don's favorite.

The guard's expression altered subtly. He regarded the cheroot with envy.

"Would you like one?" Derek offered quickly. He needed to get rid of the guard, but he wouldn't be able to do so without first allaying the man's suspicions.

"For me? You want me to smoke with you?" The guard was clearly astonished to receive a friendly offer from a gentleman so much above his social station.

"Certainly." Derek's smile locked in place as a spasm of pain traveled up his left arm. An expletive swelled in his chest. He covered it by clearing his throat. "There is no need to stand on ceremony here."

He tightened his grip. Rosa instantly stopped clawing at his hand.

The guard scanned the courtyard, evidently concerned that he would be caught neglecting his duty. "I should not."

"Come, now. Your secret will be safe with me."

"But *señor*, I couldn't take your last—"

"I have another."

The guard finally relented with a slight smile. "*Sí*, very well. *Gracias*." He pushed the rifle back over his shoulder, where it hung by its strap between his shoulder blades. Accepting the cheroot, he drew it beneath his nose and smelled deeply of the fine tobacco.

Derek pulled out the other cheroot and clamped it lightly between his teeth. He fought the urge to give in to tension and bite right through the rolled tobacco.

The guard looked at Derek expectantly.

Too late, Derek recognized the flaw in his plan. *Maybe this wasn't such a clever idea after all.* "Do you have a light?" he asked hopefully.

"No, Señor Carlisle. I thought you must have—"

"A flint. Yes, of course. In my pocket."

In his left trousers pocket, unfortunately, where it would be very clumsy, not to mention irregular, to reach across with his free hand to retrieve it. Bloody hell.

Just then, Rosa touched his wrist. Her hand trembled. It registered abruptly that he held her hair in a fierce, no doubt painful grip. Saucy and troublesome the girl might be, but he didn't really want to hurt her. Nor did he want her arrested . . . for his own reasons, of course. If she'd stolen the journal, he didn't want it to fall back into Don Geraldo's hands.

Then there was the more pressing matter of retrieving the flint before the guard became suspicious.

Only one viable solution presented itself.

Derek released the handful of black silk.

He didn't need to see Rosa's departure. He could feel her withdrawal, could somehow sense the supple strength and grace that enabled her to melt silently into the night. The dense plant growth sheltered her from the guard's view.

Frustration cut through him.

He reached into his pocket. The back of his hand stung as it brushed against the material. Derek deftly switched the flint to his right hand to conceal the half-moon cuts and the flecks of blood.

She'd certainly left her mark on him . . . in more ways than one.

Derek struck a flame. The guard leaned forward, taking a deep draw on the cheroot. The end glowed orange-gold, a tiny beacon in the darkness.

"*Excellente.*" The exhaled smoke drifted upward, dimming a grouping of stars. Raising the cheroot in a little salute, the guard added, "*Gracias.* Now, I must finish my patrol. I suggest you return to your room very soon, *señor,* just to be safe."

"Yes, thank you. I will. Do you mind if I finish this smoke first?"

The guard shook his head, then walked away.

Derek jerked a monogrammed handkerchief from his coat and tied it around his hand. His gaze scanned the courtyard. The deep shadows and profusion of concealing plants mocked him. Rosa could be anywhere, but he sensed that she was no longer nearby. She had fled, along with her booty.

The morning would alter that, he swore. He would scour Havana until he found her.

He wasn't sure what infuriated him most: the possibility that she'd managed to get her lovely hands on the journal when he had failed, the way she'd used him to make good her escape, or the evidence of his loss of control still straining against his trousers.

"DID YOU SEE what he just did?" Dickie whispered furiously from their hiding place across the courtyard, his mouth agape.

"I'm wishing I didn't," Michael growled. "Sure and I just might have to kill the son of a bitch."

"He kissed our Rosa as if she was a harlot," Esteban said, feeling deeply offended. His eyes narrowed. "*Bastardo.*"

"Not only that, he put his hands all over her—"

Esteban grabbed a fistful of Dickie's collar, cutting off his words. "Do not say it, *por favor.*"

Dickie scowled. He pried Esteban's fingers loose. "I won't. Hell, I can't even say the word. Not when we're talkin' about our angel girl."

They had just crept back from the stables, arriving at the agreed time to help Rosa down from the roof—only to find her already down and locked in the Englishman's embrace. Thankfully, she had broken free. Then the guard's arrival had cut off any chance at rescue or retribution.

"The poor colleen was so shocked she didn't even fight the rake," Michael added, shaking his head morosely.

Worse than that, Esteban lamented inwardly, she had seemed to enjoy it, the one fact none of them cared to admit aloud. To voice the suspicion would be almost akin to blasphemy. This was Rosa, their innocent darling. Unfortunately, it was her purity that left her vulnerable to such an accomplished seducer.

Esteban's shoulders slumped. "An Englishman, too. *Madre de Dios.*"

"By the saints of dear Ireland, you're right. Nothing could be worse than that," Michael moaned. He dragged his hands down his face, knocking his hairpiece askew again.

"This is horrible." Dickie automatically righted the hairpiece when Michael didn't seem to notice. "What are we goin' to do about it?"

"We must defend her honor!" Michael whispered vehemently.

With a snort, Dickie retorted, "What do you suggest we do, challenge his lordship to a duel? That bloke is almost forty years our junior. Looks quite fit, and cool as Maine ice."

"Aye, he does look like a brawny lad."

"I'll bet he's a crack shot, too. And I hope you aren't suggestin' a bare-knuckled fight. One punch to that bloated belly of yours and you'll be wheezin' for a week."

"It's sorry I am to hear you say such a thing, Dickie Hunt. Truth is, with one tiny push that lad would knock you flat, you pipsqueak."

"*Silencio!* Rosa is coming," Esteban hissed. "Let us not embarrass her by speaking of what happened. She must not know that we witnessed her humiliation."

The other men nodded briskly.

Rosa jerked in surprise when she spotted them. She glanced back over her shoulder. Esteban's mouth tightened at the fleeting guilty look that passed across her face.

She ducked down beside them. "Here you are. You are late. Did something go wrong?"

"No, *niña,*" Esteban said tenderly, resisting the urge to pull her into his arms and cradle her against his chest. There would be time for that later, when they weren't at risk of being caught. "We just do not move as fast as we used to."

"How long have you . . . um, been here?" Color stole into her cheeks. "Did you see me come down from the roof?"

"No," the three old men whispered in unison.

Rosa's brows rose.

"We just got here," Michael explained hastily.

"Did that guard see you?" asked Dickie.

"No. I . . . I eluded him."

Esteban murmured, "*Muy bien.* Let me have the bag." He took the burden from her arms. "Is this everything?"

"*Sí.* No, wait." She reached down the front of her blouse. The three men quickly averted their eyes. "Here is another piece." She handed him a circlet of pearls and gold.

After adding the necklace to the bag, Esteban said, "Michael, take Rosa ahead to the horses."

She blinked in surprise. "Why? Where will you be?"

"I do not like the fact that the guard lingers here." He nodded toward the two shadowy figures across the way, distinguished from the night by the two pinpoint orange glows of their cheroots. "Dickie and I shall remain for a short while, to make sure you are not followed."

"I think we should leave together," Rosa suggested firmly.

"Do you not trust my judgment, *niña?*"

"Of course I do, but—"

"Then go. You would not wish me to worry, would you?" He touched her face. "I will feel better knowing you are safe."

After a brief hesitation, Rosa nodded. Her reluctance was evident, but thankfully for his plan she obeyed. She and Michael moved away, crouching low. They headed for the nearby gate. Only once did she look back.

That last longing look toward the Englishman gave Esteban a renewed sense of determination. Women needed to be protected from their own troublesome yet endearing weaknesses. His great-niece needed him to protect her— from herself, but most of all from foreign rogues, too handsome and virile for their own good, who would take advantage of her innocence.

Tiny voices clamored in Esteban's head, reminding him that he'd transformed his virtuous niece into a thief, that she was the one who put food on the table. He stiffened at the stinging attack on his pride.

Well, even if he could not shield her from the ugly realities of the world and the need for money, he could protect her from the lustful intentions of men. He focused on the nagging fear that if he didn't do something to put a stop to this, Rosa and the Englishman might arrange to meet one another again. The spark of passion between them had been undeniable. It had been the same between Mercedes and Alex Wright, a powerful attraction at first sight. But Rosa's parents had been from the same social sphere. Lord Graystone was an aristocrat, arrogant and wealthy, accustomed to using women and tossing them aside like linen napkins.

Esteban would make certain the Englishman had no further opportunity to shame Rosa. She was all the family this old man had left, his only hope of love in his declining years.

Dickie eyed him suspiciously. "So, are you gonna tell me what's goin' on?"

"We should have no trouble in coaxing one of the maids to tell us where the Englishman's bedchamber is, no?"

Dickie grinned. "Now that's more like it. For once—and don't expect this to happen again—I agree with the way you're thinkin'." He reached out and explored the bag's contents through the cloth. "Did she make a good haul? What's this?" He outlined a large rectangular shape. His shaggy white brows snapped together. "Feels like a book."

Reaching inside the bag, Esteban pulled out a leather-bound book. He frowned. "Why would she burden herself with a book?"

Dickie shrugged. "Don't know. Maybe she just took a fancy to it. But since we won't get any money for a book, it's certainly one of them things we can do without."

Esteban nodded and replaced the book. Holding the lumpy bag tight so its contents wouldn't shift noisily, he and Dickie crept back into the hacienda.

DEREK DROPPED THE cheroot onto the cobblestones and ground it beneath his heel.

Two figures loomed behind him in the darkness.

"I am surprised you were able to tear yourselves away from the table," Derek said wryly. He turned, unconcerned.

Tim Rutherford, the ship's first mate and one of Derek's dearest friends, smiled. "The food was excellent."

"I was thinking more of the women fawning over you."

"There was that, too."

"They kept trying to press more wine on us," Geoffrey Stockbridge said, another trusted crewmember as well as Derek's fencing partner. "But we took care not to have more than three glasses."

"I am not surprised they made the attempt. The order to get you drunk and out of the way no doubt came from de Vargas himself."

"I don't like the sound of that," said Tim.

"How much did Don Geraldo demand for the journal?" asked Geoff.

"More than I should ever consider paying."

His two friends shared patently skeptical looks. After exploring the world with him for over five years, they were accustomed to an unlimited source of funds, either as a result of Derek's many archaeological successes or as a direct conduit from his father.

"Morally, that is," Derek clarified. "Don Geraldo can read the journal well enough to determine its link to the *Augustina*. He won't part with the journal for anything less than a full partnership in our venture."

"Ballocks," Tim said vehemently.

Geoff frowned. "Are you thinking of taking him up on that offer?"

"No," Derek replied with conviction. He stared at the gate through which that Gypsy hellion had no doubt escaped. Did she have the journal, or not? "I won't consider splitting up the treasure. The historical value alone is too substantial to ever allow half of it to be melted down or disappear into someone's private collection. Don Geraldo is only interested in the money. The wholesale recovery of a sunken seventeenth-century galleon would be unique among archaeological finds. Our crowning achievement. The copy of the *Augustina*'s manifest from the archives lists a cargo of priceless artificats, a collection the curator of the British Museum eagerly anticipates as a permanent exhibit. I want to share our prize with appreciative audiences, now and for generations to come."

Geoff crossed his arms. "Well, I'm relieved to hear you say that, old boy. But I don't believe losing half the treasure would actually be our chief concern."

"Exactly," Tim agreed. "With Don Geraldo's reputation, I'd worry more that he'd have us all killed in the end and keep the entire haul for himself."

Derek's mouth slanted bitterly. "That likelihood has certainly crossed my mind. You needn't worry, gentlemen. I don't want a nest of vipers sleeping on my ship or working alongside us in such dangerous conditions. Don Geraldo can take his ultimatum and go to bloody hell with it."

"That's what I like to hear." Tim chuckled. "Maybe we won't even need the journal."

"Perhaps the other evidence you've gathered will prove sufficient this time," Geoff said hopefully.

"I trust we'll have better luck than before. We have slightly more than two months before hurricane season is upon us. If I cannot use the journal, we'll just have to search this summer, and the next, until we find her."

Derek's two companions nodded their agreement. It humbled him that his crew of six followed him on this quest. They didn't fully understand his passion for the particular artifacts he sought, but they continued to undertake the risks out of loyalty, a love for adventure, and a fervor for the hunt.

"Get back to the ship. Don Geraldo clearly covets *Pharaoh's Gold,* and I wouldn't put it past him to attempt stealing her. Put three men on guard, heavily armed, and work in shifts."

"Aren't you coming with us?" Geoff exclaimed.

"What can be gained by remaining as the don's guest one more day?" asked Tim.

"I shall stay the night. Don Geraldo has left things open for negotiations to continue in the morning."

Tim smiled. "Knowing how you can talk a gem merchant out of his best stones, or a leading courtesan out of her gown, you might manage to convince him yet."

"Or we can wait around a few days to see if the Yanks attack," Geoff added. "Then the don might be begging you to take the book off his hands."

Derek thought of a certain black-haired thief. "I also want to nose around and ask a few questions."

He must track Rosa down and get the answers he was denied by the guard's untimely arrival. If there was any chance she had the journal, he couldn't pass up the opportunity. He'd resolved not to steal the book from Don Geraldo himself, but he would experience no hesitation in buying it from someone who had.

"Your priority is protecting *Pharaoh's Gold*," Derek stressed. "Without the ship, her equipment, and the other documents I've uncovered, our quest is at an end . . . journal or no journal. Whatever you do, don't let that bastard get ahold of my ship."

Chapter Five

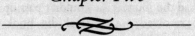

DEREK TOSSED HIS evening coat onto a chair upholstered in gold damask. The elegant burgundy and gold furnishings in the bedchamber looked particularly rich in the light of numerous candles. Everything about the hacienda was designed to showcase Don Geraldo's affluence.

Derek jerked his tie free and tossed it after his coat.

Rosa. The rose. It fit her.

She hadn't denied stealing the journal. After he met with Don Geraldo tomorrow morning, and confirmed whether or not the book was indeed missing, he would find her. With enough coins pressed into the palms of Havana's residents, he would find one person willing to talk. A woman that beautiful could hardly remain anonymous.

They had unfinished business between them . . . and he didn't mean only the journal. His body still hummed from their encounter. Her daring intrigued him. Her saucy stubbornness infuriated him. Her talent as a coquette challenged him to prove that she could never, ever, make him lose control like that again.

He was just starting to unfasten the studs on his shirt when he heard voices in the hallway. With no additional warning, the door burst open.

Four guards shoved through the opening. They took up positions on either side of the door, rifles cocked and ready.

Don Geraldo stepped between them. Locking his hands behind his back, he rocked on his heels. "Lord Graystone," he said, looking entirely too pleased with himself.

The hairs prickled on Derek's nape. Wherever this was going, he felt certain he wouldn't like the outcome.

"Don Geraldo," he replied coolly. "To what do I owe the dubious pleasure of this late-night visit?"

"Someone left an anonymous note in my chambers."

"Do you always place such reliance on a note from an individual who has some reason to conceal his identity?"

The don scowled at the thinly veiled insult. "The tip was correct in this case. My collection vault has been robbed."

"My deepest sympathies." Derek folded his arms. "But what brings you here? Surely you don't suspect me of petty theft, *señor*. You know quite well that I have deep pockets."

Don Geraldo lifted his chin, looking smug. "Except when it comes to one thing you covet. Although several items were missing, the most damning is the journal."

Derek stiffened. "Then perhaps the new owner will be willing to part with the book for a reasonable price. That is the only role I play in this little melodrama. I am certainly not your thief."

"The note I received informs me otherwise." Turning to the guards, the don ordered, "Search the room."

Although the accusations offended him, Derek watched the guards advance without concern. He knew where they could find the booty, but he certainly had no intention of telling them about Rosa. If Don Geraldo spoke the truth, she was now his only link to the journal.

Three guards spread out, one checking the polished mahogany wardrobe, another the desk, while the third knelt to search under the massive four-poster bed. The fourth man remained by the door. Derek waited confidently.

Suddenly, the guard searching the wardrobe gave a

shout. He reached into the drawer at the base. Turning, he tossed two silver carving knives and the journal onto the bed.

Derek stared at the damning evidence in shock. He was being framed for the crime, that much was apparent, but who was behind the deed?

After she had slipped away, Rosa would have had time to sneak to his room and conceal the knives and the journal while he spoke with Geoff and Tim. Could she have melted in his arms in that intoxicating way, then stabbed him in the back? Something inside him shied away from believing the worst.

What of Don Geraldo? He could have planted the false evidence himself. Perhaps the don had had the journal all along. Planting the items provided an excuse to accuse Derek of the theft and demand the *Pharoah's Gold* or his archaeological expertise as restitution.

The guard at the desk exclaimed in triumph. He tossed a glittering choker of pearls toward the bed. The necklace landed on the coverlet with a soft plop.

The sight struck Derek like an uppercut to the jaw.

Now there was no doubt. It was the same choker he'd pulled from the Gypsy's bag, the same piece of plunder she'd dropped down her blouse . . . just after he'd threatened to reveal her to Don Geraldo. Just before he'd lost his temper, acted callously, and clutched her hair in a painful grip. He'd been a fool not to assure her that he had no intention of seeing her arrested.

Rosa was protecting herself by diverting suspicion to him.

Don Geraldo would not search for the real culprit as long as he believed the thief to be in custody. It was worth the sacrifice of a few items to cover her trail. She'd given no indication that she understood the value of the journal . . . other than his interest in it. Returning it to Don Geraldo seemed a direct thumbing of her nose at the way Derek had treated her.

Her plan was concise, effective, and actually quite clever.

Nevertheless, it was a direct attack on Derek's integrity. Anger burned hot, allowing him to ignore a deeper ache that might have been disappointment.

Don Geraldo picked up the journal and tucked it under his arm. He cast Derek a self-satisfied smile. "Do you still wish to protest your innocence, Lord Graystone?"

"You think these few paltry valuables will add to my family fortune? This is utter nonsense," he snapped.

De Vargas scowled. "Even now, you are arrogant. How I hate the English." Hooking one finger through the choker, he lifted the shimmering pearls into the light. "Where did you hide the rest of the stolen pieces? Where are the two companions who accompanied you to dinner?"

"My men are gone, but they took nothing with them other than full stomachs from dinner." He stepped up to the chair, every muscle stiff with restrained fury, and scooped up his coat and tie. "Very well, you have what you came for. I shall pack my bag and be gone within five minutes."

"Allow you to leave? I think not."

"You cannot detain me. I am a British citizen."

Don Geraldo snorted. "Why should I care for that? It is only the Spanish government that honors such things. You will tell me where the items are. More importantly, you will tell me how to understand the secrets of this journal and what else you know of the *Augustina*'s location."

"Like hell I will."

"Stubborn *bastardo*." Don Geraldo signaled to the guards. "Take him to La Muerte."

The death. What the bloody blazes did that mean? "What is La Muerte?" Derek demanded.

"A place I will enjoy putting to good use in your case. An old Spanish fort facing the harbor, which I have turned into my own personal prison."

A prison. A dark, tiny cell with bars across the door and window . . . assuming there was even a window to look out upon the sky and the stars.

A closed, cramped place where he would be trapped.

The familiar cold, strangulating sensation clenched in Derek's chest. Suddenly, each breath was an effort to draw into his lungs. But the rush of fear and adrenaline also gave him new strength.

Two guards reached for him. Fighting furiously, Derek landed numerous blows. One guard dropped to the floor. Another doubled over, coughing.

Then a rifle butt slammed into Derek from behind, catching him above his right hipbone.

His knees buckled as the blow to his kidney shot pain through his lower back. Dimly, through a red haze of agony, he was aware of two guards securing his hands behind him. Each grabbed one of his upper arms. By the time he blinked and cleared the mist from his vision, it was too late.

He was a prisoner.

They dragged him from the room. The lethal end of a rifle pressed between his shoulder blades. He had thought losing the journal was the worst thing that could happen.

He couldn't have been more wrong.

ROSA DROPPED THE bag on her mattress. She plopped down on the bed beside it. Crossing her legs, she propped her elbows on her knees, dug her chin into her cupped hands, and stared at the black cloth sack as if a poisonous snake lurked inside.

To support her godfathers, she was living out the worst of the reputations that tainted her Gypsy heritage. Thievery. But she had never felt her shame so keenly as tonight, enduring Derek Carlisle's accusations and mockery even as his kisses made her body burn with desire.

Esteban, Dickie, and Michael, on the other hand, couldn't be more pleased with her success. Even now, they celebrated in the main room of the humble yet sturdy three-room house, sharing a round of whiskey. Their pride in her "accomplishment" had driven her to the refuge of her room.

She compressed her lips, pushing aside the self-pity. Her frustration didn't change the fact that three beloved, aging men relied upon her. Resolutely, she pulled the bag toward her and upended it. The contents tumbled onto the worn, clean coverlet.

Dejection vanished beneath a wave of shock.

Some items were missing. She remembered taking more flatware than these pieces. And how could she forget the lovely pearl choker after Graystone's brash threat to retrieve it from her blouse? The memory of the intense look in his eyes still sent tingles across her skin. The choker, too, was gone.

Worst of all, the book had vanished. What could have happened to it? A spasm of disappointment shot through her. Although she had known it was a wild plan, she had found hope in the book's secrets, in the potential that it might lead her to sunken treasure and provide for her godfathers' futures.

On the way home she had already begun to plan. She would need help, of course, even after learning to analyze the book. Several sea captains ranked among Dickie's and Michael's cronies at the harbor, men they could trust. Luis and Alonso dove on the large ships that came into port, making repairs and scraping barnacles off the hulls. Surely they would be interested in coming to an arrangement. She was an excellent swimmer, as well. Although complex and risky, the dream was achievable if she only pursued it steadfastly enough.

Much good those plans would do her if the book was lost. She had felt it in the bag as she fled across the courtyard. In fact, she hadn't let the bag out of her sight until—

Her eyes widened in understanding.

"*Tío!* Dickie!" she shouted. She leaped off the bed.

Her three godfathers quickly appeared at her door, whiskey glasses still in hand.

"There are items missing from this bag."

"Is that all, *niña*?" Esteban gave a nervous chuckle. "Do not give this old man such a fright."

Michael's gaze lifted, suddenly finding the peeling plaster on the ceiling extremely fascinating. The fact that he couldn't meet her eyes heightened Rosa's suspicions.

"Nothin' is gone of any special value, I'll bet," Dickie blustered.

Rosa folded her arms tightly. "Oh, really. How can you be so sure? I have yet to tell you what is missing."

Esteban jabbed Dickie's ribs with his elbow. "Let us worry about it, *niña*. You need not trouble yourself."

"I am the one who took the risk of crawling over that roof and breaking into that room. I deserve answers. Now, *por favor*."

"We needed to lighten the load—"

"We had to bribe a guard—" Esteban said simultaneously, talking over Dickie.

Their mouths snapped shut, and something clenched around Rosa's heart. They were lying to her. It wasn't the first time they'd spun stories or made excuses, but past incidents were always over something minor. Every warning instinct in her body hummed that this was far more serious.

"I want the truth. What did you do with the items?"

Michael cried out, "Faith, Rosa, it wasn't my idea."

"You would have agreed if you'd been with us, mate," Dickie snapped. "You were as mad as Esteban and I, what with all your talk about defendin' her honor."

The conversation deteriorated into arguments, accusations, and every effort to place the blame elsewhere. Words spilled out with increasing clarity, painting a disturbing picture.

"You saw Lord Graystone kiss me, didn't you?"

Michael harrumphed. "He did more than kiss you, colleen."

"Darn near tried to devour you."

For years they had judged and found all her suitors wanting. No man had ever been good enough for her.

They had chased off every man with near fanatical devotion. And now, to see a complete stranger dare to kiss her with such intimacy— Dread curled through Rosa.

"What have you done?" she whispered tightly.

Esteban lifted his chin, though his gaze suddenly flickered with uncertainty. "We made certain Lord Graystone won't bother you again."

Oh, no. "Tell me you didn't plant those missing items in his bedchamber."

Dickie sighed. "Seemed like a good idea at the time."

"You must go back to the hacienda, *pronto,* and remove those things before they are found in Graystone's room!"

"Too late for that," Dickie said dully. He swirled the whiskey in his glass, staring down at the amber liquid.

Rosa gripped the back of a chair with both hands. "What do you mean?" When they exchanged hesitant looks and remained silent, she pulled out the one threat she knew would work. "If you do not tell me, I will return to the hacienda and discover the truth for myself."

They shared another look, this one of sad resignation.

"Well . . . we, uh, that is, one of the maids slipped a note to Don Geraldo tellin' him to search Graystone's bedchamber. The don was headin' there with several soldiers as we left."

Rosa closed her eyes as a spasm of pain shot through her chest. Guilt, she was discovering, was a spiteful thing.

"Colleen, are you all right? You look a little pale."

"We were only protecting you, angel girl."

"We made certain the *hombre* would not bother you again in such a vulgar fashion. Better too for Don Geraldo to think he has caught his thief than to seek us out."

Though her godfathers were terribly misguided, they believed they had done the right thing. Their fanatical need to shield her blinded them to everything else. Their devotion assured her of their love, but it appalled her even more. She had never thought them capable of this.

"This time you went too far in protecting me. You know he is innocent of any wrongdoing."

Dickie snorted. "Not so innocent, if you ask me."

"You don't understand men of Graystone's stamp. I saw many of his ilk in Ireland. He's an accomplished seducer of women."

"A rake, like you, Michael?" When he blushed, she turned to the others. "Like all of you?"

"Now, Rosa—"

"Do you believe that over the years my ears have been shielded from tales of your amorous exploits?"

"That is why Graystone worries us so," Esteban admitted. "We understand what such rakes are capable of."

"This particular rake was capable of catching me when I fell off the roof tonight, saving me from serious injury. He also could have revealed me to the guard, but chose not to." *Though he held me prisoner himself with a cruel grip on my hair.* Her scalp still stung. Graystone had ignited her fury at the same time her body craved the excitement of his embrace.

"Oh," said Michael.

Still sounding doubtful, Dickie asked, "He did?"

"That does not excuse the way he . . . he handled you," Esteban insisted.

"An innocent man could be blamed for a crime he did not commit, simply because he had the audacity to kiss me. Yes, that deserves punishment of the highest order," Rosa snapped sarcastically. "I cannot understand why that upsets me!"

Michael cleared his throat. Esteban and Dickie shuffled their feet.

"Maybe our solution was a bit . . . extreme," Dickie murmured.

Esteban said reassuringly, "Don Geraldo may detain Graystone for a while, but soon he must let Graystone go or anger the British, no? You would not have had such powerful friends if the don had caught you instead, *niña*." He shrugged. "What else can Don Geraldo do to him?"

"We must be certain what happened. Take a cask of *cerveza* to loosen the guards' tongues. Charm them with cigars and stories of your smuggling days until they tell you something useful. This time, I am not going to clean up your mess."

WITH A CREAK and a loud click, the soldier stretched the rack another notch. The leather bindings pulled mercilessly at Derek's wrists and ankles for the second day in a row. Fresh pain shot through his joints like scorching tongues of fire. The rough wood on which he lay abraded his bare back.

Derek clenched his teeth. Don Geraldo stood beyond Derek's shoulder, just within his range of vision. He wouldn't give the bastard the satisfaction of hearing him groan.

Things could be much worse, actually. Don Geraldo could order the use of even more cruel instruments of torture hanging on the walls of the sixteeth-century fort— metal tongs that could be heated red hot to tear off flesh, thumb screws and boots designed to crush muscle and bone.

One disadvantage to studying medieval archaeology was a familiarity with the sadistic torture techniques used on heretics, political prisoners, and suspected witches. And the Spanish, with their Inquisition and determination to rip confessions from non-Catholics, had been some of the worst offenders. Derek had found the historical reading fascinating, albeit morbid.

No more. He was gaining an entirely new empathy for those ancient victims.

Perhaps worse was yet to come, if Derek continued refusing to answer the don's pointed questions.

Don Geraldo stepped closer, hovering over Derek. He stroked a thick riding crop across his left palm. A smug expression caused his eyelids to droop lazily. "Come now,

Graystone, why do you not speak? All this sad discomfort could stop if you would but tell me what I wish to know."

Derek glared at his tormentor. "Perhaps I do not have anything worthwhile to say."

"Liar. You must know something!"

"So sorry, my attention must have drifted. What were we discussing again?"

Don Geraldo's riding crop hit the wooden rack with a loud crack. A colorful curse exploded from his mouth.

Derek's dry, cracked lips slanted cynically. He gained a small measure of satisfaction from the don's temper. It meant things weren't progressing to the other man's liking, either.

"Why must you be so stubborn? It is all so simple. I want to know what other evidence you have concerning the *Augustina*."

"You keep assuming that I came here for something more than naval documents."

"Do not make the mistake of thinking me a fool, Graystone. The *Augustina* carried immense wealth. No man can resist the temptation of trying to retrieve that much money. I suspected as much the moment you asked after the nature of my collection."

"Judging my motives against the greedy nature of your own would be a mistake," Derek growled.

De Vargas snorted. "You say my ancestor was not a navigator, that his descriptions in the journal will not be adequate. Thus, you must have other information to guide your search. And the journal must contain something useful, as well, or you would not have come all this way seeking to buy it." The don leaned close. His dark eyes glittered with bitterness and greed. His breath smelled of tobacco. "You will teach me how to interpret the journal. You will take me to this location."

"Ah, yes, the proposed partnership."

Don Geraldo straightened with a sly chuckle. He stroked his fingers along the green and black leather braided over the crop. "The partnership is no longer necessary. I retain possession of the journal. I have you, and soon you shall beg me to listen to whatever you wish to say. I will find *Nuestra Señora de la Augustina* myself."

"And then what? Surely you don't think the *Augustina's* cargo sits in a convenient pile on the ocean floor after centuries of being pounded by storm after storm, do you? What do you know about salvaging a sunken ship?"

A muscle twitched alongside Don Geraldo's nose.

"You need my help, as well as my ship and equipment. From your evident frustration, I assume you haven't captured *Pharaoh's Gold*. Is my crew proving uncooperative? How many attempts have your men made to board my ship . . . and failed?"

Vivid red spotted the don's cheeks. Without warning, he whipped his crop across Derek's ribs.

The searing pain from the blow lanced through Derek. His stomach and chest muscles clenched spasmodically as he sucked in a sharp breath.

"Enough!" de Vargas raged. The last hold on his temper collapsed beneath the pressure of Derek's taunts. "You have until dawn tomorrow to tell me all I want to know."

"And if I do not?" Derek countered.

"Then you will be executed."

Astonishment flicked through Derek. "What?" he whispered.

Don Geraldo squared his shoulders. "Indeed. Executed. By firing squad."

"On what charge?" Derek demanded, finding his voice again.

"I believe the charge of aiding and abetting the Cuban rebels shall do nicely. After all, how else could you have safely passed the American blockade?"

"You have no right, de Vargas!"

"Has that stopped me from imprisoning and torturing you?"

The bastard had a good point there. Derek's neck muscles strained as he lifted his head, which he swore weighed several stone. "You are bluffing," he snarled. "This is just another tactic to get me to talk."

"Then you should hope it works. Only a fool would continue to hold out against such pain." Don Geraldo sniffed arrogantly. "If you will not speak, of what use are you to me?"

"Dead men talk even less."

"Dead men are not an inconvenience, either. In time, I will succeed in taking your ship. Then I will have all your papers and equipment without this bother."

"Papers? Perhaps I keep all my information in my head."

The don pursed his lips. "I think now you are the one bluffing, Lord Graystone." He toyed with the crop. "Remember, dawn and the firing squad will come all too soon. I suggest you choose to speak before then." Turning on the soldier at the rack and the three others standing against the wall, he snapped, "This is a waste of time. Put him back in his cell." Then he stomped from the chamber.

Derek's head sagged back against the wooden platform. He fought off a feeling of helplessness. Protecting *Pharaoh's Gold* and her contents was his crew's first priority. If they were occupied repelling attacks, they couldn't launch a rescue attempt. But his loyal men would find a way. He could endure until then.

Assuming Don Geraldo's latest threat was actually a bluff.

It must be. After the treasure was recovered Derek would be no more useful than shark bait, but in the meantime he was infinitely more valuable alive.

It made no sense to execute him.

The more Derek thought about it, the more confident he felt in his conclusion . . . though logic provided cold comfort and no relief whatsoever from the pain.

ROSA SENSED SOMETHING was dreadfully wrong the minute Michael, Dickie, and Esteban returned. Something even worse than the discovery two days ago that Lord Graystone had been sent to La Muerte. Michael twisted his favorite cap roughly between his large hands. Esteban raked his fingers through his steel-gray hair, and Dickie sighed heavily the minute he walked through the door.

Even worse, they seemed in perfect harmony with one another. Disaster must be just around the corner.

Or perhaps it had already happened! A sensation like cold, skeletal fingers clutched at Rosa's throat.

They gathered around the small dining table, each settling into a seat with weary resignation. Hoarsely, she pressed, "Well? What did you discover at the barracks?"

"It ain't good news, that's for sure," Dickie grumbled.

"Just tell me."

Michael cut in. "Well, it seems the Englishman withstood the torture—"

"Torture?" Rosa exclaimed. She recoiled inwardly, her guilt-laden imagination struck by horrifying images of Lord Graystone suffering at Don Geraldo's hands. How much agony had he suffered? Had they marred his handsome face?

"It seems they want him to talk, but he ain't tellin' them what they want to know."

"How could he?" Rosa snapped. "He doesn't know where the rest of the stolen valuables are."

"That ain't the worst of it." Dickie turned on Michael. "Why don't you tell her, you great Irish ox?"

"Oh, no, me boyo," Michael countered. He shook his head vigorously. "You can share that bit of news."

"One of you tell me . . . now," Rosa said between gritted teeth, "or I'll go down to the fort and find out for myself."

"It's just that . . ." Dickie offered hesitantly, "since the Englishman won't talk, Don Geraldo has ordered the bloke to be shot by a firin' squad at dawn."

"Madre de Dios," Rosa whispered. She braced her palms against the table as the world suddenly tilted and her heart began to pound. "Are you certain?"

Esteban confirmed the worst. "The soldiers were moaning about having to get up so early. Paolo Villarreal complained about having to fetch Graystone's last meal tonight."

Dickie tugged on his beard. "They plan on going to Señora Espinoza. Quite a cook, that woman, with that little restaurant on the west side. Not bad lookin', either, even though she's nearing sixty." He waggled his shaggy eyebrows. "Did I mention she's a widow?"

"Dickie!"

The old sailor cleared his throat. "Er, right you are. We should be thinkin' about the poor bloke. Sad thing, being executed. Maybe you could have the priest say a prayer for his soul at Sunday mass, Michael."

" 'Tis a mighty shame, to be sure," Michael agreed sorrowfully. Then, on an upbeat note, he added, "But one less Englishman in the world isn't so bad, after all."

Rosa planted her hands on her hips. She cocked her head and stared at her three godfathers, waiting with ill-concealed impatience for them to come up with the obvious.

Dickie's muttered curse broke the silence. "I suppose you might say . . . just maybe . . . that it's our fault he's in there."

Rosa drummed her fingers against her hipbones. "And what are you going to do about it?"

Esteban eyed her askance. "You are not suggesting—"

"*Sí.* It is our responsibility to get him out of there."

Michael dragged his hands down his face. "I think I'll be needing a good stout ale about now."

"Now, angel girl, think about this," Dickie cajoled. "We're just feeble old men, barely hangin' on to our wits, who—"

"Who were sneaky enough to get Lord Graystone framed for a crime I committed."

"Er, yes—I mean no! We can't break a prisoner out of that fortress! There's only the three of us."

"Four, including me."

"By the saints," Michael moaned. "I think I'll be making that a whiskey."

"It is hopeless, *niña*. The Englishman is well guarded. The only way Graystone will leave that prison is—" Esteban's voice faded.

"Is what?"

"In a coffin. Don Geraldo is determined to see him dead."

Shock rolled over Rosa in cold waves. She sank into the fourth chair. "*Dios mio,* this is horrible."

Esteban covered one of her hands with his own. "It may be small comfort, but I believe the don's hatred goes much deeper than the theft of his precious belongings. He despises all things English. His soldiers also tried to board Graystone's ship today, but they were fought off by the crew."

"We must get him out of that prison."

"I just explained—"

"In a coffin. I know, *tío.* That is the only way he is leaving La Muerte." Rosa's back straightened as a far-fetched idea struck her. "There might just be a way."

"I hope this idea don't include breakin' into that prison and tryin' to get the bloke out," Dickie said uneasily.

Rosa stood. "No, we are not going to break in. Don Geraldo is going to let us take Graystone away with his blessing."

"By the saints, I knew it," Michael moaned. "The colleen has a plan. We're doomed."

"How do you expect to trick the guards in such a way?" Esteban asked, his tone laced with doubt.

"We will smuggle Lord Graystone out."

"Smuggle?" Dickie echoed, brightening.

"Something you should all be quite familiar with."

"But how?"

"In a coffin."

Michael shuddered. "Does it have to be a coffin?"

Esteban shook his head discouragingly. "They will check inside the box. How can this work?"

"Because Lord Graystone will appear dead. Not even a doctor will be able to tell the difference."

The three men looked at each other in confusion.

Understanding dawned on Michael's face. A choking sound escaped his throat. "You wouldn't consider asking their kind for help, now would you? It gives me the shudders whenever I pass one in the marketplace."

"That is exactly what I plan to do," Rosa said firmly. "If it will prevent an innocent man from suffering and dying because of our actions, then I am willing to approach the devil himself."

"Well, you won't be far from that," Michael muttered, his tone promising calamity.

Chapter Six

A YOUNG SPANISH woman, no more than eighteen years of age, knelt before the door of the isolated hut. She set down an armful of flowers, then placed two coins alongside them. She bent her head, as if in prayer. Her fingers toyed nervously with the ivory cross and beads of her rosary.

Intrigued, Rosa stopped at the edge of the forest clearing and watched the petitioner, another who apparently was drawn to the powerful reputation of the hut's inhabitant. The girl stood, turned around three times, then took a broken piece of red brick and drew a gritty, rust-colored cross on the door.

She turned to leave. When she spotted her audience, she clapped one hand over her mouth and regarded Rosa through eyes round with horror.

Rosa smiled. The gesture apparently failed to reassure the girl, for she fled into the trees on the opposite side of the sunny clearing. No doubt she feared being excommunicated from the Catholic church if it ever became known that she sought the black magic of the *vodoun* high priestess, Mama Tienne.

Determination battled with a nagging fear of the unknown as Rosa approached the door. She lifted her chin, reminding herself that she was a practical woman, certainly not one prone to superstition. Her years of dancing flamenco had taken her behind the scenes of many types of performances, where she'd discovered that even the most amazing feats by magicians were actually just tricks and illusions. Nevertheless, she held a healthy respect for whatever mysterious deeds had gained Mama Tienne her dual reputations as gifted healer and *mambo*.

Nerves jumped in Rosa's stomach like little grasshoppers. Her own Catholic faith rebelled at the notion of seeking the *mambo*'s aid, but faith alone wasn't going to free Lord Graystone before dawn tomorrow.

Tricks and illusions were her only recourse.

She clutched the small bag at her waist. It contained the emerald ring and a pair of pure gold earrings. The delicious irony of Don Geraldo's money helping to pave the way for his prisoner's escape gave Rosa strength.

She raised her fist to the door, noting the faded images of other rust-colored crosses drawn on the weathered wood. When she first became of marriageable age, she heard young girls whisper conspiratorially of red crosses and offerings as a means to beg a *mambo*'s magical aid in procuring a fine husband.

Taking a deep breath, Rosa knocked.

A mulatto woman answered the door, her skin revealing her heritage of mixed African and Spanish blood. A voluminous cloth of olive green was wrapped around her tall figure. She looked perhaps forty, but it was impossible to determine age from the smooth skin of her face. Gold bands shaped like snakes curled around her bare upper arms. A bizarre assortment of bracelets—one of gold, another of glass beads, a third shaped from shells, and last but certainly not least, one of tiny animal vertebrae strung together— clustered at her wrists. A mass of unbound curls hung down her back in a shiny curtain of jet black.

This was the woman who'd earned a position as spiritual

leader of the descendants of African slaves brought to Cuba. Rosa had expected a wizened, dark-skinned old crone, but she immediately saw how this statuesque, proud woman had gained the respect—and fear—of her people.

"*Buenos dias,* Mama Tienne," Rosa ventured. She couldn't summon up a smile. Her face felt like cold wax.

"You seek me?" the *mambo* asked.

"Yes, I—I need your assistance." When the woman offered no response, Rosa added, "For a price, of course."

"You are not a believer."

Mama Tienne didn't miss much with that riveting dark-eyed gaze. Rosa decided that her best chance of achieving the woman's cooperation was to be forthright.

"No, I am not. My purpose for coming is more practical."

"Then you either suffer from reckless courage or much foolishness."

"I have frequently been accused of both."

One corner of Mama Tienne's mouth tugged upward. Rosa felt a sudden spurt of hope. Perhaps a sense of humor lurked beneath the *mambo*'s aloof, arrogant mask.

After a brief hesitation, Mama Tienne opened the door wider and took a step back. Rosa entered.

The hut's interior didn't fit Rosa's image of a *mambo*'s domain. Fat candles did burn on a stand, filling the room with the scent of melted beeswax, and several strange objects she didn't recognize hung on the same wall, but overall the interior was simple, clean, and neat. A small kitchen opposite the altar boasted several shelves crammed with jars of what appeared to be a variety of herbs and seeds.

Mama Tienne moved to the altar and reached into a wooden crate sitting on the floor. She pulled out the last thing Rosa expected—a four-foot-long boa constrictor. The snake offered no protest when the *mambo* lifted it over her head and draped it around her shoulders. Its camouflage pattern of brown and tan blended dramatically with mulatto skin and the olive-green wrap, making Rosa think of green leaves, damp soil, and the deep secrets of the rain forest. The snake's muscular body flexed slowly, raising its head and curling its tail upward to brush against Mama Tienne's neck.

Rosa shuddered. Although she wasn't plagued by a fear of snakes, she wouldn't want a python around her neck. Using the snake as a fashion accessory was obviously designed to discomfit presumptuous women who chose to invade Mama Tienne's domain.

The technique worked quite well.

The *mambo* stroked her pet. "What do you seek?"

Rosa cleared her throat. "I wish to purchase the potion you use to make a zombie. I am willing to pay most handsomely."

Mama Tienne's gaze hardened. "Zombies are creatures of *magie noire*. If someone angers me, I simply will it to happen." She flicked her hands in the air dramatically, causing her bracelets to rattle. The snake hissed. "Then the offender becomes the walking dead, and my slave!"

A cold shiver raced down Rosa's back. Retreat suddenly seemed an excellent notion, but she couldn't back down now. "I am not an ignorant peasant, Mama Tienne. I know that what seems like magic typically has a basis in fact. Can you prepare a potion that would make a living man *appear* to be dead?"

Mama Tienne approached slowly, then stopped just before Rosa. Her dark eyes formed a fascinating complement to the glittering gold of the snake's eyes. The python stretched its neck forward. Its glossy black tongue flicked out, coming within an inch of touching Rosa's collarbone.

Goose bumps prickled across Rosa's chest. But she stood her ground. If she lost this battle of wills, allowing Mama Tienne to intimidate her, the *mambo* would send her away with a flick of her wrist and a rattle of that bizarre vertebrae bracelet.

"You are Romany," the *mambo* said unexpectedly, breaking the taut silence. "I see it in your cheekbones."

Keeping a wary eye on the snake, Rosa answered truthfully, "My grandfather was *Gitano*, from the Andalusia region of Spain. My grandmother was from an aristocratic family, forbidden to wed outside her class. They fled to Cuba to be married."

"Such a powerful love passes good luck on to future generations."

Rosa failed to see how that held true in her case. "My father was American," she admitted.

"Still, the Romany have powerful *juju*. You have a strong aura about you. Who is this one you wish to curse?"

Curse? Rosa nearly choked in surprise. "No, no, I wish to help someone. A man."

"You wish to enslave a man?"

"Certainly not! I only wish to make him appear dead for a short time."

"You are much too beautiful to resort to magic to enslave a man," the *mambo* protested. "You should have more faith in your powers as a woman."

"But that is not why—"

Mama Tienne turned away abruptly, dismissing Rosa's protest. She sat in one of two spindly chairs by the table, then lifted the snake onto her lap. Pulling its body into a neat circle, the python rested its head on one thick coil and fixed its gaze on Rosa.

Returning its glare, Rosa couldn't resist the urge to wrinkle her nose at the python.

"Why do you stand there, Romany? Sit. I will listen."

Rosa slid into the other chair. "He is being held at La Muerte as a prisoner. I need to get him out."

"I see. There is no sense in keeping a dead man prisoner."

"Exactly. As I said, I am willing to pay you well."

"These secrets are closely guarded by the *vodoun*. If I give them to you, I will betray my calling."

"I am not asking you to reveal the recipe for the potion, only to give me some to administer to this man. Don

Geraldo intends to execute him at dawn tomorrow. Making the man appear as if he is dead is the only way to get him free."

The *mambo's* eyes narrowed sharply. She hissed, not un-like the snake in her lap. "Don Geraldo, you say?"

"*Sí.* Don Geraldo de Vargas."

"The don is an evil man. He persecutes my people." Her serene expression disappeared under a mask of righteous anger. "You wish to steal this prisoner away from him?"

Rosa leaned forward. Sensing a possible alliance against a mutual enemy, she stressed, "This prisoner is very impor-tant. It will infuriate Don Geraldo to lose him."

The *mambo* nodded. She rose with quiet dignity and placed the python back in its crate. "Very well, I shall help you."

Relief swept through Rosa. She stood as the *mambo* stepped into the kitchen. "*Gracias.* I will not betray your trust."

Mama Tienne lifted several jars down from the shelves and set them on the table. She separated out one. "This pro-duces the sleep of the dead. It comes from a fish of the sea. Very powerful *juju.* If too much is given, the victim will die."

Rosa cringed. So risky. But this way Graystone stood a chance, while if he remained in Don Geraldo's clutches un-til dawn he was sure to die. "You do know how to prepare this properly?"

The *mambo* tucked her chin and gave Rosa a stern look from beneath lowered brows.

Hastily, Rosa said, "Of course you do." Pointing to-ward two other jars, she asked, "Are these seeds?"

"Yes. *Tcha-tcha* and consigne seeds." Mama Tienne be-gan opening jars and measuring ingredients into a stone bowl.

Bending at the waist, Rosa peered into another jar. After a moment of confusion, her mind registered the nature of the brown, shriveled things with the curled-up legs. Dried tarantulas. She straightened abruptly. "Are all these ingredients truly necessary for the potion to work?"

"Not all. You only wish him to appear dead?" At Rosa's vigorous nod, Mama Tienne stated, "Very well. For the Romany I shall leave out the leaves that inflame the skin, and the dumbcane that steals the ability to speak."

"That would be good. *Por favor,* do leave those out."

The mulatto woman worked the pestle in the stone bowl, grinding ingredients together. "This man, is he handsome?"

Rosa pictured the perfect lines of Lord Graystone's face, his golden hair, his piercing blue eyes. A tiny, unbidden smile played around the corners of her mouth. "*Sí,* most handsome."

"*Muy hombre?* Virile? Strong?"

"Very," she answered, her voice oddly hoarse. Unbidden, the aching memory of glittering excitement inspired by Graystone's kiss swept through her body again.

"Ah," the *mambo* crooned, chuckling. "Mama Tienne knows these things. You want this man for your lover."

Rosa's eyes grew round with shock. Surely this woman couldn't read her mind? "I barely know him. It is simply my fault that he is imprisoned, and my responsibility to see that he is freed."

Mama Tienne smiled indulgently. "I will give you a mixture of cane sugar, yams, and zombie's cucumber that you can feed him when you raise him from the tomb. It will make this virile man confused, disoriented. He will follow you blindly, do your every bidding . . . fulfill your every desire."

Blindly fulfill my every desire. What a heady image, the idea of having such a powerful, sophisticated, gorgeous man respond to her every whim. No more mocking words. Rosa pictured Derek's hands on her body, slowly peeling away her clothes, his long fingers touching her skin. His lips would caress her wherever she guided him, a gentle coax-

ing or a whispered command all that was needed for his hot
mouth to pleasure any and every spot that ached for his attention. The tips of her breasts tightened at the thought.
Even there. The image of his mouth at her breast sent a tingling ache into her belly.

Shocked by her reaction to a silly fantasy, Rosa shook
her head to scatter her thoughts. "No, I . . . perhaps we
should just consider the potion for sleep."

"If you insist." The pestle grated against stone. "And
what of the antidote to reverse the toxin?"

Feeling foolish for neglecting the obvious, Rosa hastily
said, "*Sí*, let us not forget the antidote."

"There are things I must mix now that you cannot see.
Come back at dusk. I will tell you then how to use them."

Rosa nodded. "Gracias, Mama Tienne."

She slipped away, leaving the bag as payment on the
table.

"*BUENAS NOCHES, SEÑOR*," Rosa said in a husky purr.

The soldier carrying the tray of food stopped abruptly.
Rosa stepped farther into the golden pool of gaslight illuminating the narrow, dark street. She moved toward him,
her hips swaying provocatively.

The soldier stared, swallowing hard. She stepped up to
him, allowing her shawl to slip a bit, exposing one bare
shoulder over the low sleeves of her peasant-style blouse.

"It is a beautiful night, no?"

He blinked and nodded.

"*¿Cómo se llama?*"

"Paolo—" He cleared his throat. "Paolo Villareal."

"You work at the prison, no? You look like an *hombre*
in an important position." She deliberately resorted to flattery. She hadn't grown up around a trio of men without
learning the role ego played in undermining a man's common sense.

Paolo squared his shoulders and eyed the creamy skin

along her collarbone. "*Sí, señorita.* I guard the English prisoner."

"And all this food? Is this for you?"

"No. This is the prisoner's last meal. He is to be executed at dawn. Don Geraldo ordered the criminal fed well so he will realize what he will be missing."

Rosa shaped her mouth into a becoming pout. "How am I to talk to you with that bulky tray in the way? Don't you want to set it down?"

He looked at the tray, as if surprised to still find it in his hands. Hastily, he set it on top of a large barrel. He started toward her. Smiling, Rosa backed away, drawing him forward until the tray was ten feet behind him. He followed, grinning, believing that she played some flirtatious game.

Fool. Let him believe what he liked.

She traced a finger down a lapel of his uniform. "How do you manage such weighty responsibility?"

Grasping her hand, he pressed a fervent kiss to her wrist. "It is *nada, señorita.* I accept my duty, no matter how great the threat to my personal safety. May I say how beautifully your hair shines in the moonlight?"

Rosa peeked over his shoulder as Dickie tiptoed out from a side alley. The old seaman lifted the cover off the dinner plate, revealing a dish of steaming meat, black beans and rice, and pan-fried plantains. He picked up a plantain and popped it into his mouth. The expression on his grizzled face appeared near ecstasy as he chewed.

Rosa nearly stamped her foot in frustration.

Glancing up, he caught Rosa's glare and quickly untied the pouch from his belt that contained the powder. Mama Tienne had warned about concealing its flavor. He mixed the *mambo*'s powder into the beans and rice.

Rosa continued to distract the guard by adding, "They say the prisoner is quite mad, daring to steal valuables right out from under Don Geraldo's nose."

Paolo shrugged. "He is English. What more can we expect?"

"He must be dangerous, constantly testing your bravery."

"*Sí*. Very dangerous." Paolo tilted his chin toward the nearest streetlamp, better illuminating the left side of his face. "He tried to escape today."

A dark bruise marred the line of his jaw. Rosa stared, surprise causing her to slip from her role for an instant. Had Graystone inflicted that much damage with one blow? Warmth suffused her face as she remembered the strength of his arms when he stopped her fall from the roof.

"Did you prevent his escape all by yourself?"

"We managed to subdue him. You are quite safe. I shall protect you." He took a step closer and puckered his lips. His hands boldly reached for her waist.

Dickie finished sabotaging the tray. He replaced the plate cover and crept out of sight.

Rosa ducked Paolo's clumsy attempt at a kiss and quickly turned away with a playful little spin.

"But *señorita*," Paolo exclaimed as she danced back out of reach. He sounded keenly disappointed.

"My *dueña* will arrive at any moment. She will be very angry that I eluded her. You will be able to recognize her at a glance. She is a very large woman, with a hairy lip, and she carries a cane with a steel head."

"A cane? Is she crippled?"

"Not at all. She uses it to beat men over the head who are too forward. I would not want that to happen to you, Paolo."

"No, neither would I," he said uncertainly. "But when can I see you again?"

Rosa backed away farther, smiling. "Tomorrow night?"

"*Sí, mañana. Aquí,* in this place," he agreed, though he didn't sound happy about the wait.

Picking up the tray, he started down the street on his way to the prison. He glanced back at her repeatedly over one shoulder. Rosa waved, willing her nose not to wrinkle in distaste. She wished he would just get on with his errand so she could stop playing this ridiculous role.

Without warning, the toe of Paolo's right boot caught on a cobblestone. He stumbled.

Rosa caught her breath, horrified at the possibility of their only chance at success splattered all over the street. But Paolo caught himself, and the tray, just in time. Clearing his throat, he cast back a sheepish grin.

Rosa gave him a brilliant smile.

When he finally moved out of sight around a corner, Dickie emerged from the alley and stood by her side.

"Now what?" he whispered.

"We hurry back to the house and change for our next role . . . and pray that Lord Graystone's appetite has not been spoiled by the knowledge that he is to be shot at dawn."

Dickie grimaced. "I think that would put a damper on my appetite, yes sirree."

THE TRAY HELD a meal fit for a king. A doomed king.

The guard sneered at the condemned prisoner as he set the tray on the rickety table. Derek raised his fist and scowled. The guard backed away quickly. The metal door clanged shut.

Derek released a sigh so heavy that it threatened to turn his weary, aching body inside out. He was damn tired of the games, of maintaining a cynical, irreverent mask when he really wanted to give in to primitive blood lust and smash his fist into that guard's face. Again.

But he was also hungry.

Drawn by the delectable scents from the tray, Derek rose stiffly from the cot. Strained tendons and sore joints protested vigorously. He hobbled over to the table. Although this was deemed his last meal, he was heartily sick of the tasteless gruel they'd been foisting on him the past two days.

He sat down and lifted the cover.

A fried skirt steak accompanied a mound of black beans and rice, bread, and a glass of red wine. A square piece of cake smelled delectably of pineapple. Derek's favorite touch was what appeared to be small, sliced pan-fried bananas. He had a particular fondness for fruit.

Don Geraldo seemed determined to carry out the drama of this farcical execution to its last act, including the implication that this was truly Derek's last meal. Derek was still convinced that it was all a bluff to get him to talk.

Regardless, he breathed in the rich aromas. There was nothing like a stint in a dingy cell, accompanied by torture, to make a man appreciate the finer things in life.

Derek popped a piece of crisp fruit in his mouth. Sweetness mixed with the mellow flavor of olive oil. Suddenly realizing that he was ravenous, Derek wolfed down several bites of beans and rice. His sigh of pleasure was cut short, however, as a strange, bitter flavor began to register on his taste buds. He grimaced and spat the last mouthful of rice onto the floor.

Bloody hell. Was Don Geraldo resorting to taunting him with spoiled food?

Derek picked up another fruit and smelled it. This portion of the meal seemed fine. Perhaps the beans and rice were seasoned with an exotic spice he wasn't accustomed to.

He finished the banana-like side dish. The bitter tang lingered, however. What a pity. A swallow of wine helped obscure the odd flavor.

A strange tingling began in Derek's fingers and feet before he could start on the steak.

He grimaced. Being stretched on the rack must have had effects beyond the initial pain. His recuperative powers had always been strong, however. He seldom if ever succumbed to illness, and injuries quickly healed. Surely the sensation would fade.

His right hand suddenly went numb. The fork fell from

his fingers and clattered onto the plate. He stared at his hand, alarmed. A deep, straining effort to make a fist resulted in little more than a twitch of his fingertips.

Something was dreadfully wrong.

The numbness crept up both his forearms. A feeling of impending doom swept over him like a black cloud—images of a cold death, and blood, and being buried alive. He lurched to his feet.

His legs immediately collapsed beneath him.

Derek lay on the dirty floor in an ignoble heap. He couldn't rise, couldn't move no matter how much his mind screamed at his muscles to function. The numbness closed around his chest, as well. He tried to cry for help, but only the barest of whimpers escaped from his throat.

Had the rack damaged his spine, paralyzing him for life? His worst nightmare was coming true, but with a gruesome, mocking twist . . . rather than just being confined in some small, inescapable dark hole, he was being sucked into a trap that was his own body.

It was then that he realized the short, gasping breaths weren't just the familiar, shameful response to a panic attack. His lungs were actually shutting down, each breath more shallow than the last.

He was dying here in this foul, tiny prison cell. Eternal sleep ranked, however ironically, as preferable to being forever trapped, but did it have to be away from the sea and the brisk salt air he loved? Despair reached a new depth as he realized that his family—his father, his sister Ellie and her husband, Matt, his youngest sister, Amber—would never know what happened to him.

He struggled to cling to life.

Righteous fury sparked a red-hot flame deep inside. This was all her fault, that flamenco dancer with her ripe lips and those quick hands that were equally capable of pilfering a don's wealth and planting evidence to divert suspicion from herself.

But even the thought of wringing Rosa's lovely neck couldn't sustain him.

The last tenuous thread broke. Derek's breathing stilled.

A black void swept in to consume him.

Chapter Seven

How do I look?" Rosa stood before her god-fathers in the stolen soldier's uniform, her long hair twisted painfully tight and stuffed into a gray cap.

Esteban closed his eyes and clucked his tongue against the roof of his mouth.

Michael tapped his chin. "Well, colleen, you certainly are the prettiest soldier I've ever seen."

Rosa looked at their doubtful expressions with dismay. She stomped her foot. "This won't do at all. I must look like a man. I cannot afford to raise suspicions."

Crossing his arms, Esteban said sternly, "I told you this idea was impossible. You should not go."

"I must, *tío*. What if something went wrong? I must be there to make sure Graystone arises from the zombie sleep before it is too late," Rosa retorted. *And to make certain the three of you go through with the plan, though I would never question your manly prowess by expressing my concerns aloud.*

Dickie walked around her. "Maybe if your skin didn't look so smooth and fresh. That might help."

"*De acuerdo,*" Rosa responded eagerly. "A little dirt, perhaps?"

Esteban glared. "Do not encourage her, you old *cabrito*!"

Dickie shrugged. "Our angel girl seems determined, mate. I'd rather have you mad at me than face her anger any day."

"Maybe a little padding in the shoulders of your uniform?" Michael suggested.

Rosa grasped the sleeves and tugged them higher.

Beaming, Michael exclaimed, "That's the way. A good padding around the middle to make you look older wouldn't hurt, neither. Take Dickie, for example."

"Hah! I could strike a blow to your gut and it would be like sinkin' me hand into a pillow," Dickie countered.

"You are all *loco*, you know that?" Esteban raked one hand through his hair. "I will not take responsibility for what happens." Spinning on his heel, he paced to the other end of the room, cursing under his breath in his native language.

Ignoring the frustrated Spaniard, Dickie commented, "Padded shoulders still ain't enough to make her look like a man." He tugged on his beard while contemplating the problem.

The sight offered Rosa the solution. "Michael, give me your hairpiece."

He regarded her suspiciously. "What do you want with it?"

"It shall make an excellent mustache and beard."

Esteban stopped his pacing. He massaged his temples.

"Now, colleen," Michael said consolingly, "don't you think it will look a wee bit unnatural to have this great black thing hanging off the bottom half of your face?"

Dickie snorted. "She means to cut it up, you Irish dolt."

Michael clapped a protective hand over his head and took a step back. "Me grand hairpiece? Think what you're saying." He swallowed hard. "How will I woo the ladies? They'll be sore disappointed to be deprived of me usual dashing self."

"Don't worry, mate. They'll get used to that great bald

spot of yours. You take a woman out, and she won't even have to search for a mirror for her primpin'."

"Dickie, stop it," Rosa admonished. She laid a hand on the big man's arm. "You are dashing enough without the hairpiece, believe me. *Por favor*, Michael."

His beefy shoulders slumped. "Sure and it isn't fair when you look at me like that."

Dickie regarded him with rare and genuine sympathy. "Might as well give it over, boyo. You know you'll never win, not when Rosa has set her mind on somethin'."

Despondent, Michael dragged the hairpiece off his head. He handed it to Rosa.

She gave him a quick kiss on the cheek. "I will buy you another, I promise."

A LIGHT, MISTING rain fell steadily. Thick clouds obscured the quarter-moon and stars, casting a gray shadow over La Muerte despite the gaslights dotting the old parade ground. The weak pools of light reflected off the water on high walls and brick walkways, making the dark stones appear slick . . . almost greasy.

Esteban and Rosa huddled beneath the overhanging roof of a barracks building. Rosa's knuckles whitened around the cart horse's reins. The black gelding's entire body couldn't fit beneath the roof, but it had managed to shove its head out of the rain. The horse's breath steamed in the humid air.

Rosa shuddered. The depressing night certainly fit the mood of their desperate errand. Rain beaded on the lid of the empty coffin in the cart.

A doctor had been summoned from town.

That was their signal. They had to somehow lay claim to Graystone's "body" before the assumption that he was dead led to something truly tragic. Rosa didn't foresee any problem—after all, who wouldn't want to delegate the distasteful duty of dealing with a corpse in the middle of the night?

It was still four hours before dawn. The doctor emerged from the single-story sprawl of the adjacent building. In the moments before a soldier closed the door behind him, Rosa and Esteban could hear shouting from inside. The doctor shook his head with weary resignation, then climbed into his waiting carriage. The wheels clicked over the brick paving as he headed out the open gate and began the trip home from the fort overlooking the bay.

"The doctor looks quite grim," Esteban whispered. "Was that not Don Geraldo shouting? Do you think the potion worked?"

"Of course it did," Rosa responded firmly. Her mask of false bravado was holding, despite the worry that caused the muscles across her ribs to tremble with each breath. If she allowed her doubts to become visible, her three godfathers would cut their losses and run. Especially Dickie and Michael, who waited just outside the gate to avoid raising questions with the decidedly non-Spanish cast of their features.

"Come. It is time," Rosa said softly.

They emerged from their hiding place, leading the horse. The on-duty soldiers were inside the main building, no doubt wishing they were out in the rain rather than facing Don Geraldo's raging criticism.

Rosa tucked her chin, using the brim of the stolen soldier's cap to shield her face from the mist. Although she trusted the adhesive to hold, she couldn't afford to test it in the rain. They reached the main building and ducked beneath the porch roof. Rosa secured the horse's reins to a post. Esteban opened the door and they stepped inside.

Their arrival created the barest ripple of reaction in a room ruled by chaos.

Don Geraldo paced the length of the office, passing two battered desks and some cluttered shelves as he vented his fury in no uncertain terms. Dressed in a white uniform, he had apparently been pulled from a formal party with the news of Graystone's mysterious ailment.

The six soldiers on the receiving end of his tirade stood at rigid attention.

"You were charged with keeping Graystone alive, you fools!" the don raged. "How could you fail at such a simple task?"

The intensity of the don's reaction startled Rosa. Keep him alive? In four short hours, Graystone would have stepped before a firing squad. Whether by execution or sudden expiration, dead was dead. She frowned.

Unless Don Geraldo was decrying the lost opportunity of seeing Graystone shot. That must be it.

Rosa had no opportunity to speculate further. Without warning, de Vargas stopped his pacing. He regarded Esteban in surprise. "Are you not rather old to be serving in my army?"

Esteban snapped to attention. He offered de Vargas a sharp salute. "It is such an honor to serve *el General,* one should never be considered too old."

The don's scowl lifted. "Indeed, this is true."

Rosa let her pent-up breath out slowly. How clever of Esteban to appeal to Don Geraldo's arrogance.

Then the don turned his sharp gaze on her, and all sense of growing confidence withered. Rosa prayed the mustache and goatee she'd pasted to her face concealed her gender and her identity. At the very least, she hoped they were on straight.

"Do I know you?"

With Don Geraldo regarding her so keenly, Rosa found it astonishingly easy to drop her voice an octave.

"*Sí,* General, though I am new here. I am the nephew of your cousin, Señora Victoria de Montoya y Jimenez." Having some idea of the size of Don Geraldo's extended family, Rosa felt safe mentioning one of its members by name. Just to be on the cautious side, however, she added hastily, "On the side of her *esposo.*"

Don Geraldo hesitated. Rosa bit the inside of her lip. When he finally nodded, she nearly wilted with relief.

"So you aspire to serve in my army. You should have come to me. I find special duties for members of *mi familia*."

"I wished to work my way up through the ranks, sir."

"*Muy bien*. That is admirable." Without warning, Don Geraldo grasped Rosa by the shoulders and pulled her forward in a traditional greeting, bussing her cheeks with a quick kiss on either side. Rosa forced herself not to stiffen in dismay. The don broke the embrace just as suddenly, then spun on his heel and struck one desk with a riding crop.

"I want this stupid Englishman out of my sight. Bury him. Burn him. I care not!"

Rosa glanced at Esteban. His eyes were round with horror as he stared back at her. He twitched his upper lip, wiggling his own mustache. Understanding struck Rosa like a hammer. She covered her mouth with her hand, coughing while she secretly adjusted the mustache that Don Geraldo had knocked askew.

The don turned abruptly. "What is it, boy? Are you ill?"

Rosa improvised quickly. "No, General. I merely wished to offer to take care of the body for you."

"Initiative. I like that." He turned on one of the soldiers, a tall, slender man identified as an officer by the epaulets on his uniform. "Capitán Velásquez, see that you and your men give my cousin all the help he needs."

"*Sí*, Don Geraldo."

Nodding, the don strode away. He beat a staccato rhythm against his knee-high black boots with the crop, muttering furiously about how Graystone had had the unmitigated gall to die on him.

A sense of urgency stung Rosa. Please God, let that not be true. Let Derek . . . Lord Graystone . . . still be alive.

They must hurry now. Every moment delayed in administering the antidote risked the pretense of death becoming genuine.

THE DAMPNESS TURNED cloying in the bowels of the prison. Velásquez inserted a key into the cell door. The clank of the lock echoed through the stone passageway like a gunshot. Rosa jumped. Rusty hinges protested as the capitán opened the door.

Esteban gripped her forearm. "Wait here," he said just before following the officer and the two soldiers inside.

Rosa nodded dully. She didn't want to witness the depressing, confined space or the filthy conditions Graystone had been forced to endure because of her. Her sense of guilt couldn't tolerate any more open wounds. Her present task allowed no room for emotion.

The two soldiers carried Graystone's limp, lifeless figure from the cell.

Rosa's knees almost buckled. She had to bite the inside of her cheek to keep from crying out in dismay. If this was only a façade of death, no wonder the doctor had been fooled.

Pale gray skin gave Graystone the appearance of a waxen effigy. The healthy gloss had disappeared from his beautiful hair, leaving it as dull as straw. Thick lashes fanned against his cheeks, hiding those blue eyes that had glittered with cynical intelligence. Other than the large frame and handsome face, there was no sign of the vital, vibrant man who had warmed her with hungry kisses and brought her body to the edge of tingling anticipation with the stroking of his powerful hands.

No, he couldn't truly be dead. She wouldn't allow it, regardless of the possibility that a demise by toxin might have been more merciful than the impact of a dozen bullets ripping through his chest. She couldn't live with the responsibility for his death weighing heavily like this stone in her heart.

Silently, she led the way back upstairs to their waiting cart. The misting rain had stopped. Stars peeked through gaps in the clouds. The soldiers lifted Graystone into the coffin and replaced the lid. Esteban lit the two torches they'd prepared and thrust them into holders in the sides of the cart.

"*Gracias, capitán,*" Rosa said, saluting. "We shall deal with the matter now."

Velásquez frowned. "Is this the coffin that was prepared for the Englishman's execution?"

Alarm flashed through Rosa. "*Sí.* Word of his death travelled quickly among my fellow soldiers. The moment I heard, I gathered these things together," she improvised quickly.

"You are very young to be so ambitious," he said dryly.

She shrugged, her throat too tight to respond.

"Are you certain you have what you need to bury him?"

Rosa pointed to the spades and picks lying in the cart. "As you can see, we have the tools."

"I meant the labor." He glanced doubtfully at Esteban, who was occupied driving nails into the coffin's lid. "Perhaps I should send Manuel and Roland with you."

"No, that is not necessary," Rosa assured him. "We have two *compadres* waiting to help us."

Velásquez shrugged. "Very well. Be on your way. You will find a freshly dug grave in the cemetery down the hill."

"Freshly dug?" Rosa whispered tightly.

"We did not know it would be needed before dawn. Don Geraldo ordered us to dig the grave earlier this afternoon while the Englishman watched. The doctor believes his heart gave out. Me? I think he died of fear, the weak son of a *puta.*" Velásquez spat onto the brick walkway.

Rosa moved to the cart horse's head and took the reins between numb fingers. She closed her eyes and leaned her trembling body against the gelding's wet yet sturdy shoulder. They had forced Graystone to watch while they dug his grave. Anger coursed through her, hot and revitalizing. Don Geraldo was the one who deserved to be shot.

Then Esteban was at her side. It was time to go. Hairs prickled on Rosa's nape as she moved away stiffly, keenly aware of Velásquez watching from the porch, his thin frame silhouetted by the light from the open door.

Dickie and Michael joined them silently outside the main gate. They started down the muddy road away from the fort.

After rounding a curve behind a grove of trees, Rosa pulled the gelding to a halt. "We are stopping."

"Here?" Dickie asked nervously. "Rosa, angel, we're still mighty close to that prison."

"I know, but it has been almost four hours since Graystone ate the potion. That is beyond the time the *mambo* recommended giving him the antidote."

"Sure and he'll just have to wait a wee bit longer."

"The longer he goes without," she insisted, "the more like a zombie he'll become . . . witless, helpless, like the living dead."

"Better him than us," Dickie muttered.

Esteban interjected, "We shall be the dead ones if the soldiers catch us. It is best to wait until we get to the city."

Rosa narrowed her eyes and glared at the three of them. They had the grace to look sheepish. "That will be another thirty minutes. Our goal was to save the man."

Michael sighed. "I'm supposing the sacrifice of me fine hairpiece will be a waste if he turns up dead for real."

"Well, I value my hide a lot more than your stupid hairpiece," Dickie grumbled. He cuffed Michael on the shoulder.

"Stop it! I believe I have a solution." Three grizzled faces turned expectantly to her. "We give him the antidote now. According to the *mambo,* it takes fifteen to twenty minutes to work. By the time we are well down the road, he will be waking from his sleep."

Nodding, Esteban agreed. "Rosa makes sense. Now, hurry."

They moved around to the back of the cart.

"Pry open the lid," Rosa whispered urgently.

As the men worked the crowbars between the nails,

Rosa rolled the antidote vial between her palms. The nails squeaked slightly as they pried up the lid.

Would Graystone be all right? Were they too late?

Had she killed him?

His handsome face gleamed ghostly pale in the moonlight.

Dickie peered into the coffin, his expression openly curious. "I don't know. He looks pretty genuinely dead to me."

Esteban held his palm over Graystone's mouth and nose. Rosa craved a glimmer of hope, but her uncle's mouth tightened into a grim line. Stepping onto the cart's wheel, he bent over the coffin and pressed his ear to the Englishman's chest.

"Well?" she whispered.

Giving her a sad look, Esteban shook his head.

"The powder is supposed to slow his heartbeat until it is undetectable." She tried to hide her mounting desperation.

She opened the vial. Turning to Michael, who stood near the head of the coffin, she instructed, "Lift him up. I shall pour the antidote down his throat."

"You mean . . . touch him?" Michael shuddered. "Ugh."

"Of course she means touch him. Don't be a pansy ass."

"Sure and why don't you lift him, Dickie?"

Esteban grabbed the collar of Michael's shirt. "Do it, if you wish for us to leave this place."

Grumbling, Michael slid an arm beneath Derek's shoulders and lifted his limp body to a sitting position. "Saints, but he's heavy."

"Dead weight usually is," Dickie said dryly. He cast Rosa an apologetic look. "Sorry, darlin'."

"All of you seem to be forgetting that this is your fault," she snapped in a fierce undertone. "Now, hold his head still."

She opened Graystone's mouth, poured in the brown

elixir, then closed and held his jaw tightly. Following the *mambo*'s instructions, she blew into his face.

Nothing.

A small trickle of brown liquid escaped from the left corner of his mouth and traced a path down his jaw. Rosa gnawed on her lower lip. He must swallow the antidote.

Stroking the column of his throat, she begged, "*Por favor,* swallow it down." She blew in his face again.

Slowly, as if from a great depth, a ripple of muscle worked its way up his throat. Then his Adam's apple bobbed, and a jerky swallow drew the liquid into his body.

"You see? He lives!" Elated, Rosa cupped Derek's cheeks in her hands and planted a kiss on his cold forehead. "*Perfecto. Gracias a Dios.*"

"Rosa!" hissed Esteban in a shocked tone.

"Here now, we'll have none of that," scolded Michael. He jerked his arm out from behind Graystone's shoulders. The Englishman's body fell back into the coffin with a thud.

"Oh!" Rosa yelped, reaching out in concern. When no reaction showed on Derek's placid face, she jammed her fists on her hips and demanded, "Have you lost your minds?"

"What is going on there?" Capitán Velásquez called from the sentinel's post atop the outer wall. "Why have you stopped?"

The four false soldiers jumped guiltily.

Esteban cleared his throat. "The lid of the coffin is loose. Those fools did not put it on straight."

"Then hammer it back on. Can you idiots accomplish nothing without my supervision?" Velásquez yelled. "I'm coming down. I intend to make sure you donkeys do the job right."

"Donkeys? Who does he think he is?" Dickie hissed. "I ought to—"

"There is no need, *Capitán.* We can manage," Rosa called out frantically, but it was too late. She heard the main gate open. She thought of pulling Derek's body from the coffin and hiding him beneath the trees, but Velásquez might come around the corner and catch them in the act. She threw the empty vial into the undergrowth.

"We'll overpower him," Michael offered. "We're three against one."

Through the trees, they could see Manuel and Roland appear behind Velásquez in the arched gateway.

"Uh, never mind."

"Quickly! Hammer the lid back on. We must not give Velásquez any reason to suspect that the Englishman is still alive. Even if we get Graystone safely away, they will hunt him down and imprison him again."

"Yes, sirree, and us along with him."

Hastily, Esteban and Dickie replaced the lid and began driving in a few nails to hold it securely.

"We must cooperate for now to divert Velásquez's suspicions. Then he will leave," Rosa urged.

"How? Bury the bloke for real?"

Recognizing the inevitable, Rosa responded to Dickie's sarcasm with a grim nod.

Esteban groaned. "Rosa, how will he breathe?"

"He needs much less air in his present state. It will take a good twenty minutes before the antidote awakens him. The air in the coffin should last until Velásquez is gone and we can dig Graystone up again."

"Are you done yet?" Velásquez demanded, rounding the curve.

Michael and Dickie pulled their hats low over their faces and finished hammering in the nails.

"Let's get this over with quickly," Velásquez snapped.

Within a short distance, they reached the prison cemetery. Crooked stone markers and overgrown weeds told a story of sad neglect. As promised, a dark hole gaped, framed by piles of rain-dampened dirt. Shovels, jammed upright into the mounds, stood like gaunt sentinels.

A cold chill started along the nape of Rosa's neck and slithered down her spine.

Manuel and Roland lowered the coffin into the grave. Everyone grabbed a tool and began shoveling the slippery mud. Beneath a two-inch layer of wet dirt they found dry soil. Rosa's senses filled with the smell of damp earth, the sound of dirt filling the hole, and the feel of her pounding heart trying to burst from her chest.

Within five minutes, the grave was almost full.

Velásquez straightened abruptly. He kicked his spade into the ground. Turning to Rosa, he growled, "Is your duty shift over for the night?"

Rosa watched him warily. *"Sí, Capitán."*

"I have better things to do with my time. Finish this up, then you may go home," Velásquez declared. He issued a crisp order to the other two soldiers to stop digging. The three men withdrew to the fort.

After the gate closed behind them, Rosa said urgently, "Put out the torches."

Esteban and Dickie each grabbed a torch and shoved the burning ends into the mud. The flames sputtered and died.

They worked feverishly, shoving the spades into the grave and moving the dirt out again. When Dickie grew winded, Rosa jumped into the hole to take his place.

Her chest constricted with dread. Although she struggled for breath, she didn't slow her pace, seeking anxiously for the sound of metal striking wood.

And praying that they weren't too late.

Chapter Eight

THROUGH SHEER WILLPOWER, Derek clawed his way upward out of a dark, endless well. Something tried to hold him back, whispering seductive promises of quiet, ease, the absence of pain. But a deeper instinct told him that death lay that way.

He chose life.

He drew a sharp, gasping breath, revitalizing his lethargic lungs. He became aware of a body that weighed more than the pyramids of Giza and muscles that tingled painfully. His senses kicked in with a jolt. The scent of moist earth invaded his nostrils. Strange noises intruded—thumps, scrapes, and the sound of muffled voices.

His eyes flew open to a thick, impenetrable blackness.

Something was terribly wrong.

Forcing his weak arms to move, he reached out in front of his face. His palms encountered the rough texture of unfinished wood just inches away.

He was being buried alive.

Raw fear clutched at his heart, compounded by a sudden resurrection of terrifying memories from his childhood when he was caught under a landslide of sand. His body started to shake with those same feelings of suffocation, powerlessness, and the inability to escape.

He tried to shout, to curse, but only a croak emerged.

The air grew stale, failing to satisfy his straining lungs. He thumped weakly against the lid in desperation.

Suddenly, the barrier lifted away.

He would have shot out of that box like a twenty-pounder from a cannon, but the bizarre numbness still claimed his lower body. He lay there, overcome by gratitude, rejoicing inwardly.

A face loomed above him. Despite the mustache and goatee, the boy seemed too pretty to be real. Pale images of three old men hovered in the background, framed by the blackness of night.

The youth said, "Welcome back to the land of the living."

The husky, musical voice struck a disturbing chord of familiarity. Suspicion mixed with a dawning fury. Clumsily, Derek reached up and dragged off the youth's cap. Black hair tumbled free, falling in a thick curtain to brush across his chest.

"I know you," he rasped.

Grinning, Rosa peeled away the fake facial hair. "I am flattered that you remember."

Derek remembered all right—a false arrest, torture, and a poisoned dinner. "How could I forget?" he growled. "You are the little witch who had me thrown into that hellish prison."

The remaining numbness in his arms vanished under an onslaught of wrath. He grabbed a fistful of her lapel.

With a firm jerk, he pulled Rosa into the box.

She yelped in surprise and sprawled lengthwise along his body. The tips of their noses brushed. Gazes met, one in wide-eyed amazement and the other in pulse-pounding fury.

He instantly became aware of her breasts pressed against his chest, the sweet curve of her parted lips, the silky touch of her hair against his jaw. She was warm, supple, unarguably female. A surge of lust swept through him.

He was succumbing to her allure once again. Awareness of his deteriorating self-control swept over Derek like black, rolling clouds before a storm. He let Rosa go abruptly. His hand dropped limply to his side. Suddenly, he realized that the exertion had drained him.

"You'll pay for this," he whispered.

He let his head fall back against wood, hating her for betraying him, hating her for stirring his passion against his will.

With a groan on his lips, Derek lost consciousness again.

"DID YOU SEE that?"

"He mauled her again!"

"I'll strangle him with my bare hands," snarled Esteban.

Rosa checked Derek's pulse, reassuring herself that he'd only lost consciousness, which wasn't surprising after his ordeal. Then she faced her godfathers. She spread her arms over Derek like an eagle guarding its nest.

"You will do nothing of the sort. You promised," she said firmly, struggling to hide the fact that she could barely catch her breath after that astonishing contact. She'd felt every inch of Derek's muscular body as she'd lain lengthwise atop him. If her godfathers knew how wildly her body tingled with desire, they would conspire to keep him away from her.

"But he might try to kiss you like before," Dickie hissed.

Dear heavens, I hope so.

But not out of anger. An unexpected hurt lanced deep inside. Graystone hated her for her role in his suffering. That much he had just made clear. She couldn't blame him.

"It does not matter," she insisted. "We are responsible for his injuries, and we will see that he is restored to health.

Then we will help him evade Don Geraldo and escape from Cuba."

As she expected, her last declaration was met by stunned silence.

"Bloody hell, it's you. Isn't there someone else who can bring me food?"

Rosa paused in the doorway with the tray balanced against one hip. She allowed herself to savor the sight of Derek Carlisle—alive, safe, and thin-lipped with anger— sitting against a pile of pillows in her narrow bed. Not only had color returned to his handsome face, the hue was rather heightened at the moment. A lock of sandy hair fell across his forehead, lending a rakish quality to an otherwise cleanly shaven face.

After sealing the empty coffin and refilling the grave, they had sneaked Graystone to their house before dawn. Her godfathers had scrubbed the grime and smell of La Muerte from his unconscious body. Rosa was still rather miffed that they had excluded her from what, no doubt, would have been a fascinating experience.

After some false starts during the past six hours, in which he'd drifted in and out of consciousness, their grumpy guest had finally awakened ten minutes ago.

Graystone raked splayed fingers through his hair, proving that full mobility had returned to his arms and upper body. And what an upper body it was, Rosa thought with an inward sigh of feminine appreciation. Those broad shoulders filled out one of Michael's large shirts. The open white front gaped, providing a glimpse of a smooth, sculptured chest and ridged muscles across a flat belly.

"Actually, I should be your preferred choice at the moment." She countered his sour greeting with a cheerful tone. "Esteban wants to strangle you, Michael hopes to bloody your nose, and Dickie is debating the merits of . . . well, to put it delicately, of changing you from a bull into a steer."

"Those three old men? For what possible reason?"

"For kissing me in the courtyard, then 'mauling' me, as they phrase it, earlier this morning." At Derek's disbelieving expression, she clarified, "My godfathers are very protective."

"They are raging lunatics," Derek responded with feeling. "You all are."

She shrugged and set the tray on a table next to the bed. Let him underestimate her godfathers all he wanted. She knew better. That was why she'd encouraged the three bored men to visit their regular haunts . . . after she'd assured them that their unwanted houseguest would remain asleep for a long time yet.

Otherwise, they would never have allowed her to step foot in this room unchaperoned.

"How do you feel?"

"Oh, just smashing, as if I've been trampled by a team of horses and beaten up by a gang of thugs, all in one night."

"At least you are feeling something." He'd come much too close to the alternative for her to contemplate.

He eyed her suspiciously. "I had the worst nightmare. I dreamed I woke up in . . . no, it is ridiculous. It could not be."

"A coffin?" she said sweetly.

Derek stared at her. "Bloody hell. It is true, then."

"We had to get you out of that prison somehow. You were too closely guarded, so we faked your death."

He sat bolt upright. "The food. It was you who poisoned my dinner? I thought it was Don Geraldo in some other perverted attempt to force me to talk."

"We used a voodoo potion that slows the heart rate and chills the body, simulating death. We slipped it into your food. When you 'died,' we were able to remove your body for burial." She chuckled. "If those guards could see you now, they would cross themselves and run for their lives."

Derek paled. "I don't believe what I am hearing."

"Do not worry. The aftereffects should wear off soon." His arrogance and conspicuous lack of gratitude were beginning to fray her temper. "At least, I hope so."

"You hope! Bloody hell, woman, what if it does not? I can barely move my damn legs. What if I am like this forever?"

At the rate he was improving, she felt confident that, by nightfall, he would be further displaying his temper by stomping around the room like an enraged bull. He already had the snorting and bellowing part perfected. "Oh, stop whining. It is better than the alternative. Don Gerlado would have gladly watched your chest shot full of holes at dawn."

"I would not have been in danger if you hadn't set me up to take the blame for your crime."

She froze. How could she deny it without implicating her godfathers? Although Esteban and Dickie had planted the stolen goods without her knowledge, they had done so to protect her. Since she'd allowed Graystone to kiss her in the courtyard, and responded with an abandon she prayed her godfathers would never guess, in a way she was ultimately responsible for everything that had happened as a result.

Graystone had already chosen her as the target for his anger and resentment anyway. What could possibly be gained by exposing three fragile old men to his wrath, as well?

Her chin angled upward, proud and rigid. "It is true. I am responsible."

Without warning, he grabbed her wrist and pulled her down beside him on the bed. Rosa stared into his flashing blue eyes. She fought a sudden urge to run her fingers through his hair.

"Do you feel the slightest guilt?"

Something shifted against her hip. She glanced over her shoulder at two mountains under the blanket. He hadn't even noticed. "Your legs seem to be moving well now."

Relief flickered briefly across his face. Then he ground out, "Do not change the subject."

Of its own volition, her gaze fixed on his mouth. She licked her lips.

With a curse and a quick shove, he pushed her off the bed. She tumbled onto the floor.

Rosa rolled and jumped to her feet. "You ungrateful wretch! We saved you from the firing squad!"

"I was never at risk from the damn firing squad."

That gave her pause. "What do you mean?"

"It was a bluff, Don Geraldo's depraved way of increasing the urgency for me to talk. The torture did not work. He is not a patient man. But he had no intention of killing me."

"But . . . the soldiers, all his men, they spoke and acted as if your execution at dawn was inevitable."

"I suppose Don Geraldo led them to believe it was so it would all seem real to me. I am much more valuable to him alive."

"How can you be certain?" she challenged.

Graystone's mouth thinned. He looked away, no longer meeting her gaze despite his hostility. Bluntly, he changed the subject. "I need to get out of Cuba as soon as possible."

So, there is a kernel of doubt, Rosa thought with satisfaction. *The don is too arrogant and unpredictable for you to be certain what would have happened at dawn. He might have followed through on the threat.*

"We intend to help you escape, as soon as it is safe. Don Geraldo believes you are dead. This will make things much easier. Nevertheless, it would be wise to wait until things quiet down. Perhaps in a week—"

"No. I intend to sail tomorrow at dawn."

His words went through Rosa like an electric shock. So soon? "But how?" she asked hoarsely.

"Send someone to my ship, *Pharaoh's Gold,* with a written message signed by me. Ask for Mr. Rutherford and Mr. Stockbridge. Bring them here."

A strange tension knotted in her stomach. She wanted to be the one to help him. It was her chance to redeem her conscience for all that he'd suffered. Alone, however, she didn't have the resources to get him off the island. His crew did.

Stiffly, she nodded.

ROSA SHUT THE door behind Graystone's departing friends.

Soon, he would no longer need her. His crew would help him escape from Cuba, saving herself and her godfathers the trouble.

Well, good riddance. He was such an arrogant, ungrateful beast anyway. She was better off without him in her life.

Derek stood in the doorway of her room, one hand braced against the jamb. Although his legs were still wobbly, he'd managed to rise before the men arrived. Pure orneriness alone would have him moving freely by nightfall.

Curiosity got the better of her. "Why didn't you just leave with them?"

"Because you and I have unfinished business."

Rosa detested the leap in her heart rate. Of course he didn't mean anything of a passionate nature, not with that scowl on his face. "What do you mean?"

"I am vividly recalling false evidence planted in my room and two days of torture, not to mention coming damned close to death from your potion. You owe me, Rosa."

She couldn't deny it. "And if I do?"

"There is only one thing I want, and you are the one with the unique talent to get it."

"Talent?" Rosa asked warily.

"Thievery."

Rosa's spirits plummeted. He just wanted to use her, like everyone else. "You still want Gaspar de Vargas's book."

He visibly started. "What do you know about the book?" He advanced toward her, his brow furrowed.

Rosa stood her ground, the knowledge that he wasn't back to full strength bolstering her courage. He grasped her shoulders. Defiantly, she said, "I stole it, no? It was in my hands for a brief time."

"What did you see?"

"The first page. It was nearly impossible to read, but I could make out some words. It is an account written by Gaspar, a survivor of the sinking of *Nuestra Señora de la Augustina*. She was a Spanish treasure galleon, no?"

Muscles bunched in his jaw. "She was."

Rosa caught her breath at this confirmation of her hopes. If Graystone believed, then there must be merit to the story of sunken treasure. Wariness glittered deep in his blue eyes. He didn't trust her, but what could he do when he needed her help?

"You hope that this book will lead you to the wreck?"

His fingers flexed on her shoulders. "The journal should provide one of several clues to the site. I repeat . . . should," he said discouragingly. "There are no guarantees." He released her and took a step back. "And you ask too many questions."

She crossed her arms and tapped her foot. "Do you want me to steal it for you, or not?"

"No. I want us to steal it together."

She blinked, dumbfounded.

A bitter laugh burst from his throat. "I can hardly blame you for looking startled. I have never stolen anything in my life. Never intended to. But that was before that bastard betrayed and tortured me. Don Geraldo changed the rules of the game. I believe he owes me compensation."

"He certainly does," she agreed indignantly.

A rare smile touched the corners of his mouth. Then he grew serious. "I will not force you. If you think the risk too great, then refuse. I am willing to sail away at dawn, with nothing to show for my time on this bloody island."

He didn't suspect it yet, but she wanted that journal as much as he did. "What if the journal is not in the same place?"

"The safe? Don Geraldo thinks I am dead. He has no idea that you stole the journal the first time. What reason would he have to conceal it elsewhere? The safe is likely the most secure place in his household."

True. "Very well. I shall do it, under one condition. My godfathers are not to know of our plans."

He shuddered. "You have my word, most assuredly."

New hope surged within Rosa. Everything was falling into place, except for one thing . . . Graystone had no intention of making her a part of his larger scheme to hunt down the treasure.

She would soon have something to say about that.

"HOLD HERE, GRAYSTONE," Rosa whispered, careful to keep her voice low. "I must ask you a question."

"Now is hardly the time." Although he matched her hushed tone, impatience filtered into his voice.

Rosa disagreed. This was exactly the moment she'd planned for renegotiating their alliance . . . in her favor.

Flat on her belly, shoulder to shoulder with Derek, she peered down from the edge of Don Geraldo's second-story roof. Three soldiers patrolled the courtyard below. She clutched the pilfered journal close to her chest. Retrieving it from the safe had been child's play compared to sneaking in past the nine guards stationed outside the hacienda. The truly dangerous part would be escaping undetected with their spoils.

Derek had insisted on staying with her every step of the way. She liked to think he had done so to protect her, but logic dictated that he didn't trust her alone with the journal.

The man possessed excellent instincts.

"Nevertheless, I insist," she whispered.

"Get on with it, then."

"Could you have opened that safe by yourself?"

He looked appalled. "I told you, this is my first burglary. I am not in the habit of practicing safecracking."

"Ah. So, I have done what you asked. I provided the talent to steal this journal, no?"

"Yes," he answered after a brief pause. His eyes narrowed. "Exactly where are you going with this, Rosa?"

"I have fulfilled my part of our original bargain. My debt to you is repaid. It is time to strike a new deal."

"Now? Here?" he said in a fierce undertone. "On this roof, with a dozen soldiers patrolling the grounds?"

She smiled. *"Sí."*

"I do not agree. Give me the journal, Rosa."

She lifted the book. Instead of passing it to him, she reached out and dangled the journal over the edge—directly above the heads of the three soldiers sharing a smoke below.

"What are you doing, you little hellion?"

"Starting a new round of negotiations."

"This is not open for discussion," he hissed.

It infuriated her that he refused to acknowledge her role or take her wishes into account. More determined than ever, Rosa shifted her hand. The journal now dangled precariously between her thumb and forefinger.

Derek froze. "Rosa," he whispered, "hand over that book. Now."

"Not until we come to an agreement."

"What the blazes do you want?"

"I want you to take me, and my godfathers, with you when you leave Cuba. Our lives are in danger after aiding you. I want to be part of the search for this Spanish galleon. And when we find her, I want a share of the treasure. Half."

"Out of the question."

"I thought this book was important to you?" she coaxed. She rocked it slowly between her fingers, confident that he wouldn't make a grab for it and risk making her lose her grip.

A myriad of emotions collided in his face—fury, doubt, and seething frustration. "The historical value of the treasure goes far beyond the monetary worth. I'll not see it split up. If I was willing to take on a partner, I would have accepted Don Geraldo's offer."

"The don would have stabbed you in the back. I will not."

Muscles flexed in his jaw. "There are items in that cargo that are too unique for me to ever consider parting with."

He seemed adamant. How could she blame him, when he'd sacrificed so much in his search for this ship? Rosa's hopes started to unravel. "Do you speak of the silver and gold?"

"Of course not," he scoffed. "Other than a few prime examples, pieces of eight hardly qualify as artifacts."

"Then one piece of silver is pretty much like another?"

"Essentially. That part is of the least interest to me."

"Then I will take the bulk of my share in worthless silver and gold." His eyes blazed. She grinned, enjoying herself.

"Your gall is astonishing."

"How else do you think I have survived for seven years, caring for myself and three old men who are prone to get in more trouble than sixteen-year-old boys?"

"I am heading straight for my ship from here," he argued. "There will be no time to stop for passengers, dammit."

"My godfathers are already packed and waiting for us near the docks," she countered. At least she hoped they had followed her orders and not lingered over women or a round of drinks. She had told them that Don Geraldo had uncovered their role in Graystone's escape and would be coming for them at dawn. That should be enough to light a fire under them.

"Bloody hell. You planned this all along."

"Clever of me, no?"

He looked as if he would heartily enjoy wrapping his hands around her throat and squeezing until she turned purple.

"Decide, Lord Graystone. My hand is beginning to cramp."

"Very well," he said between his teeth. "We have a deal, but not for half. A quarter."

If the treasure was even close to the wealth envisioned by her dreams and pledged by his persistence, a quarter would prove more than sufficient to support her godfathers in comfort for the rest of their lives.

"Done," she agreed happily. "Just one more thing."

"What?" he snarled.

"I do not want you to get crafty with me. Before I hand this over, I insist on your word of honor . . . as a gentleman."

"You have . . . my . . . word." The words ground between his lips as if he was pulling out his entrails with a grappling hook.

Rosa cringed. She was in deep trouble with Graystone. For now, however, she'd accomplished exactly what she'd sought. One step at a time. There would be numerous opportunities to deal with her very large, very attractive, and very angry partner in the weeks ahead.

Chapter Nine

ROSA HANDED OVER the journal, confident that Graystone's word meant everything to him. Certainly more than she did.

They crawled to an area of the roof outside the courtyard. A large oak tree provided their means of descent, just as it had granted access half an hour before.

Three days ago, her role as an entertainer at Don Geraldo's banquet had afforded the perfect opportunity to gain entry through the less heavily patrolled courtyard. Although she'd been forced to choose the riskier route this time, Graystone had proved a far more stealthy accomplice than her godfathers.

Their horses waited at the far end of the grounds within a sheltering line of trees. The horizon hinted of sunrise. Rosa watched the sky with concern. Derek had timed the robbery so he could head straight for his ship and set sail at dawn, but perhaps he had planned things a bit too close.

They climbed down the tree, Derek first. He jumped the last few feet to the ground. Just as she'd anticipated, his mobility and most of his strength had returned before sunset.

Rosa was almost down when a deep voice shouted in Spanish.

The alarm had been raised!

Without hesitation, Derek seized her by the waist and swung her down. He grabbed her hand. They raced for the horses. Erratic gunfire erupted. Bullets thudded into the short grass behind them.

Echoing shouts sounded within the hacienda.

A curtain lifted aside in an upstairs window. Candlelight framed a tall figure. Don Geraldo yanked open his bedroom door and stormed onto the balcony.

They reached the horses and mounted. Rosa turned toward the road. Derek reined his horse around to face the hacienda.

Rosa gasped. What was he doing?

Dangerously exposed at the edge of the clearing, he lifted the journal high. His blond hair gleamed in the faint light.

"Graystone!" Don Geraldo bellowed, no doubt startled and furious to discover his nemesis still alive.

The gunfire ceased abruptly. Apparently the soldiers were just as astonished to see a former corpse come to life. Perhaps they feared Graystone's ghost had returned to haunt them.

Then Derek raised his hand to regale the don with a very speaking gesture.

Rosa's eyes widened. She hadn't thought the staid, arrogant Englishman capable of such . . . such clarity of opinion.

They turned toward Havana and the waiting ship.

"Why did you do that?" she cried over the thunder of galloping hooves. "Would it not have been better to remain anonymous?"

"Better, yes, but hardly satisfying. I wanted to make sure de Vargas knows exactly who outwitted him and won in the end."

"It will go worse for you if he catches us."

"He won't."

Derek seemed thoroughly confident that they would stay a step ahead of their pursuers. Did he know something she did not? Or was he betraying common sense to defy the tyrant who had tortured him?

THEY RELEASED THEIR winded horses at the wharf. To her immense relief, Rosa immediately spotted her godfathers. She waved frantically. They trotted over, each carrying two medium-sized carpetbags. Esteban's guitar was slung across his back.

Derek's two friends manned the oars of a waiting long-boat. Although Derek's jaw tightened in obvious annoyance, he directed his new passengers into the boat. Esteban, Dickie, and Michael climbed into the bow with the bags. Rosa sat in the middle between Derek's mates, avoiding the glowering nobleman in the stern.

"This is unexpected," Mr. Stockbridge commently wryly.

"If you only knew," Derek growled. "Now, row. We are expecting company at any moment . . . hostile company."

Half a dozen mounted soldiers clattered onto the dock within minutes after they pushed off. Still astride their stomping, wheezing horses, the soldiers snapped their rifles into position. The crack of gunfire echoed across the bay. The shifting horses spoiled their aim, but one bullet hit the longboat. A chunk of wood popped free with a load whack.

Derek cupped a hand to the back of Rosa's neck and pushed her to the bottom of the boat. She protested, but he held firm until they were out of range.

The boat surged with each pull of the oars. They rapidly approached a sleek, graceful ship, its exterior painted a light brown with the name *Pharaoh's Gold* emblazoned in gold lettering on the bow.

They bumped against the side of the schooner, and

moments later were climbing rope ladders up to the deck. The remaining crew were already hoisting the sails.

Rosa leaned against the rail. The sticky residue of salt spray clung to the dark, polished wood. A mounting breeze whipped her hair and plastered her black trousers to her legs.

The frenzied activity along the docks worried her. A carriage careened around a corner. She glanced up at Derek.

He stood with his muscular legs braced against the roll of the moving ship. His broad shoulders formed a bulwark against the wind. The reflected blue of the sky and water deepened his glittering eyes to sapphire. She felt as if she'd run a race with the devil. How could he appear so calm and refreshed?

"We haven't shaken them yet. Look!" Dickie shouted. He pointed at a three-masted brigantine pushing away from the dock. Her sails unfurled as men scrambled across the deck and up into the rigging.

"That is *La Margarita,* one of Don Geraldo's ships," Esteban offered. "His most heavily armed."

Tim Rutherford joined them and placed a spyglass in Derek's outstretched palm. Derek slid the ebony and brass tube open and raised it to his right eye.

"Is everything ready per my instructions, Mr. Rutherford?" He examined the activity on the other ship. Wind filled the brigantine's sails and the ship picked up speed.

The first mate grinned. "Aye, Captain." He pivoted on one heel and strode away.

"What instructions?" Rosa asked suspiciously.

"You shall see. Don Geraldo is on board that ship," he announced.

"Ah, hell," Dickie exclaimed. "Can't get much worse than that. Let me see that glass."

Derek ignored him, continuing to watch the pursuing ship through the tube.

"Dickie is right," Rosa said. "This is a disaster. With Don Geraldo aboard, their pursuit will be relentless. He won't allow his soldiers to give up until they capture us."

"And throw us all in that prison," Michael said morosely.

Derek turned his head toward Rosa and raised one sardonic eyebrow. "Now there is a thought."

"You would like that, wouldn't you?" she snapped. "To see me condemned to La Muerte."

Derek's resolve to maintain his dignity and avoid an argument flew out of his head. What was it about this woman that so effortlessly fired his anger? Lowering the spyglass, he retorted, "Maybe it would make you think twice before framing some other innocent for a crime he did not commit."

"You are heartless," she declared heatedly. "I sacrificed everything to get you out of that prison and retrieve your precious book. My reputation. My home. But you cannot forgive. You will carry this grudge until the day you die."

"Must everything be such bloody high drama with you?" The wind lifted her hair, floating strands around her beautiful face like black flames. Rosa was a force of nature, unfettered and undisciplined. The same characteristics that repelled him also sent shivers of sexual awareness across his skin.

"Better to be dramatic than cold and indifferent." She glared back at him.

How could she have anything left inside when she excelled at throwing her emotions to the four winds? What would it be like for her to store up that passion, sharing it only with him? Would it be fire, burning him like their kiss in the courtyard?

Derek stared down into her upturned face. A familiar heaviness invaded his lower body. The world receded.

The boom of cannon fire shattered the spell. Rosa jerked. She spun around to face aft.

Four shots exploded into the water fifty feet behind the stern, sending ragged plumes of spray shooting into the air.

"Faith and they're firing on us!" Michael shouted.

"¡Caramba! Do they intend to sink us?" Esteban cried out.

"I'm rather certain that is the general idea."

Dickie demanded, "Give me a gun!"

"Aye, and another for me," Michael echoed.

Arm these irrational old men? Derek shuddered. "You will have to count on my crew to protect you." He pointed to Tim and Geoff, who were taking up positions at the brass deck guns.

"This is it? These puny guns are all you have?" Dickie raged, his tone full of disgust rather than fear.

Derek suppressed a smile. There was nothing quite like an aging sailor spoiling for a fight. "Sorry to disappoint you, Mr. Hunt, but this is a ship of science, not of war."

"We're doomed," moaned Michael.

Esteban raked one hand through his hair. "You may be right this time."

Rosa, who to this point had remained atypically silent, dropped a bombshell. "Your ship is slowing, Graystone."

"What?" Michael and Esteban yelped in unison.

Dickie glanced up at the rigging. "Your sails aren't completely full, mate. Get this ship back on course."

"The crew are following my instructions exactly. Have you determined the range of the brigantine's cannon, Tim?"

"Sure have, Captain."

Just then, another salvo fired from the pursuing ship. The cannonballs exploded harmlessly in their wake, though definitely closer this time.

"Their range is almost on us, in case you hadn't noticed!" Dickie said furiously.

"Maintain course and speed, Tim," Derek said calmly.

"You are *loco, hombre*," said Esteban. "Don Geraldo will catch us and sink us."

Rosa stood close enough that Derek could, if he wished, have reached out and smoothed away the furrow between her brows. She watched him with a mixture of wariness and curiosity. Derek stood silent, feeling oddly breathless. He could easily ignore her godfather's blustering, but why did her confidence in his judgment seem so important?

Suddenly, her gaze shifted to fix on a sight over his shoulder. Even before he turned, he knew what she'd discovered off the schooner's bow. The Yankee naval frigate *Eagle* bore down to meet them.

"You are luring Don Geraldo out of the harbor," she said softly.

Her gaze hinted at reluctant admiration. He felt a sudden urge to trace the curve of her lips with his thumb. He stiffened.

"Indeed," he said brusquely.

Pharaoh's Gold and the *Eagle* began to pass closely, going in opposite directions.

"Hail, Captain Bancroft," Derek shouted across the gap.

The American doffed his hat and smiled. "You seem to be in a bit of a pickle there, Lord Graystone."

"Just a minor inconvenience."

La Margarita's gunners fired another round. The shots exploded into the water ahead of the advancing frigate.

Derek cupped his hands around his mouth. "It would seem the Spaniards are instigating an act of war against the Americans."

"Crossing the barricade, too, stupid bastards," Bancroft yelled back as the two ships started to separate. He grinned.

"She is all yours, Bancroft. My compliments."

The Yankee captain saluted, his expression intent and eager. He began shouting orders to his crew.

Gun ports along the *Eagle*'s starboard side snapped

open. The yawning mouths of eight cannon rolled into position. With a sharp turn of its rudder, the frigate came about.

"Fire!" Bancroft's voice rolled across the water.

The roar of cannons ripped through the air. One cannonball blasted away *La Margarita*'s bowsprit, another tore through the rigging, while a third slammed into the brigantine's side at the waterline. The others missed entirely, but no matter. The third had struck a fatal blow. *La Margarita*'s crew attempted to return fire, but the water rushing into the ship's hold caused it to list just enough that all their shots fell short of the *Eagle*. The American ship descended on her prey.

Don Geraldo stood at the rail, arms folded arrogantly. He stared at the escaping schooner, his fury evident in his stiff posture and reddened face.

The Yanks boarded the floundering brigantine, rescuing the Spanish crew from drowning even as they took them prisoner. Esteban shouted encouragement. Michael waved his hat. Dickie thumbed his nose at their former pursuers.

Derek nodded to his first mate. Tim called an order to Nigel at the wheel. *Pharaoh's Gold* shifted, catching the full force of the wind. Her sails stretched taut as she headed for open sea. Spray splashed up on either side of the bow as the schooner's sleek prow cut through three-foot waves.

Rosa glared at him. Derek braced himself. He was clearly not out of stormy waters yet.

"You knew this would happen. You arranged it. How?"

"I sent Tim and Geoff out here last night," he explained, "with a case of brandy, a bit of gold, and negotiations with the officers of a ship full of bored men eager for some action. Rowdy, impatient sorts, these Yanks."

Derek raised the spyglass, finding satisfaction in the sight of Don Geraldo de Vargas in shackles. But there was nothing indicative of surrender in the Spaniard's posture.

"The Yanks will hold Don Geraldo," he stated confidently, "or turn him over to their allies, the Cuban rebels."

Either way, de Vargas wouldn't be free to compete for the *Augustina*. The don's knowledge of the galleon's final resting place, however approximate, was a risk Derek wasn't willing to take. He had orchestrated a solution designed to put Don Geraldo out of commission . . . though he would have preferred to meet his adversary face to face one last time to settle their differences in a more direct fashion.

"And you didn't see fit to inform me of your plan?" Rosa snapped. "All this worry, and help was on the way all along? What about my godfathers? Those three old men nearly suffered heart failure thinking they were about to end up at the bottom of the bay!"

Derek's gaze slanted toward the traumatized men in question. Michael, Esteban, and Dickie grabbed one another's arms and took a few turns in a jig, celebrating their escape.

He gave her a very dry look. "They seem to have pulled through the crisis fairly well."

She folded her arms. "Thanks to the Americans."

"Perhaps your godfathers are more resilient than you think."

"They are all nearing seventy. Their health is fragile."

"I am sure once they toss back a few pints of ale they'll be feeling quite restored."

Green fire blazed in her eyes at his flippant comment. "You are insensitive."

"And you are naïve."

"You should have told me. How can we work as partners if you withhold vital information from me?"

Her criticism rankled. Partners, indeed. All of his fury at her rooftop blackmail came flooding back. He moved in closer. "Partners? I should regard you as little more than a stowaway, madam," he growled.

She stood her ground, which surprised him. No woman had ever stood firm in the face of his displeasure before. Then again, he couldn't remember the last time he'd lost his temper with a woman.

"What of our agreement? Do you intend to go back on your word?" She lifted her chin and gave him a defiant look. "How? By throwing me overboard to the sharks?"

"A capital idea."

Derek swept her into his arms and headed for the railing. Rosa sputtered in outrage.

The bow plowed into a particularly large swell. The deck jerked. Derek's arms tightened, holding her more securely as his legs braced. A fine spray blew over them, misting their hair with tiny droplets of salt water.

"You would not dare."

He held her halfway over the edge. Rosa gasped and linked her fingers behind his neck.

"Still so confident, Rosa?" he asked roughly. "I am not fully recovered from my ordeal, you know. My knees are shaking. My arms are weakening fast. I may not be able to maintain my grip much longer."

"What nonsense," she quipped. "You are steady as an oak."

"That won't help you if I decide to let go."

Her hands tightened, cupping the back of his head. "I shall just hold on tighter."

His body reacted as if she caressed him. His breath quickened; his knees genuinely weakened. "You think that will save you?" he asked huskily.

"If not, at least I will take you over the side with me." She looked at him through curling black lashes and smiled.

Was she flirting? Teasing? Or mocking him? Desire rammed through him.

Derek immediately lowered her feet to the deck. Wrenching his gaze from the provocative curve of her lips, he stepped back. Geoff and Tim immediately appeared at his side.

His friends made no attempt to conceal their curiosity.

"Gentlemen, you have met Rosa," Derek grumbled.

"Miss Rosa, I distinctly remember the pleasure," Geoff said with his typical charm. He slanted Derek a sardonic look. "We didn't realize we would have the pleasure of you joining us, however."

Grudgingly, Derek added, "Well, you may also greet her as my new—" He hesitated, finding great difficulty in pushing the unfamiliar word past his throat. "Partner. Rosa's unique skills were responsible for recovering Gaspar's journal. She and her godfathers are now part of the search for the *Augustina*."

Tim and Geoff appeared surprised, of course. He could look forward to being pummeled with questions later.

"In that case, *señorita*," Tim offered gallantly, "allow me to give you a tour of the ship."

"*Sí*, I would like that," Rosa answered readily. "I am relieved that some men here know how to act like gentlemen."

Derek scowled. "Tim, you decide on the cabin assignments. Geoff, set a northwesterly course for Galveston. Besides picking up my shipments of custom-made equipment, we could all use a couple days of relaxation before the real work begins."

"Aye, sir."

"And Geoff, meet me in an hour for a match. I feel in serious need of some exercise."

Not to mention a way to work off this sexual frustration.

"DID I HEAR Lord Graystone right, Mr. Rutherford? We are sailing for Galveston? Is that where the *Augustina* lies?" Rosa asked the first mate when they were finally alone. Tim had shown her the deck area, where he'd introduced her to Richard Blount, the ship's carpenter, Wilson Fitzpatrick, the sailmaker, and the youngest member of the crew, redheaded Nigel Buchanan. Now he headed for a narrow flight of steps leading belowdecks.

"No, ma'am. We suspect the galleon sank off the Florida Keys. But Galveston is a necessary stop to pick up special salvage equipment Derek had shipped there from Europe."

Turning at the base of the steps, he offered a hand to help her down. The lower deck vibrated slightly beneath her boots.

"And please," he added, "Call me Tim. It looks as if we'll be working together for several weeks to come. Might as well be on friendly terms, don't you think?"

Rosa smiled, charmed by his warmth as well as his elfin features. Tim Rutherford was only an inch taller than her, though he was clearly strong in a wiry sort of way. He did remind her of an elf, with his dark blond hair, expressive hazel eyes, and chin that narrowed almost to a point. The crew had welcomed her with remarkable friendliness, expressing their gratitude for rescuing their captain from La Muerte.

Apparently, the sullen Lord Graystone hadn't shared his caustic opinion of the way she'd managed his escape.

"Have you sailed long with Lord Graystone?"

"Going on six years. But Derek and I have known each other since we were boys. My father is butler to Aversham."

"Aversham?"

"The Earl of Aversham, Derek's father. Capital fellow. I was hot for the sea, much to my father's dismay. The earl bought me a commission in Her Majesty's navy. He did the same for Geoff. We served for four years before Derek convinced us to retire and join him. Geoff and I have sailed with him since."

The story emphasized how little she knew about Graystone. She was entrusting the success of this venture—her future, actually—to a veritable stranger.

"Is Graystone good at this business of treasure hunting?"

Tim chuckled. "Don't let him catch you calling it that. The captain is very serious about archaeology. He has a real nose for antiquities. If anyone can find the *Augustina,* Derek can." He turned into a narrow passageway behind the stairs and opened the first door on the left. "This will be your cabin."

Although small, a narrow bed prevented the cabin from feeling too cramped. Drawers were built efficiently into the wall. Discarded clothes lay across the bed. Men's clothes.

"Is this—" she croaked, unable to finish the question that popped into her mind. Had Derek given up his cabin for her? The idea of sleeping on his bed, inhaling his scent from the sheets, sent a strange shiver through her.

"Don't worry. I'll be moving in with Geoff."

"Oh, this is your cabin," she exclaimed, then blushed over the sound of relief in her voice. "No. I cannot drive you out."

He bowed. "The rare blessing of having a beautiful woman on board will compensate."

"Surely Graystone has invited women onto his ship before."

"Actually, before you, the only women to set foot on *Pharaoh's Gold* have been his sisters, Elysia and Amber."

Rosa felt absurdly pleased to discover that Graystone wasn't in the habit of bringing his paramours on board. Tim nodded toward a closed door at the stern end of the passageway and announced, "That is the captain's cabin, by the way."

Rosa swallowed convulsively. So close.

Tim opened a door across the hall, revealing spiral stairs and unleashing the deep thrum of machinery. "These lead down to the engine room," he explained.

They descended into the bowels of the schooner.

"Miss Rosa, this is Grady Stuart, our engineer. He has a special talent for anything mechanical."

A short, barrel-chested man with thinning brown hair loomed from a shadowed corner. His dirty appearance might have startled Rosa, except for the smile wreathing his broad face.

Grady winked. "Aye, you're the one who saved the captain. Welcome, missy. I'll spare you an offer to shake hands." He chuckled, then held up greasy palms to demonstrate why.

As Tim escorted her back to the passageway, Rosa commented, "You all appear very loyal to Graystone."

"We would lay down our lives for him, and he has proven in the past that he would risk his own for us."

They turned toward the middle of the ship. The passageway abruptly cut to the right to maneuver around an elevated room blocking the way. A set of four steps led up to a doorway.

"This is the laboratory, the heart of the ship. It's the room with the windows you see from above."

They climbed the stairs and stepped inside.

Rosa looked around in amazement. The left wall of the room was stacked with storage cabinets. The far wall held four racks of upright barrels built around another doorway. To her right, a low line of cabinets was topped by shelves, each edged with a wire railing to prevent the rows of books, jars, and bottles from sliding off during rough seas. A massive table with a surface of white marble dominated the center of the room. Drawers divided the solid base of the table into additional storage. Tools hung from what little wall space remained. The design utilized every available nook and cranny.

"What is this room used for?"

"This is where Derek examines any finds, sketches them, catalogs them, and begins the process of restoration."

"And the barrels?" She glanced at the wall through which they'd entered, likewise lined with barrels. "Do you plan on opening a tavern?"

A grin flashed across Tim's face. "We do have some ale stored in the galley, but these are empty." He knocked on one to demonstrate. "The only other wreck we've worked was a Dutch merchantman in the Philippines. We quickly learned that artifacts which have spent decades in seawater will dry out and crumble. Pottery will shatter if the salt absorbed into its pores is allowed to crystallize. It takes a long process of soaking everything in increasingly fresh water to draw out the brine. We'll store the artifacts in barrels full of seawater until we get back to England."

Fascinated, Rosa peered into a barrel and tried to imagine them full of treasures just waiting to be restored. "Will Graystone teach me how to do this?"

"You can always ask, but be prepared for a no. Derek is, shall we say, protective of working with the artifacts."

"Then I shall ask again and again, until he says yes."

With a laugh, Tim encouraged, "You do that, Miss Rosa. I can certainly see why he would have trouble saying no to you."

Rosa turned to the shelves. Her gaze scanned a row of bottles. These were the tools of a scientist, with labels like sodium bicarbonate, nitric acid, and linseed oil. On the adjacent shelf leaned a row of journals, similar to the one she'd stolen, yet much newer. All the books were bound in plain leather, except one. Its title, printed in gold foil, read *Twenty Thousand Leagues Under the Sea*.

What kind of scientist shelved fanciful tales by Jules Verne alongside his journals?

Intrigued, Rosa reached for the volume. A winsome smile curved her mouth for the book brought back memories.

Her father's shipping business had kept him away at sea for long periods. But each time he returned to Havana . . . each time he swept her into his arms and called her his "little firefly," he had brought her books from America. Geography books to tantalize her with images of faraway lands, history volumes to fascinate her with mankind's foibles as well as successes, and novels to ignite her imagination. She'd devoured them all, cherishing them as gifts from her handsome, laughing papa.

The novels of Jules Verne had been among her favorites. Verne excelled at the miraculous, with stories of trips to the moon, expeditions to the center of the earth, and adventurous travels by balloon. This one story, however, she had missed.

She opened the cover. The edges of the pages were somewhat worn, as if turned many times. She flipped through, noting the illustrations. One particular drawing inspired her to pause.

The scene depicted helmeted divers, armed with harpoonlike weapons, freely walking on the sea bottom. Floating armies of jellyfish surrounded the divers, while coral dominated the landscape like fantasy castles. And there, in the background, were the faint outlines of a sunken ship.

Excitement shivered through Rosa. She wanted the thrill of exploring the undersea world, to discover something mysterious and marvelous. She longed to be a viable part of this expedition, not just bide her time on the ship while someone else brought up the treasure.

Replacing the book, she ran one finger lightly down the spine. With the hard-hearted Lord Graystone, she stood little chance of diving to the wreck. But with the enigmatic, complex Derek Carlisle . . . a man who cherished the stories of Jules Verne . . . perhaps anything was possible.

Tim led the way through the laboratory and out the opposite door. They returned to the main passageway.

"Now we're approaching the bow. The crews' quarters are ahead. I'll spare you a tour of those. This is the galley." He pointed to a doorway on their immediate right.

Rosa looked inside. Clearly, this was where the crew dined. A small kitchen took up one end, while three narrow tables and benches bolted to the floor filled the remaining space. At the moment, one table was occupied by five men playing cards.

Apparently, her godfathers had quickly adapted to life on board and found a way to fill their idle time.

Michael slapped a hand of cards onto the table in triumph.

Esteban swore under his breath. Richard and Wilson, whom her godfathers had apparently coaxed from their duties above, groaned.

"Let that be a lesson to you, lads. Never underestimate an old man." Michael cheerfully raked in a pile of coins.

Dickie grumbled, "The luck of the Irish, my——"

"Hush, you old *cabrito*," Esteban interjected in a harsh whisper. "Rosa is here. *Hola, niña.*"

The men rose as she entered the room. Richard snatched a worn cap from his head.

Tim spoke up. "Wilson, I believe it's your turn to cook tonight. What are we having for supper?"

Her godfathers, always ruled by their stomachs, listened attentively. Rosa suddenly thought of the victuals four extra people would consume. Until the treasure was found, they were totally dependent on Graystone's largesse. Her pride felt a definite twinge.

"Fresh red snapper, caught this morning and swimming merrily in a barrel until we fillet them, rice, boiled carrots, and fresh fruit from your homeland, Miss Rosa."

"Sounds delicious, lad," said Michael. Esteban rubbed his hands together. Dickie dealt another round of cards.

"M-Miss Rosa," Richard stammered shyly. "The men . . . well, we were hoping you could dance the flamenco for us sometime."

A hint of color rose into Tim's cheeks. "I'm afraid Geoff and I described the dance you performed at the banquet. The men have been clamoring for an opportunity to see it ever since."

With a hopeful expression, Wilson added, "Do you think . . . ?"

Flamenco was one way to repay them for their kindness. Considering how she'd left Cuba with only a few belongings packed into an old carpetbag, perhaps the only way.

"*Sí*. Tonight?" At their eager nods, she added, "Very well. After dinner."

TIM AND ROSA arrived back on the main deck to the ringing sound of steel striking steel. Having grown up in a Spanish country where men were obsessed with sword arts, Rosa immediately recognized the clashing of rapiers.

"What is going on?"

"Derek's favorite form of relaxation."

Tim led the way around the rectangular shoulder-high structure that formed the top half of the laboratory. Situated in the center of the deck, the windows surrounding all sides filtered light into the room below.

Reaching the open area of deck near the bow, Tim added, "Derek taught Geoff to fence. They are a good match, though Geoff has never managed to win a bout."

"You call this relaxation?" Rosa asked skeptically.

The two men fenced with the vigor of sworn opponents. They lunged, they parried. Although they wore protective full-face masks and padded breastplates, Rosa instantly recognized Derek's broad, bare shoulders. A glossy sheen highlighted the rapid interplay of muscles and whipcord tendons in his arms. Sweat ran in a rivulet down his spine.

As if compelled, her gaze followed a thick droplet down to his lean waist. It soaked into the waistband of his black trousers. He lunged. His firm buttocks flexed.

Rosa suddenly felt light-headed.

"I would say that Derek has some anger against Don Geraldo to work out of his system," Tim said.

The swords crashed together again. The discordant sound, combined with Tim's words, sent an unpleasant jolt through Rosa.

She couldn't agree. She was indirectly responsible for Derek's imprisonment and torture. Add in a forced partnership, and she doubted it was Don Geraldo's chest he envisioned as he thrust through Geoff's guard and claimed victory with a blow to the red heart embroidered on white padding.

Chapter Ten

A MUFFLED RAPPING noise disrupted Derek's concentration. Annoyance flashed through him, especially since he'd requested not to be disturbed.

"Enter," he growled, supposing it was someone knocking at his cabin door. The tapping continued. When no response came, Derek bit back an oath and looked up from his study of Gaspar's journal.

He was surprised to note that darkness had crept into his cabin, consuming everything but the small circle of light from the desk lantern.

Then he realized the tattoo sound wasn't coming from his door, but somewhere above. What could the crew be working on this late? With a shrug, he dismissed the sound. He rolled his head, ignoring the crackle of stiff tendons in his aching neck, then bent over the journal once again. Absently, he reached for a slice of banana from a dinner gone cold.

He was halfway through translating the journal. The clues to the *Augustina*'s final resting place were sketchy, but they were indeed tucked within the scrawling script. Gaspar de Vargas described the slashing of a violent sea and the grinding impact of the galleon against a reef. The mention of the *Santa Margarita* likewise sinking to their west ranked as the most valuable clue. Archival records claimed that the *Margarita* had been salvaged by the Spaniards, soon after her loss, within sight of the Dry Tortugas. Now he need only estimate a position so Geoff could plot a—

The rapping increased in tempo, rolling like thunder.

Derek slapped his palm down on the desk. "Bloody hell, can't a man get any peace around here?"

Then he recognized the rhythm.

Flamenco.

An image of Rosa dancing on the night of Don Geraldo's banquet flashed through his mind. Was she performing for his crew? Did she dance with the same lithe, passionate grace that triggered a man's lust and turned his brain to pudding?

Derek surged to his feet.

Somehow, his invitation had been neglected.

Righteous anger took control, enabling him to dismiss the disturbing, simmering feeling of disappointment. He didn't need Rosa playing her seductive games with his crew. He would put a stop to this right away. With long, brisk strides, he headed down the passageway and up the steps.

Everyone had gathered in the open space between the laboratory and the bow. Crewmen sat cross-legged on the deck, alongside Dickie and Michael, forming a large circle. Esteban sat on a narrow bench off to one side, his nimble fingers coaxing a moving song from the guitar. The music flowed outward, claiming mastery over the night, dominating even the creaking of the rigging and the splash of the schooner's bow cutting through the waves. The rich rhythm tugged at Derek's soul. He would have loved to just sit and listen, but relaxation was impossible thanks to the fiery woman dancing within the circle of mesmerized men.

Three lanterns illuminated the scene. Although Rosa was dressed modestly this time in a red skirt and white blouse with short puffed sleeves, she lifted the skirt and petticoats almost to her knees, exposing shapely calves. Her heels drummed a staccato beat on the wooden planks. Loose, wavy hair, as black as the surrounding sea, hung nearly to her waist.

Derek stopped cold at the corner of the laboratory, shielded by a darkness the lanterns failed to penetrate. No one noticed his presence. Why should they, when a beacon of light and energy shone from the circle's center?

Her body moved with that same supple grace he remembered. Her serious expression reflected a rare intensity, as if called forth from some deep, passionate well. An aura of bliss softened her full mouth and framed her heavy-lidded eyes.

Derek's body tightened in a rush of heat. His pulse raced. He rubbed his chest with one hand, dimly aware of a burning sensation beneath his ribs and an almost overwhelming urge to charge into that circle, grab Rosa's arm in a grip that bordered on primitive, and drag her out of sight.

The reason came to him with devastating clarity. He was gripped by a feeling of possessiveness. He didn't want to share her dance with anyone else, not even his closest friends.

If he followed through on such a ludicrous urge his crew would immediately draw the wrong conclusions. He didn't want to appear . . . What? Bitter? Ill-tempered?

Jealous?

Nonsense. He wasn't the jealous sort. His true passions were reserved for archaeology. He didn't develop lasting attachments for women, certainly not emotions deep enough to lead to anything as illogical as jealousy.

Shaking his head, Derek backed away slowly. He withdrew into the night, away from the source of light, away from the shouts of encouragement and the camaraderie.

He'd known Rosa would be nothing but trouble.

If the uncomfortable fit of his trousers was any indication, the challenges to his self-control as well as his patience were only beginning.

————

FOUR DAYS LATER, dockhands tied *Pharaoh's Gold* to the Galveston wharf. Another team of workers were in the process of moving a gangplank into place. It was almost time to go ashore.

Derek's gaze shifted to the row of warehouses along the wharf. In one of those buildings, languishing in storage, awaited the salvage equipment shipped to him from Europe—two air compressors, a one-man surveying balloon of his own design, and two experimental oxygen rebreathers developed by an innovative German named Henry Fleuss. Most important of all were the two dive suits custom-crafted with special modifications, one built to fit him and a smaller one for Tim.

As a Gulf port frequented by freighters from every corner of the world, Galveston had offered an excellent solution as a destination for timely transportation of his supplies. He'd commissioned each item from a different manufacturer, some ordered months ago, with shipment deadlines calculated to meet his schedule.

Stopping over at the Texas port also provided an excuse to visit his sister Ellie and her husband, Matt Devereaux. Whereas their youngest sibling, Amber, refused to have anything to do with archaeology, he and Ellie shared a love for the science. Even Matt had developed an interest when Ellie partnered with him last year to hunt down Aztec treasure. Derek had last seen them in September, when he'd decided that the American gambler might just be good enough for Ellie.

One corner of his mouth twitched upward. Not that Matt had waited for his approval.

The gangplank settled into place. The dock foreman signaled Derek. The next stage in his plan was about to begin.

Anticipation shivered through Derek. Two days in Galveston, three at the most, then they would be on their way to their final destination. Geoff and Tim would see to outfitting the schooner with food and other supplies, leaving him free to claim equipment and visit family.

Rosa's three godfathers mounted the stairs from belowdecks. Esteban and Michael stretched in the early morning sunshine. Dickie yawned noisily. They offered a cheerful greeting and joined Derek at the railing.

"Good ol' Galveston. It's been many a year since I made port here." Dickie stroked his beard, his smile nostalgic. Then he waggled his bushy white brows. "I wonder how many of my favorite taverns are still open?"

Derek eyed them warily. "We shall be in port for three days. Do you think you can stay out of trouble for that long?"

Dickie clapped a hand to his chest with a "Who, me?" look.

"We're as harmless as wee lambs," offered Michael.

"Where shall we sleep?" Esteban asked. "On the ship?"

"No!" Derek burst out. Bloody hell, not on his ship, not when everyone would be too busy to supervise them.

During the voyage, boredom had driven the three old men to poke their noses into everything . . . excluding the laboratory, which Derek had had the foresight to lock. Twice their forays into the engine room had led to a shouting match with the engineer. Grady hadn't appreciated their efforts to experiment with the workings of the water pumps or other machinery. The third time, Derek had been forced to separate Grady and Dickie before they came to blows. A sense of dread rose in Derek's chest when he thought of Rosa's godfathers, with their love of tinkering, left alone with his expensive equipment.

Identical looks of dejection descended over their faces. Derek sighed inwardly. The manipulative old buggers had certainly perfected those whipped-puppy expressions.

He suspected they didn't have sufficient funds to put up in a hotel. Despite his cynical view, he felt sorry for them.

"I shall speak with my sister Ellie. She and her husband are leasing a large house. Perhaps she can find room."

Their faces brightened. After a brief farewell, they swaggered down the gangplank.

Heaven help the unsuspecting population of Galveston.

A coach, drawn by a fine pair of bay horses, pulled up adjacent to the ship. A handsome couple climbed out. The woman's face lit with a radiant smile. She waved.

Derek grinned. Their timing was impeccable. Ellie must have hired a spotter to send word the moment *Pharaoh's Gold* neared the port.

Rosa came up on deck. Her red skirt fluttered in the breeze. She looked beautiful and vibrant this morning. The sunshine played across her lightly bronzed skin and bleached her blouse a vivid white.

"Are you ready to go ashore?" he asked.

She nodded stiffly.

Without thinking, Derek took her elbow to steady her down the gangplank. The contact between his hand and her smooth skin triggered a shock of awareness. He noticed the attractive way she'd arranged her hair high. Black tendrils hung down the back of her neck in soft waves. By the time they reached the bottom, he was the one feeling unsteady.

He released her elbow abruptly. Then he observed how the skin across her sculptured cheekbones was drawn tight.

"You're not worried, are you? This is just my sister and her husband."

That was exactly the problem, Rosa thought nervously.

This was Derek's sister, the daughter of an earl. Tall, blond, quite beautiful, and dressed in an exquisite walking dress of pale gray with black braid trim, Elysia Devereaux represented an aristocratic world Rosa had never been part of. What if the woman snubbed her?

Reluctantly, Rosa followed Derek with her chin held high.

Ellie threw her arms around her brother's neck. Derek returned the embrace, hugging her tight.

Matt grinned. "Should I be jealous?" His wife didn't seem in a hurry to let Derek go.

"Absolutely." Freeing one arm, Derek stretched out his right hand behind Ellie's back. Matt grasped it in a powerful grip. They shook hands.

Rosa shifted uncomfortably. Such family warmth left her feeling very much the intruder.

Then Ellie stepped back from Derek and focused on her with evident curiosity.

"Hello. I am Ellie Devereaux."

"Rosa Constanza Wright, your ladyship." Not knowing quite how to greet the daughter of an earl, she curtsied briefly.

"She is quite lovely, Derek. How did you meet?"

"On my recent trip to Cuba," Derek said shortly. "Rosa joined our expedition in Havana." He performed introductions all around.

Rosa waited for him to elaborate. When he held his silence, she realized he didn't intend to admit the truth. Was he embarrassed at losing exclusive rights to the treasure, or was he ashamed of her? Rosa ignored her trepidation and said, "I am his partner in his latest archaeological search. His business partner, actually."

Ellie Devereaux couldn't have looked more astonished if a whale had climbed out of the water and walked across the dock. She gazed at Derek, blond brows arched. "A partner? This is certainly a first."

Derek grimaced. "I am well aware of that."

"This is for the *Augustina*? You are going after the galleon again this year?"

"You know I will, until I find her."

"Well, it appears you will have help this time. How very interesting." She took Derek's arm and steered him toward the coach. "You must tell me all the details."

"I wouldn't await that moment with bated breath, if I were you," Derek muttered.

Matt Devereaux offered Rosa his elbow and a friendly smile. "These Carlisles take some getting used to, don't they?"

Grateful for his friendly overture, Rosa smiled as she took his arm. At least as tall as Derek, Matt was quite handsome in a dark-haired, rugged sort of way. "Your wife is very beautiful."

Matt's gaze, full of pride, followed Ellie as she stepped into the coach. "Yes, she is."

He handed Rosa inside. They all took their seats. The Devereauxs sat close together on one side. Derek and Rosa sat as far apart as possible on the other. The coach began to move.

"My sister is looking a little wan, Devereaux. I thought you were taking good care of her," Derek challenged.

"Very good care, actually." Matt grinned wolfishly. "It's not me causing the problem. Not directly, anyway."

"Let me guess. Ellie is working too hard, obsessed with her latest archaeological quest. Have you found any sign of Jean Lafitte's pirate treasure?"

Ellie's eyes lit up. "We found a buried chest near three trees, with a bit of gold and even more interesting papers. Also, what might be the remains of Lafitte's wine cellar under a local business. When Lafitte was forced to leave the island, he burned his capital to the ground. Galveston must have been built over the remains. Other than that, nothing exciting. Much to my disappointment."

"Actually, we discovered something even better."

Ellie's brows furrowed. "We did?"

"I'm not talking about an archaeological find, sweetheart," Matt said tenderly.

"Oh, that." She blushed.

They didn't elaborate. Instead, they gazed warmly into one another's eyes. Derek drummed his fingers on one knee. When the silence stretched, he changed the subject.

"Have you heard from Father?"

"Unfortunately, yes." Matt gave an exaggerated shudder. "The earl insists on referring to me as 'that blasted Yank.'"

Derek chuckled. "I warned you not to bag more

grouse than Father when you visited him. He fancies himself an excellent shot."

"He should have tried growing up in the American West, where handling a gun was a means of survival, not just sport."

"Are you planning another visit soon, or will you wait until your work here is finished?"

Ellie reached out. Matt wrapped her hand in his.

"We'll be packing up next month and moving to England. For a while, at least," he explained.

"Near Father? Isn't that broaching the lion's den?"

"I want to be home when our child is born," Ellie said.

Derek's eyes widened. "You're . . . with child?"

Ellie laughed. "Don't look so dismayed, Derek. Just because I have a baby does not mean I cannot strap the little mite to my back and continue my work. I think we shall head for the jungles of Central America next, in search of Aztec temples."

With an expression of horror, Derek exclaimed, "Bloody hell, Elysia. I trust you are roasting me."

His sister's lips twitched with mirth.

Ellie might be joking, but Rosa took exception to Derek's high-handedness. "Why should your sister languish at home after childbirth? It is not an affliction, you know. Peasant women in Cuba carry their babies in back harnesses all the time."

"My sister is not a peasant," Derek snapped.

"Nor is she helpless," Rosa retaliated. "She is an active, strong, intelligent woman."

Down deep, she realized that a good measure of her anger came from the way Derek treated her. He preferred to keep her out from underfoot, while she wanted desperately to be a viable part of the hunt for the *Augustina*. As they glared at one another, Rosa suddenly realized that Matt and Ellie were following the exchange with interest. She quickly looked away.

Softly, Ellie interjected, "Whether aristocrat or peasant,

Derek, all women are made from the same flesh and bone." Turning to Rosa, she asked eagerly, "Tell me about this baby harness."

Derek snorted. "Don't you want to put a stop to this, Matt?"

Sitting back calmly, Matt pulled out a pocket watch. He began polishing it with a handkerchief. "What a relief to discover I understand my wife's headstrong ways better than her own brother, despite their similarities in that area. You may as well resign yourself to the inevitable, old man."

Ignoring her brother's scowl, Ellie said cheerfully, "Speaking of the inevitable, Derek, your timing is impeccable. We are scheduled to attend a ball tomorrow night. I would love for you to go with us. Everyone has been clamoring to meet my brother, the viscount."

He stiffened. "I have serious work to do, Ellie."

She smiled knowingly. "You will release your crew at night to enjoy the town. Why not yourself? What can you possibly accomplish aboard ship after dark?"

"Study documents."

"Let me spare you the eye strain. Come, enjoy yourself."

"What enjoyment can I find in a room full of strangers?"

"Not all strangers. Miss Wright will be there."

Rosa nearly fell off her seat in astonishment. "*Gracias,* but no, I could not."

Derek folded his arms across his broad chest. "So now it is your turn to look a bit dismayed," he grinned. By way of explanation to Ellie, he added, "Rosa has nothing to wear. This skirt and blouse are the nicest clothes she brought with her, if you do not count the overly revealing gowns she wears to dance flamenco."

Rosa's cheeks grew hot. She was within a hairsbreadth of jamming her heel into his ankle.

Ellie leaned across and patted Rosa's hand. "I have always wanted to see flamenco dancing. I hope you will perform for us while you are here. Perhaps you can teach me a few steps?"

Matt smiled sardonically.

Derek raked one hand through his hair.

Between Ellie's thoughtfulness and the deft way she handled her overbearing brother, Rosa liked the woman very much, indeed.

"As for a gown for the ball," Ellie continued, "we can begin right away to remedy that. I have been looking for an excuse to go shopping. What better reason than to outfit my new friend? With your lovely figure, Rosa, we can reasonably expect to find a ready-made gown that can be altered by tomorrow." Sitting back, she finished with evident satisfaction, "It is settled, then."

Derek muttered something under his breath.

Considering his aggravated expression, Rosa decided that Ellie's idea held definite merit.

"How DID IT come about that you and my brother are partners in this venture?" Ellie leaned forward, her blue eyes, so like Derek's, alight with curiosity.

The two women sat together in the carriage an hour later, on their way to the promised shopping expedition.

Rosa plucked at her red skirt. Derek didn't seem to keep secrets from his sister. Then again, during the ride home he'd neglected to regale her with the details of his time in La Muerte or how they had come to be in possession of the journal.

"I should leave that to Derek to tell you," Rosa hedged.

Ellie's lips compressed.

Rosa swallowed her disappointment. She hated to damage her budding friendship with Derek's sister. Ellie's next comment came as a surprise.

"Though it will kill me to be kept in the dark, I admire you for keeping his confidence. Derek may not appreciate it yet, but you will prove an asset to him, Rosa."

"I hope to be."

"Do you understand why I am so intrigued?"

Rosa shook her head.

"You see, my brother never, under any circumstances, takes on a partner. Not even one who is a fellow archaeologist. He is a lone wolf. However you managed the feat, I wish I had been there to witness it."

Charmed by Ellie's ability to tease and love her brother at the same time, Rosa confided, "I can tell you this . . . he was not happy about it."

Ellie laughed. "Just as I hoped. You outfoxed him in some way. No wonder you have gotten under his skin." Leaning back against the squabs, she purred, "Oh, how the mighty have fallen."

"*¿Perdoname?*" Rosa asked, confused.

"You have worked a miracle, Rosa. I only wish Amber was here to share in this."

The carriage pulled to a stop. The conveyance rocked slightly as the coachman climbed down.

"Come, we are at my favorite modiste. We shall find you the perfect gown. One that, put quite simply, will knock my brother on his ear."

Chapter Eleven

As Derek stood watching impatiently, the warehouse worker pried open the facing panel of the seven-foot-high crate. Nails began to pull free. The grating sound echoed through the cavernous dockside warehouse.

Derek glanced beyond the crates marked with his name. Along this row alone he could see huge bales of white-gray cotton stacked six high, heaps of fresh-cut lumber, and dozens of crates like his own. Galveston was one of the shipping capitals of the world. Goods flowed in and out, bringing wealth and culture to a city known for its active social life and large number of millionaires.

The loosened panel fell to the floor with a resounding crash. A fine cloud of dust kicked up, accentuating the potent scents of pine sawdust and raw cotton. It gradually settled, allowing the dim light to filter through.

The workman, a stocky fellow no taller than Derek's shoulder, with dark blond hair pulled back in a ponytail, peered inside the crate.

"Bless my mama, will you look at that! What is it?"

Derek proudly examined the yards of material folded into a tight bundle, the idle burner, and the welded metal bars that formed a complex frame around a single seat. "A rather unique balloon," he answered. Everything looked perfect, a faithful replica of the detailed designs he'd provided for a balloon manufacturer in Yorkshire.

"What's it for?"

Smiling, Derek said, "Let's open the other crates, shall we?"

The workman hurried to oblige. Another crate contained the air compressors, and yet another the oxygen rebreathers tightly wrapped in waterproof tarp, per his instructions. The second-largest crate opened to reveal his most precious acquisition . . . the round copper-and-brass helmets of two dive suits. The folded canvas suits, metal-soled boots, weights, collars, and yards and yards of air hose were all carefully packed in straw. Derek quickly checked the quick-release clamps on the base of the two helmets, an innovation he'd requested on the custom-made suits instead of the cumbersome screws that were typically used.

Everything appeared to be in good condition. Handling the equipment . . . seeing his plans and designs come to fruition . . . filled him with impatience to be on his way.

"This last crate's marked 'Explosives,' " the workman offered nervously, interrupting Derek's thoughts. The man pointed to the smallest wooden box painted with red warning messages.

"Yes, I know. Treat that one with special care."

The workman did so, gingerly prying off the lid.

Derek hunkered down on his heels. Nestled within the padded cotton were two dozen sticks of gelatinous dynamite. Alfred Nobel had been a fascinating man, coming up with dozens of patents on dynamite and nitroglycerin compounds before his recent death in 1896, including this form that could be used underwater. Fuses were coiled alongside, waterproofed with a coating of gutta-percha, a rubberlike gum from a Malaysian tree. Derek preferred not to resort to explosives, but if a key portion of the *Augustina* had become buried, he might have to set off a few charges to free the wreck.

He rose. "Seal the crates securely, if you don't mind."

"Sure. I guess the boys will be delivering them to you in the next couple of days."

"Actually, I've paid extra to have them delivered now," Derek said as he heard the sound of voices and rumbling wheels approaching down a nearby row. "These crates will not be out of my sight until they're safely aboard my ship."

THE FOLLOWING NIGHT, Derek paused before a huge mirror in Ellie's foyer, strategically installed to reflect the maroon and ivory marble floor and dramatically curved staircase. He ran a finger beneath his stand-up collar and white bow tie, grumbling at the pressure against his neck. The lack of formality aboard ship always spoiled him, making it ever harder to return to the strictures of evening attire—particularly when those clothes included a white starched-front shirt.

Many of his best clothes had been lost at Don Geraldo's. This double-breasted tailcoat had been pulled from deep in his sea chest, but it would serve. Ellie's maid had also pressed the wrinkles from the narrow trousers and restored the fashionable center crease.

Reflected movement from the staircase caught his eye. Derek froze, his gaze riveted on the mirror by a startling apparition dressed in a princess-style gown of pale blue crêpe de Chine.

He might not have recognized Rosa, if it weren't for the striking black hair gathered atop her head or the lightly bronzed skin that would make every other woman at tonight's ball appear pale and waxen. She held herself proudly erect as she descended.

The gown fit her to perfection. Small black circles of embroidery dotted the pale blue, spreading over the slight train gathered in the back. Three rows of matching narrow ribbon trimmed the scooped bodice and ran down the front of the dress. The open-front skirt revealed an underdress of white lace. A tight-fitting waist and belt of black silk accented her trim figure. Her expressive hands were bare, evening gloves being somewhat out of fashion at the moment.

His favorite touch was a choker of black velvet with a pale blue topaz dangling at her throat. The narrow strip of black triggered heated thoughts of exploring the graceful column of her neck with his lips.

He turned slowly.

If possible, she appeared even more beautiful without the mirror. She paused six steps from the bottom and boldly returned his stare.

Derek's usual repertoire of flattering comments went right out of his head. She looked like an exotic princess, beguiling and mysterious, every inch the lady. He suddenly felt privileged in the secret knowledge that beneath that outward finery lay the athletic agility of a nymph and the clever resourcefulness of a born survivor.

Her glare intensified the longer he remained silent. She planted her hands on her hips. "Go on, say whatever criticisms are burning on your tongue."

He grinned. Now this was the Rosa he knew. "Actually, I think you look superb."

She looked doubtful. "I think you are teasing me, no?"

Ellie started down the stairs just then, before he had the chance to assure Rosa that, surprisingly, he meant every word. His sister was resplendent in a gown of turquoise satin. She hooked her arm through Rosa's down the remainder of the stairs.

"Congratulations, Ellie. You have worked wonders."

"Really, Derek," she said as they reached the bottom. "The cocoon can hardly take credit for the butterfly. It merely nourishes the potential that is already there." She patted his cheek. Her grin held a hint of mischief. "You might want to claim a spot on her dance card before they are all gone. Come, both of you. I believe Matt is already waiting for us in the carriage."

"THAT'S THE WAY to go, me boyo," Michael cheered heartily. He gave Dickie a thump on the back that nearly sent the smaller man staggering. "Show that cocky Gypsy what you're made of."

Esteban glared at the arrangement of Dickie's darts on the board. Pure luck, that's what it was. He reached for his mug and downed the last swallow of frothy ale.

Tobacco smoke drifted into their corner of the Velvet Turtle, a dockside tavern. The crowd and the level of noise had grown since the sun set. The godfathers maintained squatter's rights on their privileged spot at the dartboard.

"Another game, Esteban?" Dickie leaned close and added, "Before they chase us out of here? We're almost out of money."

"Maybe we shouldn't have given so much of Don Geraldo's booty to the rebels before we left Cuba," Michael said sadly.

Esteban answered, "No, we did the right thing, *amigos*." The other two nodded. The smaller pieces they'd kept had provided a bath, haircut, and new set of clothes for each of them today. Of course, the money might have lasted longer if they hadn't chosen to gamble a great deal on dice and darts. Then again, what did it matter when a king's ransom in gold and silver awaited them from Rosa's deal with Graystone?

Dickie stroked his newly trimmed beard and sighed. "Maybe the right thing for the rebels, but I've been feelin' badly about the trick we played on Graystone."

Michael said, "Me, too, though it wasn't my idea."

A guilty feeling nudged at Esteban. "*Sí*. Me as well."

"Do you think we should apologize? After all, he's leading us to a fortune in Spanish treasure." Dickie glanced up sharply, his attention caught by something over Esteban's shoulder. "Hell, here she comes again. We're doomed, mates."

The proprietress, a large, buxomy woman whom Michael had secretly dubbed "the frigate," headed their way with a tray balanced on her hip.

"Can I get you boys something more to drink?" she asked.

Michael sighed. Dickie gazed longingly at his empty mug. Esteban swallowed against a throat that suddenly felt bone dry.

"*Gracias, señorita,* but we shall wait a while longer."

A flicker of annoyance passed over her broad face. This was the third time they'd put her off. Use of the dartboard was customarily reserved for paying customers.

She cast them a thin smile. "I'll be back." Her parting shot sounded more like a threat than a promise.

Just as she walked away, three men sauntered up—one almost as tall as Michael, another heavyset with generous jowls, and the third short with the pugnacious look of a bull terrier. Graying hair and wrinkles etched by wind and sun hinted at ages in the sixties. Their rolling strides identified them as retired sailors.

"How about you fellas let someone else use that board for a change?" the tallest one asked coldly. "We usually play at this time every night."

Michael thrust out his chin. "Sure and we're willing to . . . if you can beat us. Highest points after six rounds wins."

The heavyset man rolled one finger from his grip on a brimming mug of ale. He pointed at Dickie. "I recognize you. Haven't seen you around here for years, but I spotted you right away when you got off *Pharaoh's Gold* yesterday."

The short one scoffed, "*Pharaoh's Gold?* What kind of name is that for a ship?"

Esteban bristled. That ship was their home for now, as well as their hope for a fortune in sunken treasure.

Dickie spoke first. "Hey, now, it's a bleedin' fine name."

"It's owned by an Englishman, Lord something or other," the tall one said with a sneer.

Esteban recognized what the men were doing. They were either spoiling for a fight, or trying to intimidate them into leaving without risking the outcome of the game.

"You're Irish, aren't you," the short one taunted, pointing at Michael. "What are you doing sailing with a damn Brit?"

Michael shrugged. "I'm entitled to choose my transportation. Graystone is taking me and the lads here across the Gulf."

The heavy one gave a shout of laughter. "The Gulf? A namby-pamby Brit couldn't navigate his way across a bathtub."

"What's your problem with the Brits, mate?" Dickie demanded. "Did you and your friends fight in the War of 1812?"

"Hey! We're not that old."

Dickie snorted. "Could have fooled me."

Esteban's hands fisted, angered enough to rise to the defense. The three of them could criticize Graystone, but hearing someone else do so was a different matter entirely.

"I'd think you'd have better taste than to travel with an Englishman," jeered the tallest of the three.

Michael grabbed a fistful of the tall man's shirt. He growled, "Maybe so, but he's *our* Englishman."

He drew back his fist.

To ROSA'S ASTONISHMENT, Derek did claim a dance before the carriage reached the Winstead mansion. A waltz. Matt requested a country dance. She climbed the stone steps to the huge double doors, her confidence growing.

I think you look superb.

Had Derek truly meant the compliment? On the ride over, his lighthearted conversation had done nothing to indicate otherwise. She held his words close as their foursome was announced at the entrance to the glittering ballroom. She brandished them like a shield as she stepped into the crowd of gaily dressed women and soberly attired men.

You dance flamenco before large numbers of people, true? Ellie had encouraged. *Just pretend this is another type of performance.* Rosa lifted her chin and smiled, pleased with the opportunity to prove herself and thumb her nose at Derek's hint that she was too much a hoyden for polite company.

Within fifteen minutes, she was no longer conscious of playing a role. She was too busy enjoying herself under the flattering attention of several handsome gentlemen. They extended an effort to make her laugh, to fetch her drinks, to see she never wanted for company or an opportunity to dance.

And she danced every dance. She didn't tire . . . how could she when she had danced all her life? Although flamenco had been her focus, her father had seen that she learned other steps, as well. She flirted mildly with her admirers, excited to discover that she could hold men in thrall just as her mother had. Every man except one, that is.

Derek took to the floor on occasion, partnering a different woman each time. Rosa noticed, however, that the more she danced the more he prowled the perimeter of the floor. Although her enjoyment grew as the evening progressed, a dark cloud seemed to descend across his countenance.

She shrugged. Surely, for once, she was not responsible for his surly mood.

The time finally arrived for their waltz. Derek walked boldly into the group of five men surrounding her, as if he expected a parting of the seas at his arrival. To her annoyance, the men moved out of his way. With a curt nod, Derek took her elbow and led her to the dance floor.

He swept her masterfully into the waltz, every movement the epitome of masculine power and grace. With the firm pressure of his hand against her back, Rosa forgot her annoyance. A shiver of pleasure almost curled her toes. She could follow his steps without thinking. The same strength that had caught her when she fell from a roof moved beneath her fingertips.

"Are you pleased with your success, Rosa?"

"Am I a success?" she asked in genuine surprise.

He frowned. "You know damn well you are."

"How would I know? This is the first ball I have ever attended."

"Well, trust my expertise. You are the belle of the ball."

"Then you should be pleased, since you were concerned that I would humiliate you."

"I never said that."

"You implied it."

"If I did, then I was mistaken." He inclined his head. "Will you accept my apology?" he asked gruffly.

She pursed her lips. "I shall think about it."

His mouth slanted in a wry grin that triggered a strange fluttering of her heart. "Actually, I admire the way you can adapt yourself to any surroundings. It makes me wonder what persona you will come up with next."

Rosa smiled inwardly. His praise, however nontraditional, pleased her more than she cared to admit.

ACROSS THE BALLROOM, Ellie released a blissful sigh. "I believe Derek has noticed Rosa's popularity among the gentlemen. Just see how he is looking at her. Isn't it wonderful?"

"He looks as if he could cheerfully strangle her," Matt said dryly. He plucked two glasses of champagne from the tray of a passing waiter and handed one to Ellie.

"Exactly. That is how you looked at me when we first met."

"It must be love."

She swatted him playfully on the shoulder. "Do not tease." Then she cocked her head and shot him a look meant to challenge. "Are you saying it was not love for us?"

Rather than appearing trapped by her dare, Matt grinned rakishly. He raised her free hand and pressed warm, firm lips to the inside of her wrist as his gaze looked straight into her eyes. A heady shiver rippled through Ellie.

"I'm saying," Matt clarified, "that I've never looked at you with anything other than adoration."

"Even now, the gambler in you is showing. You can keep a poker face when speaking utter nonsense."

He winked at her, utterly unrepentant.

That mixture of arrogant man and mischievous boy was one of the many reasons she loved him so. Breathlessly, she said, "Do I see something more than adoration in your expression now?"

"Very observant, Mrs. Devereaux." He nipped one knuckle of the hand he still held captive. "Are you sure we have to stay?"

"I cannot abandon Rosa to these social sharks." She didn't try to hide her disappointment. "Besides, I'm trying to think of ways to continue throwing Derek and Rosa together."

Matt tapped his crystal flute against hers. Their glasses came together with a soft clink. "My love, they are about to be trapped together on a fifty-seven-foot ship for several weeks. I don't think your matchmaking will be necessary."

ANOTHER IN A string of admirers claimed Rosa for a dance.

Derek rolled the stem of the champagne flute between his thumb and fingers, the only outward sign of this persistent, unwanted restlessness that seemed to worsen each time another gentleman appeared smitten by Rosa's charm and beauty.

She appeared, and acted, everything that a gently reared lady should . . . which made her achievement all the more remarkable considering that just last week she'd been cracking safes and smuggling him out of prison. She maintained the appearance too consistently for it to be false. Reluctantly, he admitted that he'd underestimated her. Did he really know her at all?

"Lord Graystone?"

Derek focused on the young footman. "Yes?"

"A note just arrived. The deliveryman said it was urgent."

Derek took the proffered envelope. "Is someone waiting for a response?"

"No, sir."

"Thank you." He slipped the footman a coin.

The servant moved away. Frowning, Derek opened the note. Who would wish to contact him at this late hour? Could it be from Tim or Geoff, warning him of some accident aboard ship?

The true contents of the note proved more astonishing. Not the nature of the problem, but that Esteban, Michael, and Dickie would turn to him in their present dilemma. The note specifically requested that Rosa not be told.

He would be wise to avoid involvement in the volatile family's problems and turn the note over to her. But the plea reminded him of those times in his youth when he'd gotten into mischief. The last thing he'd wanted was to cause his sweet-spirited mother distress. Her good opinion had meant everything to him. She'd been the best of mothers, tolerating her husband's wandering spirit and abundant curiosity, frequently giving up her social life in England to travel the world on archaeological digs with the earl and their three children. Her death in Derek's late teen years had been a shocking loss.

If he could deal with the situation and spare Rosa worry—

Turning sharply on one heel, Derek left the room.

"I SEEM TO recall a promise that you would stay out of trouble while we were in port, gentlemen."

Derek walked down the stone steps of the constable's office, three sheepish old men close behind. They should be subdued. He'd just bailed them out of jail and paid reparations to the owner of the Velvet Turtle for broken chairs, mugs, and a shattered window.

He started down the street. Lamps cast evenly spaced pools of golden light into the darkness. Ellie's house was reasonably close. They could all use the walk—he to work off this nagging frustration, and his companions to dispense the odor of spilled ale clinging to their clothes.

"It started out as just a friendly game of darts, lad," Michael swore.

"Until those three old goats got ugly," Dickie offered.

"They had a bee under their bonnets where Englishmen are concerned," said Michael.

"Said a namby-pamby Brit couldn't find his way around a bathtub, much less the Gulf, no sirree."

"Those *hombres* were spoiling for a fight. We could not let them insult you."

"Let me see if I have this correct. You started a brawl in a seedy dockside tavern to defend my honor?"

"Yep," Dickie stated proudly.

Michael frowned. "Now, I wouldn't go calling it seedy, lad. The Velvet Turtle is the finest tavern on the wharf."

Derek tried to envision them scrapping with a group of equally gray-haired men. The image failed to inspire the expected amusement. Although they'd no doubt been eager for an excuse to brawl after their forced inactivity aboard ship, they had fought to protect his good name. Derek felt oddly touched.

"I appreciate your coming to my defense, gentlemen."

"Anytime, mate," said Dickie. "You're a fairly decent sort, Graystone, though we didn't think so at first."

Derek's lips twitched. "Thank you."

Dickie eyed his companions. "Ain't it time we come clean?"

Esteban sighed. "*Sí*. It grows heavy on my spirit to keep this secret."

"If we tell you . . . and it makes you mad . . . you

won't go back on your deal to include us in this treasure hunt, will you?"

Derek slanted Dickie a sidelong glance as they walked along. "My bargain is with Rosa. It would be dishonorable to break trust over something you did."

"That's a relief. Now, who's the one to tell him?"

"Faith, don't look at me. I'd left the courtyard with Rosa that night, remember?"

"Perhaps I should tell him *la verdad*."

"It was your idea in the first place, Esteban," Dickie agreed.

The course of their argument triggered a sneaking suspicion that crawled through Derek's gut. They were speaking of the night he and Rosa met in Don Geraldo's courtyard, the night certain stolen items found their way to his bedchamber.

He stopped cold in his tracks. The godfathers continued on, engrossed in their bickering, unaware that he'd stopped.

"One of you tell me," Derek growled, bringing their forward momentum to an abrupt halt. They turned, caught in a pool of light. "Now, preferably."

Esteban squared his shoulders. "We saw you kiss Rosa that night in the courtyard."

"Actually, you did a lot more than kiss her," said Dickie.

Derek winced. He remembered his hands exploring Rosa's backside, shaping her resilient flesh, pulling her tight against his arousal. Her guardians had been watching all along. Heat crept up his neck.

"So we took some of the things from her bag and concealed them in your bedchamber," Esteban added.

Dickie clarified, "Then sent a note to Don Geraldo."

"We offer our apologies," said Esteban. "We did not know you then."

"We sure didn't realize the bleedin' maniac would throw you in prison and threaten to shoot you."

"Or torture you," Michael added morosely.

The streetlamp cast their faces in stark planes of light and shadow, emphasizing regretful expressions. Stunned by the revelation, Derek stared at them. Their methods had been extreme, true. But what would he have done if he caught some man compromising Amber? Challenged him to a duel? Smashed a fist into the bloke's face?

"I accept your apology, gentlemen."

"Whew! That's a load off our shoulders," Dickie said emphatically, apparently speaking for all of them.

Mixed emotions clawed through Derek as they walked on in silence. Rosa's sense of family devotion inspired admiration. Anger instantly fired over the way her sense of responsibility had led her to shoulder all the blame. Guilt crawled beneath it all as he remembered the cutting things he'd said after jumping to the wrong conclusion. One thing was certain . . . he would find a way to make it up to Rosa for his suspicions.

ROSA STOOD ASIDE on the wharf the next morning, uncertain how to—or even if she should—be a part of the family farewells.

Derek shook Matt's hand, then kissed Ellie on the cheek. "When will you head for England?"

"By next month," said Matt.

"Pity. This is a beautiful place."

"Mr. Lafitte was a little too stingy with his treasure," Ellie interjected, sounding rather miffed.

Matt grinned. "Ellie can't be happy unless she's poking around dusty, crumbling ruins and hunting down something of historic value. You should understand that better than anyone. Good luck with your galleon."

Derek nodded. "Thank you."

Ellie turned to Rosa and held out her arms. Startled, and deeply touched to be included, Rosa glided forward and returned the hug. Even when they separated, they held hands.

"I shall miss you, my dear," Ellie said softly.

"And I, you. *Gracias* for everything, Ellie. For the lovely gown." Then, leaning close again, Rosa whispered, "And even more for the new trousers."

"My pleasure. We women of adventure should consider it our birthright to be practical." Ellie gave Rosa's hands a last squeeze, then let go. She shot Derek a hard look. "Be careful."

"I shall make sure Rosa stays safe. I promise."

Ellie responded with an unladylike snort. "I was thinking more in terms of Rosa keeping you out of trouble."

They boarded *Pharaoh's Gold.* As the crew cast off and raised sails, the schooner began to pull away.

Ellie waved. Matt curved an arm about her shoulders.

Rosa waved a handkerchief until the Devereauxs were tiny figures on the distant wharf, until they climbed into their carriage and turned for home. She'd never had a sister, nor any woman with whom a friendship had developed so naturally.

It saddened her that she would never have occasion to see Ellie again. Once the hunt for the *Augustina* was over, dissolving the arrangement with her stubborn partner, Derek would go his own way . . . never to be seen again.

Pharaoh's Gold pressed on its course into the Gulf. Rosa headed belowdecks, her throat suddenly thick with unshed tears.

THREE DAYS LATER, *Pharaoh's Gold* passed the Dry Tortugas, the last island of ancient reef west of the Florida Keys.

Thankful for Geoff's thorough nautical charts and skill as navigator, Derek watched as their hull glided safely past the patches marking the dangerous coral. The treacherous waters clearly showed why the Spaniards had feared the threat of this long chain of islands and their surrounding breakwater. He shook his head sadly, thinking of the many vessels driven against these reefs by storms.

Geoff shouted. They'd reached the designated coordinates.

Derek's heart leaped with anticipation. This was it. He headed for the canvas-covered equipment on the stern.

He found Rosa leaning over the railing. She gazed raptly into the water. "Is this the place?" she asked breathlessly.

He gazed at her profile, recalling how she'd shouldered the blame for her godfathers' trick. A strange warmth expanded deep in his chest. Her excitement for his search provided a means to make reparations for her sacrifice. He would find the *Augustina* for her as well as the British Museum, then savor her expression when he delivered her share of silver and gold into her hands.

"The best I can approximate from the journal. Unfortunately, we shall be searching an area as far as the eye can see."

She frowned, looking about. The Dry Tortugas had receded to a hazy outline on the western horizon. In every other direction stretched a solid expanse of turquoise-blue water that glittered in the sunlight. "That could take weeks."

He grinned, then realized he was actually eager to show her the newest weapon in his search arsenal.

"This should help speed things up." With a sharp tug, he pulled away the canvas sheet covering the small balloon.

Chapter Twelve

For hours, Derek manned the balloon, floating high with an eagle's-eye view of the ocean depths. Rosa watched as he soared free against the vivid blue sky, searching the reefs.

He was having all the fun.

A long tether attached the apparatus to the stern, pulling the balloon behind *Pharaoh's Gold* and allowing it to float sixty to seventy feet above water level. Nigel steered the schooner back and forth across the chosen area of turquoise water, methodically adjusting the course slightly with each tack. The balloon was equipped with some method of maneuverability as well, for now and then it dipped to one side or the other.

Whenever Derek spotted something that might indicate a sunken ship, he dropped a buoy to mark the spot. The balloon carried eight buoys attached to its undercarriage. Derek had shown her one before he went up. It consisted of a red, two-foot-long float connected to a long rope and a fist-sized lead anchor.

Each time all the buoys were dropped, one of the crew winched in the balloon. *Pharaoh's Gold* dropped anchor. Then Derek, Geoff, and Tim rowed out in the longboat for a closer examination of each marked spot.

Once, while Derek was up in the balloon, Tim explained to her what they were doing. Derek used a bucket with a glass bottom. When held against the water's surface, it provided a clear window into the world below. If he saw something particularly promising, he dove over the side to check it up close. After the men surveyed all the markers, collected all the buoys, and returned to the schooner, they loaded the buoys on the balloon and the procedure started all over again.

A neutral observer might find the process tedious. Her godfathers certainly did, spending the entire day belowdecks playing cards. Rosa found it fascinating. The enticement of silver and gold was no longer the main appeal. The thrill of exploring the undersea world, to discover something mysterious and marvelous, had captured her imagination.

She paced the deck of *Pharaoh's Gold* as the sun settled lower in the western sky. The longboat approached from its last outing, the three men aboard. A pile of recovered buoys lay heaped in the bottom.

How could she contribute to the expedition when Derek monopolized all the work? Marshaling her courage, Rosa waited for the one man who could grant or deny her wish.

DEREK CLIMBED THE rope ladder up the schooner's starboard side. He was pleased with the balloon's performance today. He wished he could say the same of the results.

Rosa awaited him the moment he stepped on deck.

"I want to go up in the balloon, Derek."

Her request caught him by surprise. "You must be joking."

"I can help search for the wreck. Let me try."

Hastily, he searched for logical reasons that had nothing to do with the twinges of worry shooting through his chest. "It is too late in the day. The sun is going down. The light is at the wrong angle to see anything beneath the surface."

"Tomorrow, then."

He folded his arms. "Absolutely not. Too dangerous."

"More dangerous than climbing across a roof and breaking into Don Geraldo's collection room?"

"If you will recall, you fell from that roof the first time. You would have the imprint of the cobblestones etched into your back now if I hadn't caught you."

"But I dared it nonetheless," she countered, undaunted. "I am not a coward."

That much he knew. "You don't know what to look for, what signs might indicate a wreck."

"Teach me."

Derek let his breath out very slowly. Did the exasperating woman have a rejoinder for everything?

"You need my help. You cannot manage this alone."

Derek's brows arched. "What brings you to that conclusion?"

"Just look at you. Your eyes are tired and very red. You've strained them by staring for hours at the ocean, with the sun reflecting off the surface and the wind hitting your face."

Was she genuinely concerned, or merely eager to get her way? "I am fine," he said gruffly, unwilling to admit that his aching eyes did burn like fire.

"Will your men go up in the balloon so you can rest?"

"Tim has an aversion to heights. The others would prefer to keep their feet firmly planted on the deck. They don't particularly trust my 'crazy contraption,' as they call it."

"Crazy? I think it a very clever idea. There is a cliff I like to visit at home where I can look down on the water. The shape of the coral, the sea life . . . I can see everything with such clarity. The advantage is in the height, no?"

Few people bothered to consider the logic behind his inventions, much less understand how they worked.

"With your eyes so tired, we might pass over an important clue that you would normally catch."

Despite the urge to grind his teeth, he admired her tenacity. She charmed, she cajoled. Would she cherish the sensation of soaring and the sparkling beauty of the ocean as much as he did? Suddenly, he wanted her to share in that joy.

"All right. Tomorrow," he agreed sternly.

She brightened.

"For a short run only."

She stood on tiptoe. With that spontaneity that always knocked the breath from his lungs, she kissed him on the cheek.

"Gracias!"

Then she danced away, as light and graceful as a hummingbird. Enthusiasm radiated from her vivid smile and sparkling green eyes. Derek's arms ached to grab her waist and pull her hard against him. But she was already gone.

He stood—bemused, silent, and totally disgusted at how quickly his randy body had responded to her.

What had he received? A peck on the cheek, of all the bloody things. The type of kiss a woman would bestow on a brother, a friend, or worse . . . a business partner. Derek winced.

He needed a bracing snifter of brandy.

Tim sauntered up instead, casting him a knowing grin. Derek nearly groaned. "Go away, Rutherford."

"I overheard," Tim said. "You gave in."

"I did not give in," Derek snapped. "I compromised."

Tim stood next to him at the rail as the sun dipped toward the horizon. Peach and gold light stretched across the low clouds. "Can't say that I blame you. She's quite charming with all that enthusiasm and persistence. Damn near irresistible."

"I would never again know a moment's peace until I agreed."

"It would be insubordinate of me to disagree, Captain."

"That hasn't held you back before."

"You know, the whole crew is rather besotted with Rosa."

Derek tensed. He would toss the first man overboard who tried to touch her. "Well, they bloody well better get over it. I don't need the efficiency of this ship deteriorating while they make calf-eyes at her."

Straightening, Tim pushed away from the rail. "I guess we'll leave the calf-eyes up to the captain, then." He grinned. "For the sake of efficiency, that is."

His first mate walked away before Derek could think of a suitable retort.

THE ALLOTTED TIME arrived the next morning.

The day was perfect, Derek acknowledged sourly as he waited next to the balloon. He'd spent a restless night dwelling on all the potential disasters of putting a woman—especially one as impulsive as Rosa—in charge of a mechanical device.

If only it would rain or blow hurricane-force winds. But the weather offered him no excuse to renege on his impulsive promise of the night before. The sky was clear, without a single cloud to spoil visibility by casting shadows on the water. The light breeze barely stirred the waves to whitecaps. Last night, over dinner, he had explained how to watch for wreck sign. This morning conditions were perfect.

He wished Rosa had slept through the morning like her godfathers.

Instead, she climbed the stairs from her cabin. She wore a white blouse and black trousers that outlined her long legs and hugged her derriere.

A low whistle sounded from the rigging. The sound jarred through Derek. He glared up at Wilson.

"You're looking very fetching this morning, Miss Rosa," Nigel called from his station at the wheel.

A blush rose in Rosa's cheeks. She responded to their flattery by dropping a mock curtsy. The men laughed.

Derek cleared his throat loudly. The two men quickly returned to work.

"I told you not to wear those. Your unladylike attire is undermining the discipline on my ship."

"Wouldn't discipline suffer a great deal more if your crew were able to peek up my skirt as the balloon rises?"

He nearly choked. "They wouldn't dare."

"How would you stop them?" She smiled. "I am not going to spend my time up there fighting to keep my skirt down."

Derek experienced a sudden, tantalizing image of long, slender legs bared by the floating bell of her skirt.

"Fine. You have made your point," he conceded roughly. "Now, get in."

She ducked beneath the balloon and settled herself in the metal carriage. Derek showed her how to fasten and release the seat's safety harness. As he turned up the burner, Rosa leaned first to one side, then the other, examining the frame.

"What are you looking for?"

"Buoys, like the ones you dropped yesterday."

"Don't worry about those," he said, deliberately evasive. The balloon filled to maximum, straining against its bonds.

"You did not replace them," she said accusingly. "There is only this one left."

"I am well aware of that. And don't get any ideas. That one is jammed. The clamp has rusted."

"Then how am I to mark anything promising that I see?"

"You don't." He released the anchors. The apparatus lifted clear of the deck and began to float off the stern. He walked alongside, guiding it away from the rigging. "You just sit there safely and enjoy the view."

Rosa gripped the armrests and glared down at him. "That was not our agreement!"

"I promised you a trial run. That is exactly what you are getting." Derek released the balloon. It rose further, floating back and away from the ship. The tether line uncoiled rapidly.

"Graystone!" Rosa yelled. "What if I see something?"

"I would prefer you not complicate matters."

Amusement curled through Derek's chest at her enraged, impotent frustration. He would have laughed outright, but worry constrained his humor. He'd manipulated the situation, but it was worth the inevitable scold to prevent her from taking unnecessary risks. The balloon was a finicky device. He preferred to keep her curiosity on a tight rein and stick to the basics this first time.

Not that there would be a second time, of course.

Pharaoh's Gold cut through the water. The balloon floated serenely behind. Derek stood motionless for an hour, watching. He told himself he was staying alert for any signs of trouble. It had nothing to do with those occasional flashes of white teeth, the smile he could just make out that confirmed Rosa's excitement and joy in the freedom of flying.

Unexpectedly, the balloon swung to its right, pivoting against the tether rope. It cut across the ship's wake. It paused, flying straight for a moment, then reversed direction and swung back to the left.

So much for keeping her curiosity in check.

Tim came up beside Derek, holding the spyglass in one hand.

"What the hell is she doing?" Derek ground out.

"Looks like she's discovered how to work the side panels."

The side panels acted as flaps that could be tilted, allowing for rudimentary steering. They were even more effective at changes in altitude.

"I determined that much for myself, thank you very much. If she turns them too sharply, she could lock up the mechanism and send the balloon plunging out of control."

Tim shrugged. "Next time perhaps you ought to explain all the details to her, instead of letting her experiment."

"There won't be a next time. The chit is worse than a cannon with a flint held to its fuse. She is going to get herself killed."

"Be patient, man. Look. She's settling down now." Tim raised the spyglass to one eye. "I think something has caught her interest. She's leaning over the side. Now she's waving."

"Let me see that." Derek took the glass and quickly located Rosa through the slender cylinder.

She definitely appeared agitated. She leaned to one side, straining against the harness in a way that sent a sickening flutter through his stomach. Then she looked all around, searching for something. Finally, she reached for the jammed buoy. She heaved on the rope, pulling with all her strength. Derek feared that her harness would break loose and she would tumble from the chair to the waves sixty feet below.

"Leave it be, Rosa," he whispered intently.

Without warning, the buoy's weighted anchor popped free of the rusted clamp. It recoiled against the force of her pull, swinging upward. The fist-sized lead anchor struck the underside of the balloon.

The impact instantly opened a foot-long rip in the fabric. The line dropped again, tangling beyond her reach in the metal framework.

Derek's grip tightened around the spyglass. He leaned forward until the rail dug into his thighs.

Rosa clapped one hand over her mouth, her eyes wide with shock as she stared up at the rip over her head. Then she looked straight at the ship. Her hand lowered to press over her heart. He could swear she mouthed the words "I am sorry."

Derek nearly smashed the spyglass against the rail. Dammit, the infuriating woman was apologizing for damaging his balloon! Didn't she realize the danger she was in?

As Derek watched, the force of the wind ripped another foot up into the balloon's delicate shell. The edges of the gaping hole flapped as if taunting him with his own helplessness.

"Ballocks," Timothy swore, expressing the shock and

fear that Derek couldn't force past his suddenly constricted throat.

The deflating balloon immediately began to lose altitude. The steady pull of *Pharaoh's Gold* worsened the problem, adding speed that encouraged the wind to shred the balloon's skin. If they could stop, Rosa might stay aloft long enough to get the longboat beneath her.

Derek practically dove to the call tube. He flipped it open and bellowed, "All stop! Dammit, Grady, all stop!"

The steady thrum of the engines ceased within seconds. The propeller stopped churning the water. Although the ship slowed, its momentum still carried them through the water.

"Lower the longboat," Derek ordered. The crew responded instantly, working the ropes to lower the boat over the side.

He jerked the spyglass up again. Rosa was fumbling with the burner controls. She managed to shut off the flame.

"Good girl," Derek murmured. An open burner would add a dangerous complication if she hit water. She was keeping remarkably cool in a crisis. As long as she didn't do anything crazy, everything would be okay until the longboat was down and he could get to her. There was still time.

Rosa's hands wrapped around the levers on either side of the chair. Her mouth set in a determined line. Then she did the last thing he expected. She adjusted the side panels to the same angle. Downward.

The balloon's angle of descent sharpened.

"What the bloody hell are you doing, woman?" he roared.

The carriage struck the surface. The heavy metal frame instantly settled deep into the water.

Fear sliced into Derek with an icy cold thrust. What if the impact had stunned her and she couldn't get the harness open? What if the carriage pulled her down with it?

The deflated balloon settled over her like a shroud, hiding her from his view.

She was pinned under the heavy fabric. Trapped. Even if she found her way to the surface, she would discover her way blocked by yards of limp, heavy balloon. Completely cut off from fresh oxygen and freedom.

The familiar sense of panic struck Derek hard, clawing up his throat and squeezing his heart.

He yanked off his shirt, then his boots, and climbed onto the stern rail.

"Wait!" Tim called out. "The longboat is almost down."

Not good enough. By the time the men climbed into the lowered boat and worked their way out to the spot where Rosa went down, it might be too late.

Flexing his knees, Derek pushed off. The water stung his knuckles as he cut through the surface.

The temperate water of the Caribbean closed over his body. Angling upward, he broke the surface and immediately settled into a distance-swallowing stroke.

His heart thundered in his ears. With each cut of his palms through water, with each kick of his legs, he prayed.

"God, don't let her drown. Save her for me . . . so I can have the privilege of wringing her neck."

THE UNDERCARRIAGE STRUCK water.

The sudden drag threw Rosa against the harness. She sat dazed for a few moments, massaging her bruised chest.

Then she realized that water was climbing up her legs. It began to lap at her waist. If she didn't get out of this balloon fast, it would pull her under. She would drown.

She was an excellent swimmer. She could tread water for an hour at least. Even if she tired, Derek would come to rescue her . . . or if her predicament didn't excite his interest, at least he would make haste to retrieve his precious balloon.

Her fingers worked the harness free. She slid into open water. The Caribbean retained a chill this early in the season, but it was warm enough to be comfortable. The waves weren't high enough to slap her in the face.

A shadow spread over her. She glanced up, confused by the sudden loss of sunlight on a cloudless day.

The deflating balloon swayed like a drunken sailor. The rip she'd caused gaped accusingly. With a sigh of lost air, the balloon tipped over and fell—straight for her head.

Limp and clinging, the balloon greedily devoured the open surface. Rosa had no choice but to go under.

The salt water stung her eyes and blurred her vision. She stroked hard, searching for the edge of the balloon and open water. But whenever she reached up, exploring with outstretched hand, she only found the unyielding weight of wet fabric.

She turned to her right. Surely it was just a little farther. She grew fearful that she was traveling the long way, the length of the balloon, and turned again.

Or had she already gone this way?

Her lungs screamed for air. Fear gripped her throat.

She struggled to stay calm.

Without warning, a dark shape emerged out of the palette of aquamarine blue. Rosa yelped, her first thought that it was a shark. Bubbles exploded from her mouth. Her arms and legs worked frantically to push her away from the threat that rapidly moved closer.

Just as she braced herself for the horror of razor-sharp teeth, she recognized the soft sway of blond hair in the water.

Derek. He was here.

She grasped his outstretched hand. He turned, swimming with a powerful stroke. She followed, kicking her own legs to help propel them into the sunlight.

Rosa gasped as she broke the surface. Treading water, she tilted her head back and allowed fresh, dry air to pour down into her starved lungs. Derek had come for her. The last remnants of fear quickly faded.

Blinking the water from her eyes, she smiled at him.

"Are you all right?" he asked gruffly.

"*Sí.* I am fine."

He grabbed her shoulders and shook her. Rosa was immediately glad they were in the water, where his feet could find no purchase, otherwise he might have managed to rattle a few of her teeth loose.

"What possessed you to do such an idiotic thing? We could have reached you in time if you hadn't turned the flaps down."

He let her go, freeing his hands to use in treading water.

"I saw something."

"Well, so did I," he snapped. "I saw you plunge into this water. I saw you nearly drown."

"I swim well," she said resentfully. "The balloon just confused me for a moment."

Although Derek's face appeared as rigid as stone, his eyes seethed with some dark emotion. "You could have been trapped," he said fiercely. In a quicksilver change of mood, he stroked his knuckles down her left cheek. Gruffly, he whispered, "I know what it is like to feel disoriented like that."

After the danger, after withstanding his sarcastic remarks, it was his concern that finally got to her.

Twin fat tears spilled over and coursed down Rosa's cheeks.

"Dammit," he said softly. "Don't cry, Rosa. You're safe." His fingers pushed back hair that clung to her brow.

She had to disagree. She was far from safe. When he bristled and pawed the ground like a proud stallion, when he stomped around with his exaggerated dignity, her own pride countered with equal stubbornness.

She had no such defense against his gentleness.

The longboat pulled alongside. Oars lifted from the water with a clatter of wood and metal. Derek urged her toward the boat, seeing to her safety before his own.

Tim and Geoff grasped her forearms and pulled her up

and over. She sat down, water streaming from her clothes. Collecting the sodden length of her hair, she shoved it behind her shoulders.

Tim and Geoff reached for Derek next. He waved them off with an impatient gesture. Gripping the edge, he hoisted himself up.

The muscles of his bare chest flexed, demonstrating the power he typically kept restrained. Every muscle and tendon in his arms tightened, defined in a display of sheer male beauty. Water sheeted from his bronzed skin. Rosa's mouth went dry as she shamelessly, eagerly drank in every bit of the view.

He looked up.

His gaze met hers, then immediately dipped lower. He swore under his breath. All strength abruptly leeched from his arms. They collapsed unexpectedly. He splashed back into the water.

Rosa blinked in surprise.

From over the side, she heard Derek demand roughly, "Did you bring any blankets, Geoff?"

"Yes, sir."

"Then hand her one, for pity's sake."

Rosa glanced down at her soaked clothes. She gasped. A warm flush pinkened her skin. Her black trousers were plastered to her legs like a second skin. The white blouse, now nearly transparent, clung to every curve and revealed the lacy texture of her lightweight corset.

Geoff's arm stretched out, his gaze averted, a brown wool blanket gripped in his hand. Rosa took the blanket and murmured her thanks. She wrapped it around her shoulders. A shiver of sensual awareness rippled up her back. Derek had reacted strongly to the sight of the wet fabric clinging to her breasts.

A slow, feminine smile spread across her lips.

He wasn't indifferent to her, after all.

She leaned forward and peered over the edge of the boat.

"Is something wrong?" she asked sweetly.

Muscles flexed in his jaw. "No!" he growled.

"Do you need any help getting in?"

"I shall manage, thank you."

Rosa sat back as he hoisted himself into the boat. The sense of satisfaction vanished when she looked at the downed balloon. The remaining air kept the contraption afloat.

"Will it fly again?"

"The balloon can be stitched and resealed. Any dents in the undercarriage can be repaired. It is the burner I'm worried about. If it has been flushed with seawater, I'm not sure we can get it to light again."

She swallowed hard. "Do you think Grady can fix it?"

"I am sure he will give it his best. Now, tell me why you wrestled with that damn buoy in the first place."

"I saw a straight line, like a dark shadow, beneath the surface. Last night, when you explained what I should watch for, you said that angles, circles, and straight lines were good signs. Anything that does not fit the natural growth of the reef. I could not lose it. I had to drop a marker."

His eyes narrowed. "Let me see if I've got this right. You saw a line, so you steered the balloon into the water rather than lose the spot?"

Inwardly, she winced. "You should have given me some buoys."

"I don't bloody believe this," Derek shouted. "Did you hear that? She wrecked my balloon to serve as a marker. She damn near killed herself because she saw a little line."

Geoff found sudden interest in the blue sky. Tim removed his hat, then replaced it with the brim over his eyes.

"It was not little," she said with offended dignity. "It was at least four times the length of this longboat."

Derek stilled. Geoff's brows rose. Tim shoved his cap back up with his thumb. They all stared at her.

Rosa hugged the blanket tighter. Disgruntled, she snapped, "What? What did I do now?"

"Where did you see it?" Derek asked tightly. Tim and Geoff were already mounting the oars. "Show me."

"The spot should be back along the line that the balloon was traveling. Not far."

The men rowed in the direction Derek indicated. He dug into the supplies in the bow of the longboat, pulling out the bucket with the glass bottom. Leaning over the side, he searched the ocean depths through the round portal.

After fifteen minutes of tedious searching and a silence that grated on Rosa's nerves, Derek abruptly held up one hand.

"Wait! This is good. Hold here."

Geoff pushed the anchor over the side. The chain rattled across the gunwale as the anchor rapidly sank.

When it stopped, Derek asked, "How deep?"

Tim checked some marks on the chain. "Twenty-eight feet."

"Excellent."

Rosa watched, fascinated by their smooth, practiced teamwork. Derek reached into the supply bag. He pulled out a pair of strange-looking glasses.

Positioning the metal and glass cups over his eyes, he tied the silk bands snugly behind his head. The curve of the glass made his eyes look overlarge. He blinked, twin magnified images of brilliant blue and sweeping sandy lashes.

He rolled backward over the edge and into the water.

Rosa leaned over as far as she could without upsetting the balance of the boat. Gnawing her lower lip, she watched the dark outline of his trousers as his legs scissored, driving him deeper. Then she lost sight of him.

A minute ticked by, then another.

Just when she thought he couldn't possibly hold his breath any longer, his blond head broke the surface twenty feet away. He pushed the goggles back on his head, causing his hair to stick up at odd angles. A broad smile spread across his face.

Rosa caught her breath. Ladled with boyish charm and enthusiasm, such a smile could devastate a woman's senses.

Derek swam to the boat and dropped two dripping items inside. He hoisted himself aboard again.

"Well? Did she find something?" Tim asked impatiently.

Derek laughed, a rich sound that rolled from his chest and vibrated down the length of Rosa's spine. "Bloody hell, she sure did. A keel scar."

Tim turned to her, new excitement lighting his face. He explained, "Sometimes when a ship hits a reef, its keel drags across and carves a groove into the coral. If the cut is deep enough, it can still be visible centuries later."

"The straight line I saw," Rosa said, amazed.

Derek said, "I can't say whether it is old enough to fit the time period of our wreck. I also found some scattered ballast stones." He picked up the items. "And these."

A tarnished spoon, so nicked and bent as to be almost mutilated, nestled in his left palm. In his right hand he held what looked like a jagged gray and black rock.

It was, by far, the ugliest rock Rosa had ever seen.

Tim let out a whoop and tossed his hat in the air, not seeming to care when it landed in the water. Geoff fell back into the bow of the boat, laughing. Derek chuckled at their antics. He rested his forearms on his knees, appearing more relaxed and happy than she'd ever seen him.

Rosa stared at them as if they'd all gone *loco*. What could they possibly find exciting in a chunk of limestone?

Disgusted, she snatched the rock from Derek's palm. He didn't protest. He watched silently as she turned the chunk over in her hands, examining the surface for some clue to their enthusiasm. Right away, she saw that this wasn't an ordinary rock. It was formed of a compressed mass of blackened discs, uneven on their edges, and cemented together by an encrustation of gritty gray limestone.

She rubbed the edge of one disc with her thumb. Some

of the crust came away. Beneath it, barely discernible, she could see tiny etchings that looked like roman numerals.

She looked up sharply.

Her gaze met Derek's bright blue eyes.

"Silver, Rosa. You are holding a clump of Spanish pieces of eight."

Chapter Thirteen

DEREK STOOD ON the deck of *Pharaoh's Gold* at noon, covered from neck to toe in his dive suit. The heavy boots clomped against the wooden deck each time he moved. The weights would hold him down beneath twenty-eight feet of water, but he would lack the ability to swim freely, denied the freedom to break for the surface whenever he chose.

He tried not to think of it as being trapped. At least he would be tethered to the ship the whole time. His watchful crew could haul him up at the slightest sign of trouble. A kerosene-powered compressor would draw unlimited air from the surface and pump it down through the air hose attached to the helmet. A release valve would prevent carbon dioxide levels from building inside and poisoning him.

Despite his own reassurances, his heart thudded erratically. Adrenaline danced through his system like a wild celebration of drunken fairies. He wished the whimsical analogy could make him smile, but the sensation was too damned unpleasant.

The brass and copper helmet rested on the deck next to Tim. Thankfully, the rest of his men weren't aware of the battle going on inside. Tim was the only one in whom he'd confided.

Rosa stood a short distance away, dressed in her red skirt and a clean white blouse. She looked beautiful and exotic, with her long black braid pulled over one shoulder and her green eyes huge and watchful in her delicate face.

He didn't want her to witness his shame should he fail to find the nerve to go through with the dive.

He glanced down at the conglomerate of pieces of eight clenched in his right hand. The wreck below could be the *Augustina,* waiting to grudgingly yield up her secrets. It was worth shutting himself inside this accursed suit and depending on a thin thread of air to the surface. Right?

"I can still go down with you," Tim said, wrenching Derek from his thoughts. He regarded Derek with a worried expression.

"Not until we are certain the other air compressor is working flawlessly. I don't like the sound of it. Get Grady to work on it today."

"I will."

"Besides, I have to prove that I can do this." Opening his hand, he stared at the indentations from the coins scored across his palm. "To myself," he added in a throaty whisper.

Tim took the clump of silver and set it aside. Then he hoisted the bowl-like helmet into his arms.

"Are you ready?"

"It will only get harder the longer I wait."

Tim lowered the metal sphere over his head.

The solid weight settled on Derek's shoulders. His only access to the world was a six-inch glass window in front of his face, two smaller ones on either side, and a hole at the top where the air hose would attach. Tim tightened the clamps that sealed the base of the helmet to the suit.

It was like being locked inside a tomb.

The panic attack struck hard. It sent a spasm through Derek's throat, then slid lower, coiling into a cold knot in his belly. His muscles went rigid. Sweat collected between his shoulder blades and slid down his spine.

"Are you sure you're all right? You look rather pale."

The urge to wrench off the helmet ripped through Derek's body. His hands clenched the base; his fingers hooked over the clamps like rigid claws.

Bloody, bloody hell. Damn this weakness, this unreasonable fear. A childhood accident shouldn't retain this much of a grip on any logical man. If he failed now, he might as well kiss his dream goodbye.

His gaze fixed on Rosa. If he jerked off the helmet, she would finally discover his pathetic Achilles' heel.

She watched him closely, her eyes bright with excitement. The envy she'd expressed by demanding her turn in the balloon was clearly etched on her face.

She considered him lucky.

Derek forced his frantic grip to open. He lowered his hands. "Just seal the damn thing," he snarled.

"Aye, Captain."

Tim squeezed his shoulder through the suit. He connected the hose and started the air compressor.

"Is it working?" Tim asked.

Cool air brushed the back of Derek's head. "Yes."

"Try to slow your breathing, Derek. You're gasping like a beached fish. You'll tire quickly like this."

As if he didn't know that. But understanding the logic and making his body respond were two different things entirely.

"Let's get on with it," Derek said gruffly.

Pulling the gloves over his trembling hands, he sealed them with straps around the wrists. He walked toward the waiting hoist. The world narrowed down, encompassing the chain that would lift him over the side, a pair of emerald-green eyes, and the thudding rhythm of his own heart.

He placed one boot into the sling and grasped the chain. *Do it now, or you will never get past this fear. Just keep moving.* He checked his tool belt—the attached rope tether, a knife, a metal paddle, and a mesh bag for samples. Taking a deep breath, he signaled to Geoff at the hoist's controls.

Two other crewmembers worked the winch. The hoist lifted Derek clear of the deck. The long arm swung him slowly out over the waves. The air hose followed, unwinding smoothly. The hoist paused, then reversed to lower him toward the surface.

Water climbed up his body, pressing against the suit as he submerged, then swept over the helmet. Derek loved the sea, but not when he was trapped in a bulky, man-sized snuffbox with weighted boots that would never allow him to reach the surface in time should something happen to his air supply.

With no one listening, he allowed his fear and self-disgust to rip from his throat in a low, guttural roar.

His descent came to a sudden, jarring stop. The howl choked off at the source. The echo of his shame faded.

As the chain went slack, he looked down at the solid footing beneath his boots. A thin white cloud of disturbed sand floated around his encased calves. *Remember the goal. You can do this.* He pried his clenched fingers from the chain and stepped out of the sling.

Shimmering patterns of aqua, blue, and white rippled across the bottom, reflecting through the silver ceiling above. Ridges of coral reef thrust upward like bulwarks against an invading army. Life teemed everywhere. More species of fish than he could count flitted through the eel grass and darted in and out of the coral.

A school of small silver fish approached. Numbering in the hundreds, they constantly changed directions, making simultaneous movements as if they shared a single mind.

Charmed by their beauty, Derek reached up a hand, wondering how they would react. They all turned on a heartbeat, darting away like quicksilver, their movements perfectly matched like an underwater ballet. Within seconds they were back.

This was amazing. The fish were as curious about him as he was about them.

In a way, this was better than free diving. True, he didn't possess the same freedom of movement in the suit, but he could stay down here as long as he pleased. He wasn't restricted to the three minutes of air his lungs could hold.

Derek forced one step, and then another. He was down here to explore, dammit. Each step became easier than the last. The panic attack began to subside, though it would never be completely gone as long as he remained in this suit.

His eyes scanned white sand and outcroppings of coral for anything out of place. He came across two, five, then nine ballast stones, a definite indication of a wreck but hardly the sixty- to seventy-foot ballast pile he would expect where a galleon actually went down. He bent, running his gloved hand over one of the smooth, egg-shaped river stones that had been the preferred material to provide stability to sailing vessels for hundreds of years.

An uneven white shape sticking up from the sand caught his attention. He squatted down and examined the broken edge, recognizing the texture of fine porcelain. Derek reached for the shard. He tugged gently. It didn't budge.

Slowly, now. Be patient. Do this the right way.

It was as if he was thirteen again, in Egypt, his father hanging over his shoulder as they excavated the tomb of one of Ramses III's high priests.

Derek unhooked the metal paddle from his belt and fanned the sand. White granules swirled away, the force of the water quickly exposing the artifact. It was a broken piece of a plate. Better yet, familiar cobalt-blue markings decorated its edge beneath the clear glaze. A graceful design of peony flowers, undimmed by 270 years in the sea, stared back at him.

Ming dynasty porcelain.

Exhilaration shot through Derek.

This was exactly the evidence he'd been praying for, mounting proof that he'd stumbled upon an ill-fated ship from the Spanish treasure fleet. But was it the *Augustina*? Nearly every Spanish galleon had carried a few cases of Chinese porcelain. Not just any wreck would do.

It was the *Augustina* he wanted, with her unique cargo. She had carried more sixteenth- and seventeenth-century Chinese decorative arts, in a greater variety, than any galleon on record. He considered Eastern artifacts his specialty.

The bottom edge of the piece was embedded in old coral beneath the sand. Derek used the knife to carefully scratch around the edges until the porcelain came free. After dropping it in his collection bag, he rose.

He must find something to identify the wreck—an anchor, a cannon with forged registration marks, silver or gold bars with assayer's marks recorded in the ship manifest. On his many trips to the archives in Seville, he'd copied down key items from the manifest of every ship lost in the 1622 fleet.

He continued to follow the thin trail of debris.

Occasional ballast stones testified to the violent death of the galleon. She must have ripped across the reef, half buoyant and half foundering, her ruptured hull spewing cargo and panic-stricken passengers at the whim of the hurricane. Few, if any, people in those days could swim. Being cast into the waves meant certain death from drowning. He trudged along, saddened, wondering what those people must have felt in the midst of such a nightmare. A certain melancholy accompanied each of his discoveries, balancing his enthusiasm with a reflection on the lives, and deaths, of real people.

The unmistakable gleam of gold caught his eye. A thumbnail-sized tip thrust from the sand. Eagerly, Derek shoved his gloved hand into the soft bed. The slender gold ingot came free, clenched protectively in his fist.

An inch longer than his hand, as big around as his middle finger, the ingot offered the perfect example of one of the wonders of chemical reactions—the same salt water that corroded silver left gold as perfect as the day it was minted.

He examined the gleaming surface.

It was smooth. Unmarked. Smuggled gold, dammit.

Disappointment sliced through him. This was the type of ingot that Spanish passengers, or even a captain and his crew, had smuggled to avoid the fifth of tax imposed by the king of Spain. Beautiful, yet useless in identifying his find.

With a sigh, Derek added the ingot to the growing collection of anonymous artifacts in his bag. Stubbornly, he trudged on, working his way between clumps of coral and schools of fish in every color imaginable.

Four times he reached the limit of the air hose. Each time his alert crew followed, moving *Pharaoh's Gold* and resetting her anchor. Yet nothing offered the conclusive evidence he craved.

The angle of the sun shifted, indicating he'd been below for almost three hours. Logic urged him to head back to the ship and plan out the next day's dive. But when he spotted the object nestled in the sand, he didn't hesitate.

Its blackened surface formed an ugly contrast to the colors of this pristine world. Grinning, Derek knelt on the seabed.

The metal bar was huge, as long as his forearm. His splayed fingers barely encompassed its width. Taking the knife, he carefully shaved away a sliver of the crusty coating.

Pure silver glistened.

The entire bar was solid Old World silver. But would it tell the story he so desperately needed?

Derek turned the heavy bar over. Thankfully, the underside was less corroded, partially protected from the brine by the sand. He brushed away bits of crust with his glove.

To a novice, the assayer's marks would make no more sense than chicken scratchings, but to an archaeologist who had studied the art, the characters carved into the surface spoke volumes. A shiver of excitement coursed down his spine.

Now, he need only compare the unique number to the detailed lists in the ship manifests.

He tugged on the tether rope, signaling that he was ready to come up. The deep thrum of the propeller vibrated through the water as *Pharaoh's Gold* eased overhead. Her shadow cut off most of the sunlight. The school of fish that had kept him company disappeared in a flash of silver bodies.

The chain lowered. Derek tied the sling around the silver bar. It was too heavy to carry up safely with him. He watched it rise to the surface, wishing he could be there to watch the crews' reactions.

Rosa would surely be pleased.

A sharp frown slashed across his brow. Why should that bother him? After all, wasn't the quest for silver and gold the very reason she'd come on this voyage?

When the chain returned, he stepped into the sling and rode to the top. The moment he touched the deck, the crewmembers operating the winch vanished. Only Tim remained.

The helmet pressed down on Derek's shoulders, reminding him forcefully of the tight, confined world of the diving suit. The buoyancy of the seawater had lightened the burden. His hunt had provided a welcome distraction. Now a fresh surge of fear slithered around his stomach and drew tight.

"Get it off," Derek ground out, twisting two of the quick-release clamps.

Tim instantly released the others. As he lifted the helmet free, he asked, "Did the suit stay watertight?"

Derek tilted his head back and cherished the open expanse of sky. He let out a long sigh. "Yes. Perfectly."

"What was it like down there?"

Hearing the envy in his friend's voice, Derek looked at Tim. "Beautiful. Serene. Fish in every shape and color you can imagine. Don't worry, we shall go together next time."

"And you? How are you holding up?"

"I shall be better after a stiff brandy." He hesitated, then added quietly, "At least I know I can do it now."

Tim nodded. "Maybe it will get easier each time."

"Bloody hell, I hope so." He peeled off the gloves. Noticing the unnatural quiet, he asked suspiciously, "Where is everyone?"

"Up by the bow, enamored of your prize. I believe we might have a severe case of treasure fever aboard."

"Blast it all! If they scratch off the sediment, they could damage some of the assayer's marks." Driven by a sense of urgency, Derek yanked his feet from the boots, stepped out of the sodden suit, and strode furiously toward the schooner's bow. He didn't take time to don a shirt or shoes.

Crew and passengers alike huddled around the silver bar.

Rosa squatted on the opposite side, gazing raptly at the bar, her red skirt gathered around her knees. Derek caught a clear view of bare feet and trim ankles beneath the bunched hem.

He froze.

Perfect toes gripped the deck, dipping into the puddle surrounding the bar. An image struck Derek of those toes stroking up his calves, then his thighs, and over his buttocks.

Rosa's gaze lifted. She stared openly at his bare chest. The tip of her tongue ran over her lips. Derek felt a thrust of desire spear through his loins.

He forgot why he was there. He almost forgot where he was.

Then Dickie leaned in close to the bar, knife in hand. The flash of reflected sunlight along the blade jolted Derek back to the present problem.

"No!" he shouted. "Do not touch it."

Dickie jumped back guiltily. Everyone turned to stare.

Amid protests, Derek stepped through the group, picked up the heavy ingot, and headed for the laboratory.

Rosa jumped up and followed immediately on his heels.

Halfway to the laboratory, he stopped abruptly and turned. "Where do you think you are going?"

"With you, of course. This is my adventure, too."

Had she invested four years of her life? Had she withstood torture for the sake of protecting the secret? "I believe you are placing too much significance on your role."

"I could have more of a role if only you would let me." Her chin set at that stubborn angle. "We are partners. Or are you going back on your word?"

"My word was given under duress."

"Does that make it any less binding?" she challenged.

It should. He could demand that threatening to drop the journal on the heads of Don Geraldo's soldiers nullified all agreements, that his life should go back to being uncomplicated, ordered, without these wild, unsettling demands on his temper or his libido. But as a Carlisle, integrity was everything.

"No, it does not," he growled. "I always keep my word. Now, this ingot is growing heavy. I have no intention of standing here, arguing with you."

"Then don't." She smiled sweetly. "You were going to your workshop, no? Lead on."

"It is called a laboratory."

"I like the way that word rolls off your tongue. Very English."

Derek mentally counted to ten, very slowly. "You are not going to follow me there."

"I want to see what you discover about the silver."

"When I finish my tests, I shall send you a written summary of my findings."

She folded her arms and cocked her head. "I think when you resort to sarcasm it is because you know I am right."

"Really." His knuckles whitened around the ingot. That secretive, feminine smile dancing at the corners of her lips was driving him mad . . . with frustration, of course. "Which only goes to show that you shouldn't jump to conclusions."

"I want to be there when you find out. Give me something useful to do. Teach me. I want to learn everything."

Her eyes sparkled with enthusiasm. He'd never had anyone interested in him as a mentor. Tim and the other members of his crew had long since learned their tasks well, but only to the extent of their individual roles. They found the overall science of archaeology tedious.

Surely Rosa would grow bored just as quickly, then leave him blissfully alone to get on with his studies.

What should have struck him as an excellent antidote to a black-haired nuisance caused a flicker of disappointment instead. The feeling confused and annoyed him. He opened his mouth to insist that certain tasks were for him, and him alone.

She curled one hand about his forearm.

Derek stiffened. Cynicism rose in his throat like the vinegar taste of bad wine. Now the feminine ploys would begin. Every woman he'd ever been involved with had cajoled for that extra set of diamonds, or a few more dresses, or begged him to spend another night in her bed before he terminated the relationship and left London behind for another voyage. What devices would Rosa employ in the attempt to get her way?

"Por favor," Rosa said simply. "I promise not to get in the way." Her gaze was fixed on him, intent and serious. No fluttering eyelashes. No sulky expression . . . though her lips *were* full and lush even without being turned down in a pout.

Heaven help him, it was her unexpected sincerity that got to him. "Very well," he found himself saying. "But do not touch anything."

Except me, he thought as she drew her hand away. *You can touch me again.*

Chapter Fourteen

HE CARRIED THE ingot into the laboratory and set it on the marble-top table that dominated the center of the room. Rosa took up a position on the other side of the table.

Derek opened a tightly sealed jar and brushed a solution of diluted acid over a section of the ingot. Bubbles foamed.

"What does that do?"

"It loosens the limestone crust so I can brush most of the debris away and see what is underneath."

Rosa wrinkled her nose. "I hope all your experiments do not smell so bad." She began to roam the room as he worked.

Derek sprinkled the ingot with baking soda to neutralize the reaction. Taking a stiff brush, he carefully worked the flaking crust loose. The outline of assayer's marks began to appear. He repeated the acid treatment, allowing the solution to work into the scratchings. This time when he cleaned out the grit, the roman numerals were clearly defined.

He copied the number onto a piece of paper.

Reaching to the shelf behind him, Derek pulled down

one journal into which he'd copied the manifests. He located the section that listed the *Augustina's* silver bars.

"What are you doing now?"

He sighed. "Didn't anyone ever tell you that curiosity killed the cat?"

"That must be an English cat. Overly cautious. Probably fat, too, fed on too much tea and scones. In Cuba, the *gato* thrives on his curiosity." Resting her elbows on the table, she leaned forward. "So, what is in the book?"

The neck of her peasant-style blouse gaped slightly, enough for him to see the cleavage between her breasts. Derek suddenly felt light-headed, as if he'd tumbled into that scented valley.

"Derek?" Rosa waved her hand across his line of sight.

He blinked. Bloody hell, he'd been staring at her chest like an adolescent.

"It will not kill you to answer me," she continued, sounding annoyed rather than offended, thank heavens. Perhaps she hadn't noticed his lapse. "Is that another journal?"

He nodded to chase the fog from his brain. "This is a copy of the manifests from the 1622 fleet. The Spanish were fanatical recordkeepers. The king and his tax collectors were always afraid of being cheated of the royal fifth imposed on everything of value. For good reason, actually, since a great deal of smuggling went on . . . gold chains, small unmarked bars, uncut emeralds. There are even stories of plating a ship's hull in gold beneath the waterline, and an anchor fashioned of solid gold then painted over."

"Very inventive."

"True, but also dangerous. Cheating the king was punishable by years in the galleys or death."

"How unfair!"

Derek sighed. She was a Gypsy by birth and a thief by choice, he reminded himself bitterly. What else would she think?

"The royal officials," he went on, "always made three

copies of each manifest. One went aboard the *capitana* of the fleet, or admiral's ship, the second aboard the *almiranta,* or flagship, and the third remained in Havana until the following year when it was sent to the archives in Spain."

"Archives? There is a library of these documents?"

"The Archivo General de Indies in Seville. A huge library, with rooms and rooms stacked with maps, books, and bound papers."

"I would love to see that," she said dreamily.

"No, you would not. It is incredibly dusty. Most of the documents are so old that they are brittle, dotted by holes from worms or termites, and nibbled at the edges by mice."

"But that would only make it more real, no? You could feel certain that you were reading genuine books and maps from that time. You would be touching history."

Her declaration stole his breath, so closely did it march with his own feelings when he dug through the archives. With a Herculean effort, Derek forced his attention back to the book.

For several minutes, he searched the lengthy manifest of the *Augustina,* running his finger slowly down the columns of numbers. Several were similar, but he needed an exact match to identify the wreck. He forced himself not to rush, but no amount of care would make the right number magically appear.

"Perhaps I can help," Rosa said, breaking the silence.

Derek swallowed hard against his disappointment. "It takes an experienced eye to draw the right comparison."

"What is so difficult?" She pointed to his slip of paper. "You are looking for this number, written in this book, no?"

"Very well," he retorted irritably. He shoved the ledger and the slip of paper across the table. "Go ahead."

Rosa bent over the book. Her hair slid over one shoulder and pooled across her forearm. He marveled at the sheen of lantern light on the ebony strands, barely noticing as she turned several pages. How would it feel to slide her hair between his fingers?

"Here it is."

Derek sat bolt upright. "Where?" he demanded.

Rosa pointed to a spot in the ledger. "Right here."

Derek's palm slapped down onto the open book. He swiveled it around and checked the number. By heavens, she was right. The assayer's number appeared in the manifest for the—

Derek slumped back in his chair. *"Nuestra Señora de Atocha,"* he grumbled.

A bright smile lit her face. "A Spanish galleon. This is wonderful. Why are you not thrilled?"

"Because it is the wrong damn ship."

"Was it carrying silver like this, perhaps gold as well?"

"According to the *Atocha*'s manifest, a great deal more. When she sailed from Havana, she was carrying forty-seven tons of gold and silver in her hold, as well as copper and tobacco."

Rosa sucked in her breath. *"Madre de Dios."*

"The *Atocha* carried one of the richest cargoes ever in the Spanish Plate Fleet. Her loss was a nearly fatal financial blow to Philip the Fourth. But I'm only interested in her sister ship, the *Augustina*. Tomorrow, at first light, we weigh anchor and begin the search again."

"Just . . . leave?"

She stared at him as if he'd lost his sanity. A voice at the back of Derek's mind whispered that perhaps she was right.

A stunningly significant archaeological find rested on the ocean bottom below his schooner's keel. But the *Atocha* was not the wreck he'd traced with almost fanatical determination for four years. The *Augustina*'s unique cargo had intrigued him from the outset, exciting his imagination and promising to provide his greatest validation yet as an archaeologist.

The discovery of the *Atocha* threatened to draw him away from his original goal. A tempting, seductive distraction.

Not unlike Rosa, with the natural sensuality that permeated her every expression, every movement, making his brain react with all the whipcord logic of raw bacon.

"Yes, pack up and leave," he answered from between clenched teeth. He wasn't going to let his dream slip away. "Decamp. Sally forth. Withdraw from the stage."

Rosa's brief glare of disgust acknowledged his blatant sarcasm. "I cannot believe you would abandon this perfectly good discovery. This is where Gaspar de Vargas's journal led you, after all."

"Then the journal is either wrong, or I misinterpreted it."

She jumped to her feet and paced restlessly on the opposite side of the table. "If the journal is wrong, then only a miracle will lead you to the *Augustina*. Perhaps she is only a phantom. You could search for the other wreck, yet find nothing, wasting your opportunity here."

"That is my decision to make."

Rosa stopped abruptly. "You know what?" She tapped her fingertips against her right temple and declared, "You are *loco*! Plain and simple."

Derek rose, his body stiff with aggravation and the effort it took to resist pulling the little firebrand into his arms.

"Perhaps I am. But I am still in charge of this expedition, where *Pharaoh's Gold* sails, and where she anchors."

Rosa tossed her hair over one shoulder in a defiant fashion. "What of your crew? Did you not promise them a reward from this voyage?"

"My crew has been with me a long time. They are accustomed to as many disappointments as successes."

"But we are talking a fortune at your fingertips here. Some of your crew have families in England. They could return home, reap the fruits of their hard work, retire rich men."

At the same time Rosa pushed him to the point of grinding his teeth, Derek had to admire her persistence.

Intelligence, too, for she put up such a good argument that he felt himself wavering. Again, dammit. How could he let this slip of a woman influence his decisions? Especially when her only purpose in being here was to grab whatever share of the wealth she could . . . then leave, never to be a part of his life again.

Anger surged unexpectedly. He crossed his arms. "Are we really talking about my crew, or yourself, Rosa? Are you afraid that if I pursue a find for purely scientific reasons, which I bloody well should be doing, that I won't be bringing up enough silver or gold to suit you? Do you fear that you will be forced to return to petty theft?"

The fire in her eyes dimmed. He was struck again by her stunning beauty, but now it held a vulnerability he hadn't witnessed in her before.

Derek's anger instantly deflated, leaving him feeling hollowed out inside. But what could he say? He'd only spoken the truth. She was a thief using his quest for further gain.

"You work hard at this," she said softly. "You take risks every day. I am beginning to understand why you love it so. But you are able to indulge your dreams because of money. Do not mock me for needing what you already have."

She moved to the door.

With one hand on the knob, she asked, "Why is the *Augustina* so important to you?"

"I have dedicated four years to searching for her," he admitted. "The *Augustina* is the one I want, and I only have time to salvage one ship before hurricane season sets in."

She watched him quietly for a few moments. Derek tensed, though he couldn't understand why he was on pins and needles for a response that would exercise no influence on his plans.

Lifting her chin, she was the picture of quiet dignity. "Very well, we should find your ship. But if we have not located the *Augustina* by the first of July, will you return to this site?"

"I will consider it." The words slipped out, unbidden.

She simply nodded and closed the door behind her.

Derek rubbed his knuckles against his chest, trying to soothe a mysterious ache. The woman's inconsistencies confused him. Where was her show of temper, the sense of high drama, the stubborn fight for her choice? Her noble agreement in the face of his anger left him feeling as if he'd just received a thorough set-down.

MICHAEL HALTED HIS stealthy progress without warning.

Dickie plowed into Michael's back, who in turn was knocked off balance when Esteban ran into him.

"Faith and what are you doing?" Michael complained in a hushed tone. "Don't be mowing a body down."

"If you wouldn't stop for no reason, you big ox, it wouldn't be a problem," retorted Dickie. "It's too bleedin' dark out here for that nonsense. The only light is that weak lantern at the stern. Can't see a bleedin' thing."

"Quiet, both of you," Esteban whispered irritably. "This will never succeed if you spoil the element of surprise." The unknown quantity of Dickie's and Michael's tempers left him nervous, not to mention his anxiety over their daring plan.

The threesome had stopped amidships, next to the structure that housed the laboratory.

"I had a reason for stopping. I heard something."

"Where?" Dickie pivoted quickly.

Cold metal touched Esteban's arm. Ever so cautiously, the Spaniard pushed the gun away until it wasn't in such nerve-wracking proximity to his heart. He didn't trust Dickie with the revolver. After all, the weight of the gun in his own hand felt clumsy and unfamiliar.

But they had to try. They couldn't allow that *loco* Lord Graystone to sail away tomorrow from a fortune in treasure!

"I don't like this," Michael muttered. "Where is everyone?"

"Yeah. What do you say to that, Esteban? I know your plan was to pick off each crewmember and tie them up until we could take Graystone hostage, but we sure can't do that if we can't bleedin' find them!"

"I do not know," Esteban admitted. "This is strange."

Michael sighed. "I wish Rosa was with us instead of tucked in her bed. I'd feel a sight better if this was her plan."

Offended, Esteban hissed, "She would not approve. At least I came up with a plan, while you two only complained."

"Hey, don't make it sound as if you're the one doin' all the work, mate. I picked the lock on the gun cabinet."

"Did you remember to put bullets in the guns?" Esteban retorted snidely.

"Sure did, but I didn't like it, no sirree. Hate to admit it, but I kind of like Graystone and his mates."

"We don't really have to shoot them to take over the ship, do we?" Michael whispered.

With a sigh of aggravation, Esteban said, "The plan is to take Graystone hostage without firing a single shot. Will you stop arguing and get on with it?"

Esteban nudged Dickie, who nudged Michael. They started to creep forward again. Suddenly, the grating scratch of several flints broke the silence. Light flared as lanterns were lit.

The three elderly men froze, caught in the glow.

Tim, Geoff, and Richard emerged from around the laboratory and came up behind them. Each man carried a rifle. Richard took the revolvers from their numb fingers.

Graystone walked calmly around the opposite corner and paused before them. Dressed simply in black trousers and a black shirt, with a revolver shoved in his waistband, he looked just like the buccaneers that populated Dickie's and Michael's more colorful tales.

"Did you . . . overhear what we were sayin'?" Dickie muttered.

"Every word," Graystone said coldly.

Esteban flinched. "What are you going to do?"

"Well, since you at least preferred not to shoot my crew, I suppose I could forgo the cat-o'-nine-tails, the keel hauling, or tossing you overboard."

Dickie and Michael swallowed convulsively.

"You were waiting for us. How did you know?"

"After my announcement this evening that we would set sail come morning, and your resultant tirades, I cautioned Geoff to keep a close eye on the gun cabinet. He discovered three revolvers missing after dark. Considering your attitudes about leaving this site, it wasn't difficult to surmise where the guns went, and why."

"It was just a little mutiny, mate. No real harm intended."

Esteban stepped on Dickie's foot, hard enough to be felt through the boot.

"You cannot mutiny, gentlemen. You are passengers, not members of my crew." Graystone glared at them from beneath lowered brows. "First the incident in Galveston, now this. I see a disturbing pattern in failing to honor your word to stay out of trouble. I cannot have you endangering my crew, my ship, my plans, or yourselves for that matter."

Michael thrust out his chest. "Whatever the punishment, you won't catch me whimpering."

Dickie squared his shoulders. "Me, neither, no sirree."

Graystone rolled his eyes. With an extended arm, he indicated the stairs that led belowdecks. "After you."

As they headed down the stairs, Esteban asked the plaintive question foremost on all their minds. "Must you tell Rosa?"

Dickie groaned. Michael ran his hands down his face.

"I suppose I shall have to," Graystone said, demonstrating that he had no mercy in his cold and heartless soul. "She will know something is wrong when she discovers that you are all locked in the brig."

"THEY ARE WHERE?" Rosa exploded indignantly shortly after sunrise.

She surged out of the chair in which Derek had invited her to sit . . . though of course he hadn't expected her to stay there when she learned of the night's events. She paced the length of his cabin. He couldn't help but notice how her energy, her very life force, brightened the room.

"Your godfathers are locked in the large storage room. I would have shut them in the brig, but I don't officially have one." *Unfortunately,* he added to himself.

"But it must be cold down there, drafty. They are just fragile old men."

"So you keep telling me." Derek leaned back against his desk and crossed his arms. "So fragile they tried to commandeer my ship."

"What if there are rats?"

"I try to maintain a clean ship, but anything is possible."

With a seething glance, she snapped, "You are heartless."

An opinion I will no doubt confirm when you discover where we are going and what I have planned. "I'll defer to your judgment, Rosa," he said wryly.

He watched her crisscross the oriental rug. Her quick, agitated stride contrasted with the rocking-chair rhythm of the ship as it pushed through the waves. The brisk breeze strained at the sails as *Pharaoh's Gold* raced toward its new destination. Time was precious, and he resented having to spend it dealing with three recalcitrant old men.

Rosa thrust splayed fingers through her loose hair, raking it back from her forehead. "I cannot believe they tried this. Guns, you said?"

"Fully armed."

"Madre de Dios."

Her distress left him feeling awkward, restless. He racked his brain for a way to comfort her, then nearly choked on that sentiment when she spoke again.

"You know they did not mean it." Stopping her pacing,

she stood rigidly, hands on hips, and gave him a look meant to challenge.

She was all too forgiving when it came to her godfathers' exploits. Those "innocent" old men had subjected him to two days of mental and physical torture, at Don Geraldo's hands. The memories of that nightmare were rapidly fading into obscurity, true, but Derek couldn't escape this daily dose of watching them manipulate Rosa. She enabled their dependency by the very nature of her compassion and strength. It really wasn't his business. Even though they were gradually stealing her youth and draining her vitality.

"They were greedy, Rosa. The only desperation came from the idea of walking away from all that silver."

"Do you intend to punish them?"

"No. I intend to be rid of them." *If you can't see that they are perfectly capable of fending for themselves, then I shall be the one to show you.*

She pressed a hand to her throat. "What . . . what do you mean?"

"Haven't you noticed that we set sail?"

"Sí," she responded warily. "I thought we were heading for your new location for the *Augustina.*"

"Unfortunately, not yet. Your godfathers' plot last night forced a change of plans." Impulsively, he crossed the room and grasped her shoulders. "Salvaging a sunken ship is dangerous business, Rosa. I cannot . . . I will not . . . risk the safety of everyone aboard by letting your godfathers run amuck on my ship."

"I can watch them. I will not let this happen again."

Even now, she took responsibility for them rather than letting the three mischief-makers pay the price for their own mistakes. Why did it matter to him so much?

"Were you able to stop last night's attempt? Did you even suspect their plans? Were you able to prevent them from planting stolen valuables in my room?"

She jerked in surprise. "How did you know?"

"They admitted as much to me in Galveston."

"Where are we going?" she whispered.

"An island east of here, farther up the chain of the Florida Keys. I intend to leave them there."

Her jaw dropped. "An island? Is it deserted?"

"Thankfully. You do not think I would inflict your godfathers on any hapless, unsuspecting inhabitants, do you? Not without fair warning, or perhaps an army at their disposal."

She wrenched free of his hands and spun away. Her pacing resumed. Derek lowered his empty hands slowly.

"You intend to abandon them? What kind of monster are you?"

"Not abandon," he said through his teeth. "Temporarily relocate."

"They will starve! They'll die of exposure! What if a hurricane strikes?"

If only she would save up this passion for him. He battled the urge to shake some sense into her.

"The island has fresh water, plant and animal life. Nevertheless, I intend to leave them extra foodstuffs."

"They will not starve?"

Derek look heavenward, asking for patience. "No."

Rosa stopped pacing. "You have been to this island before?"

"Yes. About ten months ago. Geoff and Grady are also gathering supplies and tools your godfathers can use in building a shelter."

"Build? By themselves? Are you *loco*? My godfathers are not the least bit talented with their hands."

"They may surprise you, given the opportunity."

"You do not understand at all." She walked straight up to Derek and jabbed him in the chest. "This is a disaster."

At least she was touching him. "Really? How so?"

"Without me there to control their bickering, they will kill one other. And their deaths will be on your head!"

She jabbed him again. She put lightning and crashing surf and thirty-foot waves to shame.

Desire sparked, hot and insistent.

Without pausing to think, Derek caught her hand in his. He pressed his lips to the base of her thumb.

Chapter Fifteen

ROSA'S PROTESTS STILLED instantly.

Derek gently brushed the back of her fingers along his jaw. Her expression softened. He felt her lean toward him.

He smiled gently. "Trust me, Rosa. Your godfathers will learn to depend on one another for survival."

She stiffened. "I knew it," she exclaimed, yanking her hand away. "You do think danger is involved. You believe my godfathers' very survival is at risk!"

Derek stood, stunned, one hand still raised to his chin. "Wait just a bloody minute. That is not what I—"

She spun around and stormed from the room.

Derek winced as the door slammed. If he could have kicked himself, he would have. When would he learn to keep his mouth shut while he was still ahead? He should have just pulled her into his arms and kissed her senseless.

As soon as she calmed down, he would outline his plan to her again. Rosa would see reason, dammit.

SHE SPENT THE whole day locked in the storage room with her gloating godfathers.

Derek didn't even have the satisfaction of seeing Rosa

inconvenienced for her childish protest. His crew couldn't bear the idea of her doing without . . . anything. They fetched and carried meals for four, a table, a deck of cards, her shawl, and whiskey. It didn't take a genius to determine who the latter was for. Sounds of merriment soon drifted up from belowdecks.

Derek glowered as *Pharaoh's Gold* slipped through an opening in the reef and eased into the island's picturesque bay. He had hoped Rosa would enjoy her first sight of the island with him—to appreciate its beauty, to witness for herself that it wasn't the hostile environment she dramatically predicted.

A flock of ducks flew over the palm trees, landing inland, no doubt in the natural freshwater cistern he remembered. A group of wild donkeys—perhaps descendants of animals cast ashore from a wrecked Spanish galleon—stared alertly from the undergrowth beneath the trees. Rocky outcroppings bracketed a sandy beach. On the eastern end lay a beached boat.

Derek smiled. She was still here, thank goodness. He'd been counting on the sloop as part of his plan.

Last year, when he'd been scouring the Keys for signs of the *Augustina,* a severe storm had driven them into this bay for shelter. They'd discovered another victim of the storm slowly sinking. The harried American owners of the *Lucky Lady* had welcomed the help. Working together, the two crews had hauled the lovely, thirty-foot sloop ashore. Although the damage to the hull wasn't extensive, the ship was no longer seaworthy, and more of a daunting repair task than the couple felt equipped to handle. They were pleasure boaters, not shipwrights, they moaned, and promptly requested transportation to Key West. Feeling sorry for them, and appreciating the fine lines of the sloop, Derek had bought it from them at a fair price.

He'd intended to repair the ship at some point, but for now she could serve him better in other ways.

The crew loaded the longboat with all the supplies that

could be spared. Finally, when the half-dozen crates were moved to the beach, Derek turned to Geoff and Tim.

"Bring them up." He wanted this distasteful business over with as soon as possible; then he would head for the new dive site he'd recalculated after reexamining Gaspar's journal.

Rosa climbed the stairs first, her chin raised defiantly. Michael, Dickie, and Esteban emerged behind her. They shielded their eyes from the brilliant sunlight.

Once on deck, Dickie thrust out his hands, palms up. "Okay, mate, we're ready to accept our fate."

"It's mighty ashamed we are for trying to take your ship, Graystone," Michael offered with a woebegone expression. He held out his hands, as well.

Esteban followed suit. "Do what you must."

Derek looked at their outthrust wrists and swallowed a growl of aggravation. Manipulative old coots. "Thank you for the offer of penitence, gentlemen, but shackles are reserved for dangerous felons. In your case, I think grabbing you by the scruff of the neck and hustling you ashore will suffice."

All three scowled.

"Can you not see how sorry they are?" Rosa pleaded. "Surely you can forgive them this one time?"

"One time? May I remind you that they have betrayed me twice now? Besides, I think you will discover their regret stems more from getting caught than from genuine remorse."

"Must you do this?" she whispered.

"Say your farewells, Rosa," he said curtly, avoiding her gaze. The pain in her eyes was coming disturbingly close to breaking his resolve. "The supplies are ashore. It is time."

Rosa hooked one arm through Esteban's elbow, and the other around Michael's. "I shall say *adiós* on the island. I am going ashore to make sure they are all right."

"No. You will stay aboard." The last thing he needed was additional time for these three to prey on her sympathies.

"Then I shall jump overboard and swim ashore."

Of course she would. He didn't doubt it for a moment. The whole lot of them were a bunch of theatrical lunatics. "Fine. Suit yourself," he growled.

Tim and Geoff manned the longboat, transferring everyone to the beach. The heels of Derek's brown boots sank into the coarse sand as he waited for the goodbyes to run their course. He hooked his thumbs into the waistband of his tan trousers and struggled to keep his frustration in check. When it looked as if the farewells would go on forever, he grasped Rosa's upper arm and eased her away. She acquiesced without a fight. Perhaps their performances were beginning to wear her down, as well.

"Adiós, niña," Esteban said mournfully. He sniffed.

"It's been grand, to be sure," Michael said.

"Remember us fondly, angel girl. We'll be thinkin' of you, up until the moment we—" Dickie bit one knuckle.

Derek swore under his breath. The crafty con artists managed to look like a trio of whipped puppies.

Rosa turned to him, tears sparkling on her lashes.

"I cannot do this," she said plaintively. "I cannot abandon them. *Por favor*, leave me here with them."

Bloody hell.

This would accomplish nothing. Rosa possessed too much fire and passion to be buried beneath her godfathers' clinging needs. They weren't in their dotage yet. They appeared quite capable, once motivated, to take care of themselves. Derek intended to prove as much to her.

"I can leave you here, Rosa, but who will represent your interests aboard *Pharaoh's Gold*? What incentive is there for me to return and hand over your portion of the treasure?"

Shocked silence met his pronouncement. Even Tim and Geoff looked surprised, though their gazes stayed sharp with suspicion. They, at least, knew him well enough to realize he always kept his word. And he would never abandon another human being to an uncertain fate.

Rosa's gaze flashed with renewed temper. She opened her mouth to speak, but Dickie beat her to it.

"You do have a point there, mate," he commented.

"Perhaps you ought to go with him, *niña*."

"It's up to you to protect our interests," Michael agreed.

Rosa stared at them as if they'd each sprouted an extra head. "But are you not concerned about my reputation?"

"You are a grown woman now, *niña*. We should no longer treat you like a little girl."

Michael added, "Besides, the crew is a good lot of lads."

"Yes, sirree, they're trustworthy. You can learn a lot about a man over a hand of cards. They respect you, angel girl, just as they ought."

Her jaw hung slack. "Who *are* you? What have you done with the guardians who have chased off every suitor I ever had?"

Dickie brightened. "There you have it! These boys aren't suitors. They're not interested in you that way."

Rosa blinked, confused by their complete about-face. Her wounded expression ignited Derek's anger, along with a fierce urge to protect. He swept her into his arms.

She gripped his shoulders. "No, wait."

"No more waiting."

He strode toward the longboat and seated her in the bow.

"You have your answer, Rosa. They change their tune when money is at risk."

Her lips compressed into a thin line. "They are frightened. Too old to be left alone like this."

"I have left them food, in addition to what they can hunt on the island, a source of fresh water, ammunition, shelter, even tools to repair that sloop if they wish."

"I know, but—"

She was still defending and protecting her godfathers, even after they had hurt her feelings. Such generosity was truly an admirable trait. So why did it infuriate him?

Tim and Geoff climbed into the longboat and took the oars.

"Take her back to the ship," he snapped, "then return for me. I have one last matter to see to before we sail."

DEREK WALKED BACK to the group of very disgruntled men.

They sat in the shade of a palm tree, each using a crate as a seat. Michael gloomily stared at the surf. Dickie poked a stick into the sand. Esteban massaged his temples.

Derek shook his head. When they looked like this, he almost doubted his conviction that they would thrive when faced with a challenge.

"You have about eight hours until sunset, gentlemen. I suggest you put that time to good use."

"Faith, doing what? Digging our graves?" Michael moaned.

"I was thinking more in terms of building a shelter."

"With what, I ask you?" Esteban retorted sarcastically.

"Perhaps if you opened these crates instead of just sitting on them, you might find out. The crates themselves can be broken down for wood."

Dickie glared. "There ain't enough for three shelters."

Derek hid a smile. "True. But there is enough for one."

Their looks of horror were classic.

"You mean . . . share? With these blokes?"

"Didn't you share a room in Havana?"

"There a man had room to spread out, me boyo, with his own bed. Not like some wee lean-to on a beach," Michael exclaimed.

"If this big ox rolls over, he'll crush me for sure."

Michael poked Dickie in the shoulder, knocking him off his crate. "I don't be needing sleep to best you, you pipsqueak."

Dickie jumped up and brushed the sand from his trousers. He raised clenched fists. "Try that again."

Derek rolled his eyes. This was going to take a miracle.

Unless they were forced into cooperating, however, they would never bother to try.

"I suggest you find a way. It is either that, or sleep in the rain. Storms come through here frequently."

"At least you left us enough food to survive on, no?"

"For about two weeks."

"That's all?" Dickie's face reddened above his white beard.

"Yes. I recommend hunting to extend your supplies. There is a wide variety of fish, fowl, and game. Unless it is too much trouble and you would prefer to go hungry, that is."

"But Rosa said you were leaving us plenty of food," Michael protested.

"Enough to get you started. I never claimed I was going to make this easy for you."

Dickie straightened and fixed Derek with a squinty-eyed glare. "Speakin' of Rosa, you'd best watch yourself around our angel girl, mate."

"Whatever do you mean?" They needed something to motivate them to action, rather than succumbing to their inclination to sit around feeling sorry for themselves.

Michael rose slowly. "You're a vigorous lad, Graystone. Dickie means none of that . . . you know . . . hanky-panky."

"I will admit, the thought has crossed my mind," Derek answered honestly. "More than once."

Dickie's and Michael's jaws sagged. Esteban's eyes nearly popped out of his head.

Derek shrugged insolently, seeding their imaginations. "With you stranded here, what is there to stop me from taking what I want?"

Esteban's gaze narrowed sharply. "Rosa is not for you, *hombre*. Stay away from her. Touch her, and we will find a way off this island and kill you."

"You are welcome to try," Derek countered. He pointed down the beach. "See that sloop, *Lucky Lady*? She is a honey of a ship, not too badly damaged. With some hard work, and the supplies we've provided, she will be seaworthy again."

"If you hurt Rosa," Esteban persisted, "we will hunt you down if it takes until the day we die."

"Yeah, watch yourself, Graystone." Dickie raised his gnarled fist. "We can be very dangerous men."

"Remember that, me boyo," growled Michael.

"That, gentlemen, is the only thing you have said since we've met that has earned my respect."

Derek turned away, leaving three furious men glaring at his back.

ROSA DIDN'T MOPE long. It wasn't in her nature.

It was more befitting her stubborn, impulsive, illogical nature to hatch a plot to turn his crew against him.

Derek's fingers drummed against the biceps of his crossed arms as he stood on deck, watching Rosa flirt with Richard and Wilson. She praised their work until the men blushed. She dropped hints about "convincing" Derek to abandon his current plan and return to the potential wealth of the *Atocha*.

The little firebrand was encouraging mutiny.

She just couldn't bring herself to believe that her godfathers could survive on their own. The three self-absorbed old men had spent too many years convincing her otherwise.

He didn't need to worry about his crew's loyalty. What truly bothered him was the way they received the full benefit of her charm while he was literally left out in the cold.

She had made it her life's mission to ignore him.

When she laughed at Richard's joke and gazed up at the carpenter adoringly, Derek stiffened. His vision clouded with a red haze. Before his brain could produce a single coherent thought, his body was moving toward the threesome.

His hand encircled her upper arm. "That is enough sabotage for one day, Rosa. You are coming with me," he snapped.

"Oh? What are you going to do?"

Nip at that chin that drives me mad with its obstinate tilt. Kiss those luscious lips until I silence that clever, infuriating tongue of yours. Ravish you.

He sneered. "I intend to lock you in your cabin."

Her first came flying at his face.

Astonished, Derek ducked his head to the side just in time to avoid a bloody nose. He caught her fist in the palm of his free hand. Quickly, he crooked her arm behind her back and crushed her against him.

"If you try that again, I will keep you locked up for the remainder of this expedition."

She eyed him with wary hostility. Lips parted, her breath brushed his throat in quick pants. Her full breasts flattened against his chest. Her belly fit to his in sleek, quivering perfection. Despite her bravado, she trembled.

Disgusted by his loss of control, Derek released her abruptly, before the fleeting idea of ravishment became reality.

"Isn't locking her up a bit severe?" Richard asked.

"Rather mild, actually, compared to the typical punishment for inciting mutiny."

"What is the punishment for murdering the captain?" Rosa asked sourly.

Wilson and Richard coughed into their hands, covering what sounded suspiciously like laughs.

Grasping Rosa's arm again, Derek propelled her on a straight course for her cabin. "We should reach the new site before nightfall. I will be going up in the balloon each day until I find something. I won't have you causing problems in my absence with talk of mutiny."

He reached her open door and pushed her through. She spun to face him. Derek paused, feeling a twinge of uncertainty.

"Why do you hesitate?" she challenged. "Go ahead, lock it."

Gritting his teeth, he closed the door, cutting off her glare of resentment. He turned the key in the lock.

This was the safest place for her. What mischief could she possibly get up to in her cabin?

ROSA PROWLED HER locked cabin for the third day in a row.

Was she *loco* for remaining so stubborn? All Derek required to reinstate her precious freedom was her sworn promise to make no further attempts to undermine his authority. But she couldn't forget the way he'd dismissed her most fervent pleas concerning her godfathers. Her fears . . . her concerns . . . they meant nothing to him. His indifference rankled.

Each evening he came to her doorway, offering another chance. He propped one shoulder against the doorframe in that lean, predatory, devastatingly handsome way of his. His golden grace triggered a deep, sweet pang of longing . . . until he cocked an arrogant eyebrow. He had such confidence in her capitulation. She couldn't do it. A sharp stab of frustration had sent her lunging for something to throw at him instead.

Not that she'd hit him, of course, even though her projectiles of a pewter mug one day and a boot the next had been right on target. Damn his quick reflexes. But at least she had the satisfaction of watching him storm off with a scowl.

Until he was gone and the loneliness and boredom settled over her like a heavy, suffocating blanket.

Derek was going to find something extraordinary, and she would miss out on all the excitement. If only she could spite him by escaping! He was due to visit her again in a few hours.

Her gaze drifted speculatively to the ventilation shaft. A rectangular grate covered the opening two feet above the floor. After debating the possibility for days, she finally summoned the resolve to open it. Using the knife from the lunch tray, she pried it loose.

Black emptiness stretched away into the body of the ship.

It was just as she'd feared. The shaft was barely big enough to crawl through. She didn't dread the tight confines, but there would be no way to turn around. What if she reached a dead end? The only way out would be a slow struggle backward.

Rosa set her jaw in determination. It was worth a chance to find a way out of this prison on her own terms.

She wriggled out of her bulky skirt.

DEREK ANCHORED THE flying apparatus to the deck, all eight buoys still attached. He'd seen nothing worth marking this afternoon. The balloon sagged over, losing air rapidly.

That was exactly how he felt. Deflated. Discouraged. Another full day of searching with no results. Was he giving his all to a quest destined for failure?

"Captain, I need to speak with you."

Derek spun around on one heel. Something about the odd note in Tim's voice—a bizarre cross between dread and amusement—caused goose bumps to rise on his skin.

"What is it, Tim?"

"There is something going on with Miss Rosa."

"Is she ill?"

"No . . . at least I don't believe so. Perhaps you should come see for yourself."

Scowling, Derek followed. The last thing his present mood could tolerate was another bout of theatrics from his volatile partner. At one-and-thirty, he was getting too damned old for this. He needed quiet, and solitude, and an entire bottle of brandy in which to drown his burgeoning sense of disappointment.

Tim led him down to Rosa's cabin. The door was closed.

That was how he had left her, locked in her room. At the look on Tim's face, however, doubt assailed him.

"She is still in there, correct?"

"Not exactly," Tim said flatly. "Nigel tried to bring her dinner twenty minutes ago, but there was no answer to his knock. He unlocked the door to discover this." Tim opened the door.

The room fairly shouted emptiness without Rosa's whirlwind presence. Everything seemed in perfect order, except for the dark, rectangular hole that gaped in the far wall. The grating had been removed from the ventilation shaft. Derek had included the shafts in the ship's design to provide fresh air below and protect against fire. He'd never thought—

"She wouldn't," he said harshly.

"I'm afraid she did."

"That shaft is barely big enough for a child to wriggle through."

"Somehow she managed."

With a heartfelt sigh, Derek got down on his hands and knees. He peered into the shaft. The darkness seemed to have no end and no way out. Immediately, he drew back.

"Have you tried calling to her?"

"Yes, sir."

"Did she answer?"

"In a manner of speaking."

"Well, what did she say, man?"

"'Go away, and tell that *bastardo* I hate him.'" A corner of Tim's mouth twitched. "I'm quoting directly, you understand."

"I don't doubt it for a moment." Avoiding looking directly into the coffin-sized tunnel, he called out, "Rosa?"

"Ah, the prodigal son returns," Rosa responded tartly. "I am not impressed. You deserve to be fed cactus spines rather than the fatted calf."

Her voice sounded different than he would expect, muffled rather than focused by the shaft. He assumed that was because she was facing away from him, with her body serving as a barrier to sound. Regardless, he felt an immense relief. She must be all right if peppering him with insults still ranked among her priorities. He needed to handle this situation delicately and not encourage her temper to erupt.

"What the bloody blazes do you think you're doing, woman?" he shouted.

"Whatever I *bloody* well please. Go away, Derek. I don't wish to speak with you."

"Come out of there at once."

Silence.

"Did you hear me?"

More silence.

"Rosa." His voice came out sounding like a warning snarl from an annoyed bear.

"I will not come out," she finally deigned to answer. "I prefer this to being your prisoner."

"You are not my prisoner, dammit. I was just keeping you locked up for your own safety."

A strange sound echoed down the shaft. It sounded somewhat like a snort.

Derek looked over his left shoulder and whispered to Tim, "Go to the laboratory and fetch the original diagrams for the ship's design. I stored them in the map cabinet, third drawer."

Tim hurried away.

Struggling to find some semblance of patience, Derek called into the shaft, "Can you turn around in there?"

"I do not think it would be wise to try."

Stupid question. There was no room to turn around. It was too . . . he swallowed hard . . . tight in there. "Do you see light at the end of the shaft?"

"Dimly, I think. Is the sun setting? Why is it getting darker in here?" she said plaintively. "I feel rather strange."

Perhaps she wasn't getting enough air. Derek's chest constricted in sympathy. He could feel the closeness, the pressure all around, squeezing— He gasped for air. Please don't let her faint. He didn't want to destroy several feet of deck to get to her.

"Can you move freely, or are you . . . trapped?"

"It is very snug in here."

Fear thrust through him, sharp-edged, leaving him bleeding inside. Shame followed close on its heels. After his questionable success at diving he'd thought, just maybe, he was close to conquering this fear. How arrogant to think so. Perhaps he would never be free of it.

"Of all the stupid, obstinate, idiotic things to do!"

"Then you should not treat me like a criminal, or worse, a useless child."

He sat back and raked both hands through his hair.

"You have to try to move on through the shaft, Rosa. And for pity's sake, don't let your clothes get caught on anything."

"Who said I was wearing any clothes?"

Chapter Sixteen

SURPRISE JOLTED THROUGH Derek. A quick glance confirmed her skirt on the bed. "What the devil do you mean by that?"

"Well, just suppose . . . and I am too much of a lady to confirm or deny this . . . that I decided I would fit through this shaft better without anything to restrict my movements."

Derek sincerely hoped she didn't expect him to respond to that. His voice froze in his throat as his imagination took over. He pictured her naked, wriggling through that tight place with those long, long legs and that perfectly shaped derriere.

"And, just suppose," she continued in a matter-of-fact tone, "I also thought it a good idea to cover myself in scented oil. Just so I could slide through more easily. ¿Comprende?"

Heat plunged into his groin, apparently drawing most of the blood from his brain because he suddenly felt quite light-headed. He could picture sliding, all right, but it was the slick grind of his body against hers and the kind of sliding that had her legs wrapped tightly around his waist and her panting breaths coming ever faster until her hips arched in a shattering climax.

He bit down on the inside of his cheek.

The pain brought him back to reality, though it did nothing to relieve the heavy ache in his loins. He shouldn't trust anything she said. It didn't take oil to make Rosa slippery, and daring, as well as utterly impossible. The woman was going to make him wear down the grinding surface of his teeth.

"I am not sure the oil worked, though," she added.

He cleared his throat with difficulty. "Why is that?"

"I think I may be stuck, Derek."

Trapped. Sweat broke out on his forehead. Nausea fluttered in his stomach.

Tim returned, carrying the diagrams. Derek snatched them from his hands and smoothed them out on the bed. Tim leaned over his shoulder, his expression concerned.

"Not even I'm small enough to fit through there."

"I know," Derek responded flatly. Whatever damage a rescue inflicted on *Pharaoh's Gold,* they had to get Rosa out of there. Fast, before the fist in his chest succeeded in crushing his heart. He didn't understand it. He wasn't the one trapped, but he felt her danger as if it was his own.

Tim pointed to the diagram. "Here is her cabin, and here is the shaft leading out. Where does it go?"

"Up to the deck, just aft of the laboratory."

"What about this? The ventilation system branches here and goes to—" The first mate paused in surprise.

"My cabin," Derek finished darkly. The nausea vanished. Instead, a low beat of anger throbbed in his temples.

"But that is only fifteen feet away." Tim looked confused.

Derek was beginning to see very clearly. "Exactly." Straightening, he headed for the door, his fury on low boil and gaining momentum. "Keep Rosa talking. If she asks where I am, tell her I am coming in after her."

DEREK HEARD TIM calling through the ventilation shaft. "He's coming in after you. Don't worry, Rosa."

"Hah! As if those broad shoulders will fit. Tell him I hope he gets stuck," came her sassy reply.

Now that he stood outside his own cabin door, he could tell exactly where that conniving voice was coming from. No wonder it had sounded muffled. The incorrigible little actress.

She'd made it through into his cabin. Perhaps hours ago.

She had found an excellent means of making him pay for locking her up. Thankfully, she didn't realize how much her game had brutalized his secret fear.

He turned the knob, then gave way to his wrath and shoved.

The heavy wooden door crashed against the adjoining wall.

Rosa, lounging in his chair with her feet propped on his mahogany desk, jumped half out of her skin. A glass of his best Bordeaux splashed across her forearm. Her eyes grew so wide he could see white all around the edges.

"Oh . . . I, uh . . ." she faltered.

For once her glib tongue failed her. He hoped it was his expression of barely suppressed violence that struck her dumb.

She'd certainly made herself at home. She wore one of his custom-made silk shirts over her standard pair of black trousers. Her dust-covered blouse lay discarded on the floor. Several books lay open on the bed. His wine rack had been rearranged. Dinner had apparently consisted of pistachio nuts and chocolates, for his private stashes were open and half gone.

Snidely, he imitated, "I think I may be stuck, Derek."

She gave him a sheepish smile as she set down the wine. Then, of all things guaranteed to fan the flames of his anger blue-hot, she shrugged.

To hell with his prized self-control.

He started across the room. She shot from his chair like a startled deer. He made a grab for her across the desk, but she jerked out of reach just in time. He cursed his taste in large, overly wide desks.

"Do you know what you truly deserve?" he bit out. "I should turn you over my knee and blister your backside."

She snorted. "That would be barbaric."

"I have developed a sudden taste for anything barbaric."

He started counterclockwise around the desk. Rosa moved as well, maintaining the distance between them. "Remember you are a gentleman, Graystone."

"Not today. Today I am just a man . . . and one pushed beyond the limits of his patience at that."

Balancing lightly on the balls of her bare feet, she watched him avidly. Her attitude of breathless vigilance heightened his sense of anticipation. But of what? Vengeance, or seduction? She gnawed her lower lip. His attention riveted on her mouth, and he knew. He wanted her. Despite his righteous anger, he desired her with an intensity that went beyond reason.

He feinted to the right, then lunged across the desk. She avoided him, thanks to those damnably quick reflexes of hers.

"I intend to have a piece of your hide for what you put me through, Rosa." *Starting with your lips, then your earlobe, then the sleek curve of your shoulder—*

"It should appeal to your sense of humor . . . if you had one."

"Tell that to my pounding heart, or the sick feeling that invaded my stomach," he countered harshly. He winced inwardly, taken aback by his confession. What the blazes had compelled him to blurt that out?

"Truly? You were worried about me?"

"Enough to hack through the deck, if that is what it took to get you out of there."

"Oh," she whispered, appearing rather bemused.

He took advantage of her distraction. With a quick, sideways step, he grabbed her arm. She yelped. He pulled

her around to face him, then pinned her against the desk
with his thighs pressed against hers.

"Let me go!"

"Not a chance."

He wanted that look in her eyes—not fear, but respect.
So she would stop toying with him, driving him crazy with
her antics and stubbornness and the sultry sway of her hips
that was all the more provocative for its innocence.

If he couldn't control himself, dammit, then he would
control her.

Derek kept her pinned. He planted an arm on either
side, palms flat against the desk. He leaned forward, craving
the feel of her breasts against his chest. She leaned back at
the same time, until the surface of the desk stopped her. She
braced her elbows, staring up at him warily.

The thickening bulge in his trousers pressed against her
belly. She must have felt it, for her eyes grew rounder. Now
she would take him seriously and stop challenging his temper at every turn. He'd never resorted to sexual dominance
before, but in this insane situation it seemed the only way to
subdue Rosa's wild spirit.

She glanced down.

Her eyelids lowered. Her lips parted. She looked like a
cat expecting to savor a particularly rich bowl of cream.

The sight of her looking boldly at the place where their
bodies pressed together was incredibly erotic. Molten heat
poured through Derek's veins. There was only one way
they could fit together more perfectly.

Reason and the last of his self-control spiraled away.

He rocked his hips against hers, slowly. The sudden
catch in her breath nearly undid him. Her head dropped
back. The graceful line of her throat tempted him with a
sudden urge to drag his lips down that slender column, to
suckle her skin and leave small badges of possession trailing
down her neck.

He bent low, seeking those lips that had haunted his
dreams since he saw them clamped around a rose.

"Derek? Is Rosa all right?"

Tim's voice came from just beyond the door.

Derek straightened abruptly and pulled Rosa upright in one swift move. Bloody hell, what had he been thinking? Not with his brain, obviously. The door was still ajar. He didn't want his crew to think badly of Rosa or, considering their infatuation with her, despise him for seduction.

Almost as much as he suddenly despised himself.

"As you can see, she is fine," he said briskly as Tim came around the corner. "The mischievous baggage was helping herself to my wine. She was just leaving."

Rosa's cheeks glowed a soft pink. With a mumbled excuse, she slipped from the room.

Derek subdued the urge to reach out and pull her back.

DON GERALDO PACED the stone floor of his prison cell, kicking dirty straw out of his path. His thumb nervously rubbed the spoon concealed in his hand, though he was careful to avoid the sharp end where he had secretly filed the handle to a sharp point against the stone wall.

Hearing the rumble of voices, he paused, listening. Then he relaxed, realizing the guard was still several cells down the hallway of La Muerte. There was only one at the moment. The Cuban rebels had called the others away into battle.

The rebels had thought it funny when they took over La Muerte, using it to imprison him, the crew of the captured brigantine handed over by those boorish Yanks, and the handful of soldiers manning the fort.

He would soon show them who would have the last laugh.

Despite his captivity, he couldn't imagine the war going badly for the Spanish. These Cuban rebels were the type of men who worked his plantations and acted as servants in his hacienda, not descendants of nobles like himself.

Don Geraldo resented his dirty clothes and his inability to maintain his fastidious lifestyle. He resented the tasteless food. But most of all he hated the man responsible for his humiliating capture.

Graystone would pay dearly for delivering him into the hands of the enemy . . . but not before the don exacted a special price. The English explorer had dared to steal Gaspar's journal. So be it. Don Geraldo excelled at benefiting from other people's skills.

After his one failed attempt at locating the galleon, he knew roughly where Graystone was headed. He would seek him there, wait patiently while the Englishman struggled through the work of recovering the treasure, then steal the prize.

He'd spent many hours crafting detailed plans. Once free, he would liberate his men, fixing their loyalty, then offer them a handsome reward to accompany him. Another of his ships lay idle at Manzanillo, near his sugar and coffee plantations.

His ancestor had written the journal that was leading Graystone to the treasure. He considered the treasure of *Nuestra Señora de la Augustina* his alone. He needed it to restore his wealth and power in a country torn by war.

Boots shuffled in the hallway. Don Geraldo moved quickly to the door. The narrow rectangular opening low in his door opened. The guard leaned close to slide the meal tray through.

Don Geraldo lunged, thrusting one slender arm through the small barred window. He grabbed a fistful of the guard's hair. The tray crashed to the floor.

Yanking him close, the don pressed the sharp point of his crude weapon to the man's throat. A small drop of red welled against dark skin. The man swallowed hard.

"Open this door or I shall kill you," Don Geraldo snarled.

After a hesitation that cost the guard a deeper cut, he obeyed. The key rasped in the lock.

Three more grueling days of searching produced nothing beyond a biting sense of disappointment.

Derek retreated to the bow of the ship after moonrise, embracing a bottle of brandy with one arm and a serious bout of self-pity with the other. He chose the bow because it was well away from the lanterns at the stern. Dark and isolated, the lonely spot fit his mood.

He poured a glass of amber liquid and set the bottle aside. A generous swallow burned all the way to his stomach. Leaning his elbows against the rail, he expelled a pent-up sigh. He rocked the glass slowly in the cradle of his splayed fingers.

Glittering stars punched millions of tiny holes in the black velvet sky. The calm sea reflected the waning three-quarter moon. With discouragement knotting beneath his breastbone, Derek failed to appreciate the stark beauty of the scene.

The pain went beyond his failure to find the *Augustina*. A bigger void loomed in his immediate future.

He didn't want to face the prospect of returning to England without this achievement behind him. His career was peppered with successes, but nothing that would compare with the triumph of salvaging a sunken galleon laden with Chinese artifacts. He wanted that final proof of his skill to show his father, as well as his fellow archaeologists . . . proof that it would be a damn shame to trap him in England, away from the future discoveries he might make. Just think what he had to offer the world! Great collections to grace the British Museum. Unique and priceless artifacts.

His upper lip curled in derision.

As long as he was tormenting himself, he might as well be honest and not paint his motives as noble and self-sacrificing.

Truth be told, he reveled in the hunt and the freedom.

Going home meant facing the responsibilities attributed to the Aversham heir and allowing the social drudgeries to latch onto his back and bleed him dry. During his last visit, his father had lectured him on duty, hinting heavily that Derek should return home. To stay. Permanently.

A predictable life in England held little appeal, unlike the startling discovery of a priceless artifact. He thought back, trying to recall the thrill of holding the slender gold bar from the *Atocha* in his palm. Instead, his mind formed a picture of the gold flecks in Rosa's unfathomable green eyes.

Few challenges awaited him in London. Here he faced invigorating battles against mother nature or the challenge of surviving the volatile temper of a flesh-and-blood temptress.

On the other hand, the rolling green hills of the Aversham estate wouldn't try to engulf his ship or smash it against a reef. The shining examples of English womanhood he would be expected to court wouldn't dream of cracking a safe, or mocking him through a ventilation shaft, or tapping their fingers against their temples in a sarcastic lament for his sanity.

Scowling, Derek gulped the remaining brandy and poured another glass.

ROSA HESITATED AMIDSHIPS, certain that an intrusion on Derek's vigil would be met with more of his withering sarcasm. The only question was whether she would dare anyway. Only she knew the hurt it caused each time he pricked her with that cynical scorn . . . almost as painful as the sweet stab of desire when she stole a secret glance at his handsome face, or when she bit back a moan as he pressed his hard body against hers. If only he would regard her with tenderness in his eyes rather than anger.

But tonight, throughout dinner, the look in his eyes had been bleak. Her worry continued after he'd quietly slipped away from the galley.

Derek leaned against the bow railing now, his white

shirt gleaming in the moonlight. Everything about him bespoke strength, unapproachable dignity . . . and incredible loneliness.

Rosa moved silently toward him, drawn by this new sign of vulnerability. Moonlight burnished his hair to a polished brass. Stopping directly behind his left shoulder, she fought the urge to touch the long, sleek lines of his back.

Without turning around, he growled, "If you have come to renew old arguments, Rosa, I would not recommend it. In fact, my best advice for you is to go away."

A thread of weariness wove through his voice. That additional hint of vulnerability encouraged her to ignore his hostility. "Have I ever listened to your advice, *hombre*?"

A sound erupted from his chest that bore a faint resemblance to a laugh. "Just the opposite."

"Why should I change my habits now? I prefer to remain blissfully ignorant." Crossing her forearms, she leaned against the railing alongside him.

"Or willfully obstinate."

"It is a beautiful night, no?"

He responded with a noncommittal grunt.

She tried another tack. "Have all of your discoveries been in the ocean?"

After several heartbeats of silence, during which Rosa was tempted to jab his ribs with her elbow, Derek deigned to answer.

"Actually, no. I have excavated a Viking settlement in Scotland, Inca ruins in Peru, tribal artifacts in New Guinea, and Chinese treasures near Hong Kong. My only other foray into underwater salvage was an eighteenth-century Dutch merchantman sunk in the Philippines, but we used local pearl divers. Until the *Augustina,* I've never attempted an expedition of this magnitude." The brandy snifter swayed between his restless fingers. He stared into the swirling liquid. His sigh carried the weight of the world. "I'm beginning to doubt I will ever find her. She seems destined to elude and taunt me for the remainder of my days."

Rosa hid a smile. She had heard that same miserable, discouraged tone in her godfathers' voices on many occasions, anytime something they had hoped for didn't come to fruition. It seemed that no matter what age, men could manage to sound like forlorn little boys. In Derek the quality was particularly endearing—proof that even a man so unfailing in his strength, so proud, and so rigid in his determination, could waver now and then. It made him seem more human, more approachable.

"But what of the journal and the other documents?"

"Gaspar's journal led us to the *Atocha* by accident. My earlier estimate was based on his account of seeing the *Santa Margarita* sink to their west. But what if he was mistaken? What if it was the *Atocha* he saw going down? That places the *Augustina* farther east. I can think of no other logical explanation. This new site is based on that assumption." He snorted and rolled his glass between his palms. "All my hopes are based on a best guess."

Even at his most despondent, Rosa sensed an iron core within Derek that would not accept defeat. His skill gave her confidence. His integrity and raw masculinity always made her feel safe . . . even when the temper he tried to deny boiled over.

"I know you will find it. I have no doubts."

Then his mouth twisted cynically. "Why? Because failure means that you will be without your share of the treasure?"

"No, because you do not know the meaning of the word 'defeat,' Derek Carlisle," she said softly.

"That demonstrates how little you know about me," he said roughly. Raising his glass, he drained the last of the brandy.

A bone-deep longing throbbed in his voice, tugging at Rosa's heart. What could he possibly be ashamed of? "You endure difficulties with amazing courage. I have yet to see you back away from any goal you set for yourself."

"There are certain . . . tasks . . . I find it nearly impossible to complete."

"But you are so persistent."

His head turned halfway in her direction. The moonlight heightened the planes and hollows of his face. His rugged beauty caused the pulse to flutter in her throat.

"Is that how you choose to phrase it now? In the past you've accused me of being arrogant, headstrong, and *loco*."

"You see? Those are not traits of a weak-willed man." It became a challenge, seeing how many outrageous, albeit sincere, compliments it took to restore his characteristic confidence. "You are the only man my godfathers have not managed to send fleeing in panic."

He turned sideways to face her. Leaning one hip against the rail, he drawled, "Your godfathers terrify me."

A strip of bare chest showed through the open front of his shirt. Rosa swallowed hard. Her gaze dipped, following a tempting line of bronzed flesh to the waistband of his trousers, then beyond. "I must say, you do a good job of concealing the quaking in your knees."

His voice dropped an octave. "Believe me, the effort is taking every ounce of self-control I possess."

His deep voice triggered a shiver down her spine. Were they still talking about her godfathers?

"You achieve things most men only dream of."

"Right now I can think of only one thing I want."

Derek reached for her. Rosa succumbed to his husky tone and the sudden heat in his gaze. Slipping his hands around her waist, he pulled her into his arms. His kiss demanded surrender, yet seemed endearingly sweet as his lips explored her mouth.

Rosa rose on the balls of her feet. Twining her arms around his neck, she returned his kiss, pressing her body to his with the eagerness of a clinging vine. Hard muscles rippled beneath her hands and against her breasts.

She lifted her left leg, rubbing her knee up the side of his thigh. Her bare toes explored the ridge of his shin, his knee, then curved around to brush the inside of his thigh.

A primitive sound rumbled from his chest.

He caught her knee just as it reached his hip. The solid strength of his left arm at her back kept her steady.

His hand slid down her leg. With a deft twitch, he lifted the hem of her skirt. The night breeze brushed her ankle. The cool air startled her, but it was nothing compared to the exhilarating shock of his warm hand curling around her calf.

He continued to kiss her as his fingers forged a languid trail upward, grazing the back of her knee. His splayed hand traveled farther, lightly squeezing her thigh. The work-roughened pads of his long fingers brought her skin to exquisite, quivering life.

His bold fingers slid beneath her pantalets. Her breath sucked in as his hand cupped her bare buttock, and she released a tremulous sigh. Derek took advantage of her parted lips and plunged his tongue into her mouth.

As his tongue stroked hypnotically, his fingers rubbed lightly across the juncture between her left thigh and her bottom. He started in small circles that gradually grew wider, drawing ever closer to the place where her flesh throbbed in anticipation. Wild tingles raced through her skin like a shower of sparks. Straining toward something she didn't understand, Rosa threaded her fingers through his hair and met the stroke of his tongue thrust for thrust.

The anticipation was unbearable. Just as she was about to tilt her hips and intercept his teasing fingers, he touched her gently. Her body jerked with a shock of pleasure so intense that tears pricked her eyes.

He broke the kiss, his breath coming hard and fast.

"So much passion. So perfect," he said huskily.

Rosa cupped the back of his head and tried to draw him down for another kiss. He resisted. Resting his forehead against hers, he shook his head slowly.

"What the hell am I doing?" he whispered hoarsely, like a man in pain. His hand returned to her bottom, squeezing gently.

She whimpered because it wasn't close enough. No

matter how much she molded herself to him, a chasm persisted between them, echoing the emptiness piercing her with a sweet, insistent ache. "Derek, please."

Her plea vibrated between them in the stillness.

Derek's hand slid slowly from her leg. He smoothed her skirt down, coaxing her knee to lower at the same time. Both his hands closed around her waist, flexing. He buried his face in her neck and groaned.

"Must stop. If I don't . . ." His ragged whisper drifted away.

Was he commanding her, or himself? "Derek? What is wrong?"

"We must stop, Rosa." His nose nuzzled her ear.

His warm breath teased the inside of her ear, sinking an intoxicating tremor to the marrow of her bones. Stop now? Was he *loco*? "Kiss me again."

"No. We cannot do this." His cheek stroked against hers.

A day's growth of beard brushed against her skin. She sighed, loving the difference in textures between her softness and his rugged masculinity. "But I like it."

"You are making it much harder for me to behave."

"Then do not." She didn't want it to be easy. Easy meant he didn't care, that he wasn't caught up in the same throes of desire that gripped her.

He ignored her. His arms straightened, separating their bodies with a depressing rift.

"You've been entrusted into my care," he said roughly. "I should be protecting you, not trying to seduce you. I promised Esteban, Michael, and Dickie that I would behave myself."

The mention of her godfathers' names hit Rosa like a bucket of cold seawater. She blushed. Here she was, spared their excessive watchfulness, yet she felt guilty for her wanton behavior.

"I am sorry, Rosa." Derek's mouth crooked in that boyish half-smile that made her heart skip a beat. He slid splayed fingers into her hair. His palm cupped her ear; his thumb stroked her cheek with exquisite gentleness. Warmth fanned through Rosa's belly and threatened to melt her knees. "Thank you for those sweet words of encouragement."

He withdrew his hand. Cold seeped in where all that delicious warmth had been. She didn't want him to feel sorry or duty-bound. She wanted his caresses.

He turned and walked away, noble and utterly infuriating.

Then realization suddenly dawned.

He was showing her the respect due a lady . . . not a thief, a Gypsy, or an unwanted partner. Just as she'd longed for. A shiver of surprised pleasure trickled through Rosa, making her skin hum in places still alive and sensitized by his touch.

Her eyes narrowed in frustration.

The privilege was certainly a mixed blessing.

"You might be accustomed to the last word, Derek Carlisle, but not this time," she whispered into the night.

BLINKING RAPIDLY, DEREK tried to moisten aching eyes.

He had started the seven-hour day with such high hopes. Admittedly, Rosa's faith and encouragement played no small part in that. Her enthusiasm had revived his spirit, giving him the confidence to believe in his deductions.

Her sweet passion, on the other hand, had robbed him of sleep. He no longer needed fantasies to keep him awake. The remembered texture of her agile tongue, the taste of her hot passion in his mouth, and the imprint of her straining body had kept him hard and restless throughout the night. If only . . .

But he had to push her away, before he abandoned his principles and brought to fruition a threat he'd only made to her godfathers in jest. He'd been so lost to decency that he had almost laid her down and taken her there on the deck.

He fixed his wavering attention on the water. The ocean didn't yield her secrets easily. Tomorrow he would be back, and the next day, searching doggedly as long as the weather allowed. One sliver of this vastness could conceal the *Augustina*.

He was just about to signal for Geoff to winch in the balloon when he spotted a dark shape in the water.

Derek leaned forward, his exhaustion instantly forgotten. Although the edges were indistinct, the shape was fifty, perhaps even sixty feet long and darker than the surrounding coral.

He was so astonished he almost forgot to drop a buoy.

Stay calm.

It could be nothing at all. A particularly thick growth of eel grass, an exposure of bedrock, or a ballast pile from a wreck a hundred years out of date. Logic didn't warrant this excitement bubbling through his chest.

Pharaoh's Gold sailed on, pulling him beyond the shadow.

He signaled Nigel to turn the ship and track back over the same position. It took fifteen minutes of strained patience, but finally the schooner brushed past the buoy and offered Derek another eagle-eye's view.

From the opposite angle he spotted something new that set his heart to racing. Two stubby, straight lines lay at odd angles across the darker shadow beneath.

The unmistakable shape of cannon.

Chapter Seventeen

PHARAOH'S GOLD ROCKED idly in two-foot waves, her sails furled. The mysterious shadow lay off her port side.

Fully decked out in his dive suit, Tim clung to the hoist chain and disappeared over the side. Richard, Geoff, and Grady shouted encouragement. Enthusiasm had gripped the crew.

In a moment, Derek would join Tim below and discover the truth. Was this a find that would forever alter his life, or just another crushing disappointment? The dip of the late afternoon sun left them very little time to dive, but he refused to wait another day for his answer.

Cannon were one of the most definitive ways to identify a wreck. He'd memorized the forging marks of every piece of armament registered aboard the *Augustina*. This time he wouldn't need a return trip to the laboratory and the manifests. The minute he examined the cannon below water, he would know.

Despite his resolve to keep his mind on business, Derek's gaze wandered to Rosa. Her green skirt and blouse intensified the color of her eyes. The breeze tugged curling black tendrils free of her braid and set them dancing around her face. She followed the preparations with avid interest.

Then she headed his way, and the memory of everything he'd denied himself the other night resurfaced.

"Cannon are a sure sign of a sunken ship, no?" she asked.

"Typically. But it could be a wreck from a much later period, even one from this century. I do not want you to get your hopes up."

"Too late. I have faith in what you saw."

He almost groaned aloud. There was that sweet confidence again, the same trust that had seduced him out of a foul mood and nearly gotten him into a world of trouble.

"Why?" he said testily.

"Because I saw you smiling."

He looked at her, bemused. Did he smile so seldom?

Geoff arrived before Derek could think of a suitable retort. The navigator lowered the helmet over Derek's head.

Derek watched Rosa through the viewport. He couldn't tear his gaze away as Geoff secured the clamps. She was always beautiful, but when her eyes sparkled with excitement—

In fact, he watched her so intently that the hoist had lifted him halfway over the side before he realized he hadn't reacted to the stifling confines of the helmet. Of course, as soon as he noticed, the insidious symptoms of anxiety crept in.

He grimaced wryly. Was that the cure? Remaining in a perpetual state of arousal over a woman he was honor-bound to protect, and who was only with him for the sake of money?

Tim awaited him below. Out of the dancing light and darting schools of fish, the dark mass gradually took shape. The pile of ballast lay several stones deep, an intimidating barrier of several tons to whatever might lie beneath.

It was perfect.

Carefully, they picked their way across the rocks to the ghostly, sleeping shape of the first cannon. The massive weapon lay flat, its wooden supports long since eaten away by worms. Slender clumps of eel grass had found root in the sediment across its surface.

Derek walked around the cannon. A part of his mind shouted with excitement, while another dispassionately noted the length, the trunnions, the coat of arms that disappeared under encroaching sea growth.

Derek rubbed his gloved hand over the surface, brushing away sediment. The cannon was made of brass rather than iron. His anticipation escalated. The Spanish had reserved brass for only the finest ships.

Suddenly, the head of a small moray eel emerged from the muzzle of the cannon. It waved its gray-green head and opened its mouth in a show of territorial aggression. Derek smiled, amused by the eel's choice of home. He was not amused by the twin rows of sharp teeth, however, and kept his distance.

Moving to the base of the cannon, Derek hunkered down on his heels. He chipped away clinging bits of coral with his knife. Light from above played over the raised markings. A plaque written in Latin translated "Philip IV, King of Spain." Another plaque beside it bore the coat of arms of the Spanish Catholic church. Below that were a series of roman numerals.

Joy momentarily stole his breath.

He checked, and checked again, fearful that wishful thinking distorted his perception. After all this time, all the sacrifices, he feared to believe that the answer lay right at his fingertips. But there was no denying the evidence.

The numbers matched one of the cannon from the *Augustina.*

Derek twisted around, eager to share that priceless moment of discovery. The sight of Tim made him start in surprise. The disorientation lasted only a moment, though Derek realized it was Rosa's face he'd hoped to see through the other viewport, Rosa's vibrancy and curiosity that could truly appreciate this burgeoning sense of wonder.

Tim mouthed the word "Well?"

Derek tamped down the sense of disappointment and nodded.

Tim let out a whoop that vibrated through the water.

They sought out the second cannon he'd spotted from the air. He didn't want to place all his reliance on a single piece of evidence. He was a scientist. He must rely on facts and seek corroboration.

The second set of marks also matched a cannon recorded in the ship's documents.

Standing atop the ballast pile, Derek slowly turned, surveying the site. Areas of smooth white sand stretched between ragged outcroppings of coral. The arguments he'd used to discourage Don Geraldo came back to mock him. The treasure wasn't just lying about, waiting to be picked up. Other than a few broken shards of pottery, there was no sign of the cargo at all. The lighter goods would have drifted away long ago. The heavier items would have sunk into the sandy bottom, each inch adding to the difficulty of recovery.

So many challenges. He must remain sober and methodical about this. Yet, even his cautious nature couldn't spoil the first taste of victory. An immense feeling of satisfaction began to flow through him.

At long last, he'd found the resting place of *Nuestra Señora de la Augustina*.

ROSA WATCHED AS Derek followed Tim aboard. He had barely removed his helmet when the crew surrounded him. They laughed and offered hearty congratulations to their tenacious leader. The camaraderie of these men who'd shared so many adventures had never been more apparent.

Rosa stood aside, feeling the pain of being an outsider.

You are little more than a stowaway.

It was true, she thought, the other night notwithstanding. The memory of Derek's kisses, the sudden passion that had sparked between them, left her more uncertain than ever. He had kept his distance since, as if it had never happened.

How she longed to dive with him, to recover those precious bits of treasure from their centuries-old hiding places. If she could be down there helping, perhaps Derek would regard her as something more than a nuisance.

The crew pummeled Derek with questions, most of which he waved off with a smile. He stepped out of the diving suit, exposing his bare torso and sleek muscles.

Rosa couldn't tear her gaze away. If she'd thought him handsome before, the sight of his face lighted by humor and his teeth flashing white in the sunlight took her breath away.

Derek's gaze locked with hers. The excitement in his eyes held her in thrall.

Unexpectedly, Derek took a step toward her, picked her up and spun her around. The rhythm of his laughter vibrated pleasurably through her body.

Just as abruptly he set her down, his expression reflecting astonishment at his uncharacteristic spontaneity. She felt just as dazed. Who was this appealing stranger with the buoyant, boyish charm? Who was this man with the disheveled hair and a rakish glint in his eye?

In the same instant, they both remembered their audience.

Derek took a hasty step back. Rosa pressed her right hand to her ribs, where the oddest feeling like rising champagne bubbles tickled through her chest.

"You should be pleased, Rosa. We've located the *Augustina*."

"I knew you would find it," she said breathlessly.

Derek's gaze shifted to her lips. Was he remembering their searching kiss and the hot urgency of their embrace?

"Well, gents," Tim shouted, shattering the expectant silence between them. "We've made the discovery of the century. I think that calls for a celebration!"

GEOFF TAPPED A cask of ale. Red wine flowed from a dozen open bottles. By the time the sun set, Derek's crew was well on their way to getting roaring drunk.

Grady broke out his violin. The celebration quickly evolved into lively tunes and a constant round of dancing.

Rosa never lacked for a dance partner, Derek noticed irritably. He gripped his wine bottle until his knuckles whitened. Leaning against the starboard railing, he remained just outside the circle. He took a long swallow of the velvety Bordeaux and wondered at his tense, unreasonable mood.

He should be relaxed. He should be enthused with the promise of tomorrow. They faced difficulties in the salvage, true, even potential dangers, but he'd faced challenges with every archaeological discovery. Then Rosa tossed her head and the music of her laughter tied a knot in his chest.

Ask her to dance, an edgy voice whispered in his head.

She didn't need him. She seemed to be having a bloody fine time dancing and flirting with his men.

Emboldened by a belly full of ale, Wilson cut in, ousting Geoff from his much envied position as Rosa's partner. With one hand curled tightly across Rosa's lower back, the sailmaker spun them both in an energetic series of turns. Rosa tilted her head back as they twirled. Her loose hair streamed outward like a midnight curtain of silk.

Derek set the wine bottle on the railing with a resounding thump. It was a wonder the glass didn't shatter. Something other than common sense drove him toward the group.

"The captain is claiming his turn," he announced gruffly.

Wilson stopped, but his hand remained at Rosa's waist. Derek eyed that hand with mounting annoyance.

"Now?" the sailmaker asked, clearly dismayed.

"Now."

The music stopped. The atmosphere of merriment paused as everyone watched curiously. Rosa's brows arched.

Damn, this was a stupid idea. He was playing his cards too aggressively, acting out of character. But for some reason he didn't care. Feeling absurdly obstinate, he stood his ground.

"But we just started," Wilson complained.

"I'm taking advantage of my rank. Bugger off, Wilson." Tim chuckled and muttered, "About time."

Geoff hoisted his mug in a casual salute and grinned.

Derek's gaze narrowed. What were they hinting at?

The sailmaker stepped back, relinquishing his partner.

Grady started another tune. He drew the bow across the violin in three-quarter time. A waltz. Derek felt a flash of disappointment. He'd looked forward to partnering Rosa for one of Grady's lively jigs, something that would bring a flush of color to her cheeks and that radiant smile to her lips.

"Grady," Derek warned.

"Something befitting your age and social station, your lordship," the engineer teased cheerfully. "And I believe Miss Rosa could stand a wee moment to catch her breath, too."

Grady had trapped him neatly with that last comment. How was he supposed to argue without appearing insensitive?

As they danced, she flowed like rich cream in his arms, just as she had in Galveston. She followed as if she anticipated his every move. Dancing with her was everything he remembered, and so much more.

His arms ached to pull her hard against him. He found himself wishing his crew to perdition.

The song ended, none too soon if the deep, stirring reactions in his body were any indication. Another song started, but he forced himself to release her. He executed a stiff bow and returned to his spot at the rail.

Rosa concealed her disappointment and allowed Tim to draw her into the next dance. Despite the first mate's light banter, her attention insisted on wandering to Derek.

Richard came up and tapped Tim on the shoulder.

"No!" Tim growled. "You can't steal her away."

"Sorry, mate. My turn. I'm cutting in."

"I don't think so," Tim declared, his words slurred. He set Rosa gently aside. Grinning, he gave Richard a hearty push. The carpenter retaliated in kind. Their camaraderie deteriorated into playful shoving and taunts.

With each push, Tim drew closer to the two steps leading down to the center deck. Suddenly, Rosa realized that neither man was aware of the danger. Her cry of warning came too late.

Tim's right foot came down on the lip of the top step. His boot slid off at an awkward angle. Dulled by drink, he tried to regain his balance and succeeded in making things worse. His twisted foot landed on the lower step, the full force of his weight behind it.

His shout of pain echoed in the night. The music ground to a halt.

"What's the matter with you, Rutherford?" Grady grumbled. "Your caterwauling just ruined a perfectly good song."

"What is he whining about?" demanded Geoff.

Richard said, "He's just trying to get attention."

Appalled by their insensitivity, Rosa rushed to Tim's side. His face was contorted with pain. Was she the only one sober enough to recognize the seriousness of the injury?

She touched Tim's hand. "I'm here to help."

He forced a smile. "Guess I won't be dancing with you any more tonight, Miss Rosa."

Derek knelt down on one knee beside them. "How bad is it?"

"Not good. The boot must come off before his ankle swells. But if we pull it off, it could cause further injury."

Derek's right hand slid into his pocket and emerged with a switchblade. He flicked it open. He slid the blade beneath the edge of Tim's boot and began cutting through leather.

"Damn. This is my favorite pair of boots."

"With your bonus for recovery of the treasure, you'll commission a dozen new pairs from the best bootmaker in London," Derek countered.

Tim sucked in his breath as Derek turned the knife and cut across the arch of his foot.

The other crewmembers huddled around. As the situation began to penetrate their intoxicated minds, their expressions changed from curious to concerned.

Derek eased off the boot. The flesh down the outside of Tim's ankle and foot was already discolored. Tim made no secret of his agony as Rosa prodded the swollen joint gently, searching for signs of broken bones. He cursed. He complained.

Rosa looked heavenward for patience.

Before she found the chance to voice her conclusions, Tim howled, "It's broken, isn't it. Ballocks, I knew it."

"I do not believe it is broken," Rosa reassured. "I feel no bone jutting against the skin." She glanced at Derek. "But he did tear something badly. See how fast the ankle swells?"

"Tomorrow it will be as round and black as a rotting melon," Geoff offered.

"Thank you so much," Tim retorted sourly.

The navigator chuckled.

"Tim," Derek interrupted sternly, "you will soak that ankle in cold water until the swelling goes down. Then we'll splint it to make certain you do not injure it further."

What remained of the color in Tim's face drained away. "But that means . . . What about—"

Derek raised a hand, cutting him off. His expression seemed chiseled in stone. "We'll see how it looks tomorrow."

Tim whispered hoarsely, "I'm sorry, Derek."

The ramifications of Tim's injury settled over the crew like a gray cloud. The last signs of merriment dissipated. Tim wouldn't be able to salvage the *Augustina* with that ankle, at least not anytime soon. The underwater work would fall strictly on Derek's shoulders. The second dive suit, custom-fit for the short first mate, wouldn't fit anyone else.

Any member of the regular crew . . . all tall men . . . that is.

Rosa struggled to conceal a sudden surge of hope. She felt guilty about trying to benefit from Tim's injury, but he wasn't seriously hurt. Now, all she had to do was convince a profoundly stubborn, thickheaded archaeologist of the obvious.

Derek closed his eyes and massaged the bridge of his nose. Rosa's excitement dimmed.

At the moment of Derek's greatest triumph, yet another obstacle had erupted in his path. She felt the strangest urge to embrace him, to soothe away his discouragement by stroking her fingers through his hair, to take his troubles onto herself.

Rising to his feet, Derek stared out over the sea, his expression unreadable. "Richard . . . Grady, carry Tim below to his cabin. Geoff, fetch him a bucket and some seawater. The celebration, gentlemen, is over."

If possible, Tim's ankle looked worse when Derek checked on him the next morning.

"It will be back to rights in no time at all," the first mate declared, though his voice quavered.

Tim lay on the bottom bunk, propped up on his elbows. The offending limb lay on a pillow, still swollen to twice its normal size and colored in interesting shades of black and olive green. Derek winced in sympathy.

"You will not be walking on that foot for at least a week. Diving in heavy boots will take even longer. You know it as well as I."

Tim hit the wooden side of the bunk with his fist. "I didn't mean to be so clumsy. It was the celebration, you know. I wasn't paying attention. Too much excitement."

"Too much ale, my friend." *Not to mention the dangerous*

distraction of dancing with a beautiful woman who feels like heaven in your arms.

Tim grinned sheepishly. "That, too, or so my aching head reminds me this morning." His expression grew troubled. "What do you intend to do?"

"Manage the salvage alone, for now."

"The work will go much slower than planned."

"What choice do I have? Even if the second suit would fit your taller crewmates . . . no offense intended . . . the men have made it clear that they consider submersion for hours at a time insane and unnatural. If you and I want to risk our lives, that is our affair."

"If man was meant to stay below water, he would have been born with gills."

"Richard's words." Derek squeezed Tim's shoulder. "They do not know what they're missing, do they?"

"No, they surely don't," Tim agreed sullenly. "This is all my fault. I'm so sorry, Derek."

"Apologize again and I'll stuff that pillow in your mouth." He grinned. "The *Augustina* is not going anywhere. You will be back to work, and diving, soon enough."

Tim's mouth slanted wryly. "Be careful down there. I don't like it, not being there to watch your back."

Derek left the cabin and started up the stairs.

As if he didn't face enough obstacles, Rosa awaited him on deck. The light of battle sparkled in her eyes.

She didn't mince words.

"You need a diving partner, Derek, and I am the only one who can fit into Tim's suit."

"Do I, now?" Derek countered.

"The work will go much faster with two divers."

"I can manage."

Rosa threw up her hands in evident frustration. "Must you be so stubborn? It is not healthy, you know, this need to do everything yourself. You will tire and make mistakes."

"The answer is still no."

"And why not?"

"You do not understand the dangers of diving." It astonished him, this need to protect her from those dangers.

A wave of her hand dismissed his concerns. "Will Tim be using the suit today? Tomorrow? The next day?"

"The diving apparatus is too heavy for a woman to handle."

"Tim has told me that the buoyancy under the water makes the suit feel much lighter."

"Not so light that you can handle it easily."

"I am stronger than most women. You saw this when I climbed up pillars and crawled across Don Geraldo's roof. Years of dancing have strengthened my body."

As if he hadn't noticed. She was strong, lithe, and firm in the most damnable, amazing places. Other women in his life had been pampered, soft, pillowy. He'd thought he preferred that lushness. He hadn't realized how appealing petite and athletic could be until he'd pulled Rosa into his arms.

"Morning, Miss Rosa. Captain." The sailmaker greeted them both as he walked past.

"*Buenos dias,* Wilson," Rosa answered cheerfully.

A blush rose into Wilson's cheeks. He lowered his gaze. Derek's brows snapped together. Wilson hadn't seemed the least bit shy last night as he twirled Rosa around in the dance.

"There is no logical reason for me not to go," Rosa argued.

Derek blinked, tearing his suspicious gaze from Wilson's departing back. "Go where?" What had they been talking about?

A movement from the ship's wheel caught his eye. Nigel was waving. Rosa waved back. A muscle ticked in Derek's jaw. He'd always trusted his crew implicitly . . . but that was before they faced the temptation of a beautiful, desirable woman on board.

She tapped two fingers against her temple in that infuriating way she had of implying that he was *loco*. "Have you been listening, Graystone? We were talking about the diving."

The diving. Bloody hell. "As I said, Rosa, I do not—"

Richard walked up. He snatched his cap from his head and crushed it against his chest. "How are you on this fine morning, Miss Rosa? I hope you slept well . . . I mean, that you didn't spend too much time worrying about Mr. Rutherford."

Derek's gaze narrowed sharply. Richard typically didn't bother to put that many words together for weeks at a time. And what business did he have thinking of Rosa and sleeping in the same context? Did he wonder what she wore to bed? Whether she enjoyed the feel of the fine linen sheets against her skin?

"*Gracias,* Richard. How kind of you to ask. I am concerned about Mr. Rutherford, but I slept well."

Rosa's fingers lightly touched Richard's sleeve.

That hot, unpleasant sensation crawled through Derek's chest again. He scowled, but Richard had already turned away.

Rosa looked up at him, her expression as determined as ever. "So, you see the value in my diving with you?"

Value or not, he was certainly beginning to see the necessity. Tim and Grady were married, and he'd never witnessed a hint of them considering being unfaithful to their wives. But the rest of his men were not leg-shackled. And Rosa had managed to charm them until their common sense was in shambles.

Diving for hours at a time, he would have no way of knowing what was going on right over his head.

At least if Rosa worked alongside him, he would know where she was and what mischief she was up to at all times. She wouldn't be alone with any member of his crew. That privilege would be reserved for him.

"Fifteen minutes," he bit out. "Be back on deck. You are about to receive a lesson in diving and underwater salvage. I want to make sure you know exactly what you are doing."

Rosa's eyes lit with excitement. She lifted onto the balls of her feet. Derek sensed what was coming. He quickly held up both hands. It shocked him, this aversion to another sisterly kiss on the cheek. He didn't want a show of gratitude, dammit.

Rosa harrumphed at his show of reticence. She hurried away to get ready, muttering something about British snobbishness.

Derek closed his eyes and indulged in a long sigh.

The hunt for the *Augustina*'s cargo would provide the perfect distraction. In the strong likelihood that his thoughts drifted toward something other than salvage, what could be done when he and Rosa were separated by the bulky suits?

Chapter Eighteen

THE WATER PRESSED the dive suit against Rosa's legs
as the chain began its descent the next day. Her heart thundered with anticipation. Pumped air brushed the top of her
head and filled the helmet's metal dome with a constant
hiss. The chain swayed, rocking her with the ocean's gentle
rhythm.

She moved lower. The water slid up her body like a
long, slow embrace. She loved the sensation.

It was the perfect day for her first dive, with brilliant
sunshine and moderate swells. Derek and the treasure
waited below. Now, finally, she could truly share the adventure with him. Her intensity went beyond the need to contribute. Perhaps it was this strange fascination for the man,
this need to understand what drove him, to share in his obsession.

Touching down on the sand, she stepped out of the
sling.

Despite the bulky suit, a sense of freedom engulfed her.
A whole new world stretched out before her fascinated
gaze. Fish darted about everywhere, painting streaks of
color. Upthrust coral stretched toward the sunlight, creating bizarre formations. The scene was so peaceful she al-

most forgot the surge of the restless ocean above. It was breathtaking. And it was hers to explore.

In the next instant, Derek was beside her. He peered through his viewport into her own. His gloved fingers closed around her arm.

A shiver of sensual awareness rippled through Rosa. Was she so in tune to his touch that she felt the pleasurable shock of desire thirty feet below the surface?

"Are you all right?" He mouthed the words. Derek regarded her in acute concern, as if he expected her to panic or collapse at any moment. Lines bracketed his mouth.

She nodded. Of course she was all right. Why wouldn't she be?

With evident reluctance, he let her go. He turned and moved toward a flat expanse of rocks. She followed.

Derek had described the ballast pile and the condition of the *Augustina* during her lesson. She knew what to expect. Nevertheless, it saddened her to see all that remained of the once proud galleon. The fanciful illustration in *Twenty Thousand Leagues Under the Sea* had generated hopes of a ship's skeleton, complete with crumbling decks, needlelike masts, and tattered sails streaming in the current like pale, ghostly locks of hair.

Reality was a great deal less romantic. The wooden superstructure had vanished long ago, devoured by the sea life. The ocean had adopted the *Augustina* over the years, shifting and rearranging the vessel to suit its own patterns, burying any sign of the treasure. Oblivious to mankind's definition of wealth, the fish merely considered the wreck a shelter rife with nooks and crannies, as well as a source of food.

She was anxious to get started. Somewhere amid these remains were pieces of silver, gold, perhaps even precious gems. With luck, those bits could accumulate into exactly the small fortune she relied upon to secure her godfathers' futures.

Derek caught her attention. He tapped the top of his

helmet, using one of the hand signals they had worked out beforehand. He was reminding her to be mindful of her air hose. Derek had explained how not to allow the hose to become entangled, or worse, to get caught in the sharp coral.

She waved in response. Then he pointed around, indicating that she should take her choice of where to start work. There were numerous possibilities. He'd instructed her how to pick through the ballast stones, examine the coral for encrusted objects, or sift through a patch of sand. Derek turned and made his way to a nearby mass of coral.

Rosa chose an area of sand adjacent to the ballast pile.

Her hands trembled with eagerness. She checked the tools at her belt: a metal paddle, a knife, a mesh bag for collecting artifacts, and a pick hammer for chipping away coral.

Kneeling, she carefully began to dig a two-foot-long trench in the sand. Derek had cautioned her about restraint. Impatience could lead to damaged artifacts. She must remember that everything in this world was fragile.

After a few inches, the loose, shifting sand began to flow back into the hole as fast as she pulled it out. She unhooked the metal paddle and waved it in a steady motion. The water pressure worked amazingly well, forcing the granules aside in the same way the wind would blow sand on a dry beach. The sand swirled away like smoke in the current. The trick, Rosa decided, was to work with the laws of the underwater world and not against them.

Within a few minutes, her trench had enlarged to three feet long and a foot in depth. An object poked out from one side.

Rosa gasped.

She curtailed the almost irresistible urge to grab the item and pull it out. *Fan the sand away to expose it rather than tugging on the artifact itself,* Derek had instructed.

She bent lower, waving vigorously. The concealing sand swept aside, like a curtain opening to reveal the entertainers on a stage.

The item was a dark charcoal gray. A neutral observer would no doubt call it ugly. Rosa thought it beautiful.

Reverently, she lifted the spoon and laid it across her gloved palm. It was straight, unlike the one Derek had discovered from the *Atocha*.

The significance suddenly struck her. Years ago, someone aboard the *Augustina* had used this at mealtimes, perhaps even the day of that fateful hurricane.

She shoved to her feet. How silly to feel so excited over a spoon. It wasn't silver or gold. Nevertheless, it was her first discovery.

She turned, fairly bursting with the news. For some reason, her triumph wouldn't feel complete until she'd shared this with Derek.

TORN BETWEEN ENVY and admiration, Derek watched Rosa work.

She demonstrated ease and confidence in the suit . . . those same traits he longed to discover for himself. Every time he suited up, it took a concerted effort to get past the fear and lower that helmet over his head.

She knelt to fan vigorously at the sand. A rueful smile tugged at the corners of his mouth. Such fresh eagerness. She looked . . . well, rather adorable. Leaning closer to her task, Rosa bent over the hole. The suit pulled taut across her back.

Derek's gaze riveted on the delectable outline of her derriere beneath the canvas.

She certainly did things for that suit that Tim never had.

Suddenly, Rosa struggled to her feet. She held something aloft, her posture triumphant. She tapped the knife twice against the metal paddle, just as he'd instructed her to do if she uncovered something important. He clearly heard the pinging noise through the water. She was trying to gain his attention, not realizing that she already held exclusive rights to the concentration he should be dedicating to his work.

Apparently, his apprentice had made her first discovery.

Eagerness flashed through him like an electric current. It was almost as if he could feel her excitement. Which was, of course, nonsense. Her new experience must merely be stirring his own memories, reminding him of the jade scarab that had been his first find in Egypt.

Rosa walked toward him holding up her prize. He moved to meet her. When he recognized the shape in her hand, he couldn't resist a smile. All this excitement over a spoon . . . and this from a woman with the dream of Spanish gold sparkling in her eyes.

Just when he thought he understood her, she managed to surprise him yet again.

She waved the spoon proudly. Her enthusiasm charmed him.

He took the spoon from her hand and examined it with all the deep consideration due a more significant find. Forcing his expression to remain serious, he nodded his approval. Rosa smiled radiantly. His knuckles brushed her waist as he dropped the spoon inside her collection bag. A tremor ran through his hand and up his arm.

Bloody hell. Not here, not now. Desire wasn't supposed to plague him thirty feet below the surface with these thick, clumsy suits between them.

He must focus on the salvage every possible moment. Unless he did, the diving season would soon end and the ocean would retain its grip on the *Augustina*'s secrets.

FIVE HOURS LATER, Rosa impatiently shrugged out of her diving suit with Tim's help. She was keenly aware of Derek coming aboard behind her. Exhilarated, she grabbed up her full collection bag and sought a quiet corner of the deck, eager to examine her finds.

There was nothing of any particular value in the bag

. . . in other words, nothing she could keep for herself. She had agreed to take her share of the treasure only in silver and gold. She wanted to see the fruits of her labor before turning them over to Derek.

Squatting down on her heels, she carefully arranged the items. Besides her spoon, which she set aside gently, she'd recovered two clay smoking pipes, a coral-encrusted spike, and five brass buttons. Half a dozen small glass bottles fascinated her because they were so unexpected. A fistful of corroded white-and-black balls—no bigger than the end of her finger—had looked promising, but she could see now that they were fashioned of some metal other than silver. A cross-shaped clump of white coral had caught her fancy. The only clean item in the entire batch was a piece of blue-on-white china.

A flower vine was painted across one end of the china, apparently part of a design that had extended around the border of a plate. The pattern wasn't the least bit Spanish in origin.

Below water, Rosa had thought the piece pretty, perhaps significant. Now it seemed utterly worthless. Rosa wrinkled her nose in frustration.

With a flick of her wrist, she tossed it toward the ocean.

"What the—" Derek burst out.

He lunged, his left arm outstretched. His hip slammed into the rail. He snared the piece just before it sailed over the side. For an instant his balance looked so precarious she thought he would tip over and plunge into the water. He recovered with pantherlike agility.

His scowl was as fierce as any predator's snarl.

Rosa's stomach clenched. He was obviously not pleased. He held up her discard between his thumb and forefinger.

"I assume you thought this shard was not worth keeping."

She rose. "It is just a worthless piece of china."

"Bloody hell."

Crossing her arms tightly, she persisted. "Well, it is. See the design? It is most certainly not Spanish. It cannot be from the *Augustina.*"

"That is where you are wrong. This is Ming dynasty porcelain, considered some of the finest porcelain ever made."

He stepped to within inches of her, glowering. He could be so intimidating without even trying. It took all Rosa's willpower to stand her ground.

"A great deal of Spanish cargo came from their Pacific route and trade with China and the East. They would land in Acapulco, carry the goods across Mexico by mule or horse, then join up with the Plate Fleet on the Gulf side. The bulk of the *Augustina's* cargo was Chinese decorative arts." He waved the fragment. "This is primarily what I came for. Never, ever, throw anything away. Even the smallest fragments, when reassembled, can have historical significance."

An uneasy sensation curled in the pit of her stomach. "What do you mean by the 'bulk' of the cargo? You make it sound as if the *Augustina* carried less plate than other galleons."

"Significantly less." He hunkered down and scooped up her finds, then replaced them in her bag. "Her hold was full of porcelain, silks, spices, ivory, jade, and other fine arts."

"All of it?" she asked hoarsely. Where would that leave her dream of security for her godfathers? In shambles.

He stood. "No, of course not. Even then, she still carried more bullion than you could spend in a single lifetime."

His words offered reassurance. Nevertheless, she was hurt that he hadn't shared the whole truth with her.

"Why did you not tell me?"

He glanced around the ship. The silent crewmembers watched their argument with avid interest. "We shall continue this discussion in the laboratory," he growled.

"We most certainly shall." Snatching her bag from his hand, she stormed ahead of him down the stairs.

ROSA SET THE collection bag on the laboratory table with a clank that made Derek wince. He put his own bag of modest finds aside and prepared to weather the storm. Actually, he should have given her more information early on, but he'd been too caught up in resenting the imposition of a partnership.

When she turned to face him, hands on hips, he knew he was in for thirty-knot winds and slashing rain.

"Well?" she demanded.

"I did not lie to you, Rosa."

"You led me to expect a treasure laden with silver."

Feeling defensive, he countered, "You did not seem overly interested in details when you were dangling the journal off Don Geraldo's roof and conducting your sham negotiations."

"The honorable thing would have been to tell me anyway."

"I have spent countless hours of research and four summers searching for this galleon. If I'd been seeking a partner, I would have succumbed to Don Geraldo's gracious offer."

"But you did not, even when he nearly killed you."

"Must be that stubbornness you keep complaining about."

She moved closer, stopping just inches away. "So why accept me as a partner? I did not torture you."

If only she knew. Her womanly scent triggered an ache in his loins. The battle to keep his hands at his sides was in itself a slow, insidious, ironically blissful form of torture.

"No, you did not," he said roughly. "Not exactly."

"You could have ignored my threats and attempted to wrestle the journal from me that night, no?"

Derek swallowed a groan. He really shouldn't think of "wrestle" and Rosa in the same context. "Yes, I could have, or done without the journal altogether."

"But you agreed to take me on as partner. Why?"

In pure frustration, he blurted out, "I wish I knew!"

He expected her to be angry. Her lips curved into a mysterious feminine smile instead.

To cover a sudden sense of awkwardness, Derek said, "Show me what you found today."

She spread her finds on the table. He picked up one of the small, algae-stained bottles.

"I thought these odd," she admitted.

"Unique, not odd. Every galleon carried a physician. You have uncovered his pharmacy."

"What about these?" She pointed at the large pellets.

"Lead musket balls." He spotted the cross-shaped chunk of coral. Curious, he reached for it.

Rosa's hand slapped over it. He glanced up sharply. Why was she blushing?

"Ignore this," she murmured, clearly embarrassed. "I know it is just a rock, but I thought it pretty. Silly of me."

"You need to trust your instincts. Let me see." When she removed her hand, he held the coral up in the light streaming through the high windows. Something about the shape . . .

"Are you terribly attached to this?"

"No, I suppose not."

Opening a drawer beneath the table, he pulled out a small hammer. Bracing the rock against the marble table's surface, Derek tapped once against the coral's edge, then twice. On the third gentle blow, the coral split apart in fragments.

Rosa gasped in wonder. Pushing the limestone chunks aside, she lifted out a small gold crucifix. The smooth gold and inlaid enamel gleamed in the light.

He grinned. "Coral will form around anything. Bring up any piece that seems odd in shape."

She nodded, speechless with amazement.

Her enthusiasm pleased him, reminding him of the one thing he'd resolved to do since their dive ended.

He picked up her spoon. Suddenly feeling like a fumbling adolescent, he said gruffly, "Here. This is yours."

Her brows rose. She set the crucifix on the table. "But

you keep all the artifacts of historic value. We agreed that my share was to be only a fourth of the silver coins and gold bars."

"This is different." Heat climbed up his neck.

"It is only a worthless spoon," she said, but there was no denying the wistful expression in her eyes. "I . . . I could not take it. I would be going back on my word."

"You can take it, because I am offering it."

"Why?"

Couldn't she just accept the damn thing and put him out of his misery? Despite his nervousness, or perhaps because of it, the admission rushed from his lips. "Because it is your first find. That makes it special. You should keep it."

Her gaze softened in a liquid green warmth that left him feeling short of breath. "All right. *Gracias*, Derek."

He pressed the spoon into her hand. The contact with her skin sent a shock wave up his arm. The sudden hitch in her breath made him long to throw his principles to the wind.

Boots thundered outside the door.

Derek swore under his breath and jerked his hand away, unsure whether to be grateful or furious at the interruption.

The door burst open. Geoff gripped the handle, his brows drawn together in a sharp frown.

"Captain, you need to come see this."

DEREK LOWERED THE spyglass.

Muscles rippled up his clenched jaw.

"Has she dropped anchor yet?" Derek asked Geoff, who stood at his side. They both intently watched another ship that lay idle in the water, almost two miles to the south. She was a sleek vessel, slightly smaller than *Pharaoh's Gold*, with no evidence of a name painted on her gray bow.

"No. She only arrived ten minutes ago and took up that position."

"Did you signal her?"

"Five times. No response." Suspicion laced Geoff's tone, with good reason.

An anonymous ship whose crew refused to respond to international signal flags was a clear indication of pirates. Every salvage ran the risk of the scavengers of the sea. One couldn't anchor in a fixed position for any length of time without attracting attention from other vessels in the area.

"They haven't dropped sails," Geoff observed. "They're ready to move at the slightest notice."

Derek's mouth twisted in a feral grin. "Then let's give them good reason. We shall pay them a surprise visit and demand their intentions."

Turning, Derek shouted orders for the crew to raise the anchors. Geoff and the crew set the mainsail in record time. *Pharaoh's Gold* started in pursuit as his men scrambled to hoist additional canvas.

The other ship fled before the wind, taunting Derek by maintaining its distance. He watched them through the spyglass. Suddenly, he sensed a presence at his side.

Glancing down, he said sharply, "Rosa, you really should go below." He feared for her safety. The situation could erupt into gunfire.

"Another ship?" she asked. "Where did it come from?"

"That is what I would like to know. And stop ignoring me."

"I always ignore you when you are being unreasonable," she quipped. "You consider that ship a threat, no?"

"Pirates typically are."

Her brows shot up. "Pirates? But they are running away. Do we outgun them?"

"No. They have a bow gun and two stern chasers."

After a moment's hesitation, she said seriously, "What do you think they are doing here?"

"Watching us closely. Trying to ascertain our purpose in being here. Testing our strengths and weaknesses."

Turning to the helmsman, he bellowed, "Nigel, come about!"

"We are stopping? Do you not want to catch them?"

"They are only leading us on a merry chase, a waste of precious time. Besides, I suspect their plan is to keep an eye on us, wait, then take away anything valuable by force."

Rosa's hands gripped the rail. "We cannot let that happen to our wreck," she whispered fiercely.

"*Our* wreck?"

She raised her chin. "I am working the *Augustina,* too, and I am entitled to protect her."

Her determination took him aback. Could Rosa possibly care about the *Augustina* beyond its monetary value?

He called Geoff back to his side.

"Return to the site and drop anchor," Derek ordered. "I want an around-the-clock watch. Assign the men in shifts. Make sure they are well armed." If pirates attempted to board *Pharaoh's Gold,* Rosa would be in the greatest danger of all.

"Aye, sir," Geoff said crisply. He disappeared again to carry out the instructions.

Derek's gaze stole to Rosa's profile. Her wild beauty made him ache with forbidden desire. The core of vulnerability he occasionally glimpsed beneath her mulish determination made him want to protect her all the more. There were other things on this ship as precious as the treasure.

A fierce possessiveness swept through him. Darkly, Derek muttered to himself, "I will not give up what is mine."

Chapter Nineteen

DOES HE BELIEVE the pirates will be back?" Rosa asked Tim the next morning.

Tim held her helmet in his arms. He glanced toward Derek, who stood at the bow rail, spyglass raised to scan the empty ocean at all points of the compass.

"We all do, Miss Rosa. But at least they're gone for now."

She touched his wrist. He hesitated before lifting the helmet onto her suited shoulders. "How is your ankle?"

"Coming along slowly."

Rosa detected sadness in his voice, plus a hint of envy. He was upset to be missing out on the salvage. Feeling guilty that her gain had been his loss, she said, "*Gracias,* Tim."

"For what?"

"For letting me borrow your suit. I will only experience this diving for a short time, and I am enjoying it very much."

A reluctant grin tugged at his mouth. "I'm glad. Be sure to bring up something really special today."

She smiled brightly, relieved to have his support. "I will."

DEREK SLID THE spyglass closed. He watched Rosa walk toward the hoist, fully suited up. Her hips swayed in an exaggerated fashion to move the heavy boots along. He cocked his head, admiring the way she could appear so feminine even when she looked rather comical.

Tim came up beside him. "Do you think you'll have better luck today?"

"Whatever portion of the cargo sank below us, it has sifted down several feet. We're going to need something a lot more powerful than these paddles to push aside that sand."

"How about a very large paddle?"

Derek chuckled. "Something to act along the same principles of applied water pressure." He froze. The comment had triggered a daring new idea. "What about the fire hose?"

Tim's eyes widened. "Why not?"

They hurried over to the hose rolled into a coil on the aft side of the laboratory. Designed to deal with the nightmare of fire at sea, the three-inch-diameter hose could expel water at tremendous pressure. It operated on a modified bilge pump belowdecks that drew in seawater and shot it through the hose.

"Do you think it is long enough?" Derek asked.

"You designed it to reach every corner of the ship. Forty-five feet, maybe. Given the length lost going across the side and down to the waterline, you might be a little short."

"Ready the bilge pump and lower the hose. We are going to try a new technique in underwater salvage today."

HE UNDERESTIMATED THE power of the hose.

After joining Rosa on the bottom, he signaled Tim to turn it on. The hose swelled and bucked in his hands. The sudden water jet hit Rosa in the chest, knocking her flat on her backside. Derek staggered back three steps before he regained control.

Rosa struggled to her feet. Throat tight with concern, Derek turned the hose aside and looked inside her helmet.

She was laughing.

Then she reached for the hose. The minx's eagerness to try everything charmed him, but this time she needed a lesson in common sense. He handed it over with a sardonic smile.

Her lighter weight immediately fell victim to the water's power. The hose bucked like a wild thing, knocking her every which direction. She held on valiantly, he had to give her credit for that. When he thought she'd had enough, he jerked on his tether three times. The signal he'd worked out with Tim requested a reduction in pressure. The hose calmed down.

She handed the hose back with a haste that made laughter ring inside his helmet.

She pointed to a spot adjacent to the hole she'd dug yesterday. Derek shrugged. That location was as good as any. He directed the stream onto the sand by holding the hose's muzzle two feet from the ocean bed. White shell grit spiraled upward, quickly obscuring everything in a massive cloud.

Okay, maybe he needed a modification in technique. He raised the hose to waist level. The worst of the cloud started to drift away. The influx of fresh water from the surface cleared an area directly under the jet.

The results of his impulsive idea exceeded his expectations. Within seconds, the water jet dug a hole two feet deep. His heart rate jumped. The bottom was lined with pieces of eight! The silver coins tumbled in the stream, trying to dance out of reach as Rosa grabbed at them. For every few she stuffed in her bag, the retreating sands revealed more.

A variety of fish joined the revelry, darting into the hole to grab exposed worms and small crustaceans.

Derek and Rosa worked the hole until it was four feet deep. Gradually, the supply of loose coins dwindled. Exhausted by the rush of adrenaline and the effort to hold the hose still, Derek signaled Tim to shut it off. The swirling sands began to settle. Derek assisted Rosa from the hole.

He spotted the flash of white teeth in the shadowed cave of her helmet. The *Augustina* had yielded a tidy cache of silver on only their second day of salvage. He estimated almost a hundred pieces of eight stuffed in their collection bags.

He signaled that they should go up. He hated to spoil her fun, but they must return to the ship and discuss strategy and precautions. Although this new salvage technique simplified their work, it also created its own set of potential problems.

"WHAT DO YOU mean, take things slower? Are you *loco*?" Rosa exclaimed. She planted her palms flat against the laboratory table and shot him a look of incredulity.

"Interesting question," commented Geoff while trying, with limited success, to maintain a straight face.

"Are you, Captain?" Tim joked.

Derek let out a huff of exasperation. He had called this meeting in the laboratory to discuss his salvage ideas, not to withstand a ribbing from the two lead men of his crew. Tim and Geoff were evidently enjoying the way Rosa's volatile temper and impulsive speech were creating upheavals in his life. That teasing glint in their eyes was becoming damnably habitual.

"Archaeology involves more than bringing up treasure, Rosa. It involves recording facts, sketching details, and using every means at one's disposal to re-create history."

"Really? How can we do that?"

Derek blinked, thrown off his battle plan by her ready capitulation. Her curiosity and sense of adventure—both rare traits in women of his acquaintance—amazed him.

"First, we modify the pressure of the hose so it doesn't

blast smaller artifacts out of the hole. Then you will be able to handle the hose and we can take turns operating it." He turned to his first mate. "Tim, we are going to need the metal baskets to haul up the larger pieces."

"Like more silver bars?" Geoff interjected quickly.

"And gold?" Tim asked, his gaze bright.

Derek shot them a frown. Rosa's enthusiasm had infected his entire crew with treasure fever. "If we are very lucky. Put Nigel in charge of watching the lines and pulling up the baskets whenever we signal. You man the hose pump, Tim, so the pressure can be shut off any time we find something significant. Next, I intend to work the site in sections and keep track of where the artifacts are found. We will drive metal stakes and stretch twine to lay out a grid, just as we would for an archaeological site on land. Any questions?"

Three heads shook in unison.

"Then let's gather the supplies quickly and get to work. There are a few hours of daylight left."

Tim and Geoff hurried away to collect the twine and stakes.

"What can I do?" Rosa asked.

Stand there and look beautiful, he wanted to say. *Stay out of trouble.* "Find Nigel. Work out a series of signals for the wire baskets, then help him fill several barrels from the laboratory with seawater. He'll need them to store whatever we send up."

"We are going to keep Nigel very busy, no?"

ROSA WAITED TO don her helmet while Derek finished the last of the new preparations. Clearly impatient to be back in the water, she peered over the rail longingly. A moment later, she waved wildly. What was the minx up to now? Derek thought. Did she think he could stop work and check out every minor thing she spotted? But her enthusiasm drew him irresistibly. As he reached the rail, she pressed one finger to those soft lips.

Silently, he looked overboard. His brows rose. What appeared to be a large green and brown rock floated in the softly undulating ocean. Then the rock moved, lifting an ungainly head to stare back at them. Rosa gripped Derek's arm.

The sea turtle was huge, at least four feet in length and three across. Flippers as long as Derek's arms shifted below the surface in a graceful rhythm.

"Is he not magnificent?" she whispered.

Without warning, the turtle's flippers tilted. It plunged beneath the surface. Rosa made a throaty sound of disappointment. She leaned far over the rail to track her quarry.

Derek rolled his eyes, grasped her slender waist with both hands, and set her safely back on the deck.

"Did I scare him off?"

You scare me, but it is this attraction that has me worried. "I suspect he grew bored with us and went about his business. Perhaps we shall see him below."

"Let us hurry, then." She did just that.

Derek headed for his dive suit. Rosa's fresh fascination for everything made him realize that his focus had narrowed to only the end result. He wasn't allowing himself to experience the wonder, the joyous sense of discovery. Perhaps he could learn a thing or two from her.

Ten minutes later they were on the bottom. Derek unpacked the baskets as Nigel lowered them. The same wire mesh containers that would be used to draw up artifacts served to carry supplies down. Besides the items discussed during their meeting, each basket included a black wax pencil and a slate for recording details, plus two modified crossbows armed with short, spiked arrows for protection. The activity of the fish around the swirling sand could easily draw sharks.

Another basket carried the two oxygen rebreathers

he'd picked up in Galveston. He brushed one gloved hand over the waterproofed tarp wrapping. The devices were designed to recycle the wearer's exhaled air by drawing out carbon dioxide with caustic soda. Although he'd never tried one, their effectiveness had been proven in special trials in Europe.

He just couldn't get over this nagging fear of being trapped, of some crisis leaving him thirty feet down in a heavy suit with no way to get to the surface in time. Two emergency rebreathers for two divers. He was just being practical.

Feeling foolish nonetheless, Derek glanced at Rosa. She searched for a new spot to dig. While she was thus distracted, he shoved the two packages into crevices beneath the coral.

The turtle joined them. Like an armored denizen of the deep it swam overhead, graceful despite its bulk. Rosa reached up during one pass and brushed the underside of its shell.

Laying out the grid took the better part of two hours. Each strike of the hammer to drive a metal stake sent a strident ping through the water. Although tedious, the work proved worthwhile after the last string was stretched and an orderly grid lay over the site.

The turtle didn't seem to mind the cacophony. It cruised by periodically, as if perusing the progress of their work. But primarily the massive reptile devoted its attention to devouring large quantities of small fish.

As the sun reached its zenith, Derek signaled to start the hose. The new pressure was more manageable. He started on the grid adjacent to the earlier hole while Rosa watched avidly for any sign of artifacts. Fish darted through the sandy cloud again, fighting over the choice meals unearthed.

Although the dredge uncovered a variety of small artifacts, the results failed to engender much excitement. At three feet they uncovered a large quantity of lead shot and another clay pipe. Coral-encrusted tools and a conglomerate of nails emerged at a depth of four feet.

They had just reached five feet when an ominous shadow drifted past Derek's shoulder.

He looked up sharply, but the cloud of sand obscured his vision. He directed the hose upward. The sand began to settle.

Suddenly, a silver and blue shape, almost six feet in length, dove between them. Rosa jerked back in surprise. The monster grabbed a feeding fish and lunged away from the hole.

Derek swore when he recognized the intruder.

Barracuda.

In their own way, the slender fish were more dangerous than sharks. For now the barracuda appeared interested in the smaller species feasting on the bounty of worms, but Derek had seen too many divers badly injured by the bad-tempered, aggressive predator. He couldn't trust it around Rosa.

He helped Rosa out of the hole. Handing her the hose, he indicated she should point the water jet upward, away from the sand. The last thing he needed was murky water obscuring his vision. He hurried to where he'd left the crossbows. As he bent to retrieve a weapon, the barracuda brushed his back.

He straightened and whipped around. To his horror, the fish was swimming on a direct course for Rosa.

Derek jerked the crossbow to his shoulder, then froze. Rosa was directly in the arrow's path! She took two steps back, then turned the only weapon available on the fish. The water jet punched the barracuda directly in its protruding lower jaw. The fish changed course abruptly.

Derek took aim and ended its days as a predator.

The barracuda twitched in its death throes, then turned on its side and drifted toward the bottom. Grimly, Derek watched the metallic glint of blood drift into the current. Damn. The blood would draw sharks.

Grabbing the barracuda's tail, he pulled the carcass to what he hoped was a safe distance, about thirty feet away. A ghostly shape darted through the hazy blue distance. He retreated quickly. More bulletlike shapes appeared, drawing closer with each tentative pass. Just as he reached Rosa, five sharks dove in and began to tear the barracuda apart.

Tossing aside the empty crossbow, Derek pulled his knife. He stood side by side with Rosa, watching the gruesome law of nature at work. Rosa gripped the hose. It had proven a useful defense once. Perhaps it would again.

But the sharks seemed interested only in the free meal. The moment the last of the shredded fish was devoured, the master predators of the sea disappeared into the distance.

Peace settled over the scene once more. Derek remained wary. The turtle cruised by at a leisurely pace. It cocked its head and looked at them through one lazy brown eye.

It is easy for you to look unconcerned, my friend, since you are armored like a medieval knight.

The helmets would be impenetrable to shark attack, but the canvas suits provided insufficient protection. Worse, even a minor rip would damage the integrity of the suit and allow precious air to escape.

He'd been right all along. The ocean offered too many unpredictable dangers to guarantee Rosa's safety. He would take her back to *Pharaoh's Gold,* then return to work the site alone.

He pointed up.

Rosa rolled her eyes and shook her head.

Derek jabbed his finger upward with more vigor.

She tugged on his sleeve and pointed down.

Gold gleamed in the new hole.

Derek sighed, knowing he'd lost the battle. There would be no coaxing Rosa aboard now. He wasn't sure what impressed him more—her courage or her demonstration of the same single-minded dedication to the goal that he felt.

Grasping her hand, he took charge of the hose and helped her climb down. He swore not to get caught off guard again.

Rosa's descent disturbed the sides of the trench. Sand cascaded down, concealing the intriguing glint. She plunged her gloved hands into the fine grit, sifting. When her hands withdrew, a delicate chain dangled from her fingers. Another gold crucifix shone in the slanting sunlight, but this one was attached to an exquisite rosary of apricot-colored beads.

She handed it up to Derek, her face alight with pleasure. Derek laid the rosary across his palm. Beautifully preserved, it looked as if the artisan had crafted it just yesterday. The beads were fashioned of alternating orange coral and gold, both resilient and perfectly at home in the salty sea.

He dropped the artifact into Rosa's bag. She tapped the hose. He grinned. Impatient little minx. But if she kept bringing him this kind of luck, he was happy to oblige.

The next hour revealed what luck could really bring.

They found ten gold rings with rough-cut gems set in their surface, a dented metal jewelry box fashioned of pewter, slender gold chains, and more pieces of eight. The greater surprise was three dozen crosses fashioned of gold or pewter, and several more rosaries with delicate beads carved of ivory or coral.

Derek recalled references in the manifests to religious items from China, including vestments destined for cardinals and bishops. Now he held the evidence in his hand. How ironic that Spanish Catholics, perhaps even the Inquisitors themselves, had sought out the skilled craftsmanship of Chinese Buddhists in fashioning such items.

The light began to wane. The cruising images of sharks took shape in the purplish-blue haze, moving into shallower waters at dusk to hunt. It was definitely time to retreat.

As Rosa gathered the tools, Derek tracked down a different prize he'd spotted during the day. He searched the coral, watching for the telltale signs of orange antennae waving from the crevasses. Avoiding spiny pincers, he reached in and pulled out two of the creatures. He held one aloft in each hand.

Rosa gestured in surprise. "Lobsters?" she mouthed.

He nodded. No salted meat tonight. He collected several more, then sent them to the surface in the baskets.

IT WAS WILSON'S turn to cook that night. The sailmaker outdid himself with a dinner of lobster boiled in seawater and served with fresh lime juice, plus rice, sweet potatoes, and red beans. Dessert consisted of sugared almonds. Derek ate until he could hardly move. He watched in amusement as Rosa devoured nearly as much. The hard work had given her quite an appetite.

She fell asleep on the table with her head on her arms.

A strange tenderness welled in Derek's chest. He gazed at her, bemused, until a comment jarred him from his reverie.

"I'll carry her to her cabin," Richard offered.

Wilson argued, "Forget it. I thought of it first."

"Maybe I should pull rank," insisted Geoff.

Derek rose slowly to his feet, pressing his knuckles hard against the table. His glare silenced the lighthearted argument. "Don't you all have some work to do? Now?"

Geoff hooked an arm over the back of his chair and grinned. "But that will leave only you to carry Miss Rosa, Captain."

The men rose, chuckling. They drifted from the galley, sharing a few elbow jabs and playful shoves.

A belated blush heated Derek's cheeks. They had pulled him into that trap like a raw novice. All along, their intention had been to tease him into demanding the privilege.

What kind of crazy idea had they gotten in their misguided minds? There was nothing going on between him and Rosa. He would disabuse them of that notion first thing tomorrow.

For now, he lifted Rosa gently into his arms.

She stirred. Rich pools of emerald green blinked sleepily. She felt as warm and innocent as a puppy in his arms. But there was nothing innocent about the way his body stirred, reacting to the press of her breast and the sleek length of her legs.

"Are you not tired, Derek?" she asked softly.

Her breath feathered across his neck. Pleasure rippled down his spine. "I thought I was," he said huskily.

He started down the conspicuously deserted passageway. She wrapped her arms around his neck and snuggled closer. It was all he could do not to stumble.

"Where are we going?"

To bed. He couldn't force the suggestive words past the lump in his throat. "You need your sleep."

"*Sí,*" she said, agreeable for a change. "I want to find more treasure tomorrow. A great deal more."

He chuckled. She pressed one hand to his chest. The laugh stilled as a wave of desire punched through him.

"Do not stop. I like it when you laugh," she murmured. "The sound vibrates deep in your chest, like a cat's purr."

"Should I picture myself as an orange tabby?"

"Oh, no, nothing so tame. I meant a very large cat, like a sleek, powerful panther."

He didn't know what to say. Was she flattering him? He liked the comparison. Reaching her cabin, he clenched his jaw and set her down gently on the bed.

He braced his knuckles against the mattress on either side of her head. Her unfathomable gaze searched his face. Raising one hand, she traced her fingers down his whisker-roughened cheek. His breath caught, his whole body reacting to the feather-light touch.

Derek could feel himself falling toward the bed, into her arms. To hell with the consequences.

"You are such a gentleman, Graystone," she said sleepily.

His elbows locked.

Slowly, stiffly, he pushed back.

"Good night, Rosa. Sleep well," he said hoarsely.

He *was* a gentleman, dammit, whose sense of responsibility included shielding those entrusted into his care . . . even from himself. For the first time he regretted his upbringing.

THE NEXT MORNING, Rosa took her turn at the hose. She discovered that not every day of treasure salvage could promise a resounding success.

They uncovered a stack of cannonballs, so soft and porous after centuries below water that they were like black, pasty carbon. Derek seemed thrilled over an ancient navigator's protractor, but she couldn't quite share his enthusiasm. Most of the finds in two holes consisted of everyday items: a crushed coffeepot, pewter plates, a pair of brass candlesticks, more buttons and clay smoking pipes, an inkwell, and a mortar and pestle.

Then there were the olive-jar shards. Basket after basket went to the surface filled with pieces of pottery. Derek had explained how Spanish sailors once used the narrow-bottomed earthenware jars to carry everything from wine and foodstuffs for the journey, to saltpeter and mercury as cargo, and even the pickled bodies of dignitaries being returned to their native Spain for burial.

There seemed to be no end to them.

Derek passed up another handful. Rosa gritted her teeth, quite certain she never wanted to see another olive-jar shard for the rest of her life.

Just as she gripped them, something nudged her shoulder.

Her heart jumped. A blue-gray shape moved in her pe-

ripheral vision. *Shark!* was her first terrified thought. She
pivoted quickly.

And came face to face with a bottle-nosed dolphin.

The ceramic shards fumbled from her fingers. The
hose, which had spun with her, caught one shard in the water jet and sent it flipping toward the surface. The dolphin
lunged upward. To Rosa's amazement, he grabbed the
shard in his mouth and brought it back. He dropped it near
her feet.

Rosa's mouth gaped.

The dolphin accepted the situation with perfect equa-
nimity. He paused, watching her with mutual curiosity,
then slowly did a lengthwise roll, belly up, until he came
full circle. Upright again, he seemed to be waiting for her
response.

Eagerly, she turned to Derek. If he had missed this, she
was simply going to scream.

Derek looked up from his position inside the hole.
They shared a look of wonder, a special bond that sent
a frisson of pleasure into her belly. With a shrug that
indicated "Why not try again?," he handed her the retrieved shard.

Was the incident some strange coincidence? Would
the dolphin do it again? Rosa dropped the shard in the water jet.

The dolphin repeated the performance like a trained
athlete.

This was amazing! Before she could recover from the
surprise, an entire school of dolphins arrived.

At least forty mammals glided in to join the first. Most
of the sleek, nine-foot creatures Rosa recognized as adults,
but there were six smaller youngsters that imitated every
move their mothers made.

The dolphins circled. They took turns drifting in,
nose downward, then playfully flicked their tails to dart
away. Many gently brushed against Rosa's body, making

squeaking and clicking sounds that reverberated clearly inside her metal helmet. It was almost as if they were trying to communicate.

Derek climbed from the hole. The dolphins treated him to the same friendly attention. They didn't seem alarmed by the humans in bizarre costumes, merely curious. Throughout the get-acquainted session, individual dolphins broke off the examination at regular intervals to surface for air.

Work abandoned, Derek joined Rosa in playing with the dolphins for over an hour. Not all of them participated in the game, but those who did never seemed to tire of the fun. Derek found lightweight items of different sizes and shapes to add variety. A flat shell with a glossy, iridescent mother-of-pearl lining seemed to be a particular favorite. It flashed rainbow colors as it flipped end over end in the water stream.

One particularly bold youngster broke away from its mother and chased the adults pursuing the shard. He was easy to distinguish from the other babies, with his beautiful silver skin that deepened to blue-gray along his back, and a saddle of speckles around his dorsal fin. He imitated the adults, adding quick, agitated movements, almost like a human child wriggling with excitement. He evidently wanted to participate in the game. Mother kept spoiling his fun by nudging him away. He persisted, however, and she finally seemed to accept that he would come to no harm.

Finally, the dolphins turned their attention to food. They drifted away, two or three at a time, though they didn't go far. The reef provided a generous feeding ground of fish. Just as the last of the adults swam off, the impetuous youngster sneaked back. He approached Derek, cautious yet expectant.

As Rosa watched, enthralled, Derek held out the glossy shell. Inch by inch, the youngster drew closer. Derek didn't move. Such patience was unexpected from a man driven to work, who wrapped dignity around himself like a suit of armor.

Suddenly, the youngster's mother arrived. She seemed annoyed, like any worried mother would be. Caught in his mischief, the young dolphin instantly darted forward and grabbed the shell. He swam to join the others, the prize still clamped in his slender snout.

The youngster's courage, curiosity, and daring reminded Rosa of Derek. Had her mysterious partner been so impetuous and charming in his youth? She grinned. This dolphin deserved a name. She dubbed him Oro.

Spanish for gold.

Chapter Twenty

THE DOLPHINS OFFERED a greeting the next morning by putting on quite a show. They milled around *Pharaoh's Gold*, making their peculiar whooshing noise each time one surfaced and inhaled air. Several catapulted out of the water and turned somersaults. Their whirring whistles punctuated the quiet.

While she waited for the equipment to be readied, Rosa allowed herself to be entertained. She never tired of their antics. Several members of the crew, including Derek, paused in their work to view the more daring acrobatics. Nigel and Richard shouted approval when one dolphin performed a back flip.

Rosa smiled. She would soon have the extraordinary privilege of diving among the dolphins.

"There he is!" she called out excitedly when Oro surfaced alongside his mother. Rosa recognized his distinctive saddle pattern of speckles.

Derek came up behind her. "Who?"

"The baby who took the shell from you yesterday."

"Ah, yes, the pushy one." He tried to look only marginally interested, but she saw a smile tug at one corner of his mouth.

"You enjoyed playing with the dolphins. Admit it."

"It was somewhat amusing," he said noncommittally.

He'd willingly given up over an hour of work to play with them. Determined to hear him acknowledge that he'd enjoyed himself, Rosa said saucily, "You loved it."

He grunted. "Trust you to exaggerate the situation."

"I named him Oro."

"The little dolphin?"

"See! Immediately you know which one I mean." She countered his sardonic expression with a triumphant smile.

He folded his arms across his broad chest. "You named him Gold? Why does that not surprise me?"

"It fits. He is very precious."

Derek frowned. "We cannot afford to lose that kind of salvage time today."

"What if they want to play? I do not believe you will be able to resist their charm."

"Nonsense. I am not swayed by charm."

Certainly not by my own, Rosa thought with a twinge of regret. "No? Would you care to wager on that?"

"A wager?" His brows lowered. "I do not think—"

"Do you think it too risky to wager against a woman?" she interjected, resolved to provoke him into accepting her challenge. Somehow, she would coax him into revealing that a soft heart beat beneath that shell of dense muscle and even thicker cynicism.

"I think it inappropriate, if you must know."

"You must be very worried that I am right." A hint of smug victory should sway him. The only thing predictable about Derek Carlisle was his pride.

"Do not be ridiculous," he retorted with a snort. "Very well, what are the terms of this wager?"

"What do you want if you win?"

The expression in Derek's eyes altered dramatically. His blue gaze seethed with serious intent. In a low voice that sent a delicious shiver along her nerve endings, he said, "After we have retrieved your godfathers, including

Esteban and his guitar, I want you to dance flamenco. Not for a party or a group of slack-jawed idiots who want to ogle you . . . just me."

"That seems fair," she barely managed to respond.

"And you, Rosa? What would you demand if you win?"

Impetuously, she said, "I would settle for a kiss."

"A peck on the cheek?" he said dryly. "That seems to be your usual fare."

"No," she said breathlessly. "Not exactly."

His knuckles slid down her arm. He gathered up her hand, curling it inside the strength of his own. "One like this?" Warm, firm lips pressed the sensitive skin across the back.

Rosa melted inwardly. Many men had kissed her hand. Why should it feel any different with Derek? How could something so simple feel so alluring at the same time?

"For a wager, you are supposed to demand something I am unwilling to do, or a cherished possession I am reluctant to part with."

His husky tone triggered sensations that didn't belong in broad daylight, much less before the curious eyes of his crew.

Was Derek actually flirting with her? She had watched her mother play this game many times. Men liked a challenge, a mystery. This was not the moment to indulge her first urge to throw herself into his arms. It was the time to tease, to tempt, to invite pursuit. Could she do it?

Easing her hand loose, she took two steps back. "You may be right. Perhaps I should demand another forfeit. *When* you lose, fetch my godfathers from the island by week's end."

Derek grimaced.

His long-suffering expression resurrected her sense of mischief. "Then tell them you forgive them for their mistakes."

His eyes narrowed sharply, but she detected wry respect in their depths. "*If* I lose, I will go after them. Do not expect anything remotely resembling an apology."

A dolphin surfaced nearby. It bobbed its head, then emitted a cackling sound that resembled a boisterous laugh.

Startled, Rosa and Derek both jumped. Then they exchanged an amused look and laughed, melting the tension.

For now.

"It must be a female," Derek commented dryly. "I feel as if I am being scolded for being late."

"See? I am not the only one who is impatient."

He playfully tapped one knuckle against the bridge of her nose. "Shall we dive now? You have provided me the best possible motivation to win this wager, you know."

A thrill of excitement curled in Rosa's belly. He *was* flirting with her! Even if he wasn't aware of it.

Within twenty minutes, they were below and ready to start another hole. The dolphins cruised by, occasionally brushing against them. Although they watched avidly as Derek selected a spot next to the ballast pile, the dolphins didn't seem to encourage a repeat of yesterday's game.

Then Oro darted in ahead of his mother.

The youngster held the shell in his mouth. Surely he hadn't carried it all night? He must have hidden it somewhere, Rosa concluded, then retrieved it when the divers returned. Her respect for the intelligence of these animals grew.

Oro headed straight for Derek's back and nudged his shoulder with the shell. After a quick turn to check the source of the interruption, Derek ignored the youngster and focused on the work. He signaled Tim to start the hose.

Oro eased around to the side and bumped Derek's forearm. Derek turned away. Next, Oro imitated the adults' technique from yesterday and dropped the shell at Derek's feet.

Rosa held her breath. What would Derek do? How could he resist Oro's adorable persistence?

Derek straightened. His free hand rested on his hip in a

posture of disgust. Oro shot to the surface for air, then came back, literally wriggling with enthusiasm. After a moment of hesitation, Derek picked up the shell and raised the hose.

A thrill raced through Rosa. She knew it! He couldn't disappoint the youngster. A soft heart did lie hidden somewhere beneath that gruff dignity.

Derek sent the shell spiraling upward. Oro dove after it. When he returned, he dropped the shell at Derek's feet once more. Why not? The technique had coaxed the stubborn human into succumbing last time. Rosa chuckled.

Derek repeated the game ten times, then very subtly hid the shell under a ballast stone. At first Oro seemed upset, but he proved to have the attention span of any child when Derek turned the hose onto the sand.

Oro immediately discovered a new game. He darted in and tried to grab every shiny artifact that the stream uncovered.

Rosa laughed as Derek was forced to nudge the youngster aside again and again. She joined them, helping to retrieve loose coins and porcelain shards. Soon Oro settled down, adopting the role of inspector. Derek showed the dolphin the more interesting items. Oro examined them thoroughly.

When he wasn't nose-down in the midst of the action, the youngster swam close by, surfaced for air, or occasionally left to drink milk from his mother.

As Rosa witnessed the relationship grow between man and dolphin, a strange emotion swelled in her chest. Derek tried to act reluctant, even annoyed. Yet it was clear that Oro's charm and vivacity had gotten under his skin.

When Derek pulled off one glove and ran his fingertips down Oro's side, the sight of the tender gesture shot through Rosa like a lightning bolt. A lump caught in her throat.

Without warning, her heart acknowledged the cause.

She'd fallen in love with this arrogant, headstrong, thoroughly frustrating Englishman.

If she could have slapped one hand to her forehead, she would have. Of all the *loco* things to do! Derek had shown no sign of reciprocating such deep feelings. They were from different worlds, as well. She could never measure up to the sophisticated ladies of his acquaintance.

Yet, beneath his cynicism, he harbored a wealth of secret treasures . . . just like this wreck. His kisses rocked the ground beneath her feet. Even when his temper and high-handedness frustrated her to the screaming point, she felt more aware, more full of tingling life than at any other time. Only when she experienced *duende,* that rare time in flamenco when she became one with the dance, did she come close to feeling the passion that ignited within her at Derek's slightest touch.

She was hopelessly smitten.

THREE FEET DOWN, the swirling sands parted to reveal a gleaming length of gold chain.

Rosa was away, loading some fist-sized clumps of coins into a basket. Before Derek could squat down to examine the new find, Oro swam into the clear stream to nudge the chain with his snout. Derek chuckled fondly. The little fellow certainly was drawn to anything shiny.

As Derek coaxed the youngster aside, he admired Oro's sleek, athletic shape. Designed for speed, dolphins and porpoises had followed *Pharaoh's Gold* numerous times over the years. No matter how fast the schooner traveled, they always managed to keep just ahead, slicing through the water alongside the ship's bow. They raced and played as if the sea wasn't big enough to contain their enthusiasm.

Dolphins embraced life with vigor, that much was certain.

Cupping his hand between Oro's pectoral fins, Derek lifted him safely out of the way. Oro's tendency to be underfoot should annoy him. But when Oro was gone, his absence left a void.

Derek forced his attention to the chain. Each link, as big as the end of his thumb, was intricately worked in pure gold. His excitement grew. Nothing like this was listed in the *Augustina's* manifest. It must be smuggled goods.

Rosa returned. He pointed out the rarity. As the hose moved more sand, Rosa gathered up the chain until it overflowed her hands. She held up one end, demonstrating that it was as long as she was tall, and then some.

The opposite end disappeared into the ballast pile. They would have to move a section of the heavy stones to free it. He signaled for the hose to be shut down, then handed Rosa up.

One by one, Derek moved the section of egg-shaped rocks aside. The labor soon provided another reward. The removal of each stone revealed a tiny nest of hidden treasure—scattered pieces of eight, a gold coin, rings, buttons, and other small artifacts that had sifted down between the rocks.

Rosa gathered up items as fast as he exposed them. Still busy moving stones, Derek couldn't see half of what she dropped in their collection bags. Finally, they freed the end of the gold chain. Several of the soft links were crushed, but most were remarkably intact. Overall, the chain was almost nine feet in length. A remarkable find.

Oro caught his attention. The youngster swam about excitedly, pausing periodically to dip nose-first into the hole.

Derek glanced down.

On one side, where the sliding sand had cascaded away, jutted the exposed glow of green rock.

His breath caught in raw, gut-jarring hope.

Rosa watched over his shoulder. Reverently, he lifted the large piece free. It was the first of the Chinese decorative arts he most hoped to find. The piece was a rectangular table screen, nearly two feet long, carved from solid jade. The detailed scene of a phoenix battling a dragon was stunning.

The hole revealed nothing more that afternoon, but the one find was more than worth it.

They surfaced two hours later. After a dinner of baked potatoes, biscuits, green beans, and fish fried in olive oil, Derek and Rosa headed for the laboratory to clean and record the day's finds.

Rosa had bathed and dressed in a fresh white blouse and a black skirt. With her loose hair flowing freely down her back, she looked stunning. Her feminine scent teased his nostrils.

I would settle for a kiss.

Rosa had won the wager. Although she'd changed the terms, would she still welcome a kiss? She hadn't brought up the subject of the wager at all, however. He frowned.

Sitting on opposite sides of the large table, they settled into their new routine. Rosa cleaned the items while he sketched them and recorded each description and recovery location in his logbook.

Typically Derek found comfort in the work, but tonight his attention wavered. His gaze insisted on wandering to Rosa's mouth. A twitchy, restless feeling arose in his chest, expanding until he could no longer tolerate the silence.

"You won the wager," he blurted out.

She paused in cleaning sand from the jade screen with a soft-bristle brush. "You will go to my godfathers by the end of the week?"

"Certainly." When she lowered her head and returned to work, her conspicuous silence annoyed him for no apparent reason. "I did give my word," he said peevishly.

"I know." She didn't glance up.

Derek heard a rhythmic tapping sound, then realized his fingers were drumming on the table. He slapped his hand flat. "Does that fulfill our agreement to your satisfaction?"

"*Sí.*"

"There is nothing else that you want? Nothing more?"

She blinked up at him, her expression innocent. "Assuming you follow through on your promise, what more could I want?"

Between clenched teeth, he said, "You mentioned something earlier about a kiss?"

"But I released you from that obligation."

Derek found himself moving around the table. He could have sworn his brain hadn't given his legs any such command. Regardless, he quickly reached Rosa's side.

"Thanks to our success today, I am in an excellent mood. I could consider giving you that kiss anyway."

"How very generous of you," she said dryly.

His frustration peaked. He grasped her upper arm and pulled her from her chair and against his chest. Her lips parted in a startled expression. Like a hungry wolf, he took full advantage of his prey's surprise.

He claimed her mouth in a hungry, thorough kiss designed to show her what she was missing.

He instantly discovered that he was the one living in deprivation. She tasted like sweet nectar. He slipped his tongue inside her mouth and rediscovered a warm, fragrant paradise. He explored her nubby tongue and sleek teeth, reveling in the textures and the taste that were uniquely Rosa.

Her pert tongue began to duel with his. She melted in his arms as if this was what she'd wanted all along. Desire throbbed in his veins. He was going to burst out of his skin if he couldn't bury himself inside her.

He broke the kiss, allowing them both to come up for air.

Bloody hell, this was getting out of hand. Again. To reassert his sanity, Derek slid one hand into her hair and turned her face into his chest.

She snuggled against his body. She felt so right there, fitting against him perfectly. He rested his chin atop her head. The sense of peace that came with just holding her began to calm his racing heart.

A small pile of rough, dark green stones on the table caught his eye. His pulse leaped anew.

"Rosa, where did you find those green stones?"

"Among the ballast. Do not make fun of me, *por favor,*" she said defensively. "I happen to like pretty rocks."

He set her back a step. He picked up a stone the size of a sparrow egg. "That is all you think these are?" He chuckled. "Sweetheart, this is an uncut emerald."

Her eyes grew round.

He enjoyed her astonishment. Hell, he felt pretty dumbfounded himself. She'd collected a bounty in raw gemstones without even realizing it.

"Can you find more of these?"

"*Madre de Dios,* I certainly hope so," she exclaimed.

"Next time you will know what to look for."

She smiled brilliantly. He longed to pull her back into his arms and pick up where they left off. Wisdom whispered that the distraction had been a good thing. Another such scorching kiss and things would progress too far, very quickly.

THREE DAYS LATER, dawn broke on an oppressively hot, humid morning. The sea was flat, as slick as oil. They couldn't ask for better conditions for diving.

Rosa lifted her braid from her damp neck, cherishing the occasional puffs of air that cooled her skin. It would be a relief to go down into the cool depths and join the dolphins . . . especially Oro. The youngster never tired of examining the stunning variety of treasures that had emerged since discovering the jade screen.

They had uncovered four silver ingots like loaves of black bread, plus a wide variety of rings, bracelets, pendants, and earrings delicately fashioned by the finest Chinese jewelers. More astonishing was the discovery of a great clump of silver coins, still stuck together in the shape of the wooden chest that had once held them before rotting away. A particular favorite of Rosa's was a collection of exquisitely carved ivory hair combs. Vivid blue lapis lazuli figurines fit in the palm of her hand, including an ox, horse, monkey, snake, and rabbit. There were twelve in all. Derek said they represented symbols of Chinese birth years. Rosa didn't especially care, as long as they were only the beginning of the decorative carvings that seemed to bring him such pleasure.

Right now, however, their recent success did little to quiet the worry gnawing at her stomach.

Rosa didn't need Derek or his men to tell her what was wrong. She'd grown up on an island. A storm was brewing somewhere over the northern horizon, and it was heading their way. She had braved numerous squalls, including several hurricanes, but she'd never spent one tossed about in the midst of an angry sea. The evidence of how unforgiving nature could be lay thirty feet below.

Derek and his crew had been up since first light, securing the longboat aboard, battening down the passageways and hatches, and stringing ropes strategically across the deck to give the crew a secure hold in heavy seas. The men's shirts clung wetly to their backs as they labored. Derek was no exception, for he had worked longer and harder than any of them.

His white shirt was plastered to his back and dipped into the streamlined indentation of his spine. Muscles flexed and shifted as he pulled a rope taut. With an impatient sound, he reached behind his neck and pulled the shirt off over his head.

Rosa's mouth went dry. He was so beautiful, from sun-kissed blond hair, to the streamlined contours of his back, down to snug trousers that worshiped every inch of those lean hips.

She pressed a hand to her belly, where something shivered and knotted deep inside. Every flex of Derek's muscles, every unconsciously powerful move, left her feeling more and more light-headed with desire.

Derek finished his work. They planned one more short dive this morning. She struggled to control her expression as he approached, afraid the raw wanting would be revealed.

"We are in for a blow, I'm afraid," he said.

"I know. There is not a single bird in the sky."

Rosa looked away, unable to bear the bittersweet beauty of a man whom she would never be able to claim as her own. Cold reality whispered that a wealthy English viscount could never harbor serious feelings for a Gypsy thief.

He pulled the dive suit up his bare torso. "Actually, we may be better off down there. Even after chop forms on the surface, it should be calm on the bottom. Geoff will signal and bring us up the moment it starts to get too rough. The hoist is still safe in seas up to five feet."

"*Sí*, but we must get away from the reef."

"Do not worry. Although I value the *Augustina*, I have no wish to end up like her. We will move the ship to deeper water to ride out the storm." His troubled gaze cast out over the unnatural calm of the surface. "My greater concern is that the storm will shift the sands and cover the wreck again, changing the underwater landscape. That is why my first priority this morning is to plant four marker buoys. Tim has shortened the chains so the floats will stay below the surface. I do not intend to make it easy for those pirates to locate the wreck in our absence."

His worried expression tore at her heart. His dream was in jeopardy once again. After all the work they had put into uncovering the artifacts, to have the fickle sea roar in and nullify their efforts would be a disaster. Time was running out. They didn't have the luxury of starting over again.

"Then let us go down and bring up as much as we can," she said with conviction.

Derek paused in fastening his suit. He brushed some damp tendrils of hair behind her ear, his gaze suddenly intense. "You are a wonder. Most women would be cowering in their cabins about now, demanding to be taken immediately to the nearest port and housed in a luxurious hotel to ride out the storm."

Rosa's scalp tingled from the brush of his fingers. Her heart rate jumped.

His arm lowered slowly. "Come on. We have to make every moment count before that storm hits."

ROSA RETRIEVED ANOTHER piece of blue and white porcelain and deposited it in her bag. All in all, it hadn't been a bad morning. Two dozen pieces of porcelain weighed down her bag. A conglomerate of silver coins as large as her head waited in the basket to be hauled up. She wished she could find whole articles of porcelain, or more of the sculptures Derek coveted . . . something special to lift his spirits. An eerie sensation suddenly crawled across her skin.

She swung around. The dolphins. They were gone!

After the mammals' constant company for the past few days, their abrupt absence felt like an empty, echoing hallway in a cavernous house.

Seeking out Derek, she tugged on his sleeve. She immediately gained his full attention. Sign language didn't seem adequate to convey her worry, but it was all she had. Pointing, she pivoted her arm a hundred and eighty degrees through the water.

He paused, looking. She couldn't see his expression in the dim light, but his seriousness seemed to match her own.

He nodded, then pointed toward the surface. Rosa released a long breath in relief. They were going up, but to what?

A LINE OF slate-gray clouds arched away from the north horizon, eerily resembling a crashing line of surf. A yellowish haze engulfed the sun. Deep swells rocked the schooner, though there wasn't any obvious source of wind to push them.

Tim hobbled up. "It just started building," he reported grimly. "We were about to bring you up when you signaled. What warned you?"

"The dolphins disappeared," Rosa offered.

Tim's brows rose.

Derek shrugged. "Their instincts are better than ours. I suspect they've headed for deep water until the storm passes."

A sudden gust of wind picked up a thick lock of Rosa's hair and whipped it across her face.

"Here it comes," Tim said. He moved away, shouting for the crew to haul in the anchors.

Wilson and Richard hurried to secure the storm sail. Set low on the foremast, it would serve to keep the ship running before the wind, preventing *Pharaoh's Gold* from turning sideways where it could be overturned by a big wave.

Rosa felt the deck vibrate beneath her bare feet. Grady had started the engine. The propeller would give the schooner additional maneuverability. If anything deserved her confidence, it was this sturdy ship and her experienced crew.

Derek hustled Rosa to the steps leading belowdecks. The pewter-colored seas were already kicking up.

"Go below. Stay in your cabin."

"What if I can help? You will need all hands."

"Both of my hands, actually. I don't need one dealing with the ship and the other grabbing you as some freak wave tries to wash you overboard," he growled.

She wrinkled her nose at his sarcasm. "But I do not want to be alone down there, wondering what is happening." *Wondering if you are in danger.* "I dislike feeling helpless."

"I understand, believe me. But I cannot manage dealing with the storm and worrying about your safety at the same time, Rosa. Promise me you will stay below."

She sighed, defeated by the sincerity and intensity in his gaze. "Very well."

After a quick glance around, he claimed her lips in a quick, hard kiss that left her hungering for much more.

Then he was gone.

WITH A HISSING rush, the wall of rain approached. Wind-driven drops pelted the ocean's surface, hammering so hard it appeared to smoke.

Rosa stood on the laboratory table, watching through the windows as the storm front advanced. The black clouds curled over the isolated ship. The wind began to howl. There was just time for the crew to get away from the reef before the storm was on them like all the furies at once.

The torrential downpour sheeted down the windows, cutting off Rosa's visibility. With an oath, she abandoned her post in the laboratory and hurried back to the main passageway. She could honor her promise to Derek to stay below, yet still keep a watchful eye on him. She climbed halfway up the steps, where the overhang still sheltered her from direct rain. A mist of salty spray swirled into the opening, stinging her eyes. She gripped the handrail against the roll of the ship.

The world grew ominously dark. Lightning flashed in all directions, staccato bursts that illuminated the violent scene for an instant. She watched, sick with worry, as Derek shouted orders and his crew battled the elements. But their experience showed. They worked efficiently, clinging to the ropes and maneuvering across the slick deck like monkeys.

Pharaoh's Gold rode well despite six- to eight-foot seas. Nevertheless, the schooner was taking a beating from the winds. Rigging tore free of the main and mizzen masts. A spar broke loose, plummeting to the deck with a crash that caused Rosa to squeeze her eyes shut and pray.

Unexpectedly, Rosa picked up a distant sound, a constant rumbling like a massive waterfall. It was nearly impossible to distinguish from the other sounds of the storm. She'd heard that sound once before as a child, however, and she would never forget it.

Fear sent a chill straight to her bones.

Rosa struggled to the deck, bracing herself against the howling wind. She cupped one hand over her eyes to shield them from the stinging rain.

Then she saw it.

An enormous waterspout bore down on the ship from less than a mile away.

Chapter Twenty-one

ROSA'S GAZE DESPERATELY sought the men. They continued their struggle, oblivious to the new danger above the other clamoring threats of the storm. Clinging to the ropes, she worked her way against wind and treacherous footing to Derek's side.

"What are you doing here?" he shouted. "Get below."

She gripped his dripping chin between her fingers and turned his head to face the oncoming tempest.

"Bloody hell!" he exploded. Grabbing her by the back of the neck, he pushed her down until she lay flat, snug against the port side of laboratory. "Stay here until I get back!"

Then he was gone, fighting his way to the wheelhouse. If they didn't change course immediately, the funnel would splinter *Pharaoh's Gold* into pieces no bigger than kindling.

The schooner gradually turned, angling away from the waterspout's course. Rosa held her breath as the massive funnel drew closer. They were in a race for their lives.

The funnel's narrow tail raked across the ocean's surface. The edges sucked up huge amounts of seawater. Although ocean-blue near its base, the funnel deepened in color to black as it rose into the thick clouds overhead.

The roar amplified as the monster advanced, louder than anything she'd heard in her entire life. The pressure increased until her ears ached and she had trouble breathing.

A scream built in Rosa's chest.

Derek suddenly appeared out of the rain and swirling winds. Dropping to the deck beside her, he covered her body with his own. Sparing her his full weight, he rested his left hip on the deck and hooked his right leg over her thighs. Rosa felt safe despite the threat of violent death bearing down on them.

Some kind of debris rained down, pelting them. Derek took the brunt of it. Rosa tried to lift her head, but his large hand cupped the back of her head protectively. His cheek pressed against hers.

The ship shuddered.

Without warning, the laboratory windows shattered right above Derek's back. The clinking sounds of falling glass added to the cacophony. Rosa's body jerked in shock. She was terrified that the needlelike shards had struck Derek.

"Do not move!" he growled in her ear.

She forced herself to relax. He must not be mortally wounded if he could still manage to sound so irritated with her.

Although terrifyingly close, the waterspout passed by. The roaring faded into the distance. The rain lessened.

Derek pulled her up with dizzying swiftness. He shook the glass from his clothes. She did the same. Immediately, they began examining each other for injuries. His large hands skimmed down her arms all the way to her tingling fingertips.

Rosa grabbed Derek's shoulders and insisted he turn. She ran her hands over his back, picking away the last few splinters of glass. Her breath caught on a flutter of yearning. How she wanted to linger, to explore every muscular ridge and valley. But not when he could be hurt. She quickly finished her exam down his hips and legs, which held their own dangerous appeal.

A remote corner of her mind was amazed that he stood perfectly still, rigid actually, tolerating her ministrations with uncharacteristic patience. No signs of blood.

"You are all right, thank God," she whispered.

Derek turned back. Without warning, he cupped her face in his hands. His thumbs brushed the dripping rain from her cheeks . . . or were tears of longing and relief mixed in, as well?

"Don't ever risk yourself like that again," he growled. He let her go.

They looked around at the source of the showering debris.

Hundreds of fragments of coral and a dozen dead fish littered the deck, attesting to the waterspout's destructive power. Then came the biggest surprise of all.

Three of the four marker buoys that Derek had planted on the *Augustina* that morning lay on the deck. Their chains were wrapped as tightly as a child's braid.

Derek's mouth compressed into a hard line.

"Does this mean—" she began, dreading the answer.

"Yes. The waterspout passed directly over our site."

AFTER AN ADDITIONAL hour of buffeting, the wind calmed.

Rosa dared to venture back on deck.

The sun formed a brilliant orange ball as it settled low in the sky. As she looked out to sea, no evidence remained that a storm had occurred at all. The water was as smooth as silk.

Pharaoh's Gold was a different story. Waterlogged ropes hung limply. Torn rigging and broken glass littered the deck. Rosa shuddered. The beautiful ship had taken a beating.

So had the captain and crew. Dark shadows smudged the areas below Derek's red, irritated eyes. A white, glittering film of drying salt covered his hair and clothes.

A whistle came up the call pipe in the wheelhouse. Derek stepped inside and lifted the flap. Rosa drew near.

"Tell me good news, Grady," he said wearily. He looked up, his gaze meeting hers over a splintered window.

"I wish I could, Captain. We're taking on water."

"IT'S NOT TOO bad," Grady reported after they all gathered on deck. "No holes, just a couple of split seams. The bilge pumps are keeping up with the influx of water."

Derek nodded grimly. He wasn't too worried, actually. Wilson and Nigel had repaired and raised some canvas. The untouched engine pushed them along at a tidy thirteen knots. They should reach their destination in under ten hours. *Pharaoh's Gold* needed significant repairs, but the important thing was that no one had been hurt.

"Keep her on course, Geoff."

The men scattered to continue the cleanup.

Broken glass crunched beneath Rosa's boots as she approached. Despite the salt clinging to her eyebrows and her damp hair, she looked utterly beautiful.

"Where have you been?" he asked.

"In the laboratory, checking on things."

Derek grimaced. "How bad is it?"

"Some water sloshed from the barrels, but they stayed securely upright in the racks. The journals and other papers stayed dry inside their cabinets. But the map you were using to mark the finds is destroyed. I am so sorry."

"I can reproduce it from the log."

"I was hoping you could." She hesitated, then looked at him imploringly. "Derek. I am worried about my godfathers. The storm may have hit their island, as well. I know you promised to rescue them by week's end, but can we—"

"Haven't you noticed we are heading east?"

She glanced around in surprise.

"I thought this as good a time as any to fulfill my part of our wager . . . the official part, that is," he teased.

She blushed. "What about the *Augustina*? Are you not worried about her?"

In fact, it nearly made him ill to think of how much damage the waterspout might have inflicted on the salvage site.

Feeling weary to his bones, he responded, "We must deal with the damage to *Pharaoh's Gold* first. She is our source of life out here. Your godfathers' island is as good a place as any to make repairs. Then we will head back to the *Augustina*."

And hope she hasn't been buried under a mountain of sand, he added inwardly.

"THIS DOES NOT look familiar." Rosa examined the approaching shoreline with a crease between her brows.

"There is no reason it should," Derek said warily. How was he to stop her from barging into her godfathers' camp? He was curious to see what progress the old men had made in rediscovering their self-reliance. "This is the same island, Rosa. We are merely anchoring on the opposite side. When the tide goes out, the men can start repairs on the damaged hull. We carry sufficient glass to replace the windows, too."

"Then we shall walk across." She started for the rail where Richard and Wilson were lowering the longboat.

Derek grabbed her forearm as she passed. "That is a somewhat bolder approach than I had in mind."

Her brow knit. "What do you mean?"

Heat crept up his neck. "I plan to . . . er, sneak up on them. We both need to remain silent and not reveal our presence."

"Why?"

"I believe you will understand when we get there and you can see for yourself." *At least, I hope so.* "Trust me."

Derek released her arm. He raked one hand through his hair and watched her uncertainly. Considering the constant upheavals in their relationship, why should he expect her cooperation?

Rosa cocked her head and studied his face. He fidgeted. "All right," she said softly.

DEREK AND ROSA crawled on their bellies to the top of the rise overlooking the south beach.

He believed Esteban, Michael, and Dickie had sufficient skills to muddle through the challenge he'd given them. On the other hand, if they were still wallowing around in self-pity and wasting their talents, then . . . well, it was a given that Rosa would never trust him again.

They looked down on the beach scene.

A slow, satisfied smile spread across Derek's face.

A shelter big enough for three had been erected beneath a protective stand of palms. The crates had been unpacked and the contents arranged. The *Lucky Lady* was still beached, but she had been cleaned and painted. Michael and Dickie were busy at work, repairing the hole in the sloop's bow.

The old men had adopted the roles of castaways with gusto. Esteban sat by a fire in the shade of a massive palm, his feet bare and a red cloth tied across his forehead. Michael sported trousers cut off at the knee and a hat woven of dried grasses. Dickie strutted about shirtless, the wiry white hair on his chest forming a vivid contrast to his sun-browned skin.

They looked like masters of their domain, however comical.

Their progress impressed Derek. It was certainly more than he'd expected. The camp was neat and tidy; the shelter appeared sturdy. The hole in the *Lucky Lady* was almost patched. Now all the trio needed was tar to seal the new wood, lead sheeting to cover the repairs, and canvas to rig some sails. The necessary supplies had been provided in the crates.

"They built a shelter," Rosa said incredulously, as if they had duplicated Notre Dame Cathedral.

He cast her a sideways glance. "Organized the camp, too."

Her hands clenched around clumps of grass. "They have lost a little weight, but they actually look . . . better."

"Their hunting must be proving successful. Esteban is plucking a pair of ducks right now."

"They seem to be getting along with each other," she said, amazed.

Just then, Michael said something to Dickie. One could assume the comment involved criticism, for Dickie gave the Irishman a shove. The two old rivals threatened each other with their hammers. Esteban tossed hot coffee from his cup at them. Michael and Dickie broke apart to dodge the steaming brown liquid. It fell harmlessly between them, staining the sand.

Derek closed his eyes and sighed. This was not exactly the display he wanted Rosa to witness. "Getting along in their own unique way, I suppose."

"Oh, that is nothing," she said dismissively.

Relieved, Derek opened his eyes.

She craned her neck. "They look different somehow."

He wasn't sure of her meaning. "They have adopted a rather rakish castaway fashion in clothing."

"That is not what I meant. They look more . . . fit. Younger. They have an energy I haven't seen in years."

He tensed, hoping she would see the benefits of a little sun and hard work. He'd always been proud of his own father who, nearing sixty-five, retained much of his youth through an active outdoor lifestyle. Although retired now from the pursuit of archaeology, the Earl of Aversham rode out daily in the management of his estates.

After a moment of silence, Rosa whispered, "They are proud of their accomplishments, no?"

Rolling on his side, Derek propped his head on his left hand. His gaze traced the exquisite lines of her profile. "They have a purpose, a goal. Little is left but to grow old when you do not have a goal."

"A mutual goal." She gave a ragged chuckle. "I cannot believe they are actually working together."

"And doing a bloody fine job of it, actually."

Sadly, she admitted, "They have not used these skills in recent years because I have done everything for them."

He tucked a stray lock of hair behind her ear. "They encourage you to care for them. You do so out of love."

She turned her head to meet his gaze. "You knew this would happen."

"I had my suspicions."

"How?"

His mouth slanted ironically. "Being a member of the male gender, I know how lazy and self-pitying we can be."

Her brows shot up. "Not you!" she exclaimed.

He was gratified that she didn't see him in that light. "Clubs in London are full of petulant young men who grow bored with life because their wealthy parents give them everything, middle-aged men who transform their wives into spiteful nags by ignoring them for selfish pursuits, and old men who moan that their families fail to do enough for them. Becoming dependent is a bloody easy thing for human nature to adopt."

"My godfathers always claimed they were not capable."

"Do not be angry with them. They love you, that much is obvious, and want to keep you close. I think they were . . . still are . . . afraid of losing you. Someday you will m—"

Derek stopped cold. He couldn't bring himself to say the word "marry." At the thought of Rosa with another man, his free hand clenched and ripped up a fistful of grass. Luckily, she didn't seem to notice the lapse.

"I am more mad at myself, for being so blind," she stated.

She continued to watch her godfathers work, her expression thoughtful. Her melancholy gaze held regret, but pride in her godfathers' accomplishments was foremost in her tender smile.

Derek had a sudden vision of Rosa bestowing that same

tender smile on her children. Their children. The notion sent a pang of wistfulness through his chest.

He instantly recoiled inwardly at the direction of his thoughts. Marriage? The parson's trap was something he hadn't envisioned for himself for several years to come.

"Shall we go down now and greet them?" he said brusquely.

"No," she whispered.

He wasn't sure he had heard her right. "What?"

"Not yet."

She reached for his free hand. Her warm, silky fingers intertwined with his, then squeezed tight. Derek stared at their joined hands. The urge to escape faded away. He remained silent, simply enjoying the press of her hand as she wrestled with her uncertainty.

"If we rescue them now, they will not have a chance to finish their goal. They will not prove to themselves that they can do it." She gnawed her lower lip. "How long do you estimate their food will last?"

"Perhaps indefinitely, if their hunting skills persist."

"And the boat?"

"At the rate they are going? Another week, maybe two."

She worried her lip some more. "Could we come back then?"

He smiled. This was what he'd hoped for. She had seen for herself that her loved ones weren't helpless. She shouldn't be expected to shoulder their burdens, or their entire future.

"An excellent idea. We shall return to cheer them on as they launch the *Lucky Lady*."

AS DEREK AND ROSA worked their way back toward *Pharaoh's Gold*, they passed through a landscape of thick, tropical undergrowth interspersed with rugged limestone outcroppings. They skirted the edge of a small swamp with primordial-looking trees standing high on exposed roots.

Rosa remained uncharacteristically quiet. Derek tried to lighten her melancholy mood with tales of legendary local pirates, hideaways, and buried treasure. She listened until—to his immense relief—that familiar sparkle began to return to her green eyes.

They passed through a line of palm trees and suddenly came upon a picturesque pond. A flock of startled ducks burst into flight. Three white egrets lifted off, one with a frog still gripped in its narrow beak. With long legs folded back and five-foot wings spread, the egrets sailed regally toward the rise separating them from the bay and the anchored schooner.

A lush peace settled once again. The ripples quickly settled in the cisternlike pond. Thick grass flourished around the perimeter.

"Derek, *mira!* A cave."

Like a whirlwind, Rosa led the way to a particularly large limestone outcropping. An opening, only slightly wider than Derek's shoulders, gaped in one side.

"If I were a pirate, I would have hidden my cache in a cave like this." Bending over, she braced her palms on either side of the opening and thrust her head inside.

Derek tensed, barely conquering the urge to grab the waistband of her trousers and yank her back. When she spoke again, her voice came back in an echo that made him wince.

"It goes down. I can see no end, but it is large enough." Straightening, she said excitedly, "I want to explore."

She saw adventure, mystery, and the chance of buried treasure.

Derek saw only blackness, tight walls, and no visible outlet. "Is the *Augustina's* treasure not enough for you?" he challenged grumpily.

She laughed. "Of course! But this is different. This is about pirates and tales of daring. Are you not curious?"

Grabbing him by the wrist, she tried to coax him inside.

He dug in his heels.

"Come. Where is your sense of adventure?"

When he still refused to budge, she truly looked at him for the first time. She stopped pulling. Concern instantly replaced her playful expression.

Something deep inside Derek shriveled with shame. Bloody hell, he should have realized he couldn't hide his fear from Rosa. She was too astute.

"Derek, what is wrong?"

"I simply have a dislike for caves," he said testily. *Or any other confined space that threatens to trap me.*

"Dislike?" she exclaimed. "It is more than that. You are as white as a sheet."

"Let's just go, shall we? The crew is no doubt wondering where we are."

"The crew has not given us a second thought, as well you know. They are too busy repairing the ship."

"Regardless, it is time to get back." He turned to go. Unfortunately, it was Rosa's turn to plant her feet and refuse to move. In fact, she seemed to have sprouted roots like a damn oak tree.

"You are afraid to go inside that cave."

"Do not be ridiculous," he retorted automatically.

"*Bien.* Then let us explore it."

If Rosa hadn't caught him off guard the first time, he would have concealed his dread and followed, steeling himself against the rush of adrenaline and the horrid shortness of breath. But now it was too late. She already knew. Why should he torture himself? He shook his head.

Without warning, he found himself being tugged in the opposite direction. He relaxed . . . until she sat down at the pond's edge and insisted he sit beside her.

"Tell me why."

He typically avoided thinking about that particular

story at all. In a discouraging tone, he said, "It was something that happened in my youth. A *very* long time ago."

"Not so long ago if it still bothers you."

"It is of no consequence," he said between gritted teeth.

Rosa crossed her arms over her upraised knees and rested her chin on her forearms. She stared at him, saying nothing. She simply waited expectantly.

Derek's lips tightened. His muscles twitched restlessly. She could interrogate him all she wanted, but he saw no logic in sharing his past. It revealed his most appalling weakness.

The silence stretched. Strangely enough, he felt no urge to get up and leave. That would certainly solve the present problem. Just walk away, maintain his secret. Hide his fear . . . always hiding.

It wasn't idle curiosity that burned in the emerald pools of her eyes, but genuine concern.

Suddenly, he realized he wanted to tell her. The burden of the old nightmare weighed heavily on his shoulders. He'd never told anyone before, not even his father. Tim knew of his fear of being trapped, but not the source. His first mate's aversion to heights had led to all the mutual understanding they needed.

The flock of mallards returned, landing gracefully on the opposite side of the pond. Derek stared at them as his story started to spill out from some deep, dark place.

"I was twelve at the time. Charles Umberley, the son of one of my father's cronies, was my best friend. We frequently got into a spot of mischief together, as boys will do. Our favorite forbidden place was the river on our estate. An old flood had carved a sand bar and a high embankment at one bend. It was a capital place when the water was low. We carved our names in the dirt, built forts, played at war. One day we decided to dig a tunnel into the embankment. We had progressed almost four feet when I crawled inside . . . to continue digging, you see, and—" Derek stopped. The memory alone triggered a bout of anxiety that constricted his throat.

"What happened?" Rosa coaxed.

"It collapsed," he continued thickly. "Fell right in. Over three feet of heavy sand."

"Madre de Dios."

"I couldn't breathe, couldn't move. It was only a matter of minutes before I would suffocate. I was completely dependent on my friend to get free." Derek remembered those harrowing moments. His sense of panic mounted, accelerating his heart rate. The story also picked up speed. Words tumbled out.

"The taste of sand, the scent, filled my head until I wanted to gag. Charles pulled at my legs. I screamed at him to stop wasting precious time, to dig instead, but of course the sand muffled any sound. Luckily, he realized in time. He dug frantically until he reached my waist. Then he gave a great heave and we both tumbled onto the narrow beach. He said my face was blue. It took a slap on the back to get me to draw a wheezing, coughing breath."

Rosa reached out. Her fingers slid through his hair. He began to relax . . . at least, as much as he could relax when the stroke of her fingers against his scalp triggered a sensual cascade of shivers down his back.

"Ever since then, I have suffered a fear of being trapped," he admitted. "I do not mind tight places, as long as I can be assured of a way out. When I cannot, I have these . . . feelings. I shake, my chest constricts, I can barely breathe."

Derek braced himself for Rosa's sympathy, words his pride dreaded yet his wounded spirit craved. Her first comment astonished him.

"It must have bothered you deeply to be helpless, to depend completely on someone else to save you," she whispered. "Did you and Charles remain friends?"

"No, actually." The memory of a lost friendship brought on an old twinge of regret. "He avoided me after that. The incident frightened him. He also dreaded how my father would react if he ever found out."

"Did your father discover what happened?"

"No. I've always kept the secret."

Without warning, she pivoted onto her knees, facing him. She reached out and lightly traced his lips with two fingers. A sweet, tingling shock shot through his lips and sank straight to his groin. He sat frozen, riveted by her touch and the unfathomable expression in her eyes.

Then a repellent thought intruded. Was she doing this to comfort him, to express pity? The likelihood was chilling.

He caught her wrist. "Do not do this out of sympathy."

"This is not sympathy. It is admiration."

"For what, the shape of my mouth?" he asked defensively.

Her lips curved in a teasing half-smile that was both delectable and infuriating. "That, too. But I meant your courage. Now I understand the haunted look in your eyes each time we dive. It is very difficult for you to be shut inside the suit and helmet, no?"

"It has its compensations."

"Still, it must be painful. Yet you do it anyway."

How ridiculous to react so strongly to a few words of praise. Her compliment burst through him like a warm light. Her faith pushed away the horrific memories of crushing sand and near death . . . for now.

"If I did not dread giving you an inflated opinion of yourself," she teased, "I would say that you are *muy hombre*."

His hands curled around her shoulders. "What if I assured you there was no danger of that?"

She smiled. "Then I would tell you to stop playing around and kiss me."

Raw need plunged through Derek on a wave of heat. He desired Rosa, and not just for a quick tumble to satisfy this insane lust. He ached to claim her body, to brand her as his before the world, to finally taste her passion in all its glory. He wanted to bring her to the point of ecstasy again and again, cherishing her vibrancy for the remarkable gift that it was.

At last, they were alone.

"Rosa," he rasped. "I no longer have the willpower to stop at a kiss. This is not some flirtatious game. If you intend to keep your virtue intact, you must tell me to stop now."

"I know what I want."

"What? Tell me." With Rosa, the notion of conquest filled him with distaste. He craved the surety that she was just as eager, just as needy as he felt. He must hear the words.

"I want you. Now," she whispered.

With a groan of surrender, Derek pulled her hard against his chest. He claimed her mouth in a fevered kiss. They fell back together into the thick grass.

Chapter Twenty-two

DEREK'S WEIGHT PRESSED her gently down. Rosa reveled in the sensation of strength tempered by restraint.

His kisses ravished her mouth as his deft hands peeled away her clothes. Rosa's fingers also sought out buttons, equally eager to touch the bronzed skin that her gaze had been devouring at every opportunity aboard ship. Their clothes scattered haphazardly. Soon they lay flesh to warm flesh.

Rosa shivered with pleasure. This was all too wonderful to be real. The joy of Derek's nakedness pressed close, the searching caress of his lips, the sensual admiration in his eyes as his gaze ranged over her body. She pleased him. She could tell. Then his head bent to her breasts, and she discovered that her craving could go well beyond kisses.

His tongue flicked one nipple. Both drew tight into sensitized buds, craving more. He obliged as if reading her mind, laving her nipples, the nubby surface of his tongue the perfect texture to spiral her need deeper, stronger. She moaned and threaded her fingers into his hair, holding him close. Every teasing stroke sent a strange tug deep into her belly, until the sensations concentrated into a tingling yearning between her legs.

The heat of his hand traced a path to that sweet ache. When his finger slid between the folds of her feminity, she jerked at the shock of his touch. His finger moved, circling, building sensations more wonderful than anything she ever dared imagine.

She climbed toward something waiting, something glorious, like a pure light atop some peak.

She sucked in her breath.

Then shattered in his hands. There was no better way to describe it. Her world came apart, then came back together in a shimmering cascade of rainbow light as she relaxed, happy yet somehow unsatisfied, in his arms.

He shifted his full length over her, lowering his weight gently. His belly pressed against her mound, triggering that shivering ache all over again. The silky heat of his arousal slid between her legs, brushing her upper thighs, settling against the damp nest of her hair.

A rich, deep shudder shook her body, reassuring Rosa that the pleasure was far from over. She opened heavy-lidded eyes.

Propped on his elbows, Derek looked down at her. His mouth curved in a gentle smile, but there was nothing tame about the fevered, intense look in his gaze. His eyes were so blue, with tiny white flecks, they reminded her of the sun glittering diamond-bright across turquoise-blue waters.

She doubted he even realized how unique he was. Love tightened around Rosa's heart, hugging it with boundless joy and bittersweet sadness.

Saying the words would make her too vulnerable. She didn't feel safe revealing her love when he'd said nothing about loving her in return. But she could share the depth of her feelings in other ways . . . through her caresses, greedily taking all the passion he was willing to offer . . . and giving back even more.

He raised his hips.

Rosa slid her hand down his belly. Derek froze, as if she'd earned his full attention. Muscles flexed and quivered against her palm. She hesitated, uncertain whether her urge to touch him was getting in the way of his own desires.

He brushed his cheek against hers. In a deep whisper that sent shivers down her neck, he whispered, "Yes. Touch me. Please, sweetheart."

She closed her hand around the rigid staff that spanned the gap between them. A throaty groan rumbled from his chest, a sound of vulnerability mixed with power. Emboldened by his obvious pleasure, she slid her cupped hand to his thick root, then down to the satiny head of his manhood. Blood pulsed against her fingertips. She stroked him again.

"Guide me into you," he murmured hoarsely.

She shivered, embarrassed and excited by his demand. She had no experience at such things, but she did know that spot at her feminine core that throbbed with an unfulfilled hunger. Feeling delightfully abandoned, she guided him in.

Derek slid inside her as if it was the most natural thing in the world. Slowly, carefully, he pressed inside, inch by glorious inch, creating the strangest yet most wondrous feeling of filling her, body and soul. Glittering waves rippled through her. Her back arched, lifting her hips, responding to an instinctive cry to be closer, and closer still.

He paused.

She moaned, impatient, and wriggled her hips.

A low groan wrenched from his throat. "Damn, woman, don't do that. I want to be gentle breaking your maidenhead."

He flexed his hips. A sting shot through her belly. She winced, at the same time luxuriating in the feel of him sliding all the way in. He remained motionless, allowing her to adapt. The pain faded.

He kissed her chin, her jaw. She sighed. She could almost be content to lie like this indefinitely, enjoying the satiny caress of his lips, the graze of his breath across her skin, the intimate fullness of his manhood deep inside her.

Almost.

His teeth scored the edge of her left ear, then tugged on the lobe. Her breath caught. He lifted one breast in his hand and laved the rigid nipple.

He pulled partway out, then stroked deep again.

Abruptly, all thoughts of languid enjoyment vanished. Responding to a sudden wave of hunger, she threaded her fingers into his hair and pulled his head down for a kiss.

Rosa's natural, passionate response swept over Derek like a golden flame. The sweet probing of her tongue in his mouth, penetrating him in counterpoint to the deep slide of his body inside hers, completely undid him.

His prized self-control slipped away. He let it go without regret. He wanted to experience the full measure of a passion beyond anything he'd ever known.

He gave himself over to the primitive rhythm his body demanded.

Her bare toes stroked up his calves, then across the backs of his knees. He shuddered, his body intimately aware of every detail of her explorations. Her feet traced the rigid muscles along the backs of his thighs, searching, until they grazed his buttocks. His hips flexed in immediate response, thrusting forward. He wanted her legs higher. He wanted it all.

"Hold me, Rosa," he growled.

Her legs curled around his waist, perfectly long and silky.

The world disappeared in a rush of heat.

Derek's existence narrowed down to the velvet grip of Rosa's body, the instinctive pulse of her hips meeting each thrust, the sound of her panting breaths. His rhythm escalated, trying to keep pace with his heartbeat. He sensed her pleasure coiling like a tight spring. He stroked faster, feeling a desperate need to touch her so deeply he could claim her, body and soul.

Suddenly, she gasped out his name. Her body convulsed sweetly. Her nails dug into his shoulders.

Joy swept through him at her fulfillment. The emotion surprised him. Although he'd always sought a woman's pleasure before his own, there had consistently been a distance, never a full sharing in it. Not like now.

Her body stayed taut, still on that pinnacle, still pulsing around him. He kept moving, consumed by the urge to prolong her pleasure, to hold forever in his mind the image of rapture on her face. She'd never been more beautiful. She had given this moment to him alone.

The pressure built, in his groin, in the red haze engulfing his brain, ecstasy and pain indelibly mixed. His breath hissed between his teeth.

Then he couldn't hold back the floodwaters any longer. They broke over him, sweeping him up. He arched, shuddering with a climax unlike any before in his life.

Dazed, he drifted down into her arms.

THREE DUCKS FLEW overhead. Lazy clouds drifted. Rosa lay still, enjoying the utter bliss of the moment and the tingling delight that still hummed through her body.

The light breeze gradually dried the sweat from Derek's skin as she stroked the powerful lines of his back. Although he had pulled free of her body, she cherished the sleepy, masculine drape of his torso across her own.

She felt deliciously, victoriously feminine. And hopelessly in love.

Derek finally lifted his head. He smiled. His mood seemed buoyant. She smiled back.

She glanced up at his hair. "Did I do that?"

"What?" he said huskily.

"Your hair is all mussed."

"You did that and more, you little wildcat."

She blushed and looked away. Did he think her wanton?

He hooked her chin with one finger and coaxed her to face him again. "Don't you dare be embarrassed. Your sweet, giving passion is the greatest gift I've ever known." A chuckle rumbled through his chest. "Though you nearly killed me. Maybe we should try it slower next time."

Happiness rippled through her. She loved the way he teased in this playful, sexy mood.

"There is slower?" she asked, genuinely amazed, thinking of the unhurried, exquisite, nearly torturous way he had first penetrated her.

He grinned. "Oh, yes, sweetheart, there is slower." His warm hand slid across her belly and over one hip. She gasped. "There is also faster. And if we are miraculously lucky, there might even be better."

DEREK FIXED THE spyglass on the horizon, though it seemed ridiculous to repeatedly study the monotonous line between the sea and the early morning sky.

Repairs on *Pharaoh's Gold* had taken an entire day. Now they headed west at full speed, sails straining in the wind, the engine surging.

Apprehension over the state of the *Augustina* curled his bare toes against the deck. He just couldn't purge the image of those mangled buoys from his mind. The goggles hung about his neck. His open white shirt fluttered in the wind. He fidgeted with impatience, ready to dive the moment they arrived to survey the damage left by the waterspout.

Unexpectedly, an object on the horizon slipped into view.

Derek's grip tightened on the spyglass. *Pharaoh's Gold* continued to devour distance at a brisk speed. Within minutes, the spot enlarged enough to make out the lines of a ship.

A gray ship, anchored directly over the *Augustina*.

The pirates had returned.

Derek swore under his breath. The interlopers were in

for a rude surprise. That wreck belonged to him, Rosa, and his men. He wasn't giving it up under any circumstances.

Wilson, on lookout, yelled a warning. The crew burst into frenzied activity. The schooner bore down on the other ship, drawing closer. Tim manned the bow gun.

"Fire, Tim," Derek ordered from between clenched teeth.

The bow gun boomed. *Pharaoh's Gold* shuddered under the recoil. The shot landed fifty yards short, still well out of range. The other ship didn't return fire.

"She's raising sail, Captain!" Geoff shouted.

"They're making a run for it!" Richard cried out.

Derek received the news with mixed feelings. Reclaiming the *Augustina* without a fight was preferable to risking injury. Then again, he would love to send a very clear message to those marauding vultures.

The ship pulled away, picking up speed.

Although he had the momentum to easily overtake them, Derek gave the command to stop over the site. Protecting the galleon was his first priority. Nor could he legitimately engage a ship in battle whose captain hadn't fired a single shot.

The door to the pirate ship's main cabin opened. A man dressed in a brilliant white uniform stepped into the sunlight at the stern. Light reflected from something metallic at his shoulder, flashing erratically each time the man moved.

Derek whipped the spyglass into position. The magnification enabled him to clearly recognize the man who stared coldly back across the widening expanse of ocean.

Don Geraldo de Vargas.

Bloody, bloody hell. The arrogant Spaniard had somehow escaped from Cuba.

Cold fury sliced through Derek. Storm damage was bad enough. Now he also faced the attempted theft of priceless artifacts by the greedy Don Geraldo and his men.

The crew anchored the schooner over the salvage site.

Derek burned with impatience to go below. But first things first. He bellowed a command for everyone to assemble on deck.

He spotted Rosa near the wheelhouse. She raked loose hair away from her face. The boom of the cannon must have awakened her. She looked delectably disheveled.

Hunger lanced through him. Making love to her hadn't dulled his fascination. On the contrary, his first taste of her unfettered passion had only whetted his appetite. He regretted leaving the island, losing the only privacy they'd known thus far. But since he cared for her, and didn't want to embarrass her in front of his crew, he'd once again sworn off touching her after they returned to the ship.

It was the toughest decision of his life.

His men formed a line. Rosa stood at the left end. They all watched him expectantly.

Clasping his hands behind his back, Derek began to pace. "I now know the identity of the pirates. Don Geraldo de Vargas is commanding that ship."

A shocked reaction rippled down the line, measured by dropped jaws and hearty grumbles.

"How did he get away?" Grady's brow knit in confusion.

"Although I wish I knew, it doesn't matter now. What matters is that he is here, well armed, with every intention of taking the treasure from us."

Tim asked, "But how could he have tracked us across the Gulf, to Galveston and here, without us spotting him?"

"The journal. He read it before we stole it, no?"

Rosa's softly spoken conclusion silenced the men. Derek was no longer surprised by her powers of deduction. He'd seen how her quick mind remembered details and noticed even minor clues.

"Rosa is right. De Vargas had no need to track us. He has sought the sunken galleon before based on the journal's clues. He only needed to return to this general area and wait for us to lead him directly to the trophy."

Her hand crept to her throat. "Do you think he has already been down there?"

"Yes," Derek growled. "Don Geraldo may not have the necessary salvage equipment . . . which is why he tried to force me into a partnership . . . but he does know what he is after. He wouldn't come unprepared. Among the men you saw on his ship, he no doubt has some willing to try free diving. Perhaps he even recruited pearl divers from Cuba who can better withstand the depth and hold their breath for longer periods."

"*Madre de Dios,* then why are you still here?" Rosa cried out. Stepping forward, she grasped Derek's arm and turned him toward the starboard side. The press of her fingers against his shoulder blades urged him toward the railing. "What if they stole something from your wreck? You must dive and see."

Derek grinned. Her reference to the wreck as his lightened his grim mood. She was being fiercely possessive for his sake. "You want me to go down and check on it?" he teased.

"*Sí, pronto.* The faster the better."

Unable to resist, he murmured for her ears only, "Your wish is my fondest desire, sweetheart. Remember?"

A charming shade of pink rose into her face. He trusted she was recalling her throaty pleas of the day before, and the eager effort he'd put into bringing her to fulfillment.

He tied on the goggles and stripped off his shirt. Then he took a deep breath and dove over the side.

The reef fish darted about as if nothing had changed. A school of yellow and black sergeant majors followed him as he stroked downward.

The waterspout's damage to the reef was apparent. It had snapped off branches of staghorn coral. Some sections were stripped bare of algae and spiny urchins. The storm had broken a large chunk of coral away, exposing a stubby dark mass that thrust from the pale surface of exposed limestone.

Curious, Derek drew closer. When he touched the

dark mass, part of it crumbled away between his fingers. Wood?

Astonished, he quickly pushed back and examined the damaged reef. It could be. He shook his head, amazed. If his suspicions held true, a section of the battered *Augustina* had settled here, only to be overgrown by coral over the decades.

Derek surfaced, took another breath, then dove to scrutinize the ballast pile.

Disappointment sliced through him. His carefully laid out grid lay in shambles. The holes which he and Rosa had labored over for grueling hours were filled with sand. They would have to start anew.

Nearing the limits of his air, Derek swam across the ballast pile. To his immense relief, the stones and their hidden niches of treasure appeared undisturbed. Nothing else seemed out of place. It seemed the storm had impacted Don Geraldo, as well, delaying his opportunity to reach the wreck during Derek's absence.

Derek crossed over to the north side, an area he and Rosa had yet to explore. Lungs straining, he prepared to surface.

He froze.

A large section of seabed had been stripped of almost two feet of sand. Only the storm could have accomplished such a dramatic shift in nature. Strong storms were known for moving large quantities of sand in unpredictable ways.

Ignoring his body's strident demand for air, Derek fanned at the fine sand with his hands. A piece of eight winked up at him like a coal-black eye, then another. More sand swirled away, uncovering smooth, curved edges of porcelain. Two bowls lay nestled together . . . intact bowls, their condition perfect.

Derek nearly sucked in a mouthful of water at the sight.

The other Ming dynasty porcelain they'd uncovered thus far had offered nothing better than shattered fragments. Gently gripping the bowls, he raced upward for desperately needed air.

He broke the surface, grinning like a fool.

His first thought was of Rosa. She would be pleased. The storm had given them a desperately needed head start on moving the sand. Timing was even more crucial now with Don Geraldo breathing down their necks.

DEREK CLIMBED THE rope ladder. As he stood on the deck, water pooling around his bare feet, everyone gathered to hear his report.

A burst of longing spread through Rosa's chest. Water plastered his blond hair. Black trousers clung to his body, revealing tempting details. He radiated health, energy, and an unconscious masculinity that was as natural to him as breathing. Now that she intimately knew the rough velvet texture of his skin, the feel of his tall body covering hers, the pleasure of his skilled hands bringing her to exquisite heights . . . she loved him more than ever.

Derek glanced at the gray ship lurking in the distance. Don Geraldo had only retreated out of reach this time, apparently waiting for the right opportunity to pounce.

"What did you find?" Geoff demanded eagerly.

"The site looks intact. I believe we returned before de Vargas had a chance to organize his divers." Derek's gaze focused on Rosa. He approached her, pulling out something he'd been hiding behind his back. "I also discovered these."

The porcelain bowls appeared in perfect condition. Rosa looked into his eyes. Her breath caught at the mixture of triumph and passion glittering in their blue depths.

"Will you take care of these for me? We can examine them later in the laboratory."

Deeply touched by his trust, Rosa gently took the bowls. She cradled the prizes in her hands.

"Anything else?" Tim asked.

Derek's attention shifted away. "A hull timber was exposed by a broken piece of reef. A section of the *Augustina* may be encased in the coral, perhaps even the sterncastle."

"The sterncastle? Didn't galleons typically carry the most valuable goods there, in the officers' cabins?" Tim's excitement was mirrored in the other men's expressions.

"Yes. The trick now is how to get to it."

"Embedded in coral, you say?" Grady grunted in disgust. "Hell, that would be like chipping through rock."

Geoff spoke up. "The explosives could loosen it. You brought them for this kind of situation."

Derek's mouth thinned. "Gelatinous dynamite could potentially damage the embedded section of the wreck."

"But if that is the only way to free it—"

"I know. We might have to risk it. Otherwise the whole thing will remain entombed."

"Perhaps the best part," Nigel said.

Richard offered, "You could locate some crevasses, key points that might fracture the coral without shattering it. Chisel a few holes, stuff them with dynamite, then let her go. That's how they blast rock on the surface."

In mounting horror, Rosa listened to their plans progress. "What about the fish and other reef creatures?" she burst out.

They all turned to look at her, surprised.

"The explosion will not cause extensive damage or fire as it would in the open atmosphere," Derek explained.

"But surely it must do some harm. Will it kill them?"

"I suspect the concussion will. Everything within that immediate area." Derek's voice lowered. "You know I would not try this if the dolphins were nearby, Rosa."

Nevertheless, she couldn't help her dismay. All those delicate, fanciful creatures, each a small work of art. Her temper rose. "Is there no other way?"

"Beg pardon, Miss Rosa, but they're only fish," said Richard.

"They are beautiful. I love watching them."

Wilson shrugged. "I love eating them. Maybe several will float to the surface and provide an easy meal."

Rosa flinched. "How can you talk that way?"

Derek said softly, "If there is one thing sailors learn, Rosa, it is how to deal with necessity. Even when that storm raged, we spread canvas to catch the fresh water."

"What about you, Tim? I thought you enjoyed diving for all the rich life there is to see."

"I do. But reefs, with the same types of fish, are everywhere in the ocean. There is only one *Augustina*."

The men nodded in agreement.

She swallowed hard. They could be right. Something incredibly valuable could be buried in that coral. But it didn't matter to her. Too much beauty would be lost.

Unable to bear the thought, she spun on one heel and stalked off, heading for the laboratory.

Derek drew a deep breath. Rosa's distress tore through him, not unlike having a piece flayed from his own skin. Yet his every instinct as an archaeologist demanded that the sacrifice be made to recover a significant portion of the galleon.

The silence resulting from her abrupt departure was so thick one could cut it with a knife.

Then Grady grunted and stroked his whiskered jaw. "I don't get it. Why is she so upset? They're just fish."

Were they? Derek thought uncomfortably. He pictured the life teeming over the reef, the wondrous variety of creatures, the beauty that he could watch for hours but seldom paused long enough to notice. They were important to Rosa, if not to him.

"Do you think she'll change her mind?" Nigel asked innocently.

The older men looked at him incredulously. "You've got a lot to learn about women, boy," Tim said with feeling.

Looking worried, Richard said, "I hope she won't stay mad at us the whole trip."

Derek sighed. "Don't worry, gentlemen. I do believe Miss Rosa's fury is primarily directed at me. I make the decisions."

"Well, in that case perhaps we could offer some

suggestions, Captain," Grady said cheerfully. "Not that we're experts when it comes to the fairer sex, mind you—"

Derek raked one hand through his wet hair. "Why not?" When it came to Rosa, he was beginning to think himself a complete novice.

"You might try begging her forgiveness," Geoff began.

Or I could change my mind about the explosives.

"Whatever you do, don't tell her she is being ridiculous," Tim said with a shudder and the experience of a married man.

"I could fix you a romantic dinner for two," Wilson offered.

Grady pursed his lips. "Sure wish there was something you could do for flowers out here."

Richard grunted. "A lot of stuff and nonsense. The captain has always had women falling at his feet. I think he should just kiss the lass until she forgets she's mad at him."

"Maybe he should bring something special up from the *Augustina* and make it into . . . you know . . . a gift," suggested Nigel.

"Hold on, gentlemen." Derek held up his hands. "Are the lot of you playing matchmaker?" he asked incredulously. How had they gotten from earning Rosa's forgiveness to romantic dinners and flowers, for pity's sake?

Grady chuckled. "No, sir. You've managed that much all by yourself. Do you think we're blind to the way you two look at one another?"

Every member of his crew beat a hasty retreat at that point, trying unsuccessfully to hide their grins.

Derek stared after them, aghast. They had it all wrong. He respected Rosa, desired her even more, but there was no binding commitment between them.

Then he paused, intrigued. What did Grady say about the way Rosa looked at him? Was it possible that she harbored some strong feelings?

———

ROSA SAT CROSS-legged on the foredeck an hour later, glaring at the enemy in the distance while she nibbled a breakfast of raisins, biscuits, and bacon. Don Geraldo's ship represented a threat to the men Rosa had come to care about and the treasure she was helping recover.

In a few minutes she and Derek would dive down to the storm-ravaged wreck while the crew carried on their customary work with rifles slung across their shoulders.

The halcyon days of their salvage were over.

Not only did a threat hang over their heads, she now lived in constant dread of the moment the men decided to blast.

Tim called to her. Rosa went to where he readied the dive suit. Her concern over the explosives made her more anxious than ever to work on the *Augustina*. What new wonders awaited them today?

Just as she finished donning the suit, a deep voice unexpectedly spoke up behind her.

"Give me the helmet, Tim. I will help her put it on."

At the sound of Derek's voice, a sensual shiver raced along Rosa's nerve endings like lighted gunpowder. She turned.

He wore his canvas suit. A lock of hair tumbled across his forehead, the only soft, approachable thing about his hard competence. She lifted her chin and glared at him.

One corner of Derek's mouth kicked up. How dare he find amusement in her righteous anger? Rosa stomped her foot. The heavy boot *thumped* on the deck.

"It is a good thing I am not running about barefoot at the moment," he commented dryly.

"*Sí*, a very lucky thing for your toes."

He set the helmet down.

"I have a surprise down there for you today," he said.

Her curiosity snapped to attention. "More of the bowls?"

"We shall see." He picked up her braid, which hung down one shoulder, and rubbed the end between his fingers.

The sight of his strong fingers testing the texture of her hair sent a shaft of desire through Rosa. He raised the hair to his nose and breathed deeply. The sweet ache pierced deeper. Rosa's hand shot out to snatch the braid away.

"Tsk," he scolded, deflecting her grab with his free hand. "We have to tuck this inside before the helmet can be attached."

Stepping behind her, he worked the braid down the back of her suit. His knuckles brushed her nape. Rosa shivered, then bit the inside of her cheek. This wasn't supposed to happen. She was too angry with him.

She was spared further sweet torment when he lifted the helmet and settled it over her head.

They both finished suiting up. Derek grabbed a crossbow, the slate, and the wax pencil. Rosa cast a final worried glance at Don Geraldo's lurking ship as the hoist lowered her down. Thankfully, the crew of *Pharaoh's Gold* was on full alert now.

Once below, Derek led the way to the north side of the ballast pile, opposite the spot where they'd worked in recent days. Rosa looked around, amazed. What had been a flat plain now boasted a shallow crater.

It was her turn to operate the hose. She signaled Tim, then chose a spot and aimed the water stream. The familiar white cloud lifted. She dredged deeper, uncovering fragments of broken porcelain and a few pieces of eight . . . all in all, rather disappointing finds. Then, without warning, a brown cloud swirled upward, mixing with the displaced sand. Rosa knelt, exploring the source with one glove. The hose had uncovered a layer of strange mud.

Derek knelt beside her. He gathered a handful of the brown substance and rubbed it between his fingers, releasing it to drift away in the current. Then he wrote on the slate. "Packed in tea."

Tea? The Spaniards had packed the porcelain in layers of tea leaves? How ingenious, to efficiently transport two valuable products in a limited space.

Rosa's breath hitched as realization struck. If that was the case, the presence of these decomposed leaves must mean that an intact case had settled deep in the sand, protected from the pounding force of the ocean. Only an unbroken case would have kept the tea from scattering with the ocean currents.

They must finally be close to uncovering a significant cache of Chinese artifacts.

With renewed excitement, she stood and directed the water pressure against the mud. Derek lifted out a blue and white plate, miraculously intact. It gleamed in the filtered sunlight. Before Rosa had a chance to take in the wonder of the discovery, he lifted out another, then a third. A moment later, he held up a perfect stack of five nested bowls.

Derek moved away to carry the discoveries to a basket. Rosa continued dredging. He took longer than expected to return. Just as she began to wonder where he was, he stepped into the clear stream, holding the slate against his chest.

The slate displayed a simple yet beautiful rendering of a rose and the words "I decided not to blast."

Exhilaration swept through her. She knew it! He cared too much for their special underwater world to cause any destruction. She blinked rapidly, clearing her vision of tears.

He set the slate aside and pointed to the hole. He was right. It was time to concentrate on the salvage. This area promised to unveil the most valuable finds yet.

They returned to work. More porcelain emerged.

Caught up in the magic of their discoveries, Rosa didn't sense the new arrivals until blue-gray shapes flashed by them. She looked up. Her spirits lifted even further.

The dolphins had returned.

FIVE DAYS LATER, Derek gently placed a jade carving of a boy and water buffalo in the basket, alongside a shallow rust-brown cup shaped like an open lotus flower. The resilient cup was carved of solid rhinoceros horn, thought by the Chinese to enhance the fragrance of wine.

These pieces were only a small sampling of the riches they'd unearthed on the northern face of the ballast pile. The *Augustina* had yielded Yuan dynasty bronze vases and incense burners, Ming covered jars and snuff bottles inlaid with exquisite enamel, as well as dishes, cups, brush holders, and curio boxes carved from nephrite, a pale, luminous form of jade. In terms of more traditional wealth, they'd also uncovered a barrel full of pieces of eight, eight slender gold ingots, six loaf-sized silver bars, and a solid gold disk five inches across.

But it wasn't the constant flow of artifacts that kept Derek dancing on the knife's edge between immense satisfaction and acute frustration.

It was the necessity of passing Rosa's cabin en route to his own each night, the inevitable lingering, the fist poised to knock . . . then passing by to spend the night tossing in his own bed, only to awaken aroused and sweating from erotic dreams.

He kept wondering about that look Grady had sworn was in Rosa's eyes. It ate at him that he couldn't see it. Desire flared in her gaze whenever she looked at him, but suddenly he wanted to see evidence of some deeper feeling reflected there.

The more elusive she became, the more determined it made him to uncover the truth. In the past, he'd only reserved such dogged pursuit for archaeological treasures. Now he wanted Rosa with an obsessive hunger that worsened each day.

An agile, blue-gray shape swam close, distracting Derek's thoughts. He immediately recognized Oro.

Derek frowned. What was the youngster doing here now? It wasn't yet ten o'clock, the routine time the dolphins had adopted for arriving each morning, just as they departed for places unknown at dusk.

Derek looked around for the other dolphins. Only small fish darted through the crystalline water.

Oro was alone.

The hairs on Derek's nape prickled. Perhaps it hadn't been such a good idea to encourage familiarity with a wild creature.

Derek rejoined Rosa at their latest excavation hole. Oro circled them expectantly.

The older dolphins should be here at any moment. Surely, unlike an unruly and resourceful human youth, the youngster hadn't managed to slip away completely unnoticed.

A stealthy shape moved at the periphery of Derek's vision.

He instantly recognized the lateral body movement of a shark.

Chapter Twenty-three

ANOTHER REEF SHARK appeared, and then a third. A chill slithered down Derek's spine.

They should retreat to the safety of the ship. Yet calling the hoist meant abandoning Oro to a grisly fate. Derek felt Rosa grab his forearm in a viselike grip. She'd apparently spotted the sharks. At least he could send her out of danger.

He nudged her shoulder and pointed upward. She shook her head so vigorously her whole body swayed. Turning away, she took up a defensive posture with him, back to back.

Derek growled in frustration. Of all the stubborn, pig-headed, idiotic ideas! His emotions battled between pride in Rosa's courage and a fierce urge to protect her.

He scooped up the crossbow, holding it ready.

Oro raced to the surface for a gulp of air. Then he darted back and forth between them and the silver ceiling, his confusion and mounting terror evident.

The predators cruised closer, attracted by Oro's fear and vulnerability. Their soulless eyes judged every movement for weakness.

Derek tensed. The young dolphin made easy prey. But

how to draw him within the circle of the only protection available?

He tapped his helmet with the crossbow. The metallic sound pinged loudly. The sharks jerked nervously with the staccato vibration. Thankfully, Oro responded instantly.

After one last stab at the surface, the youngster shot down to them with a flip of his tail fluke. Derek braced himself to capture the slippery dolphin one-handed, though he wasn't sure how he was going to hold Oro and battle the sharks at the same time. He didn't have to. To his immense relief, Oro ducked into the gap between Rosa and Derek and stayed there.

One shark cruised closer. Derek immediately raised the crossbow and fired. The beast shifted its course at the last second. The arrow sailed past harmlessly. With a curse, Derek tossed the useless crossbow aside.

The other two grew more aggressive, drawing near. Rosa aimed the hose at them. Rather than scaring them off, the water jet agitated the sharks. Derek signaled *Pharaoh's Gold* for a cut in pressure. The last thing they needed was the hose stirring sand and cutting visibility.

Grasping his own pick hammer, he pulled Rosa's hammer from her belt and thrust it into her hand. He preferred the blunt weapons to their knives. Drawing blood would attract more sharks.

The largest shark suddenly angled in for an attack.

Straight for Rosa.

She struck upward with her hammer, hitting the beast in the jaw. The shark jerked away violently. Its slashing tail struck Rosa a glancing blow. She staggered a step, but she succeeded in turning it away.

The predators didn't retreat. In fact, the angry thrashing of the first attacker excited the other two sharks.

Derek repelled an attack, then another, but the bastards grew bolder with each quick pass. It wouldn't be long before one attempted to ram its way inside the defensive circle. Derek's free hand curled around the grip of his knife as a last resort.

Oro's small body shifted restlessly.

Understanding struck Derek like a sharp blow. The dolphin was running out of air. Any second now, Oro would dart for the surface, desperate for fresh oxygen . . . exposed and vulnerable. The predators wouldn't hesitate to strike. But Oro had to either take his chances, or drown.

Grief clawed through Derek. This was all his fault. If he hadn't made friends with the curious young dolphin, Oro wouldn't have been tempted to sneak away from his family group.

Oro twitched, then bobbed his head in distress. Derek removed one glove and stroked his palm down the dolphin's back. His touch seemed to comfort the youngster, for Oro quieted. Then he felt a ripple of muscle as the dolphin gathered energy.

Suddenly, Oro lunged away.

The sharks turned to follow.

Derek's throat tightened, snaring his breath. He heard Rosa's muffled cry of denial carry through the water. The sound wrenched at his heart. He caught Rosa's arm and turned her. Wrapping his left arm around her helmet, he turned her viewport into his chest. She didn't fight him. She didn't want to see Oro hurt. Her arms clutched his waist in a desperate, almost crushing embrace.

The sharks shot forward like deadly gray bullets.

Derek held his breath as if it was his body about to suffer the impact and the flesh-rending grind of razor-sharp teeth.

Then he heard the most beautiful, welcome sound. High-pitched squeals sliced through the water.

Rosa pushed back, shifting her grip to his upper arms. She arched her back to look up.

The adult dolphins raced in, churning the water between the sharks, bumping them with hard blows. The attack triggered mass confusion among the predators.

The sharks fled.

The dolphins circled Oro anxiously. Except for their agitation, the ocean was quiet once again. Peaceful. Everything was back to normal.

Everything except Derek's pounding heart.

Rosa turned to him. Surface light slanted through her viewport. He focused on her face. Although tear tracks lined her cheeks, she offered him a shaky smile. Calm spread through Derek like warm rain. Rosa and Oro were safe. Although delicate tremors rippled through her body, she'd been so brave. His hands slid over her shoulder blades, keeping her within the protective circle of his arms.

He'd almost lost her.

The dolphin song changed, reverberating with an assortment of clicks and low-toned squeals. Derek looked up.

The school gathered together, surrounding the youngster. Oro appeared subdued. In whatever way dolphins disciplined their young, Derek suspected Oro was in for a severe scold.

Then, one by one, the dolphins turned and began swimming away, apparently departing this place of danger.

Joy over Oro's safety was tinged with sadness. Derek doubted he would see the mammals again.

He turned back to Rosa, flushed with energy from their victory and a hot, burning wish to take her straight to his bed and bury himself in her silken heat.

Then he noticed a silvery line extending upward from behind her left shoulder like a string of tiny pearls.

Bubbles. Dear God.

He frantically pinpointed the tear over Rosa's left hip. The blow from the shark's tail had ripped the suit. Derek grabbed her shoulders. A quick glance into her viewport confirmed the worst—her eyelids were drooping. The influx of air from the hose couldn't keep up with the loss of pressure.

Slowly suffocating, she was close to experiencing the kind of death he feared most.

Derek yanked on the tether. As the hoist lowered, he wrapped a supporting arm around Rosa's sagging body and dragged her to the chain. He arranged their feet together in the loop, clamped his arms securely around them both, and flattened one hand over the rip.

Just as he signaled for the lift, Rosa went limp.

THE SOUND OF the clamps releasing jarred Rosa from an uncomfortable sleep. The helmet slid free. A strong, lean hand cradled her head before it fell back. That, in itself, seemed strange. Why was she flat on her back in the dive suit?

Familiar voices murmured. She forced her eyes open against bright sunlight. Derek knelt next to her on the deck. He held her head, which throbbed at her temples with a nasty ache. The crew hovered in the background.

Derek looked like an angel, with the sun glinting gold in his hair and those intense blue eyes.

"Say something," he demanded harshly.

Her brows pinched together in annoyance. Why must he always be so high-handed? "If you want conversation, then explain why I am lying on the deck with all of you hovering over me like old mother hens."

Geoff chuckled. "Her sass is certainly intact."

"Sounds like she'll be just fine," Grady said.

Derek helped her climb out of the suit.

The moment she stood, her knees buckled. Derek caught her and swept her high into his arms. His scowling face appeared serious, almost frightening. Nevertheless, she felt safe as he headed below. She snuggled against his chest, taking secret delight in the fact that it was bare. He apparently hadn't taken time to dress after discarding his own suit.

"What happened?"

"That shark cut your suit. You were losing pressure."

"You mean air? That is dangerous, no?"

"Hell, yes," he snarled.

She pressed one palm against the thick muscle over his heart. Her brows rose in surprise. When he unsteadily descended the steps, her strange impression was confirmed.

"Derek, you are trembling."

"Shaking like a leaf, actually," he said between gritted teeth. He stopped at the base of the stairs.

"Because of Oro? He is safe now," she said reassuringly.

"I realize that. But you almost died down there. Twice."

He cared? Hope fluttered through her chest like dozens of butterflies. "I am fine now."

"I know," he growled. "Bloody hell, I can't stop shaking."

"Maybe you should put me down."

Disappointment flashed across his features. Then he nodded brusquely. "Of course. You are right."

Moving again, he quickly reached her cabin door. Rosa thrust out one arm and straightened both legs, blocking his way.

He cocked one eyebrow. "What are you doing?"

Her mouth curved slightly. "I did not mean here. Try the door at the end of the passageway."

A ragged intake of air swelled his chest. "My cabin is at the end."

She snuggled her cheek into his shoulder and pressed her lips against the curve of his neck. "I know."

Derek's trembling ceased abruptly. His eyes closed.

"No," he said hoarsely. "I cannot. I swore that I wouldn't compromise you."

"I thought you already had," she teased.

"That was different. Now my crew is around, men who respect you. I don't want to change the way they regard you."

Lifting her head, she stared at him. "You are trying to protect my reputation?" She was so astonished she lowered her legs, dropping the barrier.

"Yes, I am." He pushed through into her cabin and laid her on the bed. "And don't you dare call me loco."

Despite the way her body burned in hot anticipation of his touch, she was actually quite flattered.

"Get some rest," he insisted. "I'll have someone bring you a meal later."

Rosa narrowed her eyes as he closed the door. She must think of a way to be intimate with Derek again without tarnishing his sense of nobility. Time was short, and so very precious. Hurricane season would be on them in only a few short weeks, then his plans would take him back to England and out of her life forever.

A LIGHT SCRAPE awakened Derek with a start. He sat up in bed, immediately alert, searching the dark shadows in his cabin. The only light came from starlight slanting through the stern windows.

The scraping noise sounded again. His brows snapped together. He jumped to his feet. Then, with a thump, the grating fixed to his end of the ventilation shaft hit the floor. A head of dense black hair poked through the opening.

He was going to wring her neck.

In an instant, he was at her side. Rosa started to wriggle through.

"Bloody hell, woman, what are you doing?" he growled.

She looked up. Her teeth flashed white in the dimness. "Sparing you from your nobility. Your crew will not know I am here if I come through this way."

When she stretched out her hands, he quickly pulled her the rest of the way out and into his arms.

She was sleek, firm, and completely nude.

A shock went through his body, followed by a searing flash of desire. Every rational thought flew right out of his head.

Hot need gripped him.

He pressed her against the wall. His heavy arousal strained against her stomach. She murmured her approval in a deep, throaty tone that vibrated through his chest and tightened around his heart. Her arms wrapped around his neck. The tight points of her breasts rubbed against his chest.

He captured a handful of her hair. Cupping the back of her head in his hand, he kissed her, opening her with a driving need that was so intense it almost frightened him. Then he shifted lower to greedily taste the silky skin of her breasts. She moaned. The sound lanced through him. How could he want this slip of a woman so much?

Cupping her bottom, he lifted her and pivoted to face his desk. He set her gently on the surface. She looked up at him, confused, but with a hunger matching his own. When he slid her to the edge and nudged her legs apart, understanding dawned on her face . . . thankfully, since his throat was too thick to explain. She wrapped her legs around him.

Gratefully, impatiently, he plunged into her velvet heat.

A tremor coursed through him. He couldn't believe that she was already slick and ready for him.

The frenzy didn't stop there. He rocked hard, so hot for her that he couldn't slow down. She didn't help matters when she tilted her head back, dangling her beautiful hair across his desk, and moaned.

He thrust faster, taking them rapidly to a climax that exploded over both of them and almost buckled his knees.

Only then did the tumult abate. His racing heart and heaving chest began to calm. He rested his forehead against Rosa's and breathed deeply of her scent and the smell of their shared passion.

"Does this mean you aren't mad at me?" she whispered.

He groaned, swept her into his arms, and carried her to his bed. He lay back with her at his side. She snuggled against him, warm and sublimely feminine. He stared at the dark ceiling, waiting for the tingling tremors to subside and his body to return to something he recognized as his own.

ROSA LISTENED TO Derek's heart slow to a low, reassuring rhythm. She rubbed her cheek against his chest, her body satiated by his wild, surprising passion. She smiled. In bed, with her, her staid Englishman was nothing of the sort. Then again, apparently they didn't need a bed.

He stroked her hair. Rosa knew something was wrong when his chest rose and fell on a heavy sigh.

"As much as I hate to say it," he murmured, "it is almost dawn. Time for you to go."

She rolled her eyes. Not that again.

"But you are *not* going back through that ventilation shaft."

Tightening her arm across his chest, she said agreeably, "*Bien,* then I shall just stay here." Arching upward, she whispered in his ear, "We can just do this all day."

A tremor rippled through his long frame. One hand slid down to cup her buttock. He squeezed, sending a delicious shiver down to her toes. His manhood stirred against her thigh. Rosa smiled secretly. She had him now.

She underestimated his resolve.

"No," he rasped.

Rosa reluctantly let go. Although she felt certain she could undermine his determination with a little more seduction, she also cherished his protectiveness.

He rolled out of bed, then moved to the opposite side of the room. She heard one of the built-in drawers roll out from the wall. He started to rummage through it.

She stood up. Looking down, she noticed how the faint gray light painted her naked body in shades of silver.

She could at least emphasize what Derek would be missing.

Holding out her arms, she asked impishly, "What do we do about this? I did not bring any clothes with me, remember?"

Derek looked up. In the resulting silence, Rosa thought she could feel the heated touch of his gaze rake her from head to toe. Then he swore under his breath and turned away to dig in the drawer.

One of his white silk shirts flew at her out of the darkness. Rosa caught it. With a sigh, she slipped it on and pushed the dangling cuffs up past her elbows. The shirttail hung almost to her knees.

Must he have an answer for everything?

THE MOONLESS NIGHT offered the ideal opportunity for stealth.

A brisk breeze blew clouds across a starlit sky, casting shifting shadows on the choppy water. The longboat, painted black, its three occupants' features concealed with coal dust, blended into the deceptive shapes.

Cloth wrapped around the oar handles muffled any sound. The men rowed slowly, warned by their master that caution was preferable to speed. The sentry they were trying to elude paced the port side. Gradually, they approached *Pharaoh's Gold* from starboard.

Two of the men crawled up the anchor lines. The third took the longboat and rowed back the way they'd come.

The two shadowy figures slipped over the railing. They crouched, side by side, making sure they hadn't been detected. All remained quiet. No alarm was raised.

Emboldened, they crept through the darkness, then down the stairs. A low lantern burned in the passageway.

They inched toward the bow, past doors and the soft snores of sleeping men. Finally, they found a room that was silent. The door opened to the faint outline of neatly coiled rope, stacked sailcloth, and tools. They slipped inside the storage room and closed the door with a barely audible click.

The wait would be tedious, but worth it. The right timing would bring the results Don Geraldo craved and the reward he had promised to all his loyal men.

"WHAT DO YOU mean, I am not diving today?"

"Actually, I said not today or any other day."

Derek winced as a string of colorful Spanish curses poured from Rosa's mouth.

"The suit is not usable, Rosa."

"Wilson said he could repair it."

"That is not the only danger down there."

"We have faced danger every day. Why is now different?"

"The dolphins are gone. There is nothing to keep the sharks away."

She flung her hands up in disgust. "You are being unreasonable!"

Derek's mood lightened immediately. Rosa's sense of high drama used to irritate him. Now he realized her unpredictability added mystery and spice to their relationship. The wild intimacy of last night's lovemaking added even more.

Leaning close, he whispered, "I can be anything you want, as long as you stay aboard."

She hesitated. Her brows arched. "Anything?" she asked in a provocative tone.

He nearly groaned aloud. "Behave yourself."

She sniffed. "And what am I supposed to do while you are down there having all the fun?"

"I intend to send up plenty of porcelain, jade, and ivory today. Cleaning and storing them should keep you busy."

"You trust me alone with your artifacts?"

"Yes, I do. They need your tender loving care as much as I."

ROSA WATCHED DEREK disappear over the side.

Why did he have to be so stubborn? About everything!

It was dangerous to dive alone. Her mouth set resolutely. She would ask Wilson to repair the suit. Then she would join Derek, whether he liked it or not.

She headed below to find the sailmaker.

As she worked her way toward the bow and the crew's quarters, Rosa heard a thump. Curious, she drifted closer to the source. It seemed to be coming from the storage room.

"Wilson?" she called. "Is that you?"

No answer came. Her hand reached for the handle.

Without warning, the door burst open. Two dark shapes lurched into the passageway. The whites of their eyes burned within oddly blackened faces.

Rosa spun around to flee. They reacted just as quickly. One clapped a hand over her mouth. The other grabbed her elbows from behind and pinned them. She struggled, her legs kicking furiously in her black trousers, but they closed ranks and trapped her between their large bodies.

"Hold her steady, *amigo*," the one with the hand over her mouth hissed, speaking in Spanish.

"*Sí*. This must be the woman he warned us not to harm. La Perla. What do we do with her, Carlos?"

"We must tie her up and keep her here. We cannot allow her to warn the others." Leaning close, Carlos whispered with sour breath, "Do not scream, *señorita*, or we must kill every man aboard."

Rosa looked into his hard eyes and believed every word he said. That's why she didn't hesitate the instant he moved his hand. She couldn't let these predators stalk the crew with no warning.

Her knee jerked up with all the force she could muster. Carlos doubled over and clutched his groin.

"*Puta!*" he wheezed.

She kicked back, relishing the sound of her heel striking bone. The man behind her swore and staggered.

She started shouting for all she was worth.

Instantly, something hard slammed into the back of her head. The shooting pain cut off her scream. Stunned, Rosa dropped to her knees. Nausea tugged at her stomach. A coarse cloth was tied roughly around her mouth. She was dimly aware of ropes securing her wrists and ankles.

They shoved her into the supply room. She stumbled and fell to the floor . . . right next to a body. It was Wilson, similarly bound. The door closed to utter darkness.

Madre de Dios, was Wilson dead? Wincing, Rosa struggled to a sitting position. She backed up to him and reached out with her bound hands. Thank goodness, he was still warm.

Tears of fear and seething anger stung her eyes. She doubted her short-lived shouts had reached the rest of the crew.

Don Geraldo's soldiers were loose on *Pharaoh's Gold,* and her friends had no warning that they were being hunted.

Chapter Twenty-four

AN HOUR PASSED.

The door opened.

Rosa blinked at the sudden light, struggling to make out the two shapes. Hope quickened her breath.

"I told you she was not to be hurt."

At the sound of that familiar arrogant voice, Rosa's heart plummeted. Don Geraldo. His men must have succeeded in taking the ship. Was anyone hurt?

"I swear, General, she was trying to scream and warn the others," Carlos said plaintively.

"Untie her, you fool," De Vargas growled. "La Perla is an artist, a treasure of Spain."

Carlos hurried to oblige.

Rosa's hands and feet tingled as circulation flowed freely once again.

The don smiled and offered a hand. "My apologies for their rough treatment, La Perla."

Rosa kicked out, aiming for his shin.

To her fury, he avoided the blow with a quick sidestep. He chuckled. "Such spirit, like a fine thoroughbred." He twitched the gag down below her chin.

Rosa licked her dry lips. "I am not a horse, *bastardo*," she hissed.

"No, but you are as exquisite as any finely bred creature. So beautiful." Reaching down, he curled a loose lock of her hair around one finger. "Perfection. I cannot let this go to waste or deprive the world of your flamenco, though it did disappoint me to see you leave Havana with Graystone."

"What have you done with the crew?" she demanded. Dread hardened her voice.

Wilson chose that moment to regain consciousness and groan.

The don nudged the sailmaker with one polished boot. "The two men who crept aboard last night knocked them out one by one. They are like this fellow, awaiting my decision concerning their fate."

Rosa pushed to her feet, massaging her abraded wrists. She glared at him. "Which is?"

He shrugged. "I really have very little interest one way or the other. The treasure Graystone has so conveniently recovered is my goal. My men are transferring everything to my ship. But tell me, my dear, where is Graystone?"

Rosa suppressed a gasp. Don Geraldo did not know that Derek was diving below.

Careful not to reveal anything that could endanger him, Rosa said casually, "What? Has Graystone managed to elude you? I thought your men were good."

The don's jaw hardened. He glanced at Carlos. "You searched the ship?"

"*Sí.* Everywhere."

"Then search again. Graystone designed this ship. Watch for secret compartments. He must be hiding somewhere."

Rosa's mind worked furiously as Carlos hurried off. She had to warn Derek. She could break away and dive over the side, but would that only place him in graver danger? She shouldn't underestimate the antagonism between the two men. Already, she knew Don Geraldo to be capable of violence.

A large henchman stepped up behind Don Geraldo. She walked between them down the passageway. Another soldier joined them as they reached the main deck.

Geoff, Tim, Richard, Nigel, and Grady stood at the rail. Three soldiers with rifles guarded them. Richard and Nigel lowered the longboat, apparently under orders.

Two other brigands dragged a groggy Wilson on deck and shoved him in line. Rosa's spirits plummeted. So many armed men. What could any of them do? She glanced up at the sun. Its rays slanted in a way that cast the invading ship's shadow away from Derek's work area. Unless he looked up and saw the outline of the intruder, he would have no warning of danger.

As soon as the longboat touched down, the guards forced the crew to climb over the side and into the small boat.

"Wait! What about me?" Rosa cried out.

"You are coming with me, back to Cuba where you belong. I will not leave you here with these boorish Englishmen."

Geoff and Richard set the longboat's oars and began to pull away. The crew of *Pharaoh's Gold* cursed the soldiers.

"I would rather take my chances with them."

"I cannot allow that. Do not argue if you want these men to live." That gave her pause. He explained harshly, "Their lives are in your hands. Come willingly, and I will spare them. Choose not to, and my men will shoot them one by one."

"You promise not to harm them?" she whispered.

"I swear I will not kill them."

There was no other choice.

Carlos climbed up the stern stairs. "We have searched again, General. Graystone is not on the ship."

Don Geraldo turned to her, one brown eyebrow arched.

Shrugging, Rosa grasped for another lie. "Perhaps while I slept the crew murdered him and tossed his body overboard. More share of the treasure for themselves that way, no?"

"Let us hope they have not denied me that pleasure."

Rosa shuddered. Her worst suspicion was true. Don Geraldo's code of vengeance demanded he kill Derek. She must be careful not to do anything to give him away.

Taking her elbow, Don Geraldo steered her to the other side of the schooner where a plank bridge had been set across the two vessels. His men carried the barrels of hard-won treasure across. Although it seemed a betrayal to everyone's dreams, herself included, she prayed they would just take the treasure and be gone without harming anyone.

And quickly. Before Don Geraldo noticed the swollen fire hose extending over the side not three feet behind her, or the chugging air compressor just beyond that.

A slender man approached. Rosa recognized Capitán Velásquez from La Muerte prison.

"Is that everything?" Don Geraldo demanded.

"*Sí*, General." Velásquez saluted. "All the barrels have been moved."

"And the journal?"

"I found several books in the central room. We have taken them all."

"*Excellente.*" Don Geraldo stroked his goatee. "And the other task I gave you? Is it done?"

Velásquez nodded. "Indeed. We discovered something that will do the job quite efficiently."

Rosa's dread grew at their words. What did they mean? Before she could demand an explanation, Don Geraldo's gaze shifted behind her. It fixed on the water hose. "What is this?"

Still gripping her arm, he moved to investigate. Two soldiers followed.

Rosa swallowed hard. The air compressor hummed. Such an essential, faithful machine. Such a damning sound.

"Is it not time to go, Don Geraldo?" Rosa asked nervously, trying to distract him.

The don nudged the air hose attached to the compressor with the toe of his boot. His gaze followed its path over the port side. Rosa held her breath.

"Unobservant fools," he muttered sourly. Then he looked directly at her. A smirk twisted his lips.

"Graystone is down there, is he not?"

Fear constricted Rosa's throat. Forcing a nonchalance into her voice that she was far from feeling, she said, "*If* he is, then he must be working at bringing up more treasure. Perhaps his best find yet. We found a stack of gold bars yesterday that we did not have time to bring up."

"In other words, I should make sure he arrives safely aboard with more treasure in hand?" A chuckle slipped from the don's throat. "I really must learn to be content with what I already have."

The smug victory behind that laugh raised goose bumps on Rosa's flesh. "What do you intend to do?" she whispered.

Slanting a gaze at Velásquez and another man behind her, he snapped, "Hold her."

They grabbed her upper arms before she could wrench away. Then, to Rosa's mounting horror, Don Geraldo grabbed the ax from the adjacent fire station.

He raised the ax.

"No!" Rosa screamed. She tried to lunge for him, but the two men held fast to her arms.

Don Geraldo smiled coldly. "This is just too easy."

In one clean blow, he severed the hose.

DEREK FANNED THE sand aside, exposing the distinctive shape of a dragon.

The stone gleamed in a soft, muted green. His gloved fingers gently worked beneath the jade. Sand billowed away like smoke as a large drinking cup came free. The carved dragon cavorted along the outer edge of the cup's shallow rim.

Excitement tingled through his fingertips as he examined the fine art. Not only had he attained the most daring goal of his life, each new piece added to the achievement, exceeding his expectations. The morning had brought one fascinating find after another.

He lifted the cup. Light rippled across the smooth surface, reminding him of green eyes. He quelled a sudden urge to turn, to share the discovery with Rosa. Bloody hell, he missed having her at his side today. But her safety was more important. He never, ever wanted to relive the chilling horror of watching her in danger from a shark, or anything else for that matter. He would make it up to her.

Without warning, the comforting hiss of Derek's air supply suddenly ceased.

He froze, every muscle rigid. Such a small sound, really, but after working in the near silence of the deep for hours on end, its sudden loss was glaringly obvious.

There must be some mistake. Any second now, his men would fix the problem, or switch over to the other compressor.

Astonishment kept the alarm at bay, holding off panic for a few critical moments. *Stay calm. Think rationally, Graystone, or you don't stand a chance.* He reached up and closed the valves on his helmet to prevent losing the air already in his suit. As he struggled to his feet, he jerked on the air hose to signal a problem.

Forty feet of slack hose spiraled down, coiling on the sand like a black snake. The opposite end, cleanly severed, leaked bubbles in a silver stream.

It was like staring at his own tombstone.

He looked up sharply. The damning shape of another ship's keel stretched alongside *Pharaoh's Gold*.

Bloody hell! Don Geraldo and his soldiers had slipped in while he was totally engrossed in his work. How could he have been so unobservant? How could his crew have allowed them to get so close?

Rosa. She was up there, unprotected. Thoughts of her at Don Geraldo's mercy tangled a knot of fury beneath his breastbone, overriding his fear of being trapped . . . for the moment. He had to do something. But he wouldn't be any good to her dead. He forced his concentration back to his own dilemma.

Encased in a heavy diving suit thirty feet down, he was breathing his own exhalations of carbon dioxide. Within a few minutes he would die of suffocation. Weighted down by the suit, he would never reach the surface in time.

Unless he suddenly sprouted gills and could draw life-sustaining oxygen from the water, his existence was at an end.

Oxygen. Of course! The rebreather.

Although never tested, it was the only chance he had. But could he reach it in time?

He staggered toward the coral crevass where he had stashed the apparatus. Breathing was becoming difficult. The foul air brought home the truth of his greatest fear like a thunderclap—he was trapped in this suit.

The adrenaline rush hit his system like an oncoming freight train. His hands trembled. Tremors skittered down his ribs and lodged deep in his gut. Tension wrapped around his heart and squeezed. He had to think clearly. He remembered Rosa's words on the island, her admiration of his bravery.

The shaking eased. His thoughts cleared, focusing on his goal. Encouraged, he dropped to his knees and pulled out one of the watertight packages.

As he cut through the wrapping with his knife, sharp pains stabbed at his chest. He fought for a decent breath in the increasingly contaminated air. Fireworks began erupting behind his eyes, blurring his vision with tiny needle points of pain. He forced his hands to work the rebreather free. He readied the device. The memory of how to use it struggled to find purchase in his pounding head.

He shook off his gloves and tool belt. Then he was ready for the most dangerous step.

He reached for the quick-release clamps at the base of the helmet. For once, his paranoia paid off. If he hadn't feared being trapped, and designed the suit with the special clamps, he would never have been able to remove the helmet by himself.

Taking a last deep breath, he twisted the remaining clamps.

The seal broke. Water spiked through the crack in a stinging spray against his neck and chest, powered by the ocean's pressure. He bent over. With a powerful, desperate heave, he shoved the helmet off his head. Salt water slammed against his skull, making his ears ring. Brine blurred his vision. He staggered under the impact but managed to stay on his feet.

Water rushed into the suit at the neck. Before the slightest movement became impossible, he frantically tore off the collar and cut through the sealed seam down his chest. He grappled with the suit, his ears still ringing, his head aching from the pressure. He wrestled the suit down to his waist.

The struggle devoured the last of his oxygen. His lungs burned. Sheer reflex screamed through his body, demanding he open his mouth and suck in anything that was there, willing to take the risk to feed his body's unrelenting demand for air.

Groping for the rebreather, he jammed the mouthpiece between his lips.

He exhaled sharply, then took a deep breath.

Dry nothingness.

His chest squeezed painfully. He inhaled again, praying that the device only needed to be primed.

Sour-tasting air flowed into his mouth. It was awful. It was glorious. His lungs gratefully acknowledged the presence of oxygen.

Groping blindly, he fastened the straps around his chest.

He kicked out of the remains of his dive suit and swam upward.

Surfacing, he yanked the mouthpiece from between his lips. He gulped down huge drafts of the sweetest air he had ever tasted. He quickly took in the situation.

A plank bridge spanned the gap between the closely moored vessels. Don Geraldo's soldiers carried the last of the barrels containing Derek's prized artifacts across. Then they removed the plank and readied the ship to sail.

A hundred feet to the west, the crew of *Pharaoh's Gold* filled her longboat to capacity. With Geoff and Richard at the oars, they pulled away from the schooner. Two soldiers watched over them with rifles.

Rosa wasn't with the crew.

Then he saw her, standing with Don Geraldo at the stern of the Spaniard's ship. Possessive rage sluiced through Derek like hot lava.

He swam for all he was worth. Although he had a lot of distance to cover, he made up for it with wrathful energy.

The rebreather dragged at the water, slowing him down. Swearing, he stopped to take it off.

Something zipped by him and plunged into the water, leaving a narrow trail of bubbles. The unmistakable clap of a rifle's report followed immediately after. Startled, he glanced at the departing ship. The soldiers had spotted him. Another bullet zinged by, closer this time.

Rosa lunged for the stern rail. She screamed his name.

The don captured her around the waist and held fast. His arrogant face twisted in fury. He began shouting orders.

Derek dove below the waves, groping for the mouthpiece. More bullets ripped through the water. If he used the rebreather to stay down long enough, they would assume he was dead. His main worry was his crew, exposed on the surface.

He bided his time. Impatient energy poured through his muscles in his eagerness to renew the pursuit. After a few minutes, he surfaced cautiously.

The soldiers were unfurling more sail, preparing to leave. The trick had worked.

But he was too late to help Rosa.

Furious at his inability to reach Don Geraldo, Derek punched his fist through the water.

His jaw clenched until it ached. *I'll catch up with you, Don Geraldo, make no mistake of that. If you dare to harm her in any way—*

Two of Don Geraldo's men stepped up to the starboard side. Each held a large copper pot. They upturned the containers. Twin streams of chunky red poured into the sea.

Derek's insides went ice cold.

Chum. Fish entrails and blood. The perfect shark bait.

The don obviously didn't intend to leave any enemies or evidence behind.

"DEREK!" GEOFF YELLED.

His crew rowed the longboat alongside. Derek hoisted himself into the crowded boat. Hands slapped his shoulders amid vigorous expressions of relief.

"Damn, Captain. Thought for sure we'd lost you."

"Couldn't believe it when that bastard cut your hose."

"Miss Rosa would have gone straight over the side if they hadn't held her back."

"Never heard such cussing from a woman before. Too bad it was in Spanish."

Derek raised a hand. The anxious commentary ceased. "Just tell me how the hell this happened."

Every man looked away sheepishly. After clearing his throat, Geoff was the first to speak.

"They got the drop on us. Two of them, with guns. They knocked Grady and Wilson out first, lowering our numbers, then—" Geoff paused, red-faced. With a snort of self-disgust, he finished, "It was well planned, and we handled it no better than raw recruits."

"How did they get aboard my ship?"

"The best we can determine," Tim interjected, "they boarded *Pharaoh's Gold* last night under cover of darkness. Must have come up the anchor lines. Their faces were painted with coal dust. We were prepared for the approach of the larger ship. They must have used a longboat."

Richard hung his head. "It's my fault, sir. I was on watch last night."

"No recriminations, gentlemen. We all contributed to this mistake," Derek said, thinking of his own obsessed involvement with the artifacts below. He squeezed Richard's shoulder. With a hard look all around, he said coldly, "Now we get back what is rightfully ours."

The men nodded in unison.

"Don't worry. We'll catch up with them soon enough," Tim said firmly. He gave the command to row. Geoff and Richard dipped the oars into the water and started pulling toward *Pharaoh's Gold.*

"Captain? I see blood in the water," Nigel said uneasily.

"Chum. A parting gift from Don Geraldo."

A fin surfaced twenty feet away. It slid through the water then dipped out of sight. Another appeared to the east.

"The bastard," hissed Geoff.

Pharaoh's Gold rocked peacefully on the low swells. She was, without question, the faster of the two ships. They could easily catch Don Geraldo once they achieved full speed.

It wasn't like de Vargas to neglect that eventuality.

Fine hairs prickled along Derek's nape. "Wait. Hold here," he said tightly.

Geoff and Richard lifted the oars. The longboat drifted. Fifty feet of water separated them from the schooner.

"Why?" Geoff asked the question reflected in all their faces.

"I do not like this. Something is wrong."

The explosion ripped through the atmosphere with a deafening roar. The shock wave flipped the longboat like a toy, sending the seven men flying into the water.

DEREK DRIFTED, STUNNED, lost in a sensation of soft warmth.

But if everything was so serene, why did this sense of urgency clamor in his brain? He forced his eyes open. Aquamarine blue and stinging salt water flooded his eyes. He was sinking, apparently just seconds after the blast. With a powerful kick, he headed for the light.

He broke the surface . . . just in time to see the column of flame that had once been his beloved ship.

Pieces of *Pharaoh's Gold* floated on the silver surface. Everything was gone. Everything except the recovered treasure that now filled the hold of Don Geraldo's ship.

Derek forced aside thoughts of his loss. He tamped down the gnawing fury and fear over Rosa's abduction. His first priority was ensuring the safety of his crew. If any of them had lost consciousness, just as he'd nearly done—

He swam toward the overturned longboat.

Tim, Grady, and Richard clung to the small boat. All three looked dazed.

"Where are the others?" Derek demanded.

Geoff broke the surface several feet away. Dashing water from his eyes, he started in their direction.

Something thumped against the opposite side of the boat. He peered over. A drenched Wilson returned his relieved gaze.

That left only one man.

"Where is Nigel?" Derek snapped.

"Over there," Grady called out, pointing.

Nigel clung to a chunk of floating wreckage twenty feet away. Blood dripped from a gash across his forehead.

"I will get him," Derek said.

Instantly, Richard offered, "I'll go with you."

"No. It will take the five of you to flip the longboat

back over. Need I remind you that speed is crucial?" He nodded toward the burning ship. Two sharks caught too near the explosion rolled belly-up. A new group of fins angled in, half a dozen or more. In a flurry of splashing water, the newcomers ripped apart their dying companions.

Another string of expletives erupted from the men.

Derek ignored them, giving Nigel his full attention. When the sharks finished devouring the chum and each other in their feeding mania, they would branch out in search of more prey. He stretched out in a breaststroke toward the injured crewmember, avoiding any splash that would attract the sharks' notice.

Nigel's eyes rolled. He started to lose his grip. He slipped out of sight just as Derek reached him.

With a desperate lunge, Derek grabbed Nigel's collar. He hauled the helmsman to the surface.

Nigel coughed and spit up water. "Captain? That you?"

"Yes, you lucky dog. Hold on to this," he insisted, pushing the piece of wood planking beneath Nigel's arm.

Tense with urgency, Derek glanced toward the longboat. The crew had succeeded in righting the small boat. Working in pairs to balance the weight, they climbed in from opposite sides.

Derek tried to wait patiently . . . until a gray shadow shot through the water nearby. "Come on, dammit. Hurry."

Tim was one of the first in. He glanced around the boat frantically. Then he looked up. Their gazes met and held. Derek didn't need to be told the reason behind the expression of horror on his first mate's face.

The oars had fallen loose when the longboat flipped. They lay somewhere on the bottom.

Derek squeezed his eyes shut for an instant.

"Well, Nigel, it is up to us. We have to swim for it."

Nigel's red-haired head lolled weakly to one side. "Sure thing, Captain."

Derek looked at the youth's drooping eyelids and

swore. "You just relax on your back. I'll pull you. All right?"

"Yes, sir," Nigel whispered.

Looping one arm across Nigel's chest, Derek started for safety. At the same time, Tim and the other four men knelt inside the longboat. They used their arms as paddles. The gap gradually closed.

Something brushed against Derek's left leg.

He set his jaw and kept moving.

Frantic shouts of warning came from the boat. A large fin sliced through the water, still cruising, sizing them up. Sweat broke out on Derek's forehead. He kept swimming, prepared to kick out with his legs as the only defense they had.

Then the shark angled in for the kill.

Without warning, a nine-foot blue-gray body burst from the water at Derek's side. It flew over his head in a high arc, then dove in on the opposite side. Familiar squeals and clicking sounds filled the air.

A shout of joy caught in Derek's throat.

The dolphins rushed through the water. Within seconds, they drove the predators away.

Derek's chest shook with a low, rich laugh as he cherished one of God's extraordinary miracles. Renewed energy and hope washed through him.

The longboat reached his side. Eager hands reached out. Derek passed Nigel over to the crew, who pulled him safely into the boat. Those same hands stretched out again.

Derek ignored them. "Tim?"

"Yes, sir."

"Did my diving bag survive the blast?"

"It's right here. It caught on one of the hooks before it went the way of the oars."

"Hand me my goggles."

"Uh . . . don't you think it would be wise to get in the boat?"

"Not yet." Derek slipped the goggles over his eyes. "Someone has to retrieve those oars."

Taking a deep breath, he knifed his body and cut below the surface, knowing he was safe as long as the dolphins were about.

He spotted the oars several feet away. In the distance, he saw the outline of the *Augustina*'s ballast pile. Regret and anger lanced through him. His dive suit and the treasures he'd unearthed today lay on the bottom. The sea would claim them if he didn't recover them soon. But there was no room in the longboat.

The dolphins greeted him. Had they rushed to his rescue, much in the same way he had sheltered Oro? Or had they chased off the sharks merely to reclaim their territory?

It would be impossible to prove his preferred theory. But Derek knew. He just knew.

Oro darted up. He held a shell between his teeth.

Derek stroked one hand over the youngster's back.

Not today, Oro. But watch for me to return. I swear I'll be back and bring everyone. His jaw clenched in fierce determination. *Everyone, dammit. We'll finish what we started. And this time, I'll make certain she knows that I love her.*

Chapter Twenty-five

THE BOATLOAD OF men watched in grim silence as the last of the burning schooner sank below the waves. *Pharaoh's Gold* settled to the bottom, ironically less than twenty feet from the *Augustina's* final resting place.

The aura of mourning was palpable.

Their only adequate means of pursuit was gone. Derek's gut churned, thinking of what Don Geraldo could do to Rosa. He had to get her back before . . .

The men looked at him expectantly, looking for answers he couldn't provide. He didn't have all the answers, dammit.

"What now, Captain?" Tim asked.

Derek grabbed one oar, then thrust the other into Geoff's hands.

"We row, gentlemen. In shifts."

"Aye, sir. Which way?" asked Geoff.

"Which direction did Don Geraldo go?"

"South."

"Then we head due south."

"Dry Tortugas is closer, Captain. To the west."

Derek could understand Geoff's concern. With seven men and no fresh water, food, or protection from the sun, they'd be lucky to live until they reached land of any kind.

"It looks like Don Geraldo is heading home to Cuba," Derek maintained coldly, "with Rosa and the *Augustina's* treasure."

"Then south to Cuba it is!" Nigel shouted.

The others nodded in agreement.

With one last look, they bid their silent farewells to *Pharaoh's Gold*. Then they bent their backs to the oars.

Before the longboat had cleared the area of floating debris, Wilson shouted. "Sail on the horizon!"

"IT MIGHT BE Don Geraldo come to finish us off," warned Richard.

"Can't be," insisted Wilson. "The sail configuration is wrong. No topmast."

"Could be another pirate ship," Geoff said grimly.

"Could be, but I think they'll find us lean pickins, lad," Grady said dryly.

Derek watched warily as the white ship approached. If only he had his spyglass.

"What's that dark spot on her port side? Looks like someone blew a hole in her," Tim asked.

Derek smiled. "No, gentlemen, it is lead sheeting covering a hole. Say hello to the *Lucky Lady*."

ESTEBAN, MICHAEL, AND Dickie leaned across the bow railing as the sloop pulled alongside. Their eyes widened in horror as they glanced about at the floating wreckage.

Despite the recent disaster, Derek smiled with genuine pleasure at their accomplishment. Their timing also couldn't be better. With the sloop, he stood a chance of staying within a day's sail of Don Geraldo.

"Permission to come aboard, sirs," Derek called out.

"I don't know if that's such a good idea, mate," Dickie retorted saucily. "Looks to me like you didn't do such a great job of taking care of your own bleedin' ship."

"Don Geraldo blew her up," Derek said coldly.

The godfathers released a colorful variety of expletives. Esteban demanded, "Where is Rosa?"

"De Vargas took her with him."

"He kidnapped her?" Dickie exploded.

"He also stole the treasure. All of it."

Esteban waved a hand in dismissal. "Forget that, *hombre*."

"Why that low, belly-dragging, slimy scum," Dickie snarled. "He's in for the fight of his life for taking our Rosa."

Michael shook his fist in the air. "Faith and it will be a grand battle."

Derek looked around doubtfully as he climbed aboard. The sloop wasn't equipped with a single cannon. "And what do you intend to do for firepower?"

"Who needs it! We'll pull alongside and board the bleedin' ship."

"Hand-to-hand fighting. That's the ticket, lad!"

Derek hated to dump the wind out of their sails, but he cautioned, "Rosa might get hurt in a battle."

Dickie's arms dropped to his sides. Michael sighed.

"Then what can we do?" Esteban asked morosely.

Derek curved an arm around Michael's and Esteban's shoulders. He tilted his head toward Dickie in a conspiratorial fashion. They leaned forward eagerly.

"I have an idea of how to rescue our Rosa, gentlemen. We're going to need a bit of treasure, which I'm about to bring up. You get to play a pivotal role in the mission. Do you believe you are up to the task?"

THREE WAGONS LADEN with treasure pulled up outside a two-story mansion. Several windows projected beacons of light into the dark, moonless night. The house held a lonely vigil on a forested spit of land near the coast.

Rosa shuddered.

She turned to Don Geraldo, who sat on the wagon seat beside her, the reins to the two mules wrapped in his hands. Carlos and another sailor drove the other two wagons.

"Your house, I presume?" Rosa asked.

"This is one of my sugar plantations."

The don jumped down, then held up his hands. Rosa climbed down the opposite side, rejecting his help. In a flash, he was around the wagon and clutching her elbow in a painful grip.

"Do not do that again," he snarled.

She tried to shake him off, but he held fast. "I am accustomed to doing things for myself."

"Not anymore. My staff will take care of everything."

She'd discovered on board ship that Don Geraldo had an aversion to damaging her. Although he said he valued her beauty, it was as if he was obsessed over her role as a dancer. Then again, she wouldn't put it past him to murder her in a fit of temper. She'd witnessed the cruelty beneath his civilized veneer.

The nightmare of that descending ax would haunt her for the rest of her days.

He touched her cheek.

Rosa winced slightly as his fingers brushed the tender bruise beneath her right cheekbone. She'd fought furiously as his men took her off the ship in Manzanillo, earning a blow from one soldier who didn't appreciate the claw marks she'd plowed into his neck.

"The man who did this has already received forty lashes," the don said softly. Turning, he propelled her toward the house. To the men on the wagons, he said, "Bring La Perla's things inside, then meet me back out here."

Rosa climbed the steps and crossed the porch.

The blow hadn't stopped her attempts to flee. It had been the don's threat to kill anyone who offered her aid. She believed him capable of anything after he'd ruthlessly stolen their hard-won treasure, stranded the crew, and blown up *Pharaoh's Gold*. Tears pricked behind her eyes at the thought of Derek's beautiful, beloved ship . . . lost. She refused to cry for Derek, however. No, that would be acknowledging that he might be dead.

She'd seen him surface, miraculously, after his hose was cut. She hadn't seen him or the others die. She clung to that hope with fierce determination. He was still alive out there, and struggling to stay that way, in a tiny boat.

He needed her. She was going to find a way back to him. Timing was critical.

An aged black man dressed in white linen opened the door just as they reached it. He bowed deeply. Don Geraldo brushed past him without a word.

The design of the wood floor carried up the two-story walls of the foyer and the elaborately carved banister of the staircase. Halfway up the stairs, where they turned back on themselves, was a landing with a large stained-glass window. A heavyset Cuban woman hurried down the steps. She curtsied to the don, her face flushed, her attitude clearly focused on pleasing her employer.

"This is Señora Fuentes, the housekeeper. If you need anything, just ask her."

"And if I want to leave here?" Rosa asked tartly.

The woman looked away hastily. Rosa frowned, recognizing the unlikelihood of finding help among the staff. Don Geraldo was too much of a tyrant to keep servants willing to defy his authority.

"Come, I will show you to your room," the don offered by way of an answer, implying that she would not be released any time soon.

If ever.

As THEY CLIMBED the stairs, Rosa glimpsed rooms decorated with a preponderance of wood wainscoting, thick carpets, and dark drapes. The heavy, distinctly masculine atmosphere of the house clearly lacked any feminine influence.

The don opened the door to a second-story bedroom. Beige flocked paper covered the walls. Rust-colored velvet curtains hung from ceiling to floor. The deep-toned colors suited the sumptuous dark wood furniture, particularly the canopy bed with its elaborately carved posts.

Carlos arrived with her "things," which unfortunately consisted only of the brass chain they had used to secure her aboard the ship. Don Geraldo had neglected to allow her to pack in the midst of her kidnapping. Carlos attached one end of the chain to a leg of the heavy bed.

The don knelt beside her. With a sneer at the sight of her trousers, he said, "I will send Señora Fuentes to buy you some dresses tomorrow."

The shackle closed around her ankle with a resounding click.

Don Geraldo stood. "Wait for me outside." With that curt command, he sent Carlos away.

They were alone.

A cold lump sank from Rosa's throat to her belly. What did the don intend now? His hand curved over her shoulder. Her body jerked involuntarily.

One corner of his mouth twitched. "Do you believe I intend to rape you, Rosa?"

"You would have the perfect opportunity in this house where your word is law, no?"

"Very astute, my dear." He traced one knuckle along the curve of her unmarred cheek.

Although his touch made her skin crawl, Rosa forced herself not to flinch. This was a power game to him. She feared she would only lose ground if she played it his way.

"Would you fight me, Rosa? Would you struggle, and kick, and scratch?"

She lifted her chin. "Do not forget biting."

He laughed. "Ah, a woman after my own heart, willing to do whatever it takes, however messy or distateful, to win."

As Rosa stood rigidly, he walked behind her and gathered

up a thick lock of loose hair. He kept walking in a tight circle. As he passed in front of her, he raised the hair to neck level. "No, that is not the way I want it between us. I want you to come to me. I am willing to wait. I am a patient man."

Rosa watched him guardedly as he passed behind again. The implied threat of her own hair wrapped snugly around her throat did not escape her.

She wanted to scream out her hatred of this bastardo who had tried to kill the man she loved . . . and who had succeeded in crushing Derek's dream. But venting her rage could shatter the rules that maintained the don's veneer of civilized behavior.

He finally stopped in front of her. "I enjoy a challenge." His neutral expression hardened. "But remember, Rosa, when it comes to something I want, my patience is not unlimited."

He stalked out.

The key turned in the lock.

Rosa instantly began to search the room, working at the limits of the long chain. She must act quickly. The don was on his way to stash the treasure. It was critical that she follow him and discover where he hid it, not only so Derek could retrieve it later, but also for the sake of her plan.

She found what she was looking for in a small writing desk. Her fingers stroked gratefully along the slender letter opener.

Luckily, Don Geraldo wasn't familiar with her talent for picking locks.

Rosa followed the wagons at a safe distance. It wasn't difficult to trail the lanterns through the darkness. It was nearly ten o'clock. The moon had yet to rise. The incline of the land rose; the terrain grew rocky. She could smell the sea and hear the crashing of waves against rocky walls.

When the wagons stopped, Rosa crept up cautiously. The wagons huddled together in a circle. The don and his cohorts each carried a barrel. Rosa's brows knit in puzzlement. There was no sign of a building or any other structure in which to hide their booty. Suddenly, to her astonishment, the three men descended into the black ground and disappeared.

A cave. It must be! The don knew of an underground cave here where he could safely conceal the treasure.

This was her target, then, the key to her plan. Just one of the galleon's gold chains was worth a small fortune, enough to lure the captain of some ship into undertaking a rescue mission.

Rosa looked around, taking her bearings.

Derek would be furious with her for bargaining away even a portion of the *Augustina*'s wealth, of course. She would tackle the problem of his temper later, when he was secure in her arms. All that mattered was getting him, and her friends, back safely. If the hired crew succeeded, she would gratefully pay them with her portion of the treasure.

She turned back, intending to return to her room, restore the chain on her ankle, and wipe away any trace of her late-night foray. The don must suspect nothing. If he knew she was capable of escape, he would have her watched even more closely.

She would grab the first opportunity to sneak back to the cave when she knew that Don Geraldo was occupied at the house—or any place that would guarantee not running into him in the dark confines belowground. Fervently she prayed that her timing would be soon enough for seven men cast adrift in a longboat.

THE LONGBOAT BUMPED against the anchored *Lucky Lady*. Derek and Geoff helped the three godfathers climb aboard as the sun began to set.

The agile sloop had managed to keep Don Geraldo's ship just within sight during most of the voyage, confirming that the don was headed for the eastern tip of Cuba. A brief storm then slowed their progress. They lost the remainder of a day sailing around the southeastern end of the island, checking every port town until they spotted the familiar gray ship in the bay of Manzanillo.

Derek had immediately sent Esteban, Michael, and Dickie out on their critical mission. Don Geraldo's men wouldn't recognize Rosa's godfathers, thus retaining the element of surprise. The fact that the soldiers hadn't encountered them aboard *Pharoah's Gold* gave the old men the freedom to visit the wharf and the town, asking key questions.

And dropping hints.

"What did you find out?" Derek asked impatiently.

"They took Rosa off the ship last night," Dickie reported. "Don Geraldo took her, and three wagons loaded with barrels, somewhere inland."

"The don's largest sugar plantation is near here, I believe," Esteban added.

Derek shoved the anger aside. His plan required a cool head for all the intricacies to work. He couldn't afford to go on a rampage every time the image of Rosa under Don Geraldo's control burned through his mind.

"There is more," Michael said forebodingly.

Dickie explained, "The two men who helped Don Geraldo move the treasure last night haven't returned."

"What does the rest of the crew say to that?"

"Actually, they don't bleedin' care. Don Geraldo has already paid them the reward he promised, so they haven't even reported the missing men. As cutthroat a lot as they are, those mates are still afraid of Don Geraldo."

"Apparently with good reason," Derek responded coldly.

"Now what?" Esteban asked.

"Did you show the gold ingot and pieces of eight I brought up to Don Geraldo's crew?" Derek asked.

"Yes, sirree, sweet as you please. Did everythin' but wave them beneath their noses. A bit of braggin' sure gained the attention you expected."

"We hinted that we'd found a stash of them on the island," Michael added.

"That our retirement was secure," Dickie chuckled.

Esteban said grimly, "Three of the crewmen started for Don Geraldo's home just before we came here."

"Looking for an extra bonus for information, no doubt," Derek concluded. "Just as we'd hoped."

"Do you really think it will work?" Michael asked.

"If you suspected that three strangers might have discovered your cache of treasure, would you go to check the hiding place?"

"*Pronto,*" Esteban said feelingly.

"In a heartbeat," emphasized Dickie.

"Exactly. When Don Geraldo leaves the house, it will give Geoff, Tim, and I the best chance to rescue Rosa. The other men will stay here to guard the schooner." And perform other useful tasks like sabotaging the rudder of Don Geraldo's ship.

The godfathers frowned in unison.

"Now, lad, are you sure—" Michael began.

"Gentlemen," Derek interrupted quietly, "we already had this discussion. I thought you agreed that youth, strength, and speed will be essential in getting Rosa safely away." They nodded sadly. "Besides, don't you have a key task to perform, a job essential to the overall success of our mission?"

Dickie squared his shoulders and waggled his brows. "That's right. We follow Don Geraldo to the treasure."

"We shall discover where that *bastardo* hid it," Esteban stated with conviction.

Michael summed up by saying, "We take back what is rightfully Rosa's." Pink stained his cheeks and the bald area of his head. He shot a guilty glance toward Derek. "And yours, too, of course."

Derek looked between their determined faces and felt an unexpected surge of pride. Rosa's godfathers were working together, no longer exclusively focused on their own needs. He wished she was here to see this.

"You need to expect de Vargas to be armed. I want you to be careful," he admonished. Folding his arms, he regarded them sternly. "Do not try anything rash, for pity's sake. Your job is to watch from a distance, not confront the man, despite the revolvers you are carrying. One of you will then sneak away to the don's house to lead us to the right location."

"Then what happens?" Dickie demanded.

"Then I shall take care of Don Geraldo myself."

STARS WINKED FROM the indigo sky, providing just enough light for Rosa to see her way. She located the fissure in the ground that formed the entrance to Don Geraldo's cave. After one last look to make sure she wasn't being watched, she slipped inside.

She had to work quickly, before her absence was discovered.

Steps, roughly carved into stone, descended sharply. Within seconds she was underground, facing a narrow tunnel that extended into darkness.

She froze. Curiosity failed her. This wasn't her definition of adventure. Something about the tunnel sent a shiver down her spine like the brush of skeletal fingers. Perhaps it was the darkness. Perhaps it was the ominous sense of evil that lingered.

Rosa lighted the kerosene lantern she'd stolen when escaping the house. The golden glow offered a circle of relative security. She forced her feet to move along the wet floor.

The walls, of a dark gray volcanic stone, formed a passage about seven feet high. The smell of brine permeated the porous rock. The steady drip of water carried through the tunnel with a hollow, mournful sound.

The tunnel abruptly split.

Rosa stood at the juncture, torn by indecision. Which way should she go? She chose the right branch. After a short distance, the ceiling lowered until she was forced to stoop her head to pass through. Rosa paused. It didn't make sense that Don Geraldo would choose to haul the heavy barrels down this narrow tunnel. She quickly retraced her steps.

As she moved down the left branch, the water on the floor washed over her feet. Was the tunnel dipping deeper, or was the water level rising?

Then she heard it . . . the sound of surf in the distance. The far reaches of the tunnels opened to the sea.

And the tide was coming in.

A sense of urgency tingled through Rosa's muscles and sped up her feet. She didn't have much time. The water was already brushing her ankles.

The tunnel began to curve. Chains and shackles, rusted from salt water and age, were secured to the wall every ten feet. What was their purpose? Had Don Geraldo, or perhaps prior generations of his family, rid themselves of enemies here over the years?

Something moved at the edge of her circle of light.

Rosa clamped one hand over her mouth to stifle an involuntary squeak of surprise. When nothing jumped out to attack her, she cautiously lifted the lantern higher.

The two soldiers who had helped the don store the treasure last night lay on the tunnel floor. They shifted slightly. Rosa held her breath, afraid to move, dreading that her arrival had already awakened them from a sound sleep.

Suddenly, she realized the men weren't twitching in sleep. Their wrists were secured by shackles. They were floating, their dead bodies rising and falling in the gentle wash of the incoming water.

A visceral reaction jerked through Rosa's body. She swallowed convulsively, choking back the urge to scream.

She must keep going. Grimacing, she pressed herself against the opposite wall to ease past. Cool water crept toward her calves. One sailor's dead arm lifted, floating. White, curled fingers touched the toe of her right boot.

Rosa yelped and leaped beyond its reach. Shuddering, she hurried down the tunnel.

Her passage through the gruesome gauntlet was soon rewarded, however, as the tunnel abruptly opened into a larger cave. The dark rock arched away, disappearing into deeper shadows above. The steady sound of crashing waves, infiltrating through another tunnel opening at the lower end of the cave, echoed inside the cavernous room. On the opposite side, safely above the high tide mark on a natural plateau of rock, sat the rows of treasure barrels.

Holding the lantern high, she began to wade across the pool, cautiously testing the unseen ground before taking each step. She feared that the cave floor would suddenly drop before her, plunging her into deep water. But the deepest spot proved to be just to her knees as she crossed.

She discovered a set of roughly carved steps leading up to the shelf. She moved quickly among the barrels, scanning Derek's markings on the sides, searching for one of three barrles she remembered containing gold chains.

At last, Rosa located one. She set the lantern down and began digging carefully through the artifacts. She found one of the seven-foot gold chains and began to lift it free.

An unexpected sound echoed in the cavern. Rosa whirled, clutching the end of the chain to her chest.

A new source of light swelled against the tunnel wall.

Don Geraldo stepped into the cave.

Rosa gasped. She was trapped, with no time to reach the lower tunnel exiting far to her right.

The don stopped. The lantern in his left hand highlighted his astonished expression. Then his eyes narrowed sharply. He'd caught her raiding his trophy room.

Rosa swallowed hard. Don Geraldo's face finally reflected the cold ruthlessness she knew him to be capable of.

"I am very disappointed that you found this place, my dear. What a pity."

He raised his right arm.

Lantern light reflected off the revolver in his hand.

Rosa screamed in earnest.

Chapter Twenty-six

DEREK KICKED OPEN the front door from the inside of Don Geraldo's house. He strode onto the front porch and glared into the concealing darkness of the moonless night. Frustration raked through his gut like sharp claws.

Already his plans had gone awry.

Rosa had blithely decided to be absent during the critical moment of her rescue. The infuriating, clever, resourceful woman had made good her escape. Alone. Bloody hell, he should have anticipated she would somehow manage this.

She could be on her way to the port. She might be attempting to cross the island to Havana. But some deeper instinct whispered that she'd chosen neither route.

The Rosa he knew and loved would consider it her responsibility to go after their treasure herself.

Which meant that she was far from safe.

Don Geraldo was heading for the treasure, as well. When the don discovered her there—Dread coiled in Derek's stomach. His neat, logical plan to draw Don Geraldo away might very well have placed Rosa in even greater danger.

Derek's hand moved instinctively to the dagger at his waist. Worst of all, he had no idea where to look. He had yet to hear from the godfathers.

The sound of thudding feet and heavy breathing shattered the silence.

Derek burst into motion. He leaped over the three steps leading down from the porch and ran to greet Dickie.

A panting Dickie pulled to a stop when he saw Derek. He bent over, hands on knees, and sucked in drafts of air.

"It worked . . . yes sirree," Dickie reported haltingly. His voice sounded flushed with success. "Don Geraldo went for it. We followed him . . . to some kind of . . . cave."

"Did you see Rosa?" Derek demanded.

Dickie straightened abruptly. "Why should we see Rosa there? Dammit, Graystone, did you lose her?"

"In a manner of speaking," Derek growled. He quickly relayed the facts of her escape.

Grinning, Dickie concluded, "Ain't that just like our angel girl. She always was clever at pickin' them locks."

Too clever. Derek swore under his breath. "I need to know where the cave is. Now."

After leaving Geoff and Tim in charge of guarding Don Geraldo's servants and the three guards they'd overcome, Derek followed Dickie through the night.

OF ALL THINGS, why did it have to be a cave?

Derek stared at the dark, forbidding hole as Esteban lighted a lantern.

"We shall come with you, *hombre.*"

"No. Stealth is difficult enough with one. Sound will echo far along the rock walls. I won't give Don Geraldo a chance to hurt Rosa because he hears us coming." At their worried expressions, he added, "Besides, I need you out here. What if the bastard should double back?"

Michael gripped his shoulder. "We'll take care of it, lad, never you worry."

"You sure that knife will be enough?" Dickie asked doubtfully. "Maybe you should take my gun."

Derek thought about it seriously. Then he shook his head. "No, gunfire is just too unpredictable in a cave. The bullets could ricochet in any direction, hurting someone outside the line of fire." *Like Rosa.* His jaw clenched. "Besides, I do not intend to deal with Don Geraldo from a distance."

"Just you make sure he doesn't deal with you first, mate."

Derek took the lantern from Esteban. After one step down into the fissure, he faltered. The black hole extended back, narrow and confining, with no light at the far end to promise an exit. He remembered the sand collapsing upon him all those years ago, heavy and suffocating.

He waited for the anxiety to wash through his body like ice water, for his chest to constrict. Although the memory of old fears fluttered through his stomach, the choking sensations didn't come.

Relief swept through him, followed by a comprehension. He'd made it through the crisis of having his air cut off underwater. Having once survived his worst terror, he'd broken the power of his fear.

Without further hesitation, Derek ducked inside.

He was astonished to find the tunnel half full of seawater. By the time his feet touched bottom, the water was up to his hips. It filled his boots, weighing down his legs. He yanked off the boots and threw them aside.

Derek touched wet fingers to his tongue. Salt. A shock of warning jolted through him. The tide would peak within the next ten minutes.

Time itself was working against him. Urgency gripped him. He plunged forward.

He reached a fork in the tunnel. The garbled echo of voices guided him down the left. The tunnel curved, preventing him from seeing ahead.

When he saw light reflecting off the wall ahead, Derek

quickly doused his own lantern and hung it from a hook high on the wall. Soundlessly, he moved forward.

The instant the two figures came into view, Derek recognized the wet sheen of Rosa's black hair. The other lantern hung from a similar hook set high in the wall. Don Geraldo stood between them, his back turned toward Derek. The water level reached beyond his waist.

A chain stretched from a shackle around Rosa's left wrist to the wall.

A silent roar of rage lashed through Derek.

Keeping an iron grip on his temper, he crept up on his prey. Rosa's gaze suddenly slanted over Don Geraldo's shoulder. Her eyes widened.

She said nothing, but that brief flash of surprise in her face gave him away. Don Geraldo whirled. Fury twisted his face. He raised a revolver. His finger tightened on the trigger.

Derek dropped, going deep. The bullet zipped through the water overhead. With a powerful thrust of his legs, he speared through the water and collided with Don Geraldo's chest.

Breaking the surface in a rush, Derek grabbed Don Geraldo's wrists. The two men struggled, wrestling for a foothold in the high water.

Don Geraldo fired again. The revolver kicked, firing a shot that hit the ceiling with a deafening sound. It ricocheted, pinging off the rock twice before disappearing with a muffled hiss. Rosa ducked with a gasp.

"Are you all right?" Derek shouted.

"*Sí!* Hurry, Derek. Hit him!"

Derek would love to oblige her, but letting go of one of Don Geraldo's wrists might shift the balance in favor of the armed man.

He slammed Don Geraldo's gun hand against the wall, then again, and again. The man's grip finally broke. The revolver slipped free of his fingers and sank out of sight.

Derek drew back his fist and slammed a right cross into Don Geraldo's chin.

Water surged as he went down with a splash. Don Geraldo was up in an instant, grinning smugly, his own knife in hand. Blood from a split lip spread in a spiderweb pattern down into his dripping goatee.

"Now what will you do, Graystone?" the man taunted.

Derek positioned himself between Rosa and the threat. He drew his dagger.

Don Geraldo's confident smile faltered.

"Where is the key to that shackle?" Derek growled.

"Key?" Don Geraldo laughed. "I wasn't intending ever to unlock her. Why should I bother with a key?"

The last word was barely out of his mouth when he lunged.

The two men grappled. Derek felt the sharp sting of a shallow knife cut across his upper arm. But he knew he'd struck the more serious of the blows. When they broke apart, Don Geraldo clutched his shoulder and swore.

Their combined blood spread through the water.

Derek took up his stance before Rosa again. She murmured a fervent prayer behind him. Then she cursed in Spanish, consigning Don Geraldo to the devil. Derek drew strength from the blessed familiarity of her fiery temper. He readied himself for the next attack.

Don Geraldo started to back away instead. Glancing over his shoulder, he began to retreat the way Derek had come.

"I wouldn't recommend the main entrance. At least three of my men are out there, heavily armed."

"I do not believe you," Don Geraldo snapped, but another glance to the rear revealed his doubt.

Derek flashed him a feral smile. "Please don't."

The don hesitated.

"Feeling a little trapped, Don Geraldo?"

The other man scowled. "You are the one trapped, Graystone. These tunnels fill completely at high tide. I, on the other hand, know an alternate way out to the sea."

"Do you really think I'm going to let you get away that easily?" Derek asked.

Don Geraldo backed away farther. "The water is rising. It looks as if you must choose between killing me and saving your woman, Graystone."

DEREK GROUND HIS teeth, knowing Don Geraldo was right.

His enemy plunged away, quickly disappearing beyond the lantern's circle of light.

Derek spun around, dismissing the sound of splashing water and Don Geraldo's taunting laughter. It didn't matter. He had more vital concerns at the moment.

The water had risen high on Rosa's chest.

He shoved the dagger in its sheath. Although every moment was precious, he cupped Rosa's face between his palms and kissed her like a man starving.

Then he grasped her shoulders and held her at arm's length. "Are you trying to scare the life out of me?"

She smiled radiantly. "You are here. You are safe."

He groaned, devoutly wishing they were out of danger and he could continue drinking of her passion.

"Can you pick the lock?"

Rosa's green eyes sparked with frustration. "I have tried! It is too rusted from salt water. Even if Don Geraldo had a key, I doubt it would turn the lock."

He grabbed her wrist and examined the ugly metal bracelet. It was small, tight enough to prevent the bones of her hand from sliding through. "But not rusted enough to break."

He looked into Rosa's taut face. His stomach plummeted. Her wide eyes and trembling mouth confirmed that she'd drawn the same conclusion—she was caught, with no hope of escape from the incoming tide short of cutting off her hand.

Unless he could pull the chain anchor from the wall.

Planting one foot against the wall, Derek pulled with all his strength. The anchor wobbled, but refused to tear free. Two additional tries failed.

He pulled his dagger. "I'll have to loosen it."

Rosa nodded stiffly. Clamping the dagger between his teeth, Derek brushed his knuckles down her cheek. He grinned around the dagger and gave her an arrogant, reassuring wink.

A wash of water crested over her collarbone. Derek swore under his breath and ducked underwater. Urgency pounded at his temples. He drove the dagger into the porous volcanic rock. Each blow chipped away a small piece around the metal anchor. He jerked on the chain. It gradually loosened, giving him hope.

He surfaced for air.

The water level brushed the underside of Rosa's chin. Although her eyes were dark and dilated with fear, she stood patiently, believing in him. He had to free the chain on the next try or it would be too late.

Submerging again, he drove in several more blows with the dagger. Then he planted his feet and pulled.

The chain tore free. The recoil flung him against the opposite wall of the tunnel. Derek ignored the pain and surfaced immediately. The water was already to Rosa's mouth. She was forced to tilt her head back to reach fresh air.

"I'll go first and carry the chain so its weight won't drag you down. Ready?" He turned back the way they had come.

She clutched his sleeve. "It is too far that way. You know we will not make it."

"We have to try, dammit," he growled, though he knew she could be right.

"No. This way. I know a spot above the high-tide mark."

He had to trust her instincts. "Lead on, sweetheart."

She grabbed two fistfuls of his shirt and lifted herself up for a passionate kiss. It rocked Derek to his toes, but not as much as her next words.

"I love you, Derek."

He blinked in surprise.

"Hurry!" she urged.

Bloody hell, what timing. "Deep breath!"

"Just ignore the dead bodies."

Startled, he demanded, "What the devil do you mean by that?" But Rosa had already ducked below the water.

The rising water doused the kerosene lantern, plunging them into darkness.

Derek sucked in air from the black recess against the ceiling, then submerged into the unknown.

THE BRINE STUNG Derek's eyes. When he realized it was useless to attempt navigating by sight in the impenetrable blackness, he closed them. He stroked hard. The heavy chain in his right hand was not a hindrance. Instead, it offered the reassurance that Rosa was near him.

His fingertips tracked his way along the coarse stone walls. Then he encountered a bulky object blocking their way. Something soft brushed his skin. Clothing.

Gritting his teeth, Derek shoved the floating body aside, then another. Rosa followed, slipping past.

Just as Derek's lungs started to burn, the tunnel wall fell away. His strokes encountered open water. Taking a chance, he headed upward.

His head broke the surface.

A cave arched overhead. They had emerged into an open pool that filled half the cathedral-like space. Derek immediately pulled Rosa up beside him.

A golden glow arched against the opposite wall.

"*Gracias a Dios*," Rosa murmured in prayerful thanks. She smiled at Derek. "You see? This is where Don Geraldo hid the treasure. And my lantern is still burning."

Her smile wavered. She was tiring rapidly. Derek quickly helped her to the rocky shelf.

They scrambled out of the water and collapsed.

Shoving up on one elbow, Derek anxiously searched her face. "Are you all right?"

She combed her fingers through his hair and looked straight into his eyes.

"Never better," she whispered huskily.

Derek groaned, torn between desire and practicality. Grasping her hand, he helped her rise.

He glanced around. In amazement, he saw the rows of treasure barrels. It was all here. And there was more. Crates were stacked at the back. Don Geraldo had apparently used this cave before. Derek moved to examine the contents.

There were additional lanterns, tins of food and other supplies, and best of all, stacks of folded blankets and pillows.

Rosa peered over his shoulder. "It looks as if he intended to support a small army here."

"Or himself for an extended period of time. Perhaps his arrogance is not absolute. He may have prepared this place to hide if the war goes badly for the Spanish."

"We can make a meal from these tinned foods."

Derek turned her into his arms. He lowered his head and explored the silky shape of her lips. "First things first."

She smiled softly. "What would that be?"

"We find a tool to break away this shackle." His fingers went to the top button of her blouse and worked it free.

"And then?" she asked in a throaty whisper.

His fingers moved down, unfastening another button, and then another. "We get you out of these wet clothes."

IN THE SWEET aftermath of their lovemaking, Rosa lay quietly on her back, her gaze searching the shadows overhead.

"What is wrong?" Derek asked in concern. He rose on his left elbow to examine her face. It wasn't like her to look so melancholy.

"I was just thinking about your beautiful ship, our dive suits, the hoist . . . all gone."

The loss of *Pharaoh's Gold* lanced through Derek with something akin to grief. "I fully intend to build another just like her, perhaps with a few improvements, in time for next year's dive season. Everyone came through the ordeal unscathed. That is what is important. Now that we have the treasure back, my only regret is the loss of my journals and research logs."

Her head turned slightly. Her gaze traced her fingers as they followed the curve of his brow. An enigmatic smile curved her lips. "They are not lost. Don Geraldo took them along with Gaspar's journal. They must be at his home."

Elation surged through Derek. He gave Rosa a quick, hard kiss.

After a brief pause, in which he screwed up his courage, Derek asked the question that consumed his thoughts. "Did you mean it when you said you loved me?"

Rosa tensed, uncertain whether to openly admit her feelings when their future was still uncertain. "Perhaps."

"Rosa, I must know."

Blue eyes looked into hers, anxious and sincere. How could she deny him when he looked at her like that? "Yes," she whispered, then added quickly, "But do not let it go to your head, *hombre*."

"I would say it has gone straight to my heart." He gave her a crooked, endearing smile.

A myriad of emotions fluttered through Rosa's chest. Could he possibly care for her?

"Stay here," Derek said mysteriously. He rose and grabbed his dagger. He walked to the barrels. The lantern light picked out the superb lines of his lean, muscular body.

Lifting the gold chain that still hung over the side of its barrel, he used the dagger to pry open one link from the end. Then he used the hilt as a light hammer, tapping the gold against the barrel's rim.

"What are you doing?" She sat up abruptly.

"As curious as always," he teased. "Can't you demonstrate a little patience?"

A negative almost sprang to her lips, but when she saw the shape the malleable gold was taking between his strong fingers, Rosa remained silent. In fact, she was struck dumb. Hope and excitement shivered through her.

Derek headed for the spot where they'd laid out their clothes to dry.

"Where do you think you are going?"

His blond brows arched sardonically. "To get dressed and get down on my knees, ma'am, if that is all right with you?"

"Neither will be necessary," she assured. Actually, she wasn't sure she could wait that long.

"There is a right way to do this, you know."

"You expect a thief and flamenco dancer to be a stickler for propriety?" She grabbed his hand and pulled him down next to her. "No, I like it just like this."

His gaze heated in a way that stole her breath. "This must be one of those rare and precious times we agree on something."

She huffed in mock offense and tried not to let her eager gaze slide to the circlet of gold in his hand.

Derek raised the ring between his thumb and forefinger.

In a husky voice, he said, "This piece of the *Augustina* signifies a special bond between us—a quest we've pursued together, dangers faced, the victory of an unparalleled discovery. But I am no longer satisfied with that partnership." Lifting one of her hands, he placed the ring between their palms. With their fingers interlocked and their palms pressed together, he asked hoarsely, "Rosa Constanza Wright . . . will you be my wife?"

A sobering thought intruded on her burgeoning

happiness. "You are the most stubbornly noble man I have ever met, Derek Carlisle. You are not doing this be- cause . . . because it is the honorable thing, are you?"

His expression grew even more intense. "Rosa, I ask you to marry me because I cannot imagine my life without you. I want to share everything with you . . . my home, my adventures, my children. I love you."

With a gleeful cry, she threw her free arm around his neck.

In a quick move, he turned her onto her back and pressed their joined hands to the pillow above her head. He grinned. "May I take that as a yes?"

Rosa smiled. "A forever yes."

"TIME TO WAKE up, sleepy one."

Rosa made a deep, disgruntled sound in her throat. The sound vibrated into Derek's chest where her head rested. He longed to let her sleep as long as she wished— allowing him to lie here and watch her—but he anticipated three worried visitors at any moment.

"The tide is almost out," Derek persisted.

She raised her head and gave him a playful smile that quickened his heart rate. "Do we have to go?"

Tracing her lips with one finger, he said huskily, "Although I wouldn't mind staying, I would rather make love to you as my wife the next time. Surely we can find a priest on this forsaken island."

Her lips turned down in a delightful pout. "That is my home you are speaking of, *hombre*."

"Is it?"

Her gaze softened. "No, no longer," she whispered. "My home is wherever you are. I have always longed to explore the world anyway."

Turning her onto her back, he covered her ripe mouth with his lips. Then he forced himself to remember the looming possibility of interruption. With a groan, he rested his forehead against hers.

"Your godfathers were outside with me last night before the cave flooded. I expect them as soon as the water recedes enough for them to navigate the tunnel. Actually, I'm surprised they are not here already."

Rosa let out a shrill yelp and shoved him off. Derek rolled away, laughing. She leaped to her feet and grabbed for her clothes. Interlacing his fingers behind his head, he cherished the sight of her naked glory before it disappeared.

Furiously, she exclaimed, "They could come in here at any moment? Why did you not tell me?"

"I am hoping to give them no choice but to sanction our marriage."

Rosa glared at him and harrumphed. Hastily, she pulled on her dry and rather stiff clothes.

Derek arose reluctantly. He pulled on his own rumpled trousers, grimacing at the cloth made sticky by dry brine. He much preferred the satiny feel of Rosa's skin against his own. The splashes of moving feet became audible just as they finished dressing.

"Derek?"

"Rosa?"

The harsh masculine whispers echoed through the tunnel.

Derek sighed. So much for their moment of privacy.

The three godfathers burst into the cave. Astonishingly enough, they emerged from the opposite tunnel toward the sea.

"How did you get through that way?" Derek demanded.

"We followed the receding tide down the tunnel to the right. Did you know it came out on the beach?" Dickie exclaimed. He saw Rosa and brightened. "There you are, angel girl."

"By the saints, it's good to see you safe and sound, colleen."

"Did that *bastardo* hurt you, *niña*?"

She smiled reassuringly. "I am fine."

"I thought I told you to stay out of the cave," Derek growled. "It is too dangerous."

"We got tired of waiting for you," Dickie insisted, as if that explained everything.

Michael added, "One other thing. We found Don Geraldo."

Rosa gasped. Derek went rigid.

"Dead," Dickie clarified. "Drowned. His body was washing in the surf at the opening to the tunnel. It looks like he got caught by the high water and didn't make it out in time."

Derek put an arm around Rosa's shoulders. A knot in his chest loosened and relaxed. He'd intended to track Don Geraldo down and make the man pay for all the heartache he'd caused. This way, fate and Don Geraldo's own greed had made him pay the ultimate price.

"That way was too good for Don Geraldo," Esteban grumbled.

Rosa spoke up. "He is gone now. He can no longer hurt us. That is all that matters."

"As long as he didn't make off with—" Michael began.

"Look, mates," Dickie interrupted breathlessly. "There it is." His voice was rough with awe as he pointed out the barrels behind Derek and Rosa.

As if in a daze, the godfathers climbed to the rock shelf. They drifted toward the barrels, their eyes alight with wonder.

Derek ignored them and pulled Rosa into the circle of his arms. "I think we should wait to tell them the good news until they come out of their stupor, don't you?"

Her gaze searched his face. "Do you trust them around all that silver and gold?"

"Implicitly. Look what a good job they did of raising the most important treasure of all."

She looked at him through her lashes, her gaze too heated to be called flirtatious. "You are a very dangerous man, Derek Carlisle. The slightest bit of flattery from you weakens my knees."

"Hmmm. I wonder how it will affect you if I say this?" Nuzzling her ear, he whispered, "I love you, my Spanish rose."

His beloved pulled his head down for a kiss in that spontaneous fashion that promised to fill his life with light and fiery passion.

Epilogue

March 1899
Portsmouth, England

ROSA OPENED HER hands, setting the champagne bottle free. It flew outward, swinging on the attached ribbon, arcing away from the dock and across eight feet of lapping Portsmouth waters. With a crash, it shattered against the prow of the glistening, newly painted brown ship. Bubbles and crystalline liquid cascaded down over gold lettering.

Derek's hands tightened on Rosa's shoulders from behind. His deep voice christened the schooner *Pharaoh's Gold II*.

Cheers of celebration arose from the select group of well-wishers standing at the foot of the gangplank.

Reaching across the bodice of her moss-green walking dress, Rosa cupped her left hand over Derek's right. Despite their audience, she couldn't resist exploring the lean tendons and strong knuckles with her fingertips, relishing the masculine hands that could hold her tenderly or bring her to the point of mind-numbing ecstasy. He turned his hand beneath hers and toyed with the wedding band she'd worn for eight months. He'd had it fashioned from Spanish gold by a jeweler in Havana. On the outside was etched a rose, on the inside the words "My Treasure."

Together, they gazed at the new schooner, nearly a twin of the first except for a number of improvements included in its design. Tears of happiness pricked at Rosa's eyes. *Pharaoh's Gold II* was more than a ship; it symbolized the resurrection of dreams, the excitement of fresh possibilities and new adventure. Derek belonged on this ship, and she with him.

He rubbed his cheek against her upswept hair. "Perhaps we should have arranged a private celebration." Wry frustration laced his tone as they watched their guests approach.

"You were right to share this with friends and family." Turning her head, she looked up at him. His exhaled sigh brushed across her lips. "There is always later, my love."

"Later cannot come soon enough," he whispered huskily as Geoff, Tim, and Tim's wife drew near. Rosa lowered her hand. Derek continued to rest his hands on her shoulders.

Grady, Richard, Wilson, and Nigel followed close behind. The entire crew offered hearty congratulations.

"Permission to go aboard, Captain," Geoff asked, smiling.

"Granted, but you won't find much that's different from before."

Tim grunted. "That hardly matters." He slipped his arm around the petite, auburn-haired woman at his side. "The ship's new, she's almost as beautiful as our wives, and she's itching for the opportunity of a test sail. In three weeks, you said?"

"To Ireland and back, as soon as the final touches are finished on the interior."

"We'll be ready, Captain," Richard agreed heartily.

Rosa watched them fondly as they ambled up the gangplank to explore. The comfortable fortune the crew had made off the first trip hadn't dulled their appetite for another expedition.

The Earl of Aversham, Derek's father, stepped forward

to shake his son's hand. Tall and dignified, this imposing, silver-haired gentleman had welcomed Rosa into the family with a warmth that had quieted her initial trepidation.

"You will be gone soon, then?" the earl asked.

Rosa remained silent, moved by this solemn moment between father and son. She knew Winston wished Derek to stay, but after the resounding success of the *Augustina*'s exhibition at the British Museum, it was he who had urged Derek to pursue the salvage of more artifacts.

"Yes, sir. The invitation to accompany us is still open."

The earl smiled. "Tempting, but my days of living the nomad life are over. I enjoy my creature comforts too much. Archaeological expeditions are for the young." He lifted Rosa's hand and kissed it lightly. "Try not to distract this ramshackle lad too much from his work, my dear."

"If anything, she will work me harder," Derek retorted.

The earl moved away, his blue-gray eyes alight with eagerness to explore his son's ship. Matt and Ellie came forward with Derek's youngest sister, Amber, just behind them. Although Ellie looked beautiful in a striped gown of burgundy and black, it was the bundle in her arms that lent a special glow to her face.

Rosa held out her hands. Smiling, Ellie placed the baby in Rosa's arms. Erin Michelle Devereaux looked up from remarkably pure blue eyes. The baby's curling, dark brown hair was obviously a gift from Matt, considering the trio of blond-haired siblings at her mother's side.

"When do you set sail for the Caribbean?" Matt asked.

"The last week in April," said Derek. "First we head for Cuba. A fortnight there should serve well to resupply the ship."

"And to visit my godfathers. Their last letter expressed impatience for us to visit." Their correspondence over the past months had shared details of the growing success of their shipping venture, particularly with Key West and New Orleans. Business was profitable aboard the *Lucky Lady* and Don Geraldo's confiscated ship, though she suspected that much of their enthusiasm came from helping their new nation recover from war. The pride she felt in their success lessened her sadness that they had decided to remain in Cuba.

Teasingly, she added, "Derek is anxious to see them again."

Her husband rolled his eyes, but didn't offer a denial. "We sail on to the *Augustina* by the middle of May."

Ellie spoke up. "We are eager to see what you bring back. Surely the galleon has many more remarkable secrets to reveal."

"It sounds exciting," Amber offered. "I wish you both the best of luck." Moving closer, she brushed a finger lightly down the baby's plump cheek. Erin waved her arms and smiled.

A hint of wistfulness in Amber's voice surprised Rosa. Dubbed "the Untouchable," as much for her angelic beauty as the average of four marriage proposals she declined each season, Amber typically professed interest in little more than the next party.

"You could come with us, Amber," Rosa offered impulsively. She handed the baby back to Ellie.

Derek's youngest sister waved a hand dismissively. "And miss the entertainments of London? I shudder at the thought."

Rosa watched Amber curiously as the three adults moved away to explore the ship. Amber played the role of social butterfly to perfection, but Rosa sensed hidden depths in her sister-in-law.

As the last hour before sunset drifted away, so did their guests.

Derek threaded his fingers through Rosa's. "At long last, I have you to myself." With a rakish grin, he led her belowdecks.

Reaching the captain's cabin, he swung the door open and stood off to one side.

The sweep of stern windows opened onto a magnificent

view of the sunset. A sharp stab of yellow light on the horizon spread up a low line of clouds in rippling rows of orange and gold. The vivid colors lent a dramatic backdrop to the soft glow of candles on a table set before the windows. Covered dishes awaited their pleasure. Light glinted off crystal glasses of red wine.

Rosa gasped with delight. "It is so lovely, Derek. How did you manage this?"

"Wilson set it up while you were too busy to notice."

He swept her into his arms and strode boldly into the cabin—which, at her insistence, was larger than the original. Just before the table, he stopped abruptly. He stared at the bed—which, at his insistence, was a full-sized double bed. The navy blue coverlet was folded back. Red rose petals lay scattered across white sheets and pillows like a spray of rubies. Rosa's black lace shawl lay draped over the nearest dining chair.

With a crease between his brows, Derek asked, "Where did the flowers come from?"

"Ellie managed it for me, when you weren't looking." Rosa reached down and plucked the shawl from the chair.

"And the shawl?"

"A new promise. When we reach Cuba, I shall dance flamenco for you. It has been a while, no?"

"Esteban might be shocked by the way your randy husband steals you away before the dance is even finished."

She lifted the shawl between them and looked at his handsome, beloved face through the thin veil of black. In a husky tone, she whispered, "So, what shall we indulge in first tonight, *hombre*? Dinner, or bed?"

"You have to ask?"

In two long strides, he reached the bedside. Without hesitation, he fell back on the mattress, taking her down on top of him. Laughing, Rosa sprawled across his broad chest.

Love and the serious intent of seduction glittered in his blue eyes. "Did I ever tell you that I once imagined you wrapped in this sheer black lace?"

"Truly? And what else was I wearing?"

"Nothing else, thank heavens. Nothing at all."

Her mouth curved. She brushed a corner of the sheer material down his cheek and over his lower lip, treasuring the sudden hitch in his breath. "I believe that can be arranged."

Author's Note

Since Derek and Rosa barely tapped the wealth of *Nuestra Señora de la Augustina* that first trip, the sunken galleon kept them busy excavating and playing with the dolphins for three additional dive seasons. After that, Derek and Rosa expanded their roles of devoted lovers and daring adventurers to those of busy parents. Derek never got back to his first find, leaving *Nuestra Señora de Atocha* for Mel Fisher to discover in the late 1970s. Many men had searched for the *Atocha* and her reputed wealth over the centuries, but Fisher was the first to find her (officially, that is). After over a decade of salvage, and numerous professional and personal sacrifices (including the accidental death of a son and daughter-in-law), Mel Fisher and his team brought up treasure in excess of 450 million dollars.

Lucky for him that Derek Carlisle placed a higher priority on Chinese decorative arts.

For a peek at my research notes, a complete listing of all the treasure Derek and Rosa brought up from the *Augustina,* and for photographs of representative artifacts, visit my Web site at *www.kristenkyle.com.*

ABOUT THE AUTHOR

Kristen Kyle has always been a die-hard romantic. Although roses and dinner by candlelight are nice, what really ignites her imagination are stories packed with action, conflict, a headstrong heroine, a dark and dangerous hero, and, most of all, passion and love. Her goal is to provide her readers with a memorable page-turner of a book. Kristen shares her home in a suburb of Dallas, Texas, with her two teenage sons, both to-die-for heroes in the making.

Hearing from readers adds a wonderful spark to Kristen's day. Don't miss visiting her Web site for news, excerpts, contests, writing tips, research notes, and much more.

http://www.kristenkyle.com
kristen@kristenkyle.com

Kristen Kyle
P.O. Box 250
Rowlett, TX 75030–0250